The Myth
by Keith Jenkins

© Keith Jenkins. All rights reserved. No part of this publication may be reproduced or transmitted in any form or by any means, electronic or mechanical, including photocopy, recording, or any information storage and retrieval system without written permission from the Publishers. Any characters portrayed or events described in this book are entirely fictitious. Any resemblance to any individuals, whether alive or dead, or to any actual events is purely coincidental. Cover illustration by Lane Design. Kindle and Paperback edition of The Myth created by eDigital Creations Ltd. Large format and limited edition hardback available online.

Dedication

This book is dedicated to my wife, and best friend, Linda, whose ability to endure my obsession over the years has made all of this possible. Her character, Jean, appears all too briefly in this story, but if I had included her as much as her influence in my life deserved then this book would have been twice the size, and much the richer for it.

Contents

Foreword

Dedication

Acknowledgements

Part One - The Learning Curve

Preface 1

Chapter 1 - 1963 3

Chapter 2 - 1966 5

Chapter 3 - 1969 12

Chapter 4 - 1972/3 18

Chapter 5 - 1976 33

Part Two - Choosing the Path

Chapter 6 - 1979 49

Chapter 7 – 1982 67

Chapter 8 – 1986 86

Chapter 9 - 1990 110

Part Three - The Common Bond

Chapter 10 – Burghfield 133

Chapter 11- Kingfisher 154

Chapter 12 – Thirties Galore! 179

Chapter 13 – Green-eyed Monsters 200

Chapter 14 – Felcham Mere 243

Chapter 15 – A Bigger Boat 273

Chapter 16 – the Myth 297

Foreword by Dave Lane
It's a funny old thing, life.

It seems only yesterday that Keith and I were blagging our way into Harefield, our first 'proper' carp water. Totally clueless we were, at the time, but as keen as mustard, and now here we are light years further on down the line, publishing books and articles, still totally clueless I might add, but thankfully, as keen as ever.

The pen, so they say, is mightier than the sword and seeing as how Keith has never exactly had the temperament (sober at least) for a fighter; I suppose it had to fall that a writer he would eventually become. In fact, thinking about it now it seems that he has been studiously scribbling something or other ever since I've known him.

Over the long and wonderful years that I have shared with Keith, on and away from the bankside, I have witnessed the total metamorphosis from the mild mannered (if sometimes, strange-hatted) young carp angler that I first encountered, into the gargantuan, larger than life itself character that he has now become.

You would know if you had ever shared a lake with 'The Jenks', even if you were at opposing ends of Wraysbury. You would just know. The multi-coloured, wild haired, travelling chef guise that appears to have become his trademark is but a small extension of the far more outlandish personality trapped within. It does escape occasionally, however, although usually with the added influence of one embalming fluid or another.

To see Keith perform, seemingly at the drop of a cork, is a spectacle indeed. I mean, Christ, if only that air guitar were real we'd both be languishing in a rock and roll lifestyle second only to Keith Richards. Maybe he was originally destined for far greater things in life, but carp angling has him now, and I'm sure that in some strange way it will be that little bit richer for it.

One thing that has remained a constant throughout this Dr Jekyll and Mr Jenks transformation is the razor sharp wit and fluidity of prose that his friends know, and sometimes fear, only too well. It is with these talents that he will now, undoubtedly, amuse and entertain you. So sit back, pull a cork and enjoy a bloody good read!

Acknowledgments

So, where do I start without making this sound like an acceptance speech at any one of a thousand award ceremonies? Well, it's difficult not to, I suppose, but it would be impossible to acknowledge everybody who has had some influence in my life, fishing or otherwise, so to all of those I miss out, believe me, you have all meant something and are deserving of unwritten praise.

Obviously, there are people who have had a major influence, not only with this book, but also with my life. To give this some semblance of order I will start with the latter and work downwards? Upwards? Sideways? Work it out for yourself!

My wife, Linda, and children, Vincent and Christine, for making my life as stress free and happy as possible over the past three decades. My mum, for every possible thing that mums are to their sons, and for continually telling me that I could do it – whatever 'it' may be. My in-laws, Stan and Beryl, for being typical in-laws yet still treating me like their own son.

My boss, Nic, for understanding my needs and turning the odd blind eye when others wouldn't have. To all of my workmates, for being just that - mates. To Shirley and Simon, the best non-fishing friends I have, and for whose company I will give up a weekend's fishing - in the winter, at least!

To many, many authors for the knowledge that the English language can be played like a musical instrument - and the lessons are free. To musicians everywhere for giving me the hooks to hang memories on - your words appear occasionally in this book, I hope you forgive the liberty. To Steve Morgan and Kevin Knight, not only for their marvellous bait but for more help than people could imagine.

To Paul Selman and Stephen Lane for letting me do this the way I wanted to do it. To Pete Curtis, who also uses his pencil, pen and brush like a musical instrument, and is a maestro with them.

...and so, to the fishermen. The number eludes me, but some deserve special mention. To Dave 'Porky' Thouless, who had the influence on my fishing which is depicted in the book. All of the Horton syndicate, where I realised how little I really knew and began to learn much. Especially to Robbie, C.P., Tony Badham, Phil Thompson, Frogger, Sir Pete, Rob Tough and many more. To my long distance friend Mick Dickens, who is still one of the best anglers I have ever met, but will continue to suffer at the expense of my scathing wit - poor lad, someone give him a hand!

And, finally, to the three major players in my life over recent years.

To Reg, my long suffering Spurs partner, whose humour is without parallel and whose phone calls inevitably leave me gasping for breath and clutching my aching stomach.

To Chilly, who is as different from me as can possibly be imagined but who has become, in the relatively short time that I have known him, one of the very best friends I have known. Long may it continue.

And to Dave, who is the very best friend I have known. We have fished together on too few occasions of late, but when we do I realise that this situation should not continue for long - nor will it.

And, finally - to the carp, all of 'em. Small and large, common and mirror. Without them we would be very insignificant. Don't forget that.

Introduction

Hmm. A novel, eh? So what does that mean, that I'm just writing my life story under a pseudonym?

Well, not really.

The idea had been sloshing around in the whirlpool of my mind for some time, but I couldn't put flesh to the bones of that idea. Then, when Dave wrote of his 'Obsession', I realised that I could not write my 'life story' - partly because Dave had told most of it, but mainly because I knew that anything I wrote would come nowhere near to his marvellous book.

Then, at the launch of Dave's book at last year's Carp Society Conference, Paul Selman innocently asked, "So when are you going to write a book then, Keith?"

The knowledge that someone might feel the need to publish something that I had written was the flame to the blue touch paper, and the bones soon began to bear flesh.

Once I came up with the full idea, many people were influential in spurring me on to go for it fully and once it started I couldn't stop - the words kept coming and coming. I ended up writing almost twice as many as we had originally agreed on but, fortunately, Paul just kept reading, Wendy kept proofing and I kept writing. All the time, Dave and Chilly devoured everything I threw at them and kept making the right noises to encourage me to write more.

Of all the events in the book, only half a dozen (or so...) really happened, the rest have the dubious honour of being a part of my strange and inventive imagination.

Of the characters, a few are real, some are a composite of two, three or four personalities, and many are fictitious. So, if you think that you appear in these pages, the chances are that you are mistaken - probably! As for The Common, well that is obviously real (as are all the other fish), how could I possibly invent anything as wonderful? In his book, An Obsession with Carp, Dave Lane's description of the mythical Big Common is one of my favourite pieces of carp literature and was another flame that helped ignite the blue touch paper and, with his kind permission, I have reproduced part of it here ...

"In almost every lake that I have ever fished there is a big common that lurks within the myths and legends that circulate late at night, and in hushed whispers. He always seems to be about five pounds or so bigger than the biggest known fish in the lake and, of course, he has never been landed, although he has usually been lost under some bizarre set of circumstances, usually involving a punt that he happened to be a foot longer than.

Quite how he transcends from one end of the country to the other is a mystery to me unless, of course, we are surrounded by uncaught, big commons! I think it more likely that he is, in some way, omnipresent and appears to all at the same time.

It is my burning ambition to catch him one day, it wouldn't matter from where he came, for surely he would be the incarnation of all the elusive 'Big Commons' that reside in every pond, ditch or lake that has ever seen a rod and line.

Long live the Big Common, I say, for he signifies the very essence of carp angling."

This book isn't just about carp fishing, it's about a passion for anything - be it angling, football, cricket or flower arranging - and the bonds that form between people with the same passion. To describe this passion, my imagination has been stretched to limits I didn't realise I had. Now it's the turn of yours - hopefully the stretching will be much more pleasurable. Enjoy.

Part One

The Learning Curve

Preface

"Quickly, get the net! Get the net!!"

The fish surged powerfully once more and Stan, grudgingly loosening the clutch, allowed it to take a little more line. This had been the pattern for the past ten minutes and, at last, Stan's cries for assistance had been answered when Chris stumbled breathlessly into the swim and quickly obeyed Stan's command.

"Any ideas?" he enquired, in between gulps of fresh air.

"Dunno, but I can't get it off the bottom. It's been up and down these margins for about ten minutes."

Then, almost as if he was attached to a dolphin, Stan watched the line rise from the vertical to the horizontal in a matter of seconds and, suddenly, he and Chris were graced with the vision of a huge flank covered by a chainmail of golden scales glistening in the early morning sunlight.

Stan's reverie was broken by the insistent ringing of the telephone and, automatically, his arm snaked out and brought the receiver to his ear.

"Good morning, Halcyon Printing, Stan speaking."

"Yo, boy. How ya doing?" came Chris's familiar greeting, shattering the daydream like fine crystal against rock.

"Not bad, mate," replied Stan.

"What d'ya know then, fella?"

"I know I was just about to land the big Common when you rang, that's what I know," came Stan's feigned indignant reply.

"Oh dear, that's gonna be a bit tricky then, init?"

Stan could sense the smirk on the other end of the line and knew exactly what was coming but, like the stooge in a comedy duo, he dutifully played out his role,

"How d'you mean?"

"Well, that means it's gonna come out *twice* this weekend then, don't it!"

"Yep, better make sure Buzz and Sid have got plenty of film, eh boy!"

The usual chuckles came and, pretty soon, they slipped into the same conversation they had been having for the past decade or so but, despite what must have seemed like constant repetition to an onlooker, there was no sign of boredom, no hint of déjà vu from either party and they chatted for ten minutes or so as if it was the very first time that they had discussed what time they would arrive at the weekend, where they fancied fishing, had they heard the weather forecast, had they cooked enough hemp, and a myriad other formalities that constituted a telephone call about an impending carp angling session. Despite having known each other for more than fifteen years, they never became bored with their constant conversations about carp angling and a day didn't go by without at least one phone call between them, which inevitably ended with one or both of them chortling down the phone at yet another rib tickling bout of wit and repartee. The same could equally be said about their other two, long time, angling companions - Buzz and Sid.

    The four of them had been angling together for almost half a decade now, but their angling careers spanned almost four decades and, as the other three constantly reminded him, Stan's went back further than all of them...

Chapter One - 1963

The winter had been one of the harshest in recent memory but, for an eight year old boy, it had been full of snowballs, snowmen, and endless school holidays due to frozen boilers.

Now, with the eventual onset of spring, Stan's thoughts turned to things that hopped, scuttled, slithered and swam. Like most young boys he had an insatiable appetite for nature - frogs, snakes, spiders and fish being high on the list of favourites which inevitably meant that, when not at school, he could usually be found, ankle deep, in the smallest, muddiest pool searching diligently with net and jar in hand for spawn, stickleback or anything else that swam. His eventual tardy return would bring gasps of horror from his mother at the inordinate amount of mud and assorted vegetation that such a small body could carry, and a wry smile from his father when presented with the jar and its contents for perusal and approval.

It was obvious to his parents that, even at this age, Stan had a great affinity with Mother Nature and all of her kin, and they did all that they could to encourage this love affair. So it was that, when he exploded breathlessly into the kitchen at the beginning of another endless summer holiday, his mother could only stand, listen and try to decipher from the deluge of words spewing from her son's mouth what had become the latest wonder in his short life. Slowed down to half speed, it came out something like this.

"Mick's got a fishing rod and his dad said we could both use it and he's gonna take us to the common and we can catch fish so can I go? I need some bread and my jar so is it okay? We'll be back by teatime (can we have ham and chips) and I promise I won't be late. Is it okay?"

There followed a short pause, then a huge gasping as Stan refilled his deflated lungs. His mother would have no more thought of saying "no" than she would have thought of eating worms and so it was that Stan took his first fateful step onto the lowest rung of the huge ladder that was angling. That summer brought great adventures and, most importantly, it brought that first electric sensation of something alive on the other end of the line, and it was something that pulled back. Both boys caught fish, the like of which they had only ever seen in picture books, huge gudgeon and perch almost as big as their hands. These they attempted to take home to show their proud parents but it took little persuasion from these older, and obviously wiser heads that the best place for their catches was back in the pond from which they came and not gasping for their life in a jam-jar barely big enough to hold them. The return to school brought a temporary halt to Stan's fishing career but the seed had been sown in very fertile soil and it would take very little to nurture it and coax it to bloom magnificently.

The harsh winter had taken its toll on many of Mother Nature's kin and many animals, birds and plants would never see another spring and the eventual thaw brought about the least tasteful part of John Bennett's job as gamekeeper. The estate he managed was in the Avon Valley on the Hampshire/Dorset border and had suffered badly from the ravages of the worst winter in many years. He did not relish the forthcoming clean up. However, as spring's warming hands massaged life back into the land and its inhabitants, John began to once again relish his work. By mid-summer the winter was but a distant memory and, as he once more brought his handkerchief up to mop his soaking brow, John watched with relief and wonder as the fish in the mill pond thrashed along the verdant margins in their annual quest for immortality. The wonder was that there were any fish left alive in what had been, only a few months previously, a four acre block of ice. Of course, he had hoped that the deep water alongside the dam wall had remained unfrozen twelve feet down, but he had also known that there would have been very little oxygen to sustain all the fish in the pond. This knowledge had not proven unfounded and by the time the lake had thawed, the two months of constant ice blanket had brought about the demise of the bream, roach, rudd and many of the tench and carp. It was, however, the latter two that he was watching now and he had a certain admiration for these obviously hardy species. Within a week, John was studiously surveying a ball of weed which he had just dragged from the lake margins and there, on the strands of weed, he could see the evidence of the full circle of life, what Darwin had called the survival of the fittest. Thousands of eggs clung to the dripping vegetation which he was meticulously transferring into a large forty gallon tank on the back of his flat bed. This he then drove to the far end of the estate to the old trout hatchery and deposited into the rich, spring fed waters to join the dozen or so balls of weed he had already relocated.

By early autumn he could see the results of his labours flashing like silver pins amongst the now flourishing weed beds. Even at this size it was possible to differentiate between the darker forms of the tench fry and the pretenders to the throne of the King of Lakes, and amongst these, as in any animals, some were destined to be larger pretenders than others-John just hoped that they could survive the forthcoming cold months. Only time would tell.

Chapter Two - 1966

"... they think it's all over. It is now!"

Living in a South London suburb had its advantages for Stan and his mates when it came to travelling to and from their local ponds. World Cup fever was rife but this was an era before football violence had become de rigueur and their parents thought nothing of allowing these ten and eleven year olds to go by bus or bike to their favourite summer haunts. For his tenth birthday, Stan's mum and dad had presented him with a wonderful fishing rod and reel, with line, floats and split-shot all as part of the package and he regarded them as the best there ever was. The fact that all his parents could afford came under the title of 'The Junior Fishing Kit', and was not from the local tackle shop but care of F. W. Woolworth, meant nothing to their mesmerised offspring. Being a Piscean meant that Stan would have to wait for more clement weather before wetting his first line but it was not long before his float was sailing through the air to ensnare any passing vegetation, clothing, and occasionally an unwary cyprinid.

By the time that Bobby Moore was proudly holding aloft the Jules Rimet trophy for the benefit of an elated nation and Kenneth Wolstenholme's immortal words were ringing in millions of ears, Stan was a veteran at this fishing lark. He had even worked out that float fishing with 12lb line and a size 6 hook was not the way to fool loads of fish into picking up his maggots. With the help of Bob in their local hardware and fishing tackle shop, Mick and Stan had refined their tackle to 4lb line and size 14 hooks (the smallest eyed hook they could buy) and had even managed to fashion a catapult, as only young boys can. This they used to fire out their maggots but, inevitably, the maggots became missiles as the boys' patience waned and their laughter echoed through the trees and around the banks of their local pond.

Despite this obvious irreverence, they still managed to catch their fair share of gudgeon and small, suicidal perch.

Then, one day towards the end of their summer holiday, a major change took place - a change that would set Stan's small, grubby shoes on the next rung of the angling ladder.

Stan had arranged to meet Mick at their usual rendezvous spot under the big old oak outside the Old People's Home. As usual, Stan would bring the sandwiches and Mick would bring a bottle of juice and the maggots. After waiting for half an hour, Stan thought that he must have missed Mick so cycled the half mile to the pond, expecting to see his mate's bright red bike leaning against their usual tree. On his arrival, however, there was no sign of Mick or, more importantly, the bait and so Stan did the most natural thing for an angler to do when faced with the possibility of not being able to fish - he threw a wobbly! After a few minutes of ranting, raving, kicking trees and experimenting with a couple of newly acquired swear words he was suddenly aware that he was being watched.

"You should be careful about which trees you kick, you know," said the amused onlooker, "they sometimes kick back."

Despite his agitated state, Stan could not help smiling at the thought of a tree with legs and, by way of an excuse, he mumbled,

"Well, it's lucky it weren't Mick."

"And Mick is who?" enquired the tall, young man.

"He's got the maggots, ain't he?" replied Stan, as if this would be identification enough for the man to spot his errant friend in a Wembley crowd.

"Oh. Maggots. That's your problem then."

"What problem?" queried Stan, totally unaware that his black mood had disappeared like a wisp of smoke in a stiff breeze.

"Well, if you're using maggots then all you'll catch is gudgeon and small perch, but if you want to catch some real fish you should try using bread flake."

Stan was unable to stop his jaw from dropping open at this incredible feat of clairvoyance and his admiration for this prophet soared.

"My name's Jack, what's yours?" enquired the affable young man. "Stan Peacock. Have you got any bread?"

"Well, Stan Peacock-have-you-got-any-bread, nice to meet you. Do you mind if I just call you Stan?"

This level of humour was way above the young angler's head but, ignoring his obvious stupidity, Stan ploughed on in his quest for the ultimate bait that Jack had hinted at. "Yeah, that's my name. Have you got any bread' cos Mick's got the maggots? What fish do you catch with bread, then?"

Jack smiled at the lad's persistence and, walking off through the trees, he beckoned for Stan to follow. Needing no more encouragement, Stan scurried off in pursuit and almost ran into the back of his quarry as Jack stopped at the back of his swim. He had two rods set up on banksticks and so much tackle that Stan's eyes were almost out on stalks. Moving carefully through the tight swim, Jack crouched down by the waterside and pulled up a previously unseen keepnet whilst motioning for Stan to look inside. The young boy moved as if on eggshells, terrified of even touching some of the bright, gleaming fishing hardware that was scattered liberally around the swim. Because of this tightrope walk, he was totally unprepared for the bounty that was awaiting his greedy gaze at the bottom of the now fully raised keepnet. There, amongst the bright-green mesh, was a mass of silver scales, but they did not seem to be attached to the size of fish that Stan was used to seeing and as he gazed in wonderment he was able to identify, by dint of his constant reading of "The Book of British Freshwater Fishes", perch, roach and amazingly, bream. But what bream! They must have weighed five pounds each! (As it happened, they were no more than two pounds apiece, but the effect was stunning). Ogling, slack-jawed, he was almost beyond speech and was able only to utter a series of obscure sounds.

"Cor! They're .... Wow, look at that! Did you .... ? Can I, y'know, touch one?"

"Yeah, of course," chuckled Jack. "But wet your hands first so you don't damage them," he requested.

Even in his state of near ecstasy, Stan was temporarily halted by the thought that he may have caused damage to the fish he had caught, merely by the act of picking them up. Ever so carefully he dipped his hands into the pond, as though anointing them, and then reverently put them into the lucky dip bag of splashing and flipping fish. Very gently they encircled a slippery prize and, with the look of a young child on Christmas morning, he drew the fish into his hungry gaze and his eyes fed upon it like a starving man at a banquet.

"Oh, wow, it's huge," he squealed, whilst gawping at the carefully cradled bream in his cupped hands.

"Yeah. Do you want to catch one?" asked Jack casually, loving every minute of the young boy's infectious wonderment, and more than willing to give him the chance of catching the prize of his short life. While Stan attempted to take in the full possibilities that this question entailed, Jack slipped the fish back into the keepnet and lowered it back into the shaded waters. He then picked up his float rod and began readying it for Stan's use, ensuring that the float was set at the correct depth and that no shot had been dislodged in the last capture.

The fact that he was to be given a chance to fish in Jack's swim was cause enough for him to almost wet himself with excitement. When it suddenly dawned on Stan that he was to be allowed to use this obviously remarkable angler's tackle, his incontinence was complete and he rushed into the nearby bushes clutching his nether regions, much to Jack's stifled amusement. By the time he returned to the swim he was intent on only one thing. Being too young to feel any embarrassment, he ran straight over to Jack in the hope of grasping the gleaming rod before its owner suddenly came to his senses and changed his mind. Jack had no intention of disappointing the young angler, he merely needed to slow him down so that he might learn a little from what was about to transpire.

"Right, see how deep I've set the float? That's so that the bait is on the bottom, which is where a lot of fish like bream and roach and tench feed," explained Jack, relishing the role of teacher - a role he would take on professionally in the next few years. Stan nodded vigorously, having completely lost the power of speech, and just wished that he could be fishing.

Stoically trying to ignore Stan's impatience, Jack kept in control of the rod and the conversation and, picking up a nearby loaf, began the next installment of the day's lesson.

"Now, when you use bread, make sure you use the fresh stuff if you can, like the stuff your mum has in her bread bin. Then, when you want to put a bit on the hook, take it from the middle of the loaf and pinch a little piece on the eye, like this."

Taking the hook in one hand, Jack pinched off a small piece of bread flake with the other and demonstrated the method to his now rapt audience then, handing him the rod, he pointed Stan in the direction of the previously baited feeding area fifteen yards distant.

"Right, see where those bubbles are? Just flick the float out past them and reel it slowly back to that spot," explained Jack, directing Stan's gaze to the relevant spot.

Hesitantly, Stan grasped the rod and gazed out across the lake. There, as described, were the tell-tale bubbles that indicated something feeding down below and, so, taking careful aim, he executed a perfect underarm cast. 'Perfect' was, however, a relative term in the context of the situation and the two anglers watched in amazement as the float soared skywards like a Saturn 5 rocket attempting to break free of the Earth's grasp! On reaching its zenith, it hovered for a second before inevitably succumbing to gravity's insistent pull and plummeted earthwards to land in a tangled mess of hook, leads, line and float at the feet of the onlookers.

Jack didn't know what to laugh at first - the mass of tackle or the anguished look on Stan's face, as if he had just dropped a Ming vase onto concrete. Carefully taking the rod from his abashed pupil, Jack painstakingly unpicked the tangle of tackle whilst trying to calm Stan's nerves with some muttered reassurances.

"Okay, let's try again, but just relax and let the float go a little earlier," he coached. Stan took the rod again and, straining every nerve and poking his tongue into his cheek in rapt concentration, he let fly once more. This time the direction was almost perfect and the baited hook landed with the grace of a stuck-pig, five yards behind the still bubbling baited area. Jack leapt forward to prevent the inevitable bird's nest as Stan began frantically reeling the float back to the bubbles, as directed, and they both watched expectantly as the float settled, cocked and revealed an inch of luminous orange paint. Stan gripped the rod so intently that his knuckles turned white and Jack suggested that he put it down on to the rest to avoid any chance of disturbing the float. It then dawned on Jack, in a flash of foresight, the possible devastation a bite could produce and he had a vision of rod in tree, Stan on his back and a fish flapping desperately in the mud! In a bid to avoid this disastrous outcome, he began quietly chatting to his young protégé, whilst bending to pick up a handful of carefully prepared groundbait.

"Right, I'll put in a little bit more bait to keep their attention, and you keep your eye on the float, but don't strike until it goes right under."

Once again, he performed the task as described and threw three or four golf ball sized balls of groundbait around the float, rocking it with the impact. An imperceptible lift of the float alerted him to the presence of something below and he prepared to leap to Stan's aid if something should go awry. Stan, however, was just as aware of something alive in the float's vicinity and tensed every muscle in anticipation of its disappearance. Then it was gone - no pre-emptive dip of the orange tip, no mass of bubbles to indicate a fishy presence -just a small expanding ring of ripples to indicate where the float had been. Before Jack could react, Stan had jerked the rod upwards instinctively and, instead of the anticipated jolt as the hook found a fish's lips, the two of them watched in slow motion as the float arced over their heads and into a waiting branch. Unable to control himself, Jack barked out a sudden laugh, which was then overtaken by the deluge that followed and, with tears running down his face, he fell backwards onto the floor and lay there like a stranded spider. Stan's initial horror was also replaced by a series of short bursts of laughter until; shortly, the two of them were clutching their sides and wiping the tears from their cheeks. As a semblance of calm and sanity eventually returned, Jack picked himself up and stretched to retrieve the object of their hysteria and then, handing the hook to Stan, offered him the loaf of bread to re-bait it with.

Stan proved that he had paid a modicum of attention and pulled out a grape-sized piece of flake and proceeded to mould it around the hook. With subtlety, Jack removed a few pinches of bread so that the fish ·would be able to get their mouths round it, then watched as the ever improving Stan flicked the float to within a yard of the desired spot, landing it with merely a splash. A couple more balls of groundbait followed and, once again, the two new friends sat down to watch the unraveling drama. Stan's heart was pounding so hard in his small chest that he was certain the fish would be able to hear it. His worries were proven unfounded as, a few minutes later, the float was once again dragged below the watery surface but this time the ensuing strike met with a resistance so solid that it was like an electric shock along the young angler's arm and he almost dropped the rod. Retaining control, though, he began frantically reeling in the line - so quickly, in fact, that Jack thought he would lose the fish, and he leaned over to reduce the drag on the reel. This outside intervention helped avoid another disaster and, within a minute or so, Stan was guiding a fine looking bream towards the waiting net held by Jack.

"Steady now," said the netsman, "nice and steady, don't rush it, just ease it over the net, boy."

This calming advice, however, came over as "nnngkk bbblaaah, *** fnafnafna gg @@ gummmpph!!!" and Stan had only one goal in mind, which was to get the huge fish into the net NOW! And then it was, and they both let out a whelp of delight before rushing forward to admire their prize.

"Oh, wow, it's huge," gasped Stan and, not one to burst the boy's bubble of enthusiasm, Jack agreed enthusiastically even though he could see the skimmer bream was barely over a pound in weight. Reverently, the young boy picked up his silver prize in dampened hands and gawped down on it in awe, before carefully returning it from whence it came. Jack had no doubt that here was an angler for the future, and patted him warmly on the back before baiting the hook once again.

The day passed with a further three bream of similar size succumbing to Stan's baited hook before the brand new friends bade each other farewell for the day. What a day! Stan would remember this day for a very long time and, although his friendship with Jack would last only a few weeks, the effect of that relationship would mould the rest of his fishing career. The remaining days of their summer holidays passed with them fishing together on three more occasions, and Stan's knowledge increased a hundred-fold, before they both had to return to their respective schools. Jack's journey, however, was to be the greater in distance and, ultimately, in life, as he began his years at Leeds University and although he would return home for one or two weeks a year the two anglers would never meet again. But that first bream that he had cajoled into the net for Stan would be one of his finest angling achievements for many years.

For the past three years one of the most enjoyable parts of John's job was to oversee the stock in the old trout hatchery. His hopes for some milder winters had been realised and the survivors of the Big Freeze had flourished, although some had inevitably succumbed. Now, however, as the waters were warmed by the third summer's sun, the hardier carp and tench had reached sufficient size to become more than just a part of the food chain - and some had, inevitably, benefited more than others from the rich bounty available to them. The largest of the survivors, a common carp, was fast approaching double figures and was forever under the careful scrutiny of John's watchful eye. It, therefore, became more of a shock than normal when he learnt of the death of Mr. Drayton, the landowner; although it did not come as too much of a surprise that the recently ailing octogenarian had finally succumbed to the ravages of time. It was with a certain amount of surprise that John and his co-workers found out that Mr. Drayton's son, Thomas, had decided to sell the house and land to a group of property developers. They planned to turn the estate into a golf course and country house.

After his initial worries over his own welfare his thoughts went to the animals in his recent care, especially those in the trout hatchery, and it took him little time to contact his good friend Tom Watts, the secretary of the local Ringwood and District Angling Society. Tom had been badgering John for some time about letting him have some of the fish in his care to help replenish the stock in a couple of the Society's lakes. However, John had stoically refused, but he now realised that the fish would have little chance of survival if they remained in their present home. After a quiet chat over an ale in their local hostelry, John and Tom arranged for the netting and transfer of as many of the fish as possible before the bulldozers moved in.

So it was, a week later, they were surveying the fruits of their labours as the fish lay in a couple of 500 gallon tanks on the back of one of the Society member's lorries. The operation had gone relatively smoothly and they had managed to net both lakes in the space of the weekend, taking a mixture of carp, tench, trout, perch, roach and bream.

The Society had three lakes, two of which were mainly for match angling and it was these that received the bulk of the catch. The third lake, an overgrown 7 acre Pit, was already home to a few pike and carp and it was into here that Tom had decided to deposit the larger tench and the fifty or so carp for the foreseeable future. The lake was rarely fished, as the club was mainly populated by match and pleasure anglers, so the carp were to remain comparatively undisturbed for the next couple of years and would have the time and space to feed and grow.

Chapter Three - 1969

"One small step for man. One giant leap for Mankind ..."

Neil Armstrong's momentous words were like an electric shock through Stan's nervous system. For the past eighteen months there seemed to be little else on his young mind but the need to get home from school as quickly as was adolescently possible in order to keep fully abreast of every nuance of America's stride toward the moon. Today had been the culmination concerned.

The summer holidays were but a week away and, now that his present passion was temporarily spent, he could concentrate his efforts for the coming weeks in search of some more unwilling victims to fall prey to his maggot surprise. The past twelve months had seen him move to his secondary school with a new group of friends to be discovered and, in amongst them as always, he found the fisherman.

Steve Wright's birthday happened to be the day after Neil Armstrong's first steps on the moon, and six months after Stan's - a fact that Steve would continue to remind him of for the rest of their friendship - and they both had very similar tastes. Football, fishing, music and anything to do with nature were their common likes, and even their dislikes were similar, especially when it came to fellow pupils. Whether certain people have the ability to make themselves universally unpopular, or whether there is a mass consciousness that says, "He's not very nice, dislike him" is difficult to fathom. In young children especially, there is no hiding place if someone finds you distasteful, and the feeling spreads like wildfire, especially if the 'disliker' is, himself, a popular figure. Steve and Stan were fortunate because they were both on the right side of 'popular' to avoid the disapproval of the masses, but they were not beyond the hypnotic state themselves.

So it was that, a year previously, they had first met during a particularly vicious bout of pupil-baiting and the verbal abuse of a fellow student who just happened to weigh a few pounds more than was deemed adequate. Whilst offering a few snide remarks from the safety of the crowd, Steve had backed into Stan and they had both tumbled to the floor in a heap. Their initial reaction was to turn the tide of abuse onto each other but, within seconds, they both apologised to each other as that strange chemistry that forms 'friendship' suddenly bubbled away and produced a bond that would last for many years. This is, indeed, a strange chemistry and if it were something between a man and a woman it would be called love at first sight but, between two men, or boys, it has no name. That is not to say, however, that it does not exist because some friendships, a very small percentage, become so strong that it becomes an almost tangible object. At this moment in time Stan had not an inkling of this. However, during his life he would - like most people - form that indescribable bond at least half a dozen times. As is always the case in these situations, it took little time for the boys to discover their common likes and dislikes. Within a few short weeks they were sitting on the banks of the park lake where Stan had sat with Jack a few years earlier, both intent on being the first to land a fish. There were, outwardly, few similarities between the two of them. Stan was of medium height and build and, with his head of short, brown, unkempt hair, could easily be described as 'ordinary' looking and shortly to acquire many teenage spots. Steve's appearance, on the other hand, could be described as 'striking', although not for any reasons of good looks or dazzling blue eyes.

His skinny build accentuated his natural height, giving the impression of a very tall boy, and the rather gaunt lines of his face lent credence to this. But the most startling part was his hair which although cropped short and kept remarkably tidy, was obviously a concern to him. When Steve and Stan allowed their hair to flow in the coming years, Steve's natural tight curls would be seen in all their glory, giving the impression of a white Michael Jackson. The only time that this was witnessed in these early years was when the boys exited the showers after games, but Steve's withering look and rapier-like tongue stemmed any attempt at schoolboy humour from his fellow pupils.

The summer passed with the boys spending many hours together by the banks of one pond or another. A football was normally thrown in with the motley array of fishing tackle and, if the fish were more than usually reticent to accept their offer of a drowned maggot cocktail, then you could be sure that their boredom would give way first to tree climbing, then eventually, to an assault on the football.

The cement of time had strengthened their camaraderie and, by the time that the moon landing had become the third or fourth subject of conversation, their friendship had become that 'almost tangible object.' Time was also to play a big part in Stan's outlook on fishing for the next few years because, as he and Steve had reached their teens, it was now possible for them to go to football matches on their own, albeit with the grudging consent of their parents. They had been going to see local non-league teams for a year or so now and, in a crowd that was swelled by their addition, there was little to concern their parents. However, the boys' sights were set higher. Much higher! The First Division in fact and their first sortie was to be to Stamford Bridge at the start of the season. This did not interfere with the fishing of this Woodstock summer but would, over the next couple of years, change Stan's priorities a little. For now, though, the summer was before them and they had decided to make a change in their fishing as well. Not exactly a leap to the First Division, but a move to running water. They decided to jump on a train and fish the River Thames.

Their first sight of the river at Kingston must have seemed as daunting as the first sight of Old Trafford for a non-league team. Neither boy was likely to admit that to his mate so they pushed on along the towpath to an area they had been told about by their local tackle shop owner. The main benefit that Steve and Stan could see in fishing Canbury Gardens was the close proximity of the cafe and adjacent lawn - ideal for a game of football and a refreshing half-time drink. However, it was with some surprise, many hours later, that they realised the whole day had passed without a thought of a kick-about. They found the river both fascinating and daunting at the same time, and their first cast into the swiftly flowing current had both of the boys gawping at the speed with which the float was trotting from view. After half an hour of experimentation and swim swapping, they gradually started to get to grips with the speed of the flow, both opting to trot their baits in the relatively sedate water of the close margin. As he gazed across to the far bank, a quarter of a mile away, Stan wondered what monsters must inhabit those dark, churning depths and, as if to answer his question, his float was suddenly wrenched from view. The ensuing strike was slow, cumbersome but, ultimately, successful and he thrilled at the sensation of life at the end of the line. Within seconds, he and Steve were gazing down at their first river fish - a sparkling, silver fish, no bigger than a cigarette, which neither had seen the like of before. That mattered little. They had begun their river campaign successfully. Steve unloaded the keepnet from its pocket in his tackle box and dropped it into the river, securing it firmly by tying it to a convenient tree-root, lest their quarry should struggle free!

By mid-afternoon it was time for the pair to leave and, with everything packed away, they lifted the shimmering, shaking keep-net from the water and gazed down on Stan's fish and the dozen similar that had followed it into the net. They had learnt that the fish were called bleak, and were, obviously, prolific in the river. Despite this knowledge, they had both enjoyed themselves greatly and the bus journey home passed with plans for their next assault on the river and the monsters they would obviously catch. A further four trips that summer saw the boys renew their acquaintance with the dreaded bleak and by the end of their fourth trip the football had become the main part of their enjoyment as they failed to get through the hordes of hungry little fish to any other species. Despite this, they had derived great enjoyment from their trips and had learnt a new way of angling, one that they looked forward to employing in the near future. So it was that, a couple of weeks into the football season and on a weekend that Chelsea were playing away, they decided on a final trip to the Thames before they hung up their rods for the year.

Having spoken to a couple of boys on their return to school after the holidays, Stan learnt of a stretch of river a few miles away from Kingston, in front of Hampton Court Palace, and within a two minute walk of the train station. Armed with this knowledge they made the stroll along the towpath, early one Saturday morning, to a spot opposite an island. Their first impression was that there was nowhere to play football, but this initial downside was soon forgotten as they settled into their swims and took stock of the area in front of them. Unlike Kingston, they didn't need binoculars to see the far side of the river as the island was no more than 100 yards distant and swathed in trees whose branches were dipping delicately into the passing waters. The water in front of them meandered rather than rushed by and their floats took more of a leisurely stroll along the margins, occasionally snagging on some unseen sub-aquatic vegetation. By degrees, they found a better line and depth for the floats' passage and began steadily feeding maggots along it. An hour passed like a minute when, suddenly, Steve's float dipped, stopped, dipped again then disappeared. His strike met a solid resistance. Panic ensued as the fish took control of the situation, using the current in its bid to gain the sanctuary of some overhanging foliage further along the towpath. It had then dawned on Stan, like a hammer blow, that here was a fish that would need to be netted, an operation that neither of them had ever been required to perform. As Steve did his best to hang onto the leviathan on the other end of his line, Stan attempted to assemble the mesh and pole into some semblance of a fish netting device.

"Quick, get the net! Get the net!" screamed Steve as he saw the silver flash of a fish not three yards from the bank, and then almost joined it as Stan charged past him like the demented knight in a bizarre form of jousting contest. Thrusting the net into the river, the gentle flow suddenly transformed into a raging torrent - or so it seemed to Stan - and the net was wrenched to the right and almost from his grip. Quickly regaining a modicum of control, Stan was astonished to see the fish swim straight into the net and, before it realised its mistake, he scooped it victoriously into the air and once again almost tumbled Steve into the river. Laying their enmeshed prize onto the thin strip of grass along the riverbank, Stan pulled back the net to reveal a bright, silvery, monstrous roach.

Monstrous was a relative term, obviously, but at fourteen ounces it was by far the largest fish either of them had caught. Their joy was unbounded, so much so that passers-by slowed to see what all the fuss was about and then walked on, mystified at how something so small and slippery could cause such a reaction - nothing new there then! The keep net was unshipped once again and its latest occupant reverently slipped into its folds with both anglers sure that it would not remain in solitary confinement for long. Their confidence was not wholly unfounded for they both hooked roach in excess of a pound, unfortunately neither angler realised this as they both lost out in the battle between line and snag; the roach escaping the hookholds whilst the young anglers tussled with the sub-surface vegetation. The inevitable bleak joined the lone captive in the net, and the day ended with a brace of suicidal perch falling to Stan's rods. All in all, a very successful outing and one that they would continually remind each other of during the footballing winter that followed. They spent the next two or three seasons fishing together on the river, and a few small ponds, but two things were to temporarily stem the tide for both of them in that time - goals and girls!

Since their introduction into the neglected gravel pit the carp had remained exactly that - neglected. They were, therefore, able to utilize their formative years to the utmost, doubling and, in some cases, trebling their weight. But this sort of increase in size could not go unnoticed indefinitely and, so, in the spring of that moon-walking year, the sounds and vibrations of anglers became a regular part of the bankside disturbance. Although quite overgrown, the pit was still relatively young, having been dug in the early '50's and, so, was in the adolescent years of a gravel pit. The pH of the water had stabilized sufficiently to promote the necessary plant and invertebrate life, which in turn sustained the higher members of the food chain. This was why the carp, and other fish species, had thrived so well. But, now, the highest member of the food chain had arrived to, metaphorically, set its place at the table. A small group of anglers, having researched the rumours diligently, had decided that the large pit would be worth some serious attention. Not only for the carp, for they were still considered by some as almost uncatchable, but also for the bream and tench of which there were a few impressive specimens resident in the pit. As the temperatures rose during the close season, the band of four anglers were evident more often along the banks of the Pit, pinpointing areas of interest and regular fish activity. As June arrived, they set about pre-baiting some likely areas in readiness for their midnight start a fortnight later.

The inhabitants of the pit were totally unprepared for these new food offerings and soon their natural curiosity overcame their inbred caution and the larger denizens joined the already gluttonous shoals of roach and rudd in disposing of the mashed bread, maggots, and corn feast that was set before them. Little wonder, then, that after a dozen such feasts they continued to feed greedily despite the addition of hook and line amongst the, now, acceptable but unnatural fare, and by dawn of the first day of the season almost two dozen fish had felt a hook point for the very first time. Amongst them, the largest inhabitant of the lake - The Common - had been one of the earliest to give in to its greed and fought all the way to the net in a bid to rid itself of the frightening *and unnatural feeling. Once landed, the anglers treated this most welcome prize with great care and, after recording a weight of almost fourteen pounds, they released it back into its now less than secure sanctuary.*

This initial surprising success had merely filled the anglers with greater enthusiasm and they fished the pit regularly for the rest of the year, changing their maggots for deadbaits with the arrival of winter, and changing their quarry from carp and tench to pike and perch. Prior to this assault on the lake's predators, The Common allowed its defences to drop once more, this time exceeding its previous weight by almost a pound, but it found these experiences greatly disturbing and they were embedded deeply, instinctively within itself. It would be much more cautious in future.

Chapter Four - 1972/73

"Turn that row down, will you!" bellowed Stan's dad for the umpteenth time. "..... aaaaAAAHHHH Wham! Bam! Thank you Mam!" replied Mr. Bowie, lyrically.

Grudgingly, Stan leant forward and turned the volume control fractionally to the left, thus reducing the decibels from an ear-bleeding level, to a mere teeth-shattering level! Teenage rebelliousness had manifested itself in Stan in much the same way that it had in most of his friends, by increasing the length of his hair tenfold and bestowing upon him the ability to listen to screaming guitar solos and still retain the power of thought! His bedroom walls were testament to this change in him, and were adorned with images of Ozzy Osbourne, Jimi Hendrix, David Bowie, Paul Rodgers and the 1971 Spurs team.

In the corner stood his fishing rods and reels, primed and ready for their annual summer outing. This summer, however, would be the last that he would spend as a student, for that time in his life had come to an end and a new period was about to begin because, in September, he would join the Great British Workforce. He and Steve had successfully navigated the stormy waters of O-Level examination and had both gained employment with H.M. Customs and Excise but, before that could happen, they had their last six weeks of freedom to enjoy.

The previous three years had seen major changes in their lives, not least with regard to the opposite sex. Although both boys had indulged in some adolescent fumblings, Stan had been wholly unsuccessful in keeping a girlfriend for any length of time. He felt that he was missing something very important when it came to dealing with girls, like there was a hidden agenda that he was not privy to. In later years he would realise that there was, indeed, a hidden agenda and as to being privy to the secrets therein - forget it, not only was it in a different language, it was in a code that made the German 'Enigma' machine look as complicated as Cockney rhyming slang! But that realization was another three stages of man away, for now he would just like to be able to find a girl to talk to without having his tongue feel like a potato sack.

Then, a month or so before sitting his O-Levels, he had met Jean at a party. She was as pretty as a picture and built like a Playboy model. She and Stan had hit it off straightaway and, even if the glowing description of her was mainly in Stan's head, she was pretty enough to turn boys' heads and make Stan wash regularly, even dragging a brush grudgingly through his complaining hair once in a while. Steve already had a 'steady' girlfriend. With Steve that meant he could remember her second name! The last six week holiday the boys would ever experience was split between doing the things that boys do - like skipping the fares on the train to Box Hill, and climbing every tree to the top of the Hill, then trying to push each other down the other side! Then doing the things that girls like to do, like going swimming, getting on a train to London and walking down Carnaby Street, and strolling around the gardens of Hampton Court. In between these activities, Stan and Steve managed to fish together only four or five times. Two of these trips were memorable for very different reasons.

They had spent much time on the banks of the Thames, either at Hampton Court or, latterly, further downstream at Walton. Their catches had not improved overly, but they had been consistent in their capture of bleak, perch, roach and, on a couple of occasions, some small but greedy chub. They had also spent a few sessions by the banks of their local park lake, but the familiarity was becoming contemptible and their concentration was apt to lapse very quickly if they did not receive action early in the day. The rods were invariably left to fish for themselves whilst the two would-be anglers found the nearest piece of flat grass to use as a makeshift football pitch. For the last joint full summer's fishing, they had decided on two radical courses of action. The first was to be their maiden night fishing sortie, the second was to fish a lake a few miles further away that was reputed to hold some monstrous fish. The only problem was that it was in the grounds of a convent and therefore very private. In other words they would need to poach it.

Their first couple of summer outings were spent on the banks of the Thames and it was here that they decided to night fish. Their favourite swim at Hampton Court was within a quarter of a mile of the bridge which was, naturally, fully illuminated throughout the night and so afforded a certain amount of ambient light. They were also very familiar with the banks, and any snags were well known to them, so they approached their coming soiree with brash teenage confidence. How soon that was to be shattered! Steve's dad was a fisherman, so was able to lend advice and a Tilley Lamp, the latter was accepted with gratitude, the former viewed with disdain - as if a night by the riverbank would hold any fears for these two brave hunters! They were within a short stroll of civilization, they would have the necessary comforts of a blanket and a garden chair each, and it was the middle of summer. What on earth could go wrong?

The walk from the station was more tiring than usual due to the excess baggage they both had to carry, but both thought it would be worth it in the end. On their breathless arrival, they disencumbered themselves of their heavy loads and gazed out triumphantly across the slowly churning waters, to the island. It was a balmy Wednesday afternoon in mid-August and the river looked like the best possible place on Earth to be at that moment.

Though not busy, the towpath had a steady procession of couples, children and dogs in various states of haste strolling along it, so the lads took their time setting everything up in readiness for the night ahead.

They had both brought along a garden chair and a blanket, which they deposited unceremoniously against the hedge at the far side of the towpath until they were required. Stan had brought some sandwiches and a bottle of drink which were both quickly opened and partly devoured to quench hunger and thirst. The next step was to set up the Tilley Lamp for, even though the sun was high in the sky, they had to be sure that the lamp was working. After a few false starts the thing lit spectacularly, sending Steve sprawling with a very smoked look about him, much to the great amusement of Stan and a few passers-by.

"I could have been bloody burnt alive!" blurted the prone Steve, indignantly. This outburst only served to swell Stan's laughter to greater heights, and the other onlookers moved on in amusement, confident that no real harm had come to the boy. Desperately trying to regain a semblance of dignity, Steve got to his feet, brushed some dirt from his hands, and did his best to make his saunter over to the Tilley Lamp as casual as possible. Bending to relight it, he lifted the lamp by its side, only to have the realisation brought painfully home that their previous attempt to light it had, indeed, been successful. This time it was the lamp itself that was sent tumbling as Steve dropped it like the proverbial hot potato. Resembling, momentarily, a recently beheaded farmyard fowl, Steve quickly recovered his wits and plunged his throbbing appendage into the cooling waters of the river. By this time Stan was incapable of speech, sight and the ability to breathe, issuing a stream of meaningless squawking noises from his flapping mouth. Steve's cursing did little to stem the tide of this babble and it took many minutes before anything like a semblance of sanity was resumed, invariably being punctuated by a bellow from Stan as he re-ran the movie in his head. It was many minutes later that Steve realised that his speedy release of the lamp had left it sputtering on its side, spilling forth its lifeblood onto the grass, and he cautiously bent down and flicked it upright with a nearby twig. Nothing seemed to be broken and little fuel appeared to have been lost so they left the lamp well alone for a while, concentrating their efforts on, firstly the bottle of drink and then, at last, on their fishing tackle. This was something they felt much more at home with, but because they were night fishing they had to change their float tackle for leger tackle. Neither boy was greatly enamoured with legering as a method of fishing, preferring the sight and constant movement of a float, and the excitement its disappearance gave. They knew they could not night fish by sight alone so had had a few practice runs on the river over the previous couple of weeks with a modicum of success. The main problem they envisaged was that of bite indication for although during the day they could watch the rod tip this was obviously not feasible at night so they had devised a seemingly foolproof method of bite indication. The idea was quite simple but required a relatively large fish to make it work - the leger was cast out, the line pulled quite tight and the rod tip set at ninety degrees to the river i.e. facing along the bank much the same as swing-tipping. However, rather than being set on a rod rest the rod tip was laid on the ground behind a pile of stones and on the other side of the pile of stones was a small metal plate - now you're getting the picture!

When the fish tugged on the leger, the rod tip would pull round, knocking over the pile of stones onto the tin plate thus alerting the possibly sleeping anglers. Brilliant! Well Stan and Steve certainly thought it was and nothing as minor as the possibility of a drop back or a fish too small to move the leger was going to cloud their thinking - why, they'd even brought along a couple of tin plates especially for the job!

The day had, by now, moved into evening, and the passers-by diminished in number, so the lads set about making everything ready for the night. Steve's bright green fishing brolly was rested at forty five degrees and the two chairs placed either side of the centre pole, Stan's to the right, Steve's to the left and the Tilley in between. Each of them had a small flask of soup and an assortment of sweets and cakes for the night, along with what was left of the drink and the sandwiches. As the shadows lengthened they made their casts into the lake, laid down their rods, and built their bite indicators. Everything was ready and they talked excitedly of what could await them, for it was a well-known fact that only BIG fish fed after dark and, as a sudden afterthought, Stan hurriedly made up the landing net, for it was bound to be required. Whilst Steve carefully lit the Tilley Lamp, Stan chuckled away at the earlier events of the day and was soon joined in the merriment by a relieved Steve, flippant now that the lighting of the lamp had been successfully accomplished. No sooner had they settled into their chairs than Stan's wall of stones came crashing down and the clatter of flint on tin almost sent them into cardiac arrest. Chairs, sweets and blankets were sent in different directions as Stan groped blindly for the rod, eventually finding it by using the time honoured method of kicking it along the floor and, having found it, heaving it skywards lest there be any doubt that the hook hold was insecure (a method of striking he would continue to employ for many years). Hook hold, however, there was none for, unbeknownst to the night blind anglers, the stones had been dislodged by a passing rat who was, by now, halfway across to the island with the rat equivalent of "What the **** was that?" going through its tiny mind! Stan wound frantically, only to feel everything go solid when the lead lodged in the tip ring and realization dawned on him that the weight on the end that he was playing was just that, the weight on the end. He peered into the night and made a rudimentary inspection of his worm and maggot cocktail before casting it back into the inky, black depths then laid his rod down and began groping around for his specially selected stones. It was now that a few doubts came into his mind about how prepared they really were for this night fishing lark. Neither of them had thought to pack a torch for occasions like this but, after a few abortive but noisy attempts, he managed to rebuild his alarm, and rejoined Steve under the glowing brolly. Now was also the time when they both realised that warm in the day does not necessarily mean warm at night and, as the temperatures fell, they both hitched their blankets up around their shoulders in an attempt to retain some body heat.

The next few hours passed uneventfully but, due to lack of warmth and aching backs, neither boy was able to sleep and took turns in mumbling some inanity or another in a bid to be the one who stayed awake all night. As a new day took over from the old, a totally unconnected string of events transpired which ensured that neither boy succumbed to sleep. Without warning, and seemingly inches from their heads, an owl hooted, bringing screams of panic and a string of expletives forth into the night. Within seconds, they were both laughing and joking nervously and shouted derision at the unseen predator when it repeated its call a few minutes later but, inwardly, they were a little chilled. A feeling that was enhanced shortly afterwards when the flame in the Tilley Lamp began to flicker, evidence that it had lost more fuel than previously suspected in the earlier fracas. Despite Steve's shaking and cajoling, the flickering got worse and the flame was obviously not going to offer much more comfort that night. Then, as the light dimmed and the owl hooted derisively, there was a noise as of a thousand cymbals crashing in an echo chamber - Steve's wall had been tumbled down and the resultant crescendo of sound nearly shattered Stan's backbone! Still shaking, both from fear and cold, Steve jumped up and heard a further sound, that of something being dragged across stones - he had a fish on and it was making off with his rod. Groping around on hands and knees proved a better method of rod location than Stan's and, soon, Steve could feel the rod bucking in his hand as something pulled back on the other end. The fight was strange in the darkness but from where Stan stood he could see Steve and the rod silhouetted against the lights from the bridge in the distance and this faint illumination helped a little when it came time for Stan to perform the netting ceremony. Steve seemed to have a modicum of control over his unwilling adversary and it was not long before they could hear the splashing sound of something quite large on the end of the line. Stan squinted into the reflected lights until he could see the splashing and swirling in the arms of the net, then lifted it victoriously, only for Steve to yell that he had missed it.

Three more unsuccessful attempts left him believing that this fish must be able to swim backwards, and Steve believing that his ex-mate would not see the light of dawn if this fish came off. Girding his loins for one more attempt, Stan instructed Steve to keep walking backwards until they were sure the fish was netted and, within a matter of seconds, the ploy worked and they heaved their prize onto the bank. The flame from the lamp was barely a candle glow but, by laying the net right in front of it they were able to discern the identity of their prize - and in doing so they nearly jumped out of their skins.

"It's a bloody snake!" exclaimed Stan from a much safer distance. The net writhed and glistened as its captive tried, sinuously, to escape.

"No it's not, it's an eel," replied an equally apprehensive Steve. Neither of them had encountered Mr. Anguilla before and had no idea how to handle it. Allowing natural instinct to take over, Steve picked up his rod, bit the line a yard above the wriggling captive, and hurled it unceremoniously back into the swirling depths - a fish larger than either of them would catch for a couple of years and they had no idea.

Steve couldn't be bothered to retackle. He realised just how cold he was and, after draining the last few mouthfuls of tepid soup from his flask, he wrapped the blanket around him and curled up as small as possible in his chair, willing the sun to rise. Stan was of much the same mind, even to the point of willing his pile of stones to remain upright as if cemented together - no way did he want to be entangled with one of those greasy hydras. The light had totally gone now, as had the food and drink, and fingers of cold were gradually insinuating their way into the warmth of his paper thin blanket. He started singing the words of a Beatles song in his mind. "Here comes the sun, here comes the sun, and I say - it's alright." Oh, please let the sun come, he thought as he slipped into a fitful sleep.

And then it was there, glaring into their faces from above the trees on the island - the sun. Their bones ached, their stomachs rumbled and their throats felt parched and so, by subconscious mutual consent, they slowly packed their things away, and shuffled disconsolately back to the station to sit and wait for the first train to arrive, an hour hence.

A couple of days later they were sitting upstairs on a double decker bus, in transit for the Crystal Palace Bowl where an open air concert was due to take place. It was from their lofty, mobile perch, that they spied the tell tale glint of sunlight on water - an ability all anglers unconsciously develop over time. As the bus stopped for a minute to collect new passengers, the boys peered intently through the trees at their find. The lake was in the grounds of a convent, surrounded by an eight-foot high fence. However the woods that dominated this area of common land formed a barrier at the back of the convent grounds, and also surrounded the lake on three sides. It was this possible entry route that gave the eager anglers some hope and, as the bus moved off, they started planning a campaign that could lead to them fishing the lake. Their plans were put on hold for the rest of the day as they revelled and rocked at the Bowl but, on their return journey that evening, they peered intently from the bus as they passed the convent. By the time they had completed the four mile journey home, they had formulated a plan of action which involved a further bus journey the following morning to reconnoitre the woods and to see if there was a way into the convent and thereby the lake.

They alighted from the bus just before midday and did their best to control their urge to run, full pelt, into the woods and to the perimeter fence surrounding the grounds. Their eagerness was almost bursting from them and, as soon as they entered the shade of the trees, they broke into a run and raced each other through the woods to the beginning of the fence. The talk on the bus journey had been of the uncaught monsters that obviously lay in wait for them, why else would someone have gone to the bother of putting up such a fence? So, when, within a minute or so of their walk along this boundary, they found a loose board they could not help but squeal with delight. With no thought of stealth or silence, Steve quickly pulled the board to one side and allowed Stan to pass into the hallowed grounds, following his friend as though tied at the hip. The woods extended into the grounds, as they had seen from the bus, so afforded ample shelter from possibly prying eyes. The two interlopers made their way quickly but more carefully through them until they saw the sun glinting off the surface of the water through the last few trees. Once by the water's edge they stayed behind the trunk of a large oak and took stock of their surroundings, revelling in the danger and excitement. The lake was about two acres in size and surrounded on three sides by trees, however, the fourth bank, opposite their present position, had a lawn leading from the water's edge to the convent building some hundred yards distant. At present there was no one evident but the two or three small benches overlooking the lake was proof that the nuns did frequent the area for some pleasant meditation. This was not the place to be fishing so, moving back into the shelter of the trees, Stan followed his friend through the undergrowth as they made their way further left and away from the lawn and, after a hundred yards, they found exactly what they were looking for. Here, the bank jutted out into the lake a little and then swept back ten yards or so, forming a small bay but affording enough cover to allow someone to be invisible from prying eyes. Steve turned, smiling, and gave Stan the thumbs up and they both pushed through the undergrowth to the water's edge. The bay was rimmed with reeds which added to the cover and Steve pushed apart this vegetation whilst crouching down on his haunches. However, his friend preferred a loftier viewpoint and so, spying an adequate looking limb, he shimmied up a nearby trunk and took up station six feet above Steve, high enough to give him a good view of most of the lake but still hidden from sight by the surrounding trees. From his lofty perch Stan could see the odd ripple where small fish were dimpling the surface and it was whilst he was peering across the lake to the far bank that he heard a tremendous splash and an appropriate exclamation from below.

"Jesus!" shouted Steve, involuntarily, and Stan looked down fully expecting to see his friend in the lake but all he saw were Steve's bulging eyes looking up at him and his arm extended, pointing out into the lake.

"Did you see that?" he inquired in a very poor attempt at a stage whisper. Stan put his finger to his lips in a bid to silence his animated friend, and then began to descend from the tree. As his foot was resting on the last branch before the ground, his gaze flicked across the bay just as the perpetrator of the previous splash repeated the act. A huge black fish slid through the surface film and hung, seemingly for hours, in mid-air before reentering the lake with an even louder splash. This time it was Stan's turn to use one of the most popular words in their present surroundings and he dropped to the ground unceremoniously, whilst babbling inanely to Steve, as if his friend had seen nothing of the incident.

"Jesus! Did you see that? It was huge. Did you see it?"

"Course I did, I just told you about it," replied Steve. Stan was still staring at the spot in the vain hope that the fish, a carp, would give him one more glimpse and, as if reading his thoughts, it left the water for the third and last time, in full view of the two open mouthed onlookers. To the boys it was, indeed, huge. Although it weighed no more than four pounds, by the time they returned home to tell Steve's dad of the incident the fish had grown to biblical proportions weighing probably as much as Clarissa, which they had seen in London Zoo the previous summer. But, for that moment, they were speechless and just looked at the lake, then each other, then back at the lake again. Finally, Stan broke the silence.

"Tomorrow morning. We've got to come back tomorrow morning."

"Yep," replied Steve, "first thing. Before the nuns wake up. We'll have to come on the bikes and hide them in the woods."

Once the dam was broken, the words came in a torrent and shortly, with one last hopeful glance back at the lake, they made their way back to the fence, whispering intently about how they were going to go about their assault on the lake. The bus journey home passed with them making plans, dismissing them, and making other plans. Then, when they arrived at Steve's house and told his dad, they did not make the mistake of ignoring him this time. His advice of heavier line and larger hooks was immediately heeded and his tackle box immediately raided and divested of some size ten hooks, one hundred yards of six pound line and a large disgorger. The plan was for Stan to stay the night at Steve's, and for the two of them to leave before sunrise with the minimum of tackle, so Stan returned home to collect his rod and reel and a duffel bag for items such as bait and food.

The evening was spent readying everything for an early departure and when it came to the question of bait they once again took Steve's dad's advice, "If it's carp you want to catch you should take some worms."

Within minutes the two of them were scrabbling around in the half-light of evening at the end of Steve's garden, with a couple of tablespoons and a small maggot box. After half an hour it became too dark to see and they returned to the kitchen with their rather sorry collection of a dozen straggly worms. These were added to the half pint of maggots they were taking and this concoction, along with a small bag of groundbait, was to be the carp's downfall - or so they fervently hoped. Sleep came with difficulty and the strident ringing of the alarm clock seemed to wake them far too early but, once up and dressed, the excitement was almost palpable and they took little time grabbing the bare necessities and mounting their bikes.

The sky was still dark as they set off but in the three quarters of an hour it took them to cycle the four miles to the lake the sky had turned a dark pink and the sun was not far below the horizon. Trying to contain their eagerness, they pushed their bikes through the still dark woods until they came to the broken fence. After untying their rods from the crossbars, they pushed the bikes a little further along and hid them behind a large bush that was growing next to the fence. Once into the convent grounds, Steve took the lead and they crept stealthily through the undergrowth to the water's edge and then followed the contours of the bank along to the bay. Just as they came to the tree that Stan had scaled, Steve surprised a waterfowl and its startled cry and subsequent skittering departure across the lake nearly gave the pair of poachers' heart failure. After taking a few seconds to regain his composure, Steve turned to Stan and motioned with a nod of his head for them to continue on and within a few short strides they were behind the reeds that fringed the bay. Steve moved forward and to the left and settled himself down in front of a small tree that he utilised as a backrest and Stan did much the same thing five yards to the right of his friend. Although the woods were still cloaked in darkness, the boys were able to discern certain features on the far bank, as night once more gave way to day, and it took little time for their eyes to become accustomed to the gloom. Stan had elected to use worms from the start but his friend had still to recover from the eel incident and was convinced that worms were synonymous with those dark, slithering creatures so was loathe to use them again, opting instead for the safer maggot option. Not knowing the depth of the lake, and not wanting to waste any time in finding out, they had decided that Stan would fish at a depth of three feet and Steve at two. When they cast out it was evident that the lake was a little less than three feet deep for Stan's float did not cock properly, but sat at a forty five degree angle whilst Steve's settled perfectly, revealing a mere inch of red tip above the surface film. Stan was undecided whether to leave his float as it was but, before he could make his mind up, he saw his friend strike and shortly bring to the bank the ever present small perch, which decided him in favour of leaving things as they were. The next ten minutes saw Steve repeat his actions another three times and, although the boys loved to catch these striped predators, now was not the time for such sport so Steve decided on a change of bait and grudgingly slipped a small worm onto his hook. Stan, meantime, had made up a little groundbait and had lobbed a couple of small balls of it around his float and, as the light gradually strengthened and the woods resounded to the sounds of waking birds, he could see that his offerings had attracted some attention. Small, pinprick bubbles began breaking in the surface film surrounding his semi-cocked float. Still unsure whether to adjust the depth of the float, he was startled at the sight of the quill suddenly rising out of the water and lying on its side but, as he had never encountered a lift bite before, he did not know what course of action to take. This decision was taken out of his hands, almost literally, when the float just as suddenly righted itself then disappeared below the surface and his instinctive strike was unnecessary as a line of bubbles shot to the surface as an indication of the escape route the unseen fish had taken. The power of the fish was such that it pulled a bemused Stan to his feet but, never having had to discover the workings of the clutch on his reel before, he had no idea how to react. The fish just carried on going and, within seconds, Stan found himself dumped on his arse as the tortured line could take no more and parted with a crack. The bewildered angler could only stare at the line of bubbles that exited the bay and try to still the pounding of his heart.

"Bloody hell! What was that?" exclaimed Steve, looking at the same stream of bubbles.

His friend was not capable of an answer at that moment in time, having not quite recovered from the stunning power of whatever he had hooked.

"If you hook a carp, you'll know all about it," Steve's dad had warned them. Stan was certain that he did, indeed, know all about it.

"I think it was a carp," he eventually managed to reply, tonelessly.

"Right!" said Steve, "what depth were you fishing?"

He proceeded to move his float further up the line, flicking it back out a yard or so closer to Stan than previously. This spurred Stan into action and he quickly re-tackled, rebaited and recast to the same spot, lobbing another couple of balls of groundbait around his float and its new neighbour. The sun was above the horizon by now and the sights and sounds of morning assailed the anglers' senses. The wood was alive with birdsong, as were the banks of the lake and Stan watched, mesmerised, as a moorhen ushered its brood of spikey-haired offspring across the lake to a far reed bed, fussing continuously and stridently hurrying them to the safety of the marginal vegetation. For the next half an hour the bay remained still, and the floats bobbed infrequently from the small perch that worried the worms. Then, out of the corner of his eye, Stan caught sight of a small explosion of bubbles ten yards to his right and three yards from the point of land that formed the right-hand perimeter of the bay. Reeling in his worm, he shuffled along to the next tree and, ensuring that he was still hidden from view, flicked his float out to the slowly disappearing bubbles. In his eagerness he had snagged some reeds to his left so the float dropped into the margins at his feet, leaving the worm in the offending reed stem. Worms were now in short supply so he broke one in half and slid it, with a maggot, onto his hook and, taking greater care, flicked the offering just behind the bubbles. Either the lake was deeper here, or he had not set the depth the same when he had retackled but, for whatever reason, his float settled perfectly, revealing the barest minimum of red tipped quill. A ball of groundbait and a handful of maggots followed it and he sat back against the trunk of the tree, expectantly. Barely had a few minutes passed when the first telltale bubbles popped to the surface near his float and he sat up, hand hovering above his rod butt in readiness for anything. When the red tip disappeared his strike was immediate and he waited for the surge of power to wrench him from his sitting position, but it did not materialise. Instead there was a frantic shaking on the other end and, with a twinge of disappointment, Stan reeled in what he was sure was a perch but a sudden flash of gold belied that supposition. Very soon, he and Steve were gazing down on a fish that shone like a bar of gold in the ever-strengthening sunlight.

"Wow, what is it?" enquired Steve.

"Dunno," replied Stan, "but ain't it lovely? It looks like a goldfish, don't it?"

Steve nodded in agreement at this identification, and neither boy was far from the truth because it was a crucian carp, a very close relation to the goldfish.

"Let's weigh it then," demanded Stan. They quickly drew out an old pair of spring scales and a cloth bag that Stan used to take his plimsoles to school in. Wetting and weighing the bag first, like Steve's dad had shown them, they slipped Stan's prize into it and soon agreed on a weight of twelve ounces. Stan, smiling, slipped the fish back into the lake.

The next couple of hours saw the boys land a further four crucians of similar size. Their much larger cousins did not seem like entering the bay again so, as sounds of life emanated from the convent building, Steve decided on one final recce of the left hand margin in case he could find anything larger to try for. Taking the last sandwich with him, he crept through the trees that lined the bank and emerged fifty yards further along, behind a large weedbed. He peered into the lake whilst polishing off the final mouthful of ham and pickle, casually throwing the last bit of crust into the lake, at his feet. A minute or so later he was about to move on when he heard a sound at his feet. Looking down, he gazed in astonishment as a large pair of rubbery lips attempted to engulf the pieces of sodden bread that had settled against a reed stem, completing the task with a noise like water going down a plug hole. Ignoring the need for silence, he whistled across to Stan and motioned for him to come round, staring intently into the lake until his partner in crime joined him.

"What's up? What have you seen?" asked his friend, quizzically.

"Have you got any food with you?" was Steve's puzzling reply.

"What!" said Stan, frowning at his obviously demented friend. "Have you got any food, you know, sandwich, biscuits. Anything?"

Assuming Steve's dementia had come about by near starvation, he searched through his pockets until he found a scrunched up crisp packet with minimal remains of the contents.

"That'll do," said Steve, snatching the packet from Stan's grasp. He then opened out the bag and, extending his arm out over the water, upended the packet and watched the crushed remains scatter onto the surface.

"Watch," he commanded and Stan, totally bemused, did as he was bidden. The reason for Steve's 'dementia' became all too evident very quickly when, first one pair of lips then another slurped greedily at the floating harvest. Steve watched Stan's reactions triumphantly, knowing that they mirrored his own. Within a few short seconds the crisps were gone and all that was left to show that the carp had been there were the slowly expanding ripples.

Once again, words were unnecessary and after a quick look into each other's eyes, the boys made off hurriedly in the direction of their rods, all thoughts of caution forgotten. This proved foolhardy for, as they reeled in and spoke in less than hushed tones, a shout from the lawn froze them in their tracks. Looking across the lake they could see three cassocked figures peering back at them.

"What are you doing there? This land is private, what are you doing over there?"

The shouted enquiry shook them from their trance and, suddenly, everything moved at speed as they grabbed their belongings and crashed headlong through the trees to the exit, all thoughts of silence and stealth banished. They grabbed their bikes and ran them through the woods for a quarter of a mile until they were certain they had no pursuers, then peddled along the dirt path until they came to the main road, a full half mile away from the convent. This last, desperate, escape made the whole affair a marvellous adventure and, although they did not manage to put a bait to those carp, the myth of their size grew with every telling.

They returned to the woods in the last days prior to employment, but were deflated to see that their antics had brought about a strengthening of the defences around the convent. There was barbed wire across the top of the fence and a brand new fence where they had made their entry and exit. They would never get to fish the lake again, but Stan would never forget that surge of power and, although the next few years would see a lessening in his vigour, subconsciously Stan's fishing future had just been re-routed.

The Common had indeed been more cautious over the previous couple of years, but the natural instinct to feed was almost as strong as that of the need to flee from danger, so it was no surprise that it had slipped up on a couple of occasions. The first such occurrence had seen it avoid capture due to the fact that the angler was fishing only for roach and perch so his two pound line had snapped like cotton within seconds of The Common feeling the hook. The second time was at the end of the previous season when it had fallen foul of one of the group of four anglers, and he was very prepared to do battle with a fish of that size. Even so, he was stunned at the increase in size the fish had shown, pulling the scales down to an ounce or two under twenty pounds.

The four of them had agreed that this was to be their last season on the water, and what a way it was for them to end it. A couple more waters in the locale had been producing some good results so they had decided to try their hands on these new pastures. This left The Common and its brethren almost undisturbed and, with the pit becoming steadily more mature, the natural larder was full of everything sweet and sticky - in carp terms.

The fish had benefited in a different way from the changing moods of Mother Nature, for their numbers had diminished a little since the turn of the decade. This was due, in the main, to the severe winter the country had suffered the previous year. Many lakes had remained frozen for weeks and the countryside had been cloaked in a white blanket for almost the same amount of time.

Many animals and birds had seen their last spring due to the severity of the icy conditions and the lack of food to sustain them through this harshest of times, and the inhabitants of the pit were no exception. Being a relatively shallow pit, the lack of oxygen under the ice was exacerbated, forcing the fish to congregate in the few, deeper holes in a bid to eke out their existence until the solid roof above them was removed, and it was almost a month after the first fingers of ice crept across the lake that the weak winter sun eventually dappled on wind rippled waters again. By that time, many of the less hardy denizens of the deep had succumbed and the carcasses of bream and roach littered the deepest parts of the lakebed - the pike would feed well this year. As usual, the tench and carp proved to be the hardiest breed, although they were not without casualties and The Common found itself with fewer competitors for food when the sun rose higher in the sky and signalled the change of season a month or so later.

Whether it is a natural thing in animals or not, it is difficult to say, but it certainly seems that in fish, and especially carp, the largest of that particular species spend a lot of time together, gravitating towards each other as the years pass. The Common, therefore, had been accompanied by a mirror of similar size for the past couple of years and they had regularly been seen by the anglers, feeding and basking together during the summer months. The Mirror, though not quite the size of The Common, had a voracious appetite and had allowed itself to be banked on half a dozen occasions due to this greed. On each occasion, bar one, he had been landed by one of the specimen hunters and had been treated with due deference and care, but the other capture was by an angler who had never even dreamt that fish like this existed and was totally unprepared to deal with it on the bank. It was fortunate for the fish that all it suffered was some minor grazing when the angler attempted to lift it but was unable to hold the fish when it flipped from his hands, landing flapping on the gravel at his feet. It was fortunate, also, that the angler realised his limitations and thought more of the carp's welfare than for his own pride so, lifting it gingerly he carried it quickly to the water's edge but was powerless to stop the fish leaping once again from his hands and back into the safety of the lake. Such was the force of its re-entry, however; that the carp skidded along the shallow margin and felt the pain of a tree root rip along its side. The whole incident left The Mirror shaken and scared but, within a few days, natural instinct once again took over and the affair faded into distant memory - all it had to show for its traumatic experience was a steadily healing scar along its back which would act as an identity for the foreseeable future.

By the time that Stan and Steve were pedalling frantically away from the convent, the two largest inhabitants of the pit had enjoyed a peaceful, almost angler-free summer, and had more than made up for the enforced fasting of the previous winter. But the days of peace and tranquillity were rapidly coming to an end as, once again, their size had become the lure for another group of specimen hunters and the next few years would see their vigilance stretched to the limit.

Chapter Five - 1976

"I do."

"I now pronounce you man and wife."

Their wedding at the beginning of June was the culmination of a four year love affair for Stan and Jean and marked the most major change in their young lives so far. Although the physical attraction had been great for Stan, one of the main things he loved about his new bride was her dissimilarity to most of the women he knew. She was not one of those flapping females who screamed at the sight of a spider or any other multi-legged crawling creature. She didn't think that snakes were slimy, and had been quite calm about holding a grass snake called Humphrey that Stan had kept as a pet, albeit for a short time before it made good its escape. And she would sit quite calmly with a frog balanced in her cupped hand, before stroking its back and initiating the leap back into the pond. But most of all she loved fishing. Allow me to qualify that statement. She loved Stan, Stan loved fishing so anything that he loved, she loved also. That's a rather romantic way of saying, "If you can't beat 'em, join 'em!" But she did enjoy it. She loved the great outdoors, and the first holiday that she and Stan had taken together had been a cycling and camping holiday on the Isle of Wight. She did not think that fishing was cruel, especially when she saw how gently her boyfriend handled his captives. Although she was not greatly enamoured by the sight of a container full of writhing maggots, she was quite happy to hold some of the smaller fish and lower them carefully back into the pond or river, elated at the silver flash as they sped away to freedom.

The times spent by the waterside for Stan had been few since he had started work and he had managed only four or five short trips during each summer. This had normally been with Jean for company which inevitably meant that the fishing was taken less seriously than other activities that may have been on offer! Another reason for his apathy towards the sport was his enthusiasm for football. Since starting work, Stan had joined the football team and had found most of his Saturdays from September onwards spent in one collision or another in pursuit of a leather ball. His time at H.M. Customs had lasted a couple of years but the romance of the airports was the domain of a privileged few and the tedium of constant and repetitive office work was not his idea of a lifetime's vocation. He had, therefore, taken little time to accept the offer of a job at a local printing firm which a friend of his dad's owned.

This was much more to his liking as, with a much smaller workforce, he did not become just another face in the crowd. After serving the apprenticeship of the struggling bar, the long wait and the left handed screwdriver, he was soon accepted into the clique of printers and apprentices that made up most small companies. Within six months he was also an essential part of the firm's football team and it was not long before he was playing twice a weekend and drinking with his new found friends. As previously, it did not take him long to find the fisherman amongst his new work mates either, and although Perky had little love for football, he and Stan soon found two things that they had in common - their musical tastes and their love of the riverbank. For Stan, here was someone who had been more adventurous than he and Steve in their fishing. Dave Pink had been a member of a local fishing club since his early teens - six or seven years now - and profited from all that has to offer. He had fished a number of matches and learnt well from his elders, and he had also had the benefit of fishing private lakes and stretches of river that were out of bounds to most anglers. He was, therefore, a source of great knowledge to Stan and also an entry ticket onto those hallowed banks because, as a senior member, he was allowed to take a guest fishing four times a year.

They had managed one trip during Stan's last year as a single man and, although Perky was able to pass on some tips, the trip had ended with just a few bleak and roach to the pair of them. But they had certainly had some fun and. Stan soon cajoled his new pal into agreeing to take him on a few trips to a couple of lakes in the new season. So it was that, a month after becoming a married man, he and Perky found themselves making their way along the banks of a mist shrouded lake at dawn. The lake was just outside Dorking, a half-hour car ride away, and was mainly a day-ticket water. However, the club that Perky belonged to had sole rights to fish a four hundred-yard stretch of bank on the far side from the car park and that was where the pair were headed. Perky had spoken in glowing terms of Old Bury Hill Lake for the past couple of months. Stan had looked forward to this visit more than the wedding if truth be known, but he would never let his new wife know that. He was beginning to learn a little about the fairer sex after all!

Perky had collected Stan just before dawn, as arranged, and they had crammed everything into his Mini Cooper and set off through the deserted suburban streets, arriving at the lake as the sun was painting the sky in a vivid array of colours. The walk to the far bank took five minutes and, despite the early hour and lack of heat in the sun, they were both sweating healthily on their arrival at the gate that marked the day ticket boundary. Once through there, Perky guided Stan through the still dark woods and across a rickety wooden walkway that took them through six foot high bullrushes to the far bank.

Once there, they immediately unshipped their rod bags and creels and slumped to the ground, panting like a couple of mountaineers on their arrival at an oxygen-deprived summit. Pretty soon, the blood stopped pounding in his ears and Stan could make out the more acceptable sounds of early morning. A skylark soared to new heights and let out its triumphant call to inform the world, and a coot squawked a tuneless warning to an interloper. A thousand sets of avian tonsils were tested for another day's auditioning in the nearby woods - and a great fish crashed at the back of the nearby lily bed. This last spurred the anglers into action, and they were soon loaded up for the last leg of their journey.

"Where we going, man?" enquired Stan, eager to cast a bait into this new wonderland. Perky had told him of the fantastic fishing to be had at the lake, of the huge bags of bream that could be taken in a morning's fishing, of the hard fighting but very catchable tench, and of the omnipresent, uncatchable monster carp.

"Just along here. There's a couple of swims in the reeds that we can fish from the same landing stage, they're normally good for tench at this time of day. Did you bring the corn?"

This last question was reference to the wonder bait that he had been telling Stan about over the past few months. Sweetcorn. Stan had never even seen the stuff, let alone thought of using it for fishing with, but he had dutifully gone to his local shop and, sure enough, there next to the tinned peas were cans of yellow sweetcorn. He was still a little unsure of this new bait so had brought along the ever reliable maggot and worm cocktail, as well as a small loaf of bread. This latter would be used to supplement the guys' diet if the fish were slow on the uptake but, for now, he was just happy to be on the bank at dawn whilst the rest of the world slept. They crept along the wooden boards that led out to the landing stage, twenty feet out into the lake. As they appeared from behind the reeds, they startled another angler who screeched loudly and, with a flap of its great grey wings, soared off across the water to alight in a distant, vacant reed bed.

"Jesus, I thought it was a bloody pterodactyl!" exclaimed Stan, almost startled to death by the departing heron. Perky could not stifle his amusement at his friend's horrified look and chuckled loudly.

"Yeah, it's usually here at this time of day," he commented between gritted teeth.

"You bastard! I wondered why you let me go first. You bloody well knew! You bastard!" Stan's look of indignation only added to Perky's amusement and, pretty soon, they were both trying to stifle each other's laughter.

"Okay! Okay!" commanded Perky. "Let's get fishing, boy."

"Okay, boss, after you," agreed Stan, and they both set about preparing their tackle for the day ahead.

Stan took up station to the left and immediately noticed bubbles rising by the edge of a bed of lilies, fifteen yards away, and closer inspection showed him that the pads were being knocked by something below, thin ripples drifting out from the leaves. Indicating this to Perky, his companion nodded and pointed to some pads in his own swim that showed similar activity. Suddenly, all thoughts of the prehistoric heron were banished and Stan couldn't tackle up quickly enough, but his doubts about the use of sweetcorn were still nagging him so he opted for maggots as an initial teaser for the fish. He heard a 'plop' behind him and turned to see his friend's float emerging from a ring of expanding ripples, inches from one of the lily leaves. 'Good cast,' he thought, and watched as a small handful of the yellow grains rained down around the float, which was then twitched back a little until the barest fraction showed above the surface.

"Be ready for lift bites," advised Perky and, remembering his last incident of such, Stan prepared himself to be lifted off his feet again. He flicked his float out with a little too much force and watched as it landed on a lily leaf, turning abashed to see if his friend had noticed.

Perky was staring intently at his float but, without a glance to his left, suggested, "That's okay, just slide it off the leaf and let it drop there."

'Good idea,' thought Stan, and did just that, raining down a couple of handfuls of maggots on and around the leaf. His float settled as he watched a couple of maggots spend their last few seconds of life wriggling towards the edge of the leaf and certain death. Then he heard a 'swish' and a splash and turned to see his fellow angler's rod bent at an alarming angle. There followed a brief struggle, a flash of dark green and then, finally, the lifting of the landing net and there in its folds lay one of the biggest fish Stan had seen on the bank. A year or so earlier he had witnessed the capture of a five pound barbel whilst fishing with Steve and Jean at Teddington, but this was the first time he had seen a fish of this size caught by one of his mates. The contrast of the red eye against the emerald green of the body made this three pound tench one of the finest fish he had ever seen and he stroked its smooth flank whilst Perky carefully removed the hook and slid the fish into the waiting, and voluminous keepnet.

"Where's your float?" asked Perky, urgently.

Spinning round, Stan saw only water and water lilies and instinctively lifted his rod skywards. Instead of the anticipated rod bending thump, he felt that all too familiar flapping of a small, greedy perch on the end of his line and he swung it in, unceremoniously, to his waiting hand. He then had to carefully remove the gorged hook with the all too often required disgorger.

"Not a bad start, eh?" said Perky, cheerily, and dispatched his float fished sweetcorn to the same spot as previously with, a few minutes later, the same result and another fine specimen of a tench followed its predecessor into the waiting net.

Stan was mightily impressed by this and was desperate to land one of these dark beauties himself but his maggot offering was still only attracting the attentions of the spiked predators, albeit larger specimens than he was previously used to, so it was no surprise that, after a further two tincas fell foul of Perky's rods, Stan was delicately mounting a couple of the yellow grains onto his hook, as Perky had demonstrated. The sun was gaining height and strength and it would not be too long before their shadowy corner felt the first of the day's rays and with them, so Perky forecast, the end of the tench action. Time was short as Stan's sweetcorn offering landed delicately by the lily bed and he quickly followed his friend's lead by dispatching a handful of grains into the immediate vicinity of his hookbait to, hopefully, supplement the bed of groundbait already there. The odd bubble had continued to rise since their arrival on the landing stage, but there seemed to be little pattern to them and Stan was convinced that they were just the product of gases issuing from the lake bed. Then, a few minutes after his second introduction of a handful of corn, he spied a dozen or so pin-prick bubbles appear between the lily leaves behind his float, then two more, then another three. Then his float rose from the lake like a Saturn 5 rocket and toppled over like a felled spruce. 'Be ready for lift bites,' Perky had advised, and this was the 'liftiest' of lift bites he had ever seen and, before he could stop himself, that old instinct took over with Stan trying desperately to pull the fish's head off. If the perpetrator of the bite had been the usual palm-sized perch they would probably have had to climb the tree behind them to get the hook out of the fish's mouth. As it was the fish was considerably larger but still had vegetation to use against the angler. After the initial shock of contact, it used the stretch in the line and the inadequacy of the angler to its advantage, ploughing through the jungle of lily stems and making good its escape as the line could stretch no more. The whole thing had taken a matter of seconds and the more experienced Perky was powerless to help his friend who was totally unprepared for the tench's initial surge of power.

"Bump the line up a bit," he advised. "The lily stems are a real bugger. Here, put some five on."

He handed Stan a spool of five pound line and showed him how to tie the two lines together, then wound thirty yards or so onto Stan's spool. Stan re-tackled a little despondently, especially as the first rays of the sun were just entering their leafy glade. He felt like a vampire who knew he would melt at the touch of the morning sun on his skin, and busied himself to get his bait back in the water. There was still evidence of sub-surface activity as, every few seconds, a small group of bubbles would pierce the surface film and Stan's float landed less delicately in the vicinity of the last set as he tried to make the most of the final moments of the tench's breakfast. This time, however, he had no time to scatter the free offerings around his float because it was once again attempting to leave the earth's orbit but, unlike before, Perky was in attendance and offered immediate and telling advice.

"Strike and pull to the right," was his barked command and Stan willingly obeyed, pulling the rod around to the right and seeing the tip bending back from whence it had just come. He felt the tench angrily shake its head in a bid to turn and enter the sanctuary of the lily stalks but the stronger line and the test curve of the rod acted as an absorbing buffer. After a few short runs, the fish was spent and Perky slid the net under his friend's prize. Stan was beside himself with joy and voiced the usual inanities all anglers do at this time.

"Yes! YES! How big is it? Bloody hell, look at it, it's huge! How big do you reckon, man?"

His friend attempted to calm him down whilst readying the scales and weigh sling, and ensuring that the fish was not going to regain its freedom prematurely. Stan was like a tit in a trance and didn't know what to do as this was by far the biggest fish he had ever caught but, at Perky's behest, he knelt down and put a protective hand on the side of the tench. The fish was then slipped into the weigh sling and up on to the Salter scales.

"Two pounds twelve ounces," declared Perky and Stan squealed with delight before taking the fish and ever so carefully lowering it back into the lake, to be followed by the four that Perky then released from the keepnet. The sun was bright in their eyes now and it would have been cruel to retain the fish any longer. The pair moved swims for the remainder of the morning but it seemed that nothing, not even the normally suicidal perch, was willing to feed in the midday sun and it was a considerably sweatier pair of anglers that made the return trip to the car early in the afternoon.

To Stan, the whole day was a complete success and all thought of the lost fish was totally extinguished by the memory of the one that didn't get away. He told everyone, his wife, his parents, his workmates, and Steve. Since leaving Customs, Stan had not seen a great deal of Steve, who had left their employ and was working for an accountant in the City. They had stayed in contact enough for Steve to be Stan's best man, and for Stan to return the favour a fortnight later when Steve married a girl he had managed to stay with for over a year. Unlike Stan, however, Steve had taken the plunge even deeper and had, with the help of his parents, managed to get a mortgage on a house in South East London. Although not a million miles away from Stan's

Wimbledon home, it was no longer the five minute walk away and the two school friends would never be as close again. But, for the moment, Steve was really pleased for his friend and, although his love of the sport had waned since his move to the City, he still had enough memories to understand how Stan felt.

Despite his elation, it had not escaped Stan's notice that the weather was taking its toll on the world around him and rumours of water rationing were becoming more common. He had also noticed the effect the heatwave and lack of rainfall was having on his local lake and, by the time he had tempted the tench, the water level there was down by over a foot. It became imperative, therefore, that he talk Perky into one more trip to Dorking before drastic measures were taken by the authorities and it did not take him long to convince his benefactor that they were indeed running out of prime fishing time. A date was set, therefore, for the last Saturday in July to be their next and possibly last trip to the lake for the foreseeable future. Stan could not wish the week away quickly enough until, at last, he was standing bleary-eyed at his front door straining to see the headlights of Perky's car in the gradually receding darkness of early morning. By the time it had become unnecessary for the use of headlights, Stan was pacing up and down like a caged tiger, fuming at the non-appearance of his chauffeur and when eventually Perky did arrive, an hour later than scheduled, Stan was barely capable of speech. He merely tossed his tackle through the opened car door, deaf to his friend's apologetic grovelling. They made the journey in silence apart from, of course, the usual Pink Floyd accompaniment to the steady engine noise.

By the time they pulled into the Old Bury Hill car park, Stan's mood had lightened and he was once again receptive to Perky's efforts at recompense, offering Stan the first choice of swim. The day was already threatening to follow in the flip-flop steps of its predecessors and become the warmest one this summer. By the time the two be-decked anglers had made the tortuous journey to the gate and across the bridge, they were pumping sweat and breathing like a couple of asthmatics. After the customary collapse onto the grass and gulping of air by the lungful, they slowly arose and took in their surroundings. Due to their late start the sun was already making steady progress above the horizon and the swim they had fished previously showed little in the way of shade and looked entirely less inviting than before. Perky motioned his companion forward and moved on behind the wall of reed, past a couple more landing stages, until he finally came to a halt at an area of grassy bank between two beds of bullrushes. The swim offered a thirty yard cast to the edge of a further stand of reeds that formed a barrier at the back of it. There was room enough for both anglers to settle on the grass, Stan once again choosing to fish to the left-hand side. The swim was sheltered from the rays of the sun by the overhanging branches of a small copse of birches at its rear, and this canopy would offer welcoming shade until early afternoon - a good four or five hours fishing time. Looking out, Stan likened the area in front of him to a corral, with reeds forming a seemingly impenetrable barrier on three sides and the grassy bank a fourth. However, from the constant knocking and bending of the stems he could tell that the fish found them anything but impenetrable and a loud splash to his left, in the depth of the reed jungle, startled him from his reverie and spurred him into action. A flash of blue and a piping call indicated that he had not been the only one startled into action and he marvelled for the split second it took the kingfisher to pass across from left to right, banking hard to the left and disappearing with another shrill whistle. That sight alone had made his morning for he loved these brief glimpses of nature almost as much as the fishing itself but, to business. The day was wasting and he would catch nothing whilst gawping at the jet stream of a passing halcyon bird.

As usual, Perky was swiftly into his angling and before Stan had even pulled his rod from its sleeve, his partner was dispatching a handful of corn in the direction of his settling float twenty yards out and a yard from the right hand reed bed. Unlike the previous session, Stan could see no immediate signs of fish in the swim. He set about preparing a little groundbait and, mixing in a few grains of corn, lobbed three or four balls of the mixture close to the back of the swim, at the corner of the 'corral.' He then followed that with his float-fished corn offering and sat back to regain a little composure after the frenetic activity of the past couple of hours. He leaned back against his creel and lazily unscrewed the top to his thermos before pouring himself and Perky a very welcome cup of tea. Minutes passed as if they were wading through treacle and Stan's mind gradually slowed to the pace of life by the lake, soothed by the hypnotic buzz of a thousand beating insect wings and the lilting call of a nearby song thrush. All these sounds served to lull him and he drifted into a peaceful half sleep, reassured in the knowledge that there was no need to worry about anything, not even that awful buzzing noise. What was that noise? It sounded like a metallic bumble bee.

"Stan, quick! Your rod. Your rod!"

He was suddenly bolt upright, not sure whether he was dreaming or ballooning. Perky's sudden call had wrenched him from his reverie and he had no idea what was happening.

"Your rod, Stan," his friend repeated loudly. "Grab your bloody rod, you've got one on."

As the instructions ploughed their way through Stan's sleep-addled consciousness, he looked down to see his rod sliding across the grass towards the lake and only managed to save it from a watery start to the day by diving forward and grabbing the butt with outstretched fingers. Then, getting a firmer grip on it, he lifted the fibre glass wand up and gazed out curiously at where his float should have been but all he could see was a large patch of bubbles and a great commotion in the reeds behind them. Feeling the rod buck in his hand, he was suddenly fully aware of what was happening, and also that he was too late, when he felt the jolt of the hookhold losing purchase. Disconsolately, he reeled in his empty hook and glanced sheepishly over at Perky.

"Well, at least they're here," he said, and went about the corn hooking process once more, vowing not to rejoin the realm of sleep until well after dark.

A further biteless half hour passed before Perky was required to strike at his first bite of the day and it was all he could do to stop the fish from gaining the sanctuary of the right hand reeds, applying as much side-strain as he dared until, very gradually, the rod's power began to tell and with a swirl of its tail, the fish gave into the pressure and moved away from the stems. The job was now done and Stan slipped the net under a huge looking, dish shaped fish. Their first thoughts were of one of the lake's many bream but, once the mesh was removed, Stan immediately recognised that golden glow.

"It's a bloody great crucian," he ventured, and Perky was not about to disagree. It was the largest crucian that Perky had ever seen and it was his turn to question whether he was dreaming or not. Stan, it was then, who took control and confidently slipped the fish into the dampened weigh sling, hoisting it onto the scales and up above his head.

"Two pounds twelve ounces, same as my tench," he declared, although both anglers knew that Perky's capture was much more meritorious and he was glad that he had decided to bring his Instamatic along on this occasion. Stan clicked off a couple of shots before his pal released the fish back into the ever warming waters of the lake. Even in the shade of the trees the temperature was noticeably rising and Stan knew that he had very little time in which to become the subject of photographic composition.

It was with much relief, therefore, that he watched Perky slip the net under a very welcome tench, ten minutes later. Stan had been fully awake and vigilant when the float disappeared and the fish had no hope of reaching the reedy sanctuary as Stan applied frightening pressure to guide it into open water. At a few ounces less than his companion's fish, it was still Stan's second biggest fish and he revelled in the photo-taking, smiling hugely for the camera. The trip that had started so disastrously had certainly ended well and the pair gradually started thinking about the horrendous journey they had to undertake to get back to the oven that was Perky's Mini Cooper.

There was still one more trick of the tail and as Stan gazed out dreamily, this time with realistic thoughts of fine tench in his mind, he noticed some reeds knocking, halfway along the left hand boundary wall. Staring intently at the spot, he noticed small vortices and the odd bubble rising to the surface so, very carefully, he slowly reeled his float back, leaning his rod over to the left to ensure that the float settled just perfectly, its red tip peeking through a foot from the twitching stem and, as he moved to grab a handful of groundbait, Perky stuck out a restraining hand and shook his head.

"Don't put any out, you might spook it," he suggested, having noticed Stan's sudden alertness.

Stan refrained from any baiting up and stared intently at the still twitching reed stem and the ripples emanating from it that were lightly knocking the tip of his quill. This activity continued for the next two or three minutes and, every now and then, a sudden twitch of the float would have the distraught angler stabbing forward to his rod, only to relent as the float stilled once more. This happened on a number of occasions so Stan was a little unprepared for the sudden disappearance of the tip below the surface and the violent rocking of the reed stem. His strike was still swift enough to stop the perpetrator from gaining any immediate advantage and, for a few seconds, they just hung there - the irresistible force and the immovable object. Stan knew that he could not allow the fish to gain any line so increased the side-strain to such an extent that his friend winced, and prepared to avoid the splinters of shattering fibre glass that would inevitably shower down upon him. Amazingly, though, the shower did not arrive and he watched in astonishment as the strain of the rod began to tell on the fish. The bend became less alarming, and the realisation suddenly dawned on him that he could well be required to net what was very obviously the biggest fish Stan had ever caught. His friend seemed remarkably calm and in control and Perky looked on in admiration at the accomplished way he was playing the fish, and gave himself a mental pat on the back for a job well done. Then, an even more amazing thing happened. Rising like a marlin, a great carp leapt clear of the water in a final bid to free itself of the hook, belly-flopping back onto the lake surface with a noise that sent the resident coots and moorhens into a cacophony of startled cries. It careered off into the nearby reed bed, parting the stems like a rogue elephant stampeding through the African brush - free.

The line had parted with a snap that had been drowned out by all the other noise and the two anglers looked on in disbelief, jaws slack. Stan turned to his pal and mentor and simply said,

"I think we need a bigger boat!"

There was no more to say and, with the swim devastated, they slowly and silently packed away in preparation for their final nightmare of the day. The walk back was tortuous and the drive home little better but, as they neared Stan's house he asked, "Fancy a quick pint?"

Without a word, Perky guided the car into the nearest pub car park. Once inside, the cold lager seemed to act like a verbal laxative and the words poured forth from Stan's parched lips. How big? Did you see? Played it well. Bloody big. Ten pounds? Should have used heavier line. Fancy another? Thought I had it. Bloody huge!

And so it went for the next couple of hours, but they could not repair the damage and it was still only 'the one that got away' to anyone who would listen. But to Stan it was the beginning of a quest, even though he didn't know it yet, and having been re-routed previously, the path of his angling had taken a more certain direction.

The weather did indeed curtail any further angling for the pair of them that summer. Stan was once again bitten and also determined to right the wrongs done to him by certain members of the carp family and the next time he met one of their kin, he vowed that it would be third time lucky.

"So what do you propose we do then, Tom?" enquired Seth Thomas.

"We've got to move as many as we can to Stanton's, and as quickly as possible before we lose too many more," replied Tom Watts to the committee in general.

He had called an emergency meeting of the Ringwood and District Angling Society in a bid to finding a solution to the severe drought problems they were having. Already, barely a month into the season, they had lost a frightening number of fish from many of their seven lakes and ponds. With no sign of substantial rainfall in the foreseeable future, a few of the members had decided that the time had come for some drastic measures to be taken. Of the seven waters that they leased, two of the smaller ponds were stream fed directly by the River Avon and so seemed unlikely to suffer as badly from the adverse conditions but, due to their size, it was deemed foolhardy to stock too many more fish into them. Therefore the Society had the major headache of having to find a suitable new home for the inhabitants of five lakes - and the sooner the better as casualties of the blistering heat were being found daily.

An ideal candidate for a certain quantity of the ailing stocks was a large, disused gravel pit ten miles north of town. At twenty five plus acres and with an average depth of twelve to fourteen feet, the pit offered ideal conditions and a seemingly perfect haven for a number of fish. Naturally, there were dissenters.

Inevitably it was the guys who fished two or three times a year but had been a Society member 'thirty years, man and boy' that were the loudest in their disagreement with the rescue plan.

"How am I gonna get out there with my back?"

"Twenty five acres, more like a bloody inland sea. You'll never catch 'em in that depth!"

"Old refuse dump, that be. Rats as big as cats, and vicious too!"

These, and a hundred more, were the sort of objections that were being put forward by the minority of members but, as in all clubs, the general apathy towards any sort of meeting meant that, come any show of hands, they were inevitably in the majority. Add to this apathy the fact that the prolific River Avon flowed past their doorsteps and it was easy to see why this proposal to move the bulk of the fish to a safer, if temporary, home was balked... After much shouting, swearing, shaking of heads and hands the committee finally acceded to the wishes of the 'majority' and agreed to move the stock from the three small match lakes into the two stream-fed pools, despite the obvious fact that they were already over-stocked. This left the remaining two sparsely stocked and therefore less popular pits to be dealt with and it was decided, with much less of a furore, that the stock from these would be moved into the twenty five acre Stanton Pit.

For The Common and its mirror companion, this was the culmination of a three year period in their life that had proved both demanding and rewarding. Following the departure of the four specimen hunters the fish had enjoyed almost a year of angler-free tranquility and in that time the fast growing carp had made the most of this freedom and steadily increased their knowledge of the world around them, and their body weight. Amongst the many things that Mother Nature threw at them in order to assist their survival instinct one of the most traumatic and physically demanding was, indeed, the main driving force in any creature s need to survive - the need to procreate, and when carp spawned the earth certainly did move! For almost ten summers, now, The Common had been driven by the same urge as its kin, and for a mad couple of days once, or maybe twice a year it could be found in amongst a melee of crashing, thrashing and leaping bodies as the will to breed surpassed every other instinct. The fact that nearly all the participants of these annual orgies survived to breed another year was another of nature s miracles, but many of them bore the scars of their endeavours and The Common was amongst the 'branded' number, having lost a small number of scales on one shoulder whilst performing with excessive vigour one particular summer. This was one of the means of identification used to single it out from the lake's other common carp, as if its size wasn't enough! The reason for this scrutiny occurred two summers prior to the big heatwave and the scrutineers were a group of three anglers who were more than specimen hunters, they were carp anglers and their sole aim in life was to catch carp, and the bigger the carp the better.

They had picked up rumours of the carp in this pit from the previous successful anglers and, as fish of their alleged size were very rare in that area of the country, they thought it rude not to investigate. Close season visits to the lake had proven very rewarding and so they had joined the club in order to fish for these obviously large specimens and had brought with them new and exciting food to titillate the carp's senses. It was unsurprising, therefore, that the beginning of the season found the three anglers on the banks of the Pit, full of confidence having watched a number of carp feeding on their mixture of hemp seed, black eyed beans and maple peas - and prominent amongst the ravenous carp and tench could regularly be seen The Common and The Mirror. Unsurprising, also, that The Mirror was one of the first to fall foul of an anglers tackle after midnight but the captor and his mates were not prepared at all for the size of the fish, turning the scales to an awesome twenty five pounds. How big was The Common? They found themselves doubting the possibilities. That year, The Mirror visited the bank on a further three occasions, although never exceeding its initial weight but its larger and wiser companion avoided capture, much to the consternation of the would-be captors. The following year saw no letting up in their persistence but still their elusive prey avoided capture, although it did let its guard down once, days after spawning, and foolishly accepted a tasty floating morsel, ridding itself of the unpleasant but vaguely familiar sensation by using the power of its huge tail to propel it through some lily pads and into some bankside snags. The strange pressure disappeared immediately, as did the nagging ache in its mouth after a couple of days of rubbing it in the gravel.

The knowledge that the Pit may well be closed early in the new season was a great disappointment to the anglers who felt that they had failed in their quest to capture what would have been, without doubt, the largest carp any of them had caught. Then, a day prior to the Committee meeting, one of them had been strolling disconsolately around the Pit, stripped to the waist in the soaring early afternoon temperatures, when he had spied half a dozen carp basking in the shade of an overhanging branch. Halfheartedly flicking out some bread crust, he was amazed to see first one, then two, then a whole host of rubbery lips slurping at the surface and the slowly sinking bread. Amazed at this stroke of good fortune he flicked out another crust, this time with his hook in it, and within seconds was grudgingly releasing the pressure on his clutch as an angry carp made off across the lake. Thirty minutes later carp and carp angler were lying exhausted on the ground, each in a different, highly emotional state. It was The Common and, once the ecstatic captor's friends arrived, it was weighed at a few ounces over twenty seven pounds, the last time it would ever be caught by hook and line from that lake.

Although Stanton's Pit was large and relatively empty of resident fish, the new arrivals huddled together in a deep shady hole beneath a huge overhanging willow, quite close to the point of their introduction into the pit a few days earlier. They were still very stressed from the trauma of the netting and subsequent lorry journey to their new locale. Quite a number of fish had perished during the move, either through stress, damage or lack of oxygen but once again the carp and tench proved the hardiest, although their numbers were also a little depleted by the episode. Along with the fish from the Common Pit, the club had also introduced some fish from another smaller, sparsely stocked pit and amongst the stock they had discovered three large pike, a number of surprisingly large perch (considering their decimation only a few years earlier) and one very large and previously uncaught mirror carp.

Despite the trauma of the move, it did not take long for the fish to settle down into a natural rhythm and soon they were investigating their new home in great detail. Instinctively they sought out Mother Nature's larders and mentally marked them for further investigation and soon, as the relentless heat at last showed signs of receding and the promise of rain grew ever greater, the carp began settling back into a normal way of life, all memory of the recent events but a distant blur. Quite naturally, the larger carp sought out each other's company and the trio soon became a common sight around the pit - if there had been eyes to see. News of the move and the many casualties led people to believe that the hardships to be endured to fish the pit were really not worth the effort. By the time the Society once again allowed its members to cast a line on its waters come the end of September, thoughts of fishing Stanton's were all but forgotten.

Once again The Common, and its new companions, had been given a brief reprise and once again they could benefit from the rich, natural harvest that Mother Nature was about to set before them, for the coming year would see the food-chain benefit greatly from the parched earth that had lain fallow for many months, just waiting for the life-giving rains to wash the nutrients back into the hungry water of the lake.

Part Two

Choosing the Path

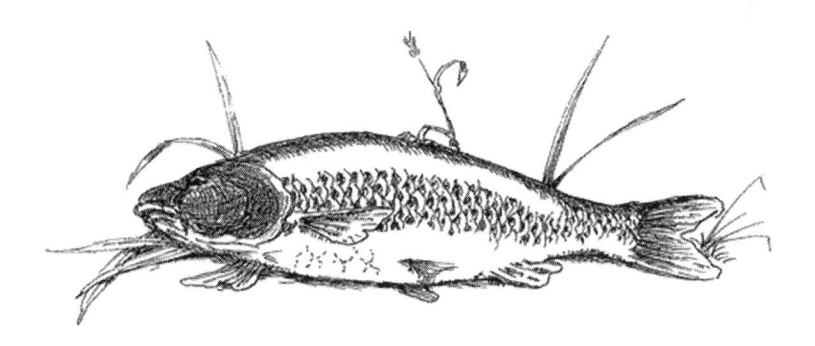

Chapter Six - 1979

"Congratulations, Mr. Peacock. You have a lovely baby daughter!"

The nurse's words brought a huge smile to Stan's face and, as he rushed in to see his wife and daughter Laura, he was vaguely aware of the completion of a series of major changes in his life over the past couple of years.

After their marriage in 1976 it had taken little time for Jean to conceive and their son, Stephen, had been born the following June. This had been the start of a certain amount of pressure in their lives as, not only were they a young, newlywed couple with a baby they could barely afford, but they were, at the present time, still living at Stan's parents' house in Wimbledon. Although large enough to cope with the extra personnel, the proximity of all those adults was inevitably beginning to cause some friction. The young couple did their best to save enough to put down as a deposit on a flat but, with Jean out of work, it was extremely difficult to find the money to feed them, let alone to think about taking a further commitment.

When Jean announced she was pregnant again, the pressure rose rapidly and voices became raised regularly. It was hugely fortunate, then, when an uncle of Jean's lost his mother. This was not as callous as it sounds for she was in her eighties and had been ill for a few years prior to her death - she also left her son a small house just outside Guildford. It was these premises that Jean's Uncle Bob offered them as their very first home of their own. Although only a small two bed-roomed cottage, it was ideal for the couple and Bob agreed to rent it to them for the first year, with a view to their purchasing the property thereafter. This was a godsend, and after a trip down the A3 to see the place, they gratefully accepted his offer and made plans to move into the house in the spring of '79 with the help of assorted friends and parents. The house was in need of total redecoration and so the next months were spent not by the lakeside or on the football pitch, but with paint and paste, screwdriver and hammer in order to transform some of the house before welcoming the latest addition to the Peacock family.

Stan's favourite pastimes had gone through a major change in the last twelve months as well for, in a short three month period in the middle of '78, he had caught his first carp and suffered major injury on the football field.

The first had taken place at the start of the fishing season on a farm in Kent where a couple of his footballing mates had taken him. Mick and Malcolm had told him on a number of occasions of their friend Johnny, a somewhat notorious South London character who had needed to get rid of a large amount of money legally, and so had bought a small farm near Headcorn in Kent. He used it as a weekend retreat for himself and a few friends, who would indulge themselves in the traditional country pastimes of shooting, drinking and dodgy dealing. Mick and Malcolm would normally join in on the pheasant shoot and the subsequent trip to the local pub but, when it came to the dodgy dealings, they took a rain check. They passed the rest of the weekend fishing on one of the three small lakes that made up three of the ten acres of land that belonged to the farmhouse. Stan loved to hear the stories they told on their return, especially when they spoke of the carp and tench they would catch and so it was with great enthusiasm that he accepted their offer of a weekend in the country at the beginning of the season.

The trio arrived at Headcorn and were greeted by Johnny, his wife and a huge breakfast and were told to make themselves at home as Johnny had to be somewhere else that weekend - they asked no questions! Stan was very grateful for the food and the fine hospitality but he could not contain himself for long before blurting out, "Okay then, let's do some fishing!"

The other two smiled at him and, bidding their host farewell, ushered Stan outside to the car in order to don their wellies, and then around the back of the farm building and across the field to the first of the three lakes.

Stan could not hide his disappointment at this muddy puddle and said so. "You're joking! This isn't it, is it?"

Malcolm laughed and followed the slowly disappearing back of Mick.

"Not for now, but there's a bloody great pike in there, y'know," he called over his shoulder.

Stan eyed the waterhole suspiciously and decided not to go for the bait, just in case. As they topped a small rise, Stan spied the second lake and, just through a distant copse of trees, the third. The middle lake, although four times the size of the previous one, was still very small in Stan's eyes and the thick weed that covered two thirds of it made it seem nigh on impossible to fish. Stan's initial enthusiasm was lessening with every step until, as they neared the first of the trees surrounding the last lake, he almost felt like turning round and heading straight for the pub. Within a few short steps, however, that was the furthest thought from his mind and his eyes greedily consumed the vista before him. This was more like it and, as he closed the gap on his companions, he busily collated as much information as his mind could cope with in that short space of time.

The lake was surrounded on three sides by trees but, unlike the convent lake, they were not thick and dark, more of an arboreal 'fence' that circled the banks. Of these sentinels there were a few that had been unable to withstand the storms of recent years and their carcasses littered the far bank, skeletal limbs trailing into the lake and offering sanctuary to the resident wild carp population. The bank nearest to the farm, a half-mile distant, was devoid of cover and muddy hoof prints were evidence of Johnny's two horses regular visits to this spot to drink, a good reason to set up in the cover of the trees, Stan surmised. Though much larger than the other two ponds, this third still only covered about two acres. However, Stan was sure that the stories that he had begun to recently doubt had every chance of coming true in the water before him and, once again, he was egging on his pals in a bid to get into contact with the hard fighting inhabitants of this lake.

Within half an hour Stan was making his first cast, flicking his bread paste offering along in front of the overhanging branches to his left, as directed by his battle hardened companions. The water was no more than two feet deep here and he doubted their wisdom but this doubt was soon brushed aside when a fully plated wildie leapt clear of the water not ten feet behind his float. He stared so intently at his float that he nearly went boss-eyed. It was, inevitably, the one occasion in over ten minutes when he had taken his eyes off the water that the float actually disappeared and, as he looked over to the spot, he was just in time to see it re-emerge. Cursing himself, he renewed his vigilance, but Malcolm comforted him with the knowledge that when he got a bite from the carp he would know all about it, and memories of a similar prediction from Steve's dad came flooding back. Sure enough, after recasting a little further along the margins, Stan's chance came an hour after his first cast and the bite was blistering. No pre-emptive dip of the float, no lift bite, just gone! The strike was unnecessary and the scream of the clutch heart-stopping but, despite Stan's certainty that he would never be able to cope with the carp's power, it took only a matter of minutes for Mick to slip the net under Stan's first carp. He reveled in his young friend's elation at the capture. The fact that the carp was smaller than the tench he had caught with Perky mattered not a jot - this was a carp and he had never felt such power. What must one of those monsters he saw in the Angling Times fight like and how could anyone land a fish that large and powerful? For the moment these thoughts were filed into his subconscious whilst he pondered the more immediate problem of how to stop himself shaking in order to rebait his hook!

Rebait he did and, over the next few hours, enjoyed sport the like of which he hadn't even dreamt of. He hooked a further five torpedoes and successfully brought three to the bank, all of similar size to the first. By early afternoon, Mick and Malcolm had to threaten him with physical violence to get him to join them down the pub, assuring him that there would be further fish to catch before they returned home the following afternoon. The fishing for the day came to an end because on their return from the pub, a few pints the worse off, they were capable of only one thing - sleep!

The following morning found Stan by the lake again, but this time he was shaking for a different reason and it took a few cups of very strong coffee before he and his partners were capable of concentrating on the float without feeling slightly nauseous! Once he had overcome this initial, minor set-back, it was not long before Stan was battling once again to halt another carp's escape. After the second two pounder of the morning, he started to feel restless and soon realised that he was becoming bored with catching the same sized fish. He craved the power of a fish twice the size, or larger - the slumbering giant that was a specimen hunter was slowly starting to stir.

Stan then began to take notice of another feeling that had crept into his subconscious, like a half heard whisper. He realised that, for the third or fourth time in as many minutes, he was staring across the lake to one of the fallen trees, and more importantly to a small bay that two of its half-submerged branches had formed. As this thought became more prominent he began devising, in his mind, a method of presenting a bait and soon decided that, if the water was shallow enough, he could wade to the edge of one of the branches and easily present a float fished bait in to the beckoning bay. As is the way with these things, once the idea had been given flesh there was no way to stop the inevitable enactment of the plan. Scooping up the requisite items of tackle, he left his slumbering companions and made his way around the lightly wooded margins to the point of entry he had selected. The water was, as he had hoped, quite shallow and if entered carefully would not deposit any water into Stan's knee high wellies. Leaving the small tackle box and carrier bag full of bread on the bankside, he picked up his baited rod and his landing net and slowly made his way through the deepening water to the edge of the drowned limb. Water gradually shipping over the top of his wellie indicated that he had gone as far as he could. He carefully took one step backwards before laying the landing net on the branch and deftly flicking the float fished bread paste three or four yards to the centre of the small bay. The water here was obviously quite a bit shallower than in his previous swim as the float lay flat on the surface. He declined to reel it in to readjust the depth lest he should cause any further unnecessary disturbance, resting the top section of the rod on the branch and settling his weight onto his other leg. The occasional bubble pimpled the surface film, but nothing to suggest the presence of carp in any numbers.

Stan started to question his reasoning as a wave of nausea swept over him, as if it had been left behind by its mates and was in a rush to catch them up! The feeling soon passed but left Stan with a sudden, unquenchable thirst. Water, water everywhere .... he thought and tried desperately to think of something else when, suddenly, that task was performed admirably for him by the rise and fall of his float and the vicious tugging of his rod tip. In a nanosecond his need for water was gone and was replaced by the wish that he had not suddenly rushed forward to strike, resulting in a boot-full of lake. The fish powered away strongly but, instead of heading out into the lake as Stan had hoped, it had, instead, taken a route straight through the trailing branches on the far side of the bay and had found sanctuary five yards past them. Stan had no experience of this sort of battle and the realisation soon dawned on him that he had given no thought whatsoever to how he was going to land any fish he should hook. The battle was short but far from sweet and it was not long before Stan was sitting on the bank, emptying lake water from his boots prior to retackling and carefully re-entering the lake in damp and uncomfortable boots. This time he reset the float to the correct depth and cast another knob of bread four or five yards from the branch, striking purposefully when it disappeared five minutes later ... his bully tactics paying dividends this time. He was soon slipping his net under another hard fighting carp, but his hope of a bigger fish was dashed as he peered down on another of the plague of two pounders which he unhooked and slipped straight back into the warm water. A further ten minutes passed before he was again forced to tread water as an obviously larger fish made good its escape through the grasping dead limbs of the far branch and Stan slapped the surface in anger and frustration.

It was obvious, now, that any decent fish that he should hook would attempt the same escape route so he had a couple of options. He could hold as hard as possible to prevent the fish from reaching its wooded sanctuary, but the combination of six pound line and the carp's power made him doubt that course of action. He could negotiate the fallen tree and come out at the back of the bay at the point where both branches met, thus approaching the carp from behind and hopefully forcing them out onto open water. Or he could go back to his swim, get a drink of coffee and sit out the remainder of the morning on a nice comfy chair, catching two pounders!

'So how do I get along this tree, then?' he asked himself - the slumbering giant stirred once more.

Precarious was a word very much on Stan's mind a couple of minutes later as he carefully tried to inch himself along the fallen tree trunk to his desired position at the back of the small bay. The whole affair seemed to take forever, with the grasping branches constantly snatching at his rod tip, float and hook but, eventually, he found himself settled on the unyielding bark of the trunk contemplating his first cast from this new perch. The usual knob of bread below a quill float was flicked a mere five yards to the farthest point of the bay and, as the float settled, Stan adjusted himself a little in order to sit more comfortably. Across the other side of the lake, he could see his mates drinking coffee and gazing around in search of their errant charge. Then Mick's eyes caught sight of Stan in the branches and he pointed across to him whilst exclaiming to Malcolm, "There he is, he's in the bloody tree!"

Stan waved, carefully, and smiled at their consternation - if only he could land one of the biggies now that his mates were awake, that would be great. It took only a couple of minutes before he was given the opportunity to do just that as the float, once more, made a dramatic exit and the rod hooped over alarmingly under the powerful charge of another scaly combatant. It was all Stan could do to stop himself from being pulled from the tree into the lake, such was the force of the carp's first bid for freedom. He was encouraged to see that his ploy had worked as the fish spurned the snaggy sanctuary to the left, making a bee-line for the far bank instead. Despite its initial, ferocious charge (or maybe because of it) the carp soon slowed and gradually succumbed to the pressure that Stan was exerting and, just as he was about to congratulate himself for a job very well done, he realised an awful truth - the landing net was lying peacefully on the grass, ten yards and a wooded barrier away! What an idiot! His mind was a whirr of possible solutions but none of them bore any relation to logic but then, just as he was on the point of resigning himself to losing another good fish, a knight in shining armour appeared.

"I think you might need this," came Mick's voice from behind him, and he glanced over his shoulder to see his friend's smiling face beaming from behind an outstretched landing net. Like a drowning man grabbing a lifebelt, Stan gratefully grasped the net and quickly manoeuvred it into position in front of him, suddenly realising that he still had the carp and the snags to contend with. But he need not have worried. The fish was obviously totally bemused by what was going on and, instead of utilising Stan's lack of concentration to make good its escape, had probably decided that the young angler deserved a little good fortune and glided easily between the outer branches and straight into the waiting net. Stan let out a whoop of joy that sent the tree's other feathered occupants wild with startled cries and caused Mick's face to crease with another smile. Uncaring of wet footwear or clothing now, Stan waded around the branch and back to dry land. Mick had been joined by the third of their merry band and it was Malcolm who took the proffered net whilst Mick heaved the victor out of the margins, patting him soundly on the back.

They all gazed down at Stan's prize and it gradually dawned on them that this was the biggest fish any of them had ever caught. Stan was beside himself with joy and babbled in a very similar fashion to a young child, many years ago, who had caught his first bream.

"Bloody hell, it's huge! How big d'you reckon? It's huge! YEEEEHAAAHH!!!" His two companions could not hide their glee either and all three of them were soon sharing a mental age of seven - and not for the last time, either!

"Where's the scales?" asked Mick. This query brought about a semblance of sanity and they quickly decided to take the fish to the scales, back at their original swim. Stan reverently carried the netted fish along the bank and, on his arrival, Malcolm transferred the fish to a large, plastic carrier bag and hooked it onto the scales that Mick held. Mick hoisted them up and the spring was pulled down to reveal a weight, bag and all, of five and three quarter pounds and more whoops of joy rent the warm, summer air. Stan dispensed with his sopping wet boots before reentering the lake, barefooted, to slip his jewelled prize back - slapping the surface with glee, not anger, once it had disappeared from view. What a day! What a day! The three anglers smiled and shook hands and smiled some more before Mick declared that it was time to leave. There was no disagreement so they quickly packed away their assorted tackle, knowing that the weekend could not have ended any better. As they slowly made their way back to the farmhouse, Stan glanced back for one last look at the place where, he would later realise, the slumbering giant had first awakened.

The next few weeks found him unable to think or speak of little else but, despite a new, almost brash, confidence, he was unable to add to his tally of carp in the three or four visits he made to Old Bury Hill. By the time that the new football season was upon him, he had become more accustomed to the ways of tench and bream rather than carp. This, however, still enthused him and he was certain that it would only be a matter of time before he was joined in arm-aching battle with one of that lake's plated warriors. For now, though, there were other battles to be joined and it was away with rod and reel and out with boots and ball as September heralded the start of the new season. Confidence in the team was high as they had finished the season in third place and, as was the peculiar way of Sunday league football, had gained promotion in doing so. By now, Stan was playing on both days of the weekend so there was little chance of any further fishing until next year but, within a month of the off, all thought of football and fishing became secondary.

It wasn't a rash challenge. He always played hard and went for every fifty-fifty ball with the sole intention of winning it but, unfortunately on this occasion, so did his opponent. Stan was a fraction of a second quicker and managed to flick the ball past the left back, however the left back carried on as if the ball was still there, but it wasn't - Stan's outstretched leg was. For the second time in a few months, Stan let out a yell that startled the occupants of the nearby trees, but this time it was agony not ecstasy that brought about the cry.

"I am afraid you won't be playing football for the rest of the season, Mr. Peacock." The words chilled Stan as he lay in his hospital bed, his right leg held at forty five degrees and balanced by a dangling weight. Broken tibia and fibula that needed a metal plate to hold them together seemed bad enough, but the worst of it was the damage to the knee ligaments. This was many years before keyhole surgery would make that operation a mere formality and Stan knew that he would need to be very lucky if he was going to be able to play again.

By the time that he and Jean had moved into their new house, six months later, Stan had accepted the fact that he would not play competitively again. With a new addition to the family due and the move to a place that seemed to be surrounded by lakes and rivers, that acceptance was made much easier. The endless decorating also helped to take his mind off his injury, although Stan would always be one of those people who maintained that D.I.Y meant do it yourself! Due to this paper-hanging apathy, it did not take long before Stan was poring over an O.S. map of his new environs and beginning to appraise himself of the wealth of water that was within casting distance of his front door - well, almost. Laura's arrival in early August was the culmination of almost a year without Stan wetting a line and when, a couple of weeks after giving birth, Jean suggested that he go fishing for the weekend whilst she visited her mother's, he almost jumped for joy. Their new house was a mere twenty minutes away from Old Bury Hill and, after a quick call to Perky, he began preparations for the ensuing Saturday. It was nice just to get the rods out again and it was a surprise to him how much he had missed it, especially when the first tench of the day sunk his float and made his heart leap.

'I love this,' he thought to himself, not for the first time that weekend, 'but I wish I could catch one of those carp.' By the end of a tench-filled weekend, he vowed to go angling as much as wife and baby would allow, and began making plans for an assault on the lake's carp population. Both he and Perky agreed that their usual swims in amongst the reeds were not the place to fish for the carp as the fishes' obvious power in such an enclosed space would make landing them almost impossible. So, after packing away their tackle on the Sunday, they went for a stroll further along the bank leaving the tall reeds behind them. After a few hundred yards of open water they came upon a stretch of bank that faced the lake's only island and subconsciously came to the same conclusion. This was where they should start their campaign for carp.

Prudence and a screaming baby dictated to Stan that an immediate return to the lake was unwise and so it was not until early September that he once again made the muscle-stretching journey to the far bank.

'If I can do this,' he thought, as he trudged across the rickety wooden bridge, 'I must be able to play football, surely?'

But this was just idle, mental banter. He had long since decided that this was the sort of exercise he craved for his future weekends, and within a few minutes he was gulping in huge lungfuls of oxygen whilst surveying the tree draped island, some sixty yards distant. The sun was rising later as the year neared its end but, no matter what the time, Stan still loved the dawn and drank in the tranquility of the misty morning, the silence broken only by the inevitable calls of moorhen, coot and mallard. And the crashing of some unseen leviathan under the island trees. Peering through the slowly swirling mist, Stan sought out the source of the disturbance and was shortly able to discern the tell-tale ripples emanating from a point a third of the way along the right hand edge of the island. Then, as the mist cleared slightly, the perpetrator of the initial leap repeated the process for its slack-jawed audience.

"Bloody hell, that was a monster!" he exclaimed, but there was no one to acknowledge this declaration. Stan was alone today as Perky had a wedding to attend, but his absent friend had filled him with enthusiasm following the capture of a seven pound carp the previous week, the story of which was still fresh in Stan's mind. It was from this very swim that Perky had taken the monster. Unable to contain himself any longer, he unshipped his rods and hurriedly made them up. Along with his normal float tackle, he had assembled a very simple running leger rig with which he hoped to reach the far island but, as he once again peered across the lake, he doubted his ability to cast such a distance. Threading on three grains of corn, he held the rod above his head and, with an almighty swish of fibre glass hurled his one ounce lead as far as he was able. Unfortunately, his ability fell twenty yards short of the island and a further half a dozen attempts proved equally inadequate, leaving him cursing and frustrated at his lack of ability. However, after a few calming minutes, he elected to put out his float, thus enabling him time to compose himself and come up with a fresh idea. Whilst watching the red tip settling amongst the almost mist free water, he hit upon a plan that could not fail and so, after casually striking, playing and landing a small tench, he set about putting his foolproof plan into operation.

It was obvious that, in order to cast the required distance he would need a heavier lead, but one ounce leads were all he possessed, so he would use two of them - simple! Excited at this brilliant idea he quickly set about tying up a running leger with two leads on the five pound tail. Then he slipped the swivel onto the line above the hooklink, placing a swan shot six inches from the hook to prevent the leger affair from fouling the hook - how had he never thought of such a thing before?

The first cast went like a dream and landed ten yards up the tree on the island! The next, after having tied a new leger set-up, landed five yards short, but he had seen the sweetcorn come off and, on retrieval, was dismayed also to find that the swan shot had slipped down to within two inches of the hook.

Another try, with two swan shot, prevented the swivel slipping but could not prevent the sweetcorn free-falling into the lake and frustration was, once again, starting to rear its ugly head - more float fishing was required.

Once again, the calming sight of that red tip dancing in the steadily rippling water acted like a balm to his frustration and he soon had a new, improved plan. The lead and swan shot was working, so all he had to do now was to devise a method of keeping the corn on the hook and, as another hungry tench snaffled his float fished offering he came up with the obvious solution - use a different bait. Brilliant! But what? Bread, like sweetcorn, had a tendency to explode in mid-air if cast too hard so the obvious answer was maggots, but he had none. What he did have, however, was their big brothers - worms - or at least he would have after a little gardening. Deftly unhooking the tench and slipping it back, he scrabbled in the still damp grass and quickly unearthed three or four suitable wrigglers, slipping a couple onto his size twelve hook before carefully taking aim at the far tree-line. His recent casting exploits had taught him the necessary force required, but it was with wonder and pride that he saw the whole jangle of tackle and bait land with an audible splash beneath the outstretched branches of the very tree where the early morning carp had shown. It was more by luck than any sort of judgement. With a skip in his step, he set his rod down on the rests and attached a small dough bobbin on the line between reel and butt ring as Perky had shown him, and sat back to await events, dispensing with the float for the moment so that he could concentrate on the island rod. It was then, after being at the lake for almost two hours, that he realised how hungry and thirsty he was, so set about rummaging through his bag for something suitable to eat. Underneath the shade of the island trees, a couple of carp moved slowly forward to investigate the sound that usually registered an easy meal dropping from the branches above, or from the tufts of grass that overhung the bank. Soon their sensitive barbules picked up the signals that signified that breakfast was being served. It was just a matter of to whom.

Whack! The dough bobbin hit the rod butt with such force that Stan thought someone had fired a pistol and, so, deposited a cup of hot tea in his lap. Then, before he had a chance to register any pain to his thighs, he registered, instead, the sound of the clutch of his reel spinning like a dynamo and instinctively grabbed the rod before it became airborne. As he lifted the rod above the horizontal he could see his line cutting through the water from left to right, a thousand tiny droplets of water sparkling in the early morning sun as they sprayed from the tortured nylon. What had he hooked? The power of this fish made his legs weaken and his heart pound as if he had just completed a hundred yard sprint. However the sprinter was not him and it did not seem that it would be content with a mere hundred yards in which to vent its fury, and so Stan just hung on and hoped for the best, or at least some respite. As is always the way, respite was close at hand and after its initial, dynamic burst of power, the carp's energy was sapped and it slowed to a sedate gallop. The realisation that he was suddenly close to some sort of control was like a slap round the face to Stan. He quickly resumed the guise of someone who knows what they are doing, glancing over his shoulder like you do when you have just tripped in the street and you wonder if anyone saw you. The fight was a much more orderly affair, now, but Stan could tell by the weight, and the frightening signals coming back up the line as the carp angrily shook its head that this was by far the biggest fish he had ever dreamt of, let alone hooked. He tried desperately to calm himself.

'Oh, Perky, where are you when I really need you?' he thought, but that did him no good so he grabbed the net and prepared, like a first time aviator, for a solo landing. The carp was very tired by now and was slowly cruising up and down the margins, so Stan slipped the net into the lake, only to wonder how the fish would fit in there after he saw it roll impressively on the surface. But, fit in there it did and ten minutes after the initial gunshot, the race was over and Stan, the victor, let rip his victory cry once more and gazed down in wonderment at the vast amount of carp that was in his woefully small net.

"I think I need a bigger boat!" he gasped. He laughed aloud at that remark, and at life in general.

"I just love this!" he bellowed, and assorted waterfowl screeched their agreement.

The next few minutes were a blur and, when later relating the whole story to everyone within earshot, he was unable to remember anything from the netting to the weighing. The weighing he remembered, oh yes indeed! The spring balance creaked under the strain but, as much as he willed it, would go no further than nine and three quarter pounds. Nine and three quarters! He was beside himself with joy and wished that Perky, or anybody for that matter, was there to witness it. His wish was shortly granted when a voice from behind shook him from his reverie.

"Blimey what was all that noise? I thought someone had fallen in or something," said the newcomer.

Stan turned to see a middle aged guy with a beard and glasses standing a couple of yards away.

"I've just caught a carp," said Stan, by way of explanation, "and it's blooming huge!"

'Heard it all before,' thought the other but, when he looked into the sack that Stan was holding, all semblance of cockiness was gone and he gasped, "Bloody hell, how big is that?"

"Nine and three quarters," replied Stan, proudly. "Can you take a photo for us?" he requested.

The bemused newcomer took the proffered camera and clicked off a couple of poor shots of a cuddled common carp, and Stan accepted the stilted congratulations without realising the first stirrings of something that would become too evident in future years -jealousy.

For Stan, the season consisted of two more visits to the lake, either side of the end of September. No more carp graced his net due mainly to the fact that they had moved into deeper water at the back of the island, a fact that Stan and Perky were totally ignorant of. Perky did hook one more, on worms, but the hook pulled before he had any idea of what size it might have been and he soon reverted back to the tench fishing that he loved. Stan, however, could never again be content with catching something that did not double his heartbeat and so, once again, he would soon find himself fishing with different but like minded partners. This seed was planted before the year was out and, on a mild October day just prior to the clocks changing and heralding the end of British Summer Time, Stan met someone who would be the next leg of the relay race that was carp angling.

The Ordnance Survey map of Guildford and environs was well thumbed and marked with pen circles and scribbled notes, the bulk of which Stan was studying intently on the kitchen table for the umpteenth time that week. A visit to a local tackle shop had borne fruit and, armed with the knowledge from there, he had searched out the lakes that he had been told contained the treasure he was seeking - carp. He had singled out three possible venues for next year and had decided that, rather than fish for the last couple of weeks of this season, he would visit these lakes in order to learn a little more about them. What did they hold? Who owned them? Could he get a ticket? Did they excite him?

The first, a five acre lake near Farnham, seemed quite acceptable but the two or three anglers that he spoke to were less than helpful and succeeded in putting him off completely. The second, however, was much more encouraging - so much so that he did not bother visiting his third choice for more than a year. The lake was a classic estate lake. Fifteen acres in size and vaguely triangular in shape, it had a dam wall at one end where the water was about twelve feet deep. At the far end the lake narrowed down to a silty area that was no more than two feet deep but would obviously be an area that fish visited in the warmer, summer months. Being in the middle of Pirbright

Common, it was surrounded on three sides by woodland from where Stan could hear all manner of birdsong, including the repetitive tapping of a woodpecker. As he looked across the remnants of a large lily bed, he saw the flash of blue that marked the flight of the resident kingfisher - he liked it here.

His first visit to the lake had been one evening, after work, and his initial impression had been favourable but he had seen no fishermen on the banks so had decided to return at the weekend in order to glean some information about the lake's inhabitants, hopefully. So it was that he was walking the heavily wooded east bank on Saturday morning just as one of the weekend anglers was landing a fish. Stan strolled over, casually, not wanting to disturb the guy but desperate to see what he had caught. He need not have been so sensitive for the angler, a tall, dark haired man in his mid-twenties, was more than eager to reveal the contents of his landing net to anyone who was passing. Looking round, he spied Stan standing by a tree at the back of the swim and motioned him forward.

"What yer got?" Stan enquired, eager to look into the sunken folds of the landing net.

"A carp," came the breathless reply. "And a good 'un, as well."

Stan's pulse quickened a fraction and he leant forward in rapt anticipation as the excited angler lifted the net. It seemed to Stan that, at that precise moment, the sun appeared from behind a cloud and a host of skylarks burst into joyous song. What a fish! The first thing he noticed was the lack of scales - this was a mirror carp, the first he had seen on the bank. The angler carefully laid the net onto the grass and peeled back the mesh to reveal the wonderful, golden flank that was speckled here and there with small, penny-sized scales. Clucking with delight, the excited young angler carefully folded the mesh back over the fish before quickly extracting scales and a sling from beneath his chair.

"How big d'you reckon?" he asked of Stan.

"Dunno. I had one of nine and three quarters a little while ago but this looks bigger than that, I'd say."

Seeing his visitor in a different light with this news, Paddy (for that was his name) carefully removed the hook from the carp's rubbery bottom lip before slipping the fish into the homemade but very efficient weigh sling. With a grunt, he lifted it to eye level and read aloud the resulting weight.

"Twelve pounds and... Twelve pounds four. Woooohh!"

Laying the carp carefully back down, he punched the air with joy and proceeded to dance a little jig around his swim.

"Personal best!" he exclaimed, as if a grinning Stan needed any explanation for this show of elation. "You any good with a camera?" enquired the similarly grinning Paddy.

"I'll have a go. My name's Stan, by the way."

"Good to meet you, Stan-by-the-way. Mine's Paddy. I'll just call you Stan!"

They both laughed at this remark, but Stan had a tremendous sense of déjà vu. Oh, it was probably nothing. He took the compact camera and listened to Paddy's brief instructions, then waited eagerly for the captor to fully reveal his prize, mentally gasping when he did. What a magnificent fish, the likes of which he had only ever seen in the weekly angling papers, the likes of which he would dearly love to be holding, soon. Stan clicked off four or five shots, as instructed, then enviously watched as Paddy slipped the gleaming fish back into the lake, laughing maniacally as its great tail splashed water all over him in its bid for freedom.

"Yeeesss!" he screamed, and grabbed Stan's extended hand to aid his exit from the lake.

Now was obviously a good time for Stan to prise as much information about the lake from the bemused Paddy and so, over the next half an hour or so, he gleaned as much knowledge about Manor Pond as he could. By the time he bade his soon-to-be friend farewell, he knew exactly where he would be fishing next season and what for. The lake held carp in excess of twenty pounds, according to Paddy, although the largest he had seen caught was a mere eighteen pounds. Eighteen pounds! Stan's head spun at the thought of such a fish and his journey home was filled with daydreams of himself and the beast in a wonderful embrace.

The controlling club was run by one of the guys who worked in the tackle shop and membership would be no problem. So it was that, as the decades changed, Stan took the next big step in his carp angling career - a step that would be quite awkward to negotiate, but one that, if taken with care, would set him firmly on the ladder to carp beyond his wildest dreams.

Almost two years of neglect, coupled with a more stable climate, had benefited all the creatures that used Stanton's as a home and not least amongst these was the lake's carp population. Of the sixty or so fish that had made the strenuous journey two summer's earlier, three quarters of that number had survived and were now flourishing in the nutrient rich water increasing their weight considerably with little outside interference. Naturally, the bigger the carp, the bigger the weight gain, or so it would appear if the fish at Stanton's were any yardstick, and the trio of monsters showed every sign of benefiting hugely from the previous couple of years of rich harvest. However, this could not go unnoticed forever and so it was no surprise when more than the usual, casual float angler made the onerous trip from car park to lakeside on the last June 16th of the decade.

Dean and John had heard casual rumours at their local tackle shop, the previous autumn, of some bream and tench anglers who had seen a couple of huge carp cruising the margins of the little-fished Stanton's Pit over the course of the summer. These rumours had been compounded when a well-known and respected local angler had been unable to stop a large fish from snapping his eight pound line like cotton. Dean had made some concerted enquiries over the winter and had tracked down a couple of the anglers one frosty, December morning whilst they were spinning for pike on the banks of the Avon. Strange how, in these adverse conditions, anglers seem to gravitate towards each other as if the battle against the elements is a common bond that brings them closer together. If the same group of men had happened upon each other in similar, summer circumstances you could be sure that they would have barely acknowledged each other's existence, but Dean knew this to be so, and used the situation to his advantage. It was no coincidence that his tackle bag contained a huge flask of steaming broth, nor that he just happened to have three cups in the depths of that same bag. So it was that, within an hour of passing the first casual 'Hello', Dean had manoeuvred the conversation gradually onto the subject of the Stanton monsters.

"I'll tell you something I've heard, but you mustn't breathe a word of it to anyone," he confided, mysteriously. Like anglers everywhere, this was as alluring as feathers to a mackerel and the two prey took the bait before they even realised they were being fished for.

"Won't tell a soul, will we, Ned?" said the one, almost crossing his heart as evidence of his oath of silence.

"Not a soul, young fella, you have my word on that," confirmed Ned, with honour.

Dean flicked over the bail arm.

"Well, you know that big pit outside town, Stepton's or something?"

"Stanton's," corrected Ned, pecking at the bait.

"That's it. Well, I've heard that there's s'posed to be a couple of good sized carp in there. Mate of mine, Bob, reckons some bloke lost a twenty pounder in there but I reckon he's pulling my leg."

The bait was twitched enticingly along the floor. Ned looked at his companion, who nodded imperceptibly then darted forward to grab the bait lest it should disappear.

"Twenty pound and more, young fella, and it's not the only one!" Strike!!

Time to reel 'em in, thought Dean, gleefully.

"Oh, now you're really having me on," he goaded.

It was suddenly a matter of who could speak quickest as the two raconteurs vied for first place in the landing net. Ned won by a short breath.

"Oh no he's not, lad. I've sin 'em with me own eyes on more than one occasion and I was there when old Ted got broke up by one of 'em. Went off like a rocket, and there was no stopping him. Left a wake behind him like a speedboat, he did."

Suddenly, Dean felt himself being played like a fish, but he felt that this bait was not an artificial lure, as his had been, but as natural as a worm! He spent the next half an hour coaxing as much information from the two ever willing informants, risking hypothermia whilst plying the others with the remains of the tongue-loosening broth. But later, as he gradually thawed out in front of a roaring log fire and sifted through his newfound knowledge, he realised that the risk of frostbite had been worth it. 'Here there be monsters!' he thought, dramatically.

John took some convincing, but was willing to give his friend the benefit of the doubt and agreed to a few close season walks along the ever-burgeoning banks of the large pit. So it was that, a month prior to the start of the season - and just as Stan was putting paper to wall some hundred miles east - the two budding carp anglers first set eyes on The Common and The Scarred Mirror, and were almost speechless at the sight. These were by far the largest carp either of them had ever seen and, momentarily, they were a little scared but that feeling was shortly replaced by one of anticipation and, eventually, boyhood excitement. Very soon, one of them would be holding a carp in excess of thirty pounds, of that they were absolutely certain, 'as long as it's me first,' they both privately hoped.

A further two sightings strengthened their resolve, especially as it appeared that another fish of similar size was present in the lake. Although never seen as clearly as the other two, the big scaled mirror seemed to frequent the same area of lake as the other two, just a few yards further out and deeper down. Let the baiting commence.

With the new breed of carp anglers came a new breed of bait - protein baits. Although Dean and John were not totally up to date with the latest ideas, they knew enough people and had enough knowledge of their own to put together an acceptable and enticing bait with which to tempt their prey. With copious amounts of hemp and sweetcorn to act as a groundbait, they scattered their paste offerings liberally around the margins of the lake in the weeks leading up to that last June 16th of the decade and on that day one of them had his wishes granted when he was the first to land one of the monsters as, once again, The

Scarred Mirror could not control his appetite and made the first of three visits to the bank that summer. As was usual with that particular fish, its first visit was its heaviest and, at a shade over thirty one pounds was more than the angling companions could ever have imagined from their first session on the lake. If only they had known that carp's position in the lake's hierarchy they may have been more careful about whom they told of their success. Within two short weeks it became very apparent to them that the lake's inhabitants had not been a complete mystery. It had just been that some people preferred to wait for someone else to do all the hard work and confirm the rumours before these parasites showed themselves at the lakeside and, inevitably, reaped someone else's reward – ever would it be so!

By the end of September the carp-vine had worked its magic and news of the lake's huge denizens had spread far and wide, attracting anglers from as far as Kent, Hertfordshire and Wales. The further captures of The Scarred Mirror had been spectacularly overshadowed when an angler from Kent, who had been camped on the lake for four days a week, enjoyed a success that not even he could have dreamt of. In a three day period at the end of July - a week prior to the birth of Stan's daughter, Laura - he caught carp of eighteen, twenty one, twenty six and, ultimately, The Big-Scaled Mirror at a stunning weight of thirty two pounds and a few ounces.

If there was any doubt of the lake's potential, this capture dispelled it and, very soon, the club was being inundated with requests for tickets which it, at first, dispensed with relish, accepting gratefully this unexpected bounty. But soon, and for once beneficially, the dissenters in the small club made their displeasure at this influx of new and unwelcome members known and, as the waters were being stirred, a series of unrelated events occurred to confirm these words of doom.

The first was probably nothing to do with the new members but more to do with the usual summer combination of lack of oxygen and spawning frenzy. The appearance of a couple of dozen dead bream and roach in the swim of one of the oldest club members set the drums beating. The second was definitely a cause of the increase in anglers, and it always will be, and that was litter. At first a small amount that gradually grew if not to a mountain, then to an eyesore that caused offence and brought about the third, and most unwanted addition to the lake's fauna rats. But not just rats. Rats in the Club Secretary's swim whilst he was angling with his wife and young child. That was the final straw, an Extraordinary General Meeting was called, but what was strange was that only the locals heard about it and attended, for once, in full force. The 'thirty years, man and boy' man did not even have to speak, his views were aired by all present and the subsequent proposal was passed unanimously. And the proposal? No members outside a ten mile radius of the village church,

65

effective immediately. All those who were outside this boundary would have their money refunded and their tickets confiscated, despite the short term financial damage to the club - this would be rectified by a small increase in club funds and a couple of fund raising events over the next couple of months. The effect on the club would, eventually, be very little. However, the effect on the denizens of the lake would be profound for, once again, man had stepped in to alter their destiny - this time for the better, but it would not always be so. What of The Common, though? Strangely it once again dropped its guard when within sight of salvation and, once again, it was its predilection for a surface bait that was its downfall. Fittingly, I suppose, it was Dean who was to be the captor of one of the largest common carp in England, at the end of September, and as the Club Secretary was trying to calm his distraught wife, Dean was watching incredulously as a huge pair of lips engulfed his floating crust and a back like a Labrador's broke the surface and cleaved a wake like a speedboat across the lake as it tried, in vain, to shed the hook. Although the battle was long and fraught with drama, the angler was eventually the victor and gasped, with many other envious onlookers, at the size of his prize as it was laid gently onto the sponge mat that Dean had made for this sole purpose. Unfortunately he had not quite grasped the scale of the carp!

"Thirty four pounds six ounces," rang out John's voice like a town crier's.

Hands patted a back and cameras clicked until, finally, the great fish was returned to the lake's depths to recover whilst its grateful captor took his deserved plaudits.

So ended the decade and the lake, once again, was returned to a modicum of peace and serenity. But it would never be the same because there were anglers in the local club who had seen what bounty it held and they saw that it was good. They, however, had much to learn about the ways of large carp and the tackle and tactics required to vanquish them, but learn they would. It was just a matter of time. The problem was that it was also just a matter of time before one of Nature's little bombs became primed and ready to explode. For now, it was laying dormant - waiting.

Chapter Seven - 1982

"I counted them out, and I counted them all back in."

Peter Sisson's chilling recounting of a small part of the Falklands' conflict held the nation rapt with attention and anticipation. Thankfully their attention span was not extended too much and the crisis was over in the space of a close season, if only the same could have been said for those who had to uphold the honour of Queen and Country, but their story would remain unheard for many years.

For Stan, this close season seemed to have been postponed for a couple of years and he had never been more excited by the prospect of the new season and what it may hold. His decision to quit football had been a little premature. During the first winter of the new decade, he had realised that he could not just stand on the sideline and watch his team mates give their all whilst he, occasionally, ran the line and waved his flag as impartially as he could. No, his career was not finished as long as he still had the will to play and, so, he began training again whilst the lakes froze and his eagerness to be by the lake was lessened by the temperature. So it was that, in 1980, Stan looked forward to the beginnings of two seasons the first on the 16th of June and the second less than three months later.

The start of the fishing season found him at the Manor Pond for the first time. Despite only landing two small tench, he felt that he had begun his carp angling journey in fine style when he was on hand to land a mirror carp of just over ten pounds for Paddy. Little did the pair realise that, as they sat and toasted the rising moon with a steaming brew, carp angling history was being made just a few hundred miles away.

"Record Carp," screamed the headlines of the angling papers on the following Wednesday, and Stan beamed all the way to work at the news that Dick Walker's twenty eight year old record had finally been bettered. A guy called Chris Yates (whom Stan had never heard of) had been at Redmire Pool (of which Stan had heard much) and had landed a massive mirror carp of fifty one and a half pounds. Fifty one! He found it difficult to imagine any fish of that size, let alone one of the carp that he fished for. The following weekend, the lake was abuzz with the news and many copies of the Angling Times and the Anglers' Mail were being handed around as proof to the non-believers. Stan, Paddy and a couple of Paddy's mates spent most of the day discussing how long it must have taken to land. What amazing tackle the guy must have had, what bait he was really using - sweetcorn, oh sure! If only they had known!

The next few weeks saw many new faces at the lake and Stan soon became a little disconsolate at the lack of action his rods were receiving from the local carp population - if only he was still fishing for tench, then he would have no complaints. Paddy, on the other hand, could not stop catching carp and, although he had yet to repeat his first day's success, he was making up in numbers what he was lacking in size. He could not help noticing Stan's waning enthusiasm, however, so decided to give him a bit of assistance in the shape of a can of luncheon meat. After showing him how best to use this innovation in bait, he was as elated as he could be when Stan caught his first carp from the lake on the very next weekend. Stan had realised that the pads at the far south end of the lake were home to carp at every time of day or night, but had been constantly frustrated, on his arrival at the lake, by the lack of swims available in the area. So he had decided to have a day off work on the following Friday and arrive at the lake at dawn of that day, twenty four hours earlier than usual. The plan worked admirably but, unfortunately, Stan's lack of experience at playing such powerful fish in such a demanding swim left him ruing the loss of four carp by the time Paddy arrived in the early evening. Stan was planning to leave by midday on Saturday and did not relish playing any carp during the hours of darkness as they had been impossible to land in daylight! He allowed Paddy to move in next to him and fish the pads whilst he moved his rods a little further along the bank and dropped his luncheon meat offerings beneath the branches of a couple of overhanging trees either side of his new swim. Inevitably, Paddy hooked three carp during the night, landing the last and filling Stan with envy as he showed him his double figure prize - a pound larger than Stan's personal best and a mirror to boot.

As the sun made its first impression on the day, Stan had a brace of tench to show for his night's vigil and was snoring tonelessly when, at last, an errant carp happened upon his last, hastily cast bait. Stan knew little of the ensuing fight except that his head ached terribly from its collision with the brolly pole, and also that something was trying desperately to pull his arm off, and so it was with total bewilderment that he found himself gazing down upon his first carp from Manor Pond. He let out a whoop of delight and was soon joined by an equally bewildered Paddy who had also been enjoying some well-earned snoring time. The pair looked first at the carp, then at each other and then back at the carp before jumping around as if they were at Redmire and had broken the record anew. Stan's fully scaled fish was a little over a tenth of the size of the Redmire monster, but he cared not a jot and smiled brightly in the early morning sunlight as Paddy pointed the Instamatic in his direction. With this renewed vigour, Stan was able to endure a further month of abstinence before landing his second, and last carp of that season and although a pound or so bigger than the first and the same smaller than his personal best, he did not feel the same elation. He puzzled over this for a week or so but then his apathy was explained completely when he laid eyes on the last fish he was to see that season. This was a stunning fourteen pound linear mirror that was Paddy's personal best, and his excitement was almost as tangible as the captor's. This was what he craved.

The next season followed a similar pattern, with Stan venturing to the lake on half a dozen occasions before the lure of a football dragged him away from the bankside once more. He approached the season with a renewed confidence, which was quadrupled, by the end of June, following the landing of his first mirror carp. He had managed to secure a swim in the ever-popular pads area and had, once again, been undone on two occasions by the power of the fish. On the third occasion that a carp fell prey to his luncheon meat offering, his luck and line held and he was soon gleefully caressing and weighing an eight pound mirror carp whose flanks were scattered here and there with penny-sized scales - never had he seen a prettier carp. His confidence was sky high, and he arrived each weekend knowing that he was going to hook a carp or two, it was just a matter of landing them. And hook them he did. Over the following three weekends he hooked three carp but failed, on each occasion, to land the hard fighting fish and soon realised that he was doing neither himself nor the fish any good by constantly hooking and losing them in the pads. So he decided that, for the remaining three weekends prior to the start of the football season, he would explore the rest of the lake. It took a little time for him to realise that he had been limiting his chances greatly over the previous month or so. Although he caught nothing on his first two trips, he witnessed the capture of the largest carp he had seen on the bank when a young angler fishing a couple of swims to his left landed a mirror carp an ounce or two under sixteen pounds in weight. This was obviously the guy's personal best and, though envious, Stan could not help being infected by the captor's joy and shook his hand warmly following the release of the fish back into the lake. He also glanced carefully at the hooklink and bait as he left the swim. There was something different about the hook and line, and the bait looked for all the world like a couple of brown peas but Stan dismissed this as some form of delusion, concentrating instead on the memory of that glorious fish. How long would it be before it was his wet hand that was being shaken and his face that was split by a victorious smile?

The answer to that was almost a week. Not 'almost' as in time, but 'almost' as in tangibility.

His sweetcorn offering was picked up and, being in relatively open water, Stan had little to concern him apart from the power of the fish. It was this power, however, that was Stan's undoing. When the fish made one final surge towards the overhanging rhododendron branches to his right, Stan could only watch in horror as the line disappeared into that tangled jungle ten yards along its length and, seconds later, felt his heart sink as the line went slack. Shaking and disconsolate, he could not bring himself to retackle and rebait for more than an hour and when he did it was with a sense of resignation, casting the lead as far as he could in order to vent some of his pent up frustration. Why had he let it go along there? He had told himself that the last place he should let the carp go was to his right, so why had he let it go there? In the midst of these recriminations he was aware of a buzzing sound and looked down in amazement to see the spool spinning furiously on the recently cast rod. He picked up the offending wand and struck forcefully. The resistance was encouraging but, within minutes, he knew that this was no comparison to the recent escapee and soon led the offender into his waiting net. Peering down, his heart skipped a beat when he momentarily thought that here was his yearned for double, but that milestone would wait for another day as this carp missed that target by a mere six ounces. Stan's joy at this common a mere two ounces below his previous best was tempered a little with the certainty that 'the one that got away' was well in excess of that particular landmark. He still felt, though, that he was starting to get to grips with this trying water - more was the pity that the football season began next week. Still, maybe next season.

By the time that the opposing forces were readying themselves for battle in the South Atlantic in the early months of 1982, Stan had decided that his 'comeback' had been a foolhardy decision and, although not aggravating his injury, it was his pride that had suffered. The team had, a season before, amalgamated with another well-known local team and the ensuing influx of players had meant that Springwater's were able to field three teams, the second of which Stan had been drafted into. This demotion had worried him little, but the splitting up of his old pals into the three different teams seemed also to have split the team spirit and, within a few months, players had started to leave for pastures new. Stan decided to stick it out but, by the spring of the New Year, had made up his mind that this would be his last season - definitely. The nail was hammered firmly into the coffin in the penultimate game of the season. Due to injuries in the first team squad, three of the second team had been 'promoted' to first team duty, Stan amongst them, but instead of pride at this move, they all felt annoyed and used. The first team was wallowing in mid table and was going for neither promotion nor relegation. The seconds, however, had every chance of achieving runners up spot in their division if they could win their last two games. Despite these arguments, the first team took priority and the players, too. The firsts drew 1-1 with the bottom of the table team, the seconds lost 2-1 to a team ten places below them and with that defeat the chance of promotion was gone. Feelings ran very high that night in the clubhouse and it was then that Stan knew his decision to quit was, indeed, the correct one.

Within a month of Christmas, Stan's decision to leave had begun forming in his mind and, so, he had subconsciously begun moving towards fishing again. This manifested itself mainly in his desire to read as much as possible about carp angling and, pretty soon, he was amassing a small fishing library containing anything he could find to do with fishing. Trout, tench, gravel pits, float fishing, but mainly carp fishing. Dick Walker's Still Water Angling was read from cover to cover on numerous occasions as were Basic Carp Fishing, Carp and the Carp Angler and, most avidly Quest for Carp. He found himself lost in the words and sentences and paragraphs. He felt as if he was Alice and the white rabbit was a huge, elusive common carp, and by the time that he removed his studded boots for the last time, his mind was a blur with possibilities and daydreams of huge carp in voluminous landing nets. The close season was spent, not only walking the banks of his local lakes and ponds, but also building up a new armoury of tackle - stronger, shinier, more powerful and very costly - and by the beginning of June he was ready to do battle with the King of Carp.

He had also read closely about the methods and rigs that were required to vanquish these beasts and had spent many hours re-spooling his new Mitchell reels with eight pound line, onto which was slipped a link-leger of one and a half ounces.

Finally, a rig consisting of a swivel, twelve inches of the same line and a size 6 Jack Hilton hook. All was ready for his first, real onslaught on the local carp population - they didn't stand a chance, was it fair even to cast out! Oh, poor, deluded child!

On the couple of sorties he had made to Manor Pond he had seen, from his lofty perch, a number of fish in the pads, some of which took his breath away - especially when they had greedily accepted the latest weapon in his armoury. Stan had been sure that he was merely scratching the surface when it came to bait, especially after Paddy's luncheon meat revelation, and this supposition was borne out tenfold by the lists of possible baits that could be used to catch carp - who would ever use cat food, I ask you! His initial scepticism, however, gave way to stunned belief when his free, close season offerings were wolfed down by the ever hungry diners at Cafe Manor, and all of the other small ponds he visited in the last fortnight before the off. It was on one of these last minute visits that he was, once more, reacquainted with Paddy who seemed to have a few offerings of his own for the lake's carp, and they talked in earnest about the forthcoming season. Paddy seemed genuinely pleased that Stan was to concentrate solely on his carp fishing for the foreseeable future, and pleasantly surprised at the knowledge that Stan had gleaned over the winter.

"What's in the bag?" he enquired of the new carp angler.

"Trout pellet paste. What d'yer think?" replied Stan, proffering the opened carrier bag for Paddy's perusal. Sticking his face into the bag, like carp anglers everywhere, he inhaled deeply.

"Smells disgusting," grimaced the sniffer. "Must be good stuff. Here, have a sniff of these," he suggested, whilst thrusting his own bag of evil smelling wares forward for Stan's approval.

Stan repeated the smelling ceremony, yanking his head out sharply lest the odious contents should disable his nervous system!

"What the hell ... !" he choked. "That is disgusting, what on earth is it?"

Paddy seemed pleased with the effect his concoction had had on the smeller and chortled happily.

"Kit-e-Kat, anchovy paste, semolina, eggs and a couple of secret ingredients. Good, innit?"

'Good' was not the description that Stan would have used but, seeing his friend's supreme belief that this was indeed what it was, Stan nodded and smiled.

"Yeah, really good! But do the carp like it?" he added as a caveat to his agreement.

"Watch this," Paddy suggested, and crept carefully up to the water's edge. Glancing left and right like a strange Green Cross Code man, he made sure that there were no diners present before depositing a couple of handfuls of the foul smelling balls into the lake. Motioning for Stan to follow, he led the way to a convenient climbing tree and scurried aloft, quickly followed by Stan. They had barely had a chance to settle on their respective perches before the first of the carp cruised into view, followed shortly by another three, and as if of one mind, all four homed in on Paddy's bait and commenced devouring it lest some other fish should appear. Appear they did, though, and soon the only thing that the watchers could see were massive clouds of silt with the odd tail waving frantically from within. Stan had never seen the like of this before, although the description from different books was embedded in his cranium, now he could see what they meant by this feeding frenzy, this total preoccupation with one food source. Just to see if he was wasting his time, he emptied the remainder of his bait bag down on the carp below, like a brown hard rain, but they seemed little perturbed, merely turning from their existing feast to take in the new dessert. Stan was most pleased with this result and felt, somehow, vindicated, as if this was an approval of his good works. They stayed aloft for a further hour, waiting for the clouds to recede so that they could identify individual fish in amongst the throng. They speculated as to the size of the few fish that dwarfed many of the others and, by the end of the afternoon, they had convinced each other that, by the evening of the 16th, they would both have caught carp of immense proportions. They arranged to meet at the lake on the 15th, both having arranged time off work, and bade each other a hearty farewell.

The next three days were like all the Christmas Eves that Stan could ever remember. He slept barely a wink such was his excitement and anticipation. His plan to arrive at the lake on the afternoon of the 15th went straight out of the window and it took little for him to gain another day's holiday so that he could arrive at the lake in the early morning, lest all the swims were taken! That sleep would be impossible on that night was not a doubt. Whether he would actually go to bed, however, was seriously in question and so it was no surprise to the amazingly patient, and soon to be long-suffering Jean, that she felt the weight rise from the mattress to leave her alone for the first of a thousand nights or more. Had she bothered to look at the clock she would have doubted her sleep muddled eyes - surely not three o'clock? Surely not! Stan crept about the house as quietly as a church elephant, gathering his tackle and food and depositing it into the waiting Escort, quietly closing the door behind him before setting off through the dark country lanes on the fifteen minute journey to the lake. What time did the sun rise, he wondered, having forgotten a similar journey the previous year? But last year had not been like this. Last year he was still just a fisherman, this year he had transformed into a carp angler. As the lanes rolled by, lit by a three quarter moon, he mused to himself, paraphrasing a favourite poem of his, "The road was a ribbon of moonlight across the purple moor, and the carp angler came riding, up to the dark lake shore."

Smiling at his revision, he repeated it a number of times, trying to remember how the rest of it went. He lost patience with this as soon as he came to the fork in the road that led to the track that led to the rough car park that led, at last, to the lake. The cooling engine ticked and clicked a few times but that was the only sound that broke the silence at the edge of the pine wood. Stan stood stock still, drinking in the heady atmosphere and filling his lungs with gallons of molten elation. Ever so gradually he could see the black changing to a dark blue in the sky to his left and he knew that the day would soon be alive with birdsong. There was the first, a single call. Then another, was it a blackbird? He had no idea but had heard it said, by some who professed to know, that it was that dark bird who initiated the dawn chorus, others equally qualified to a point of view disagreed, naturally. No matter, this was the throat-clearing before the morning's great aria and Stan was soon unable to distinguish between the tumult of whistles, squeaks, peeps, warbles and caws that made up the cacophony of noise that was Nature's No 1 hit. By the time that he had taken a leisurely stroll along the lake's West Bank, thus benefiting from the ever increasing light emanating from the east, the world was wide awake and ready for breakfast. As he neared his desired swim, he could just make out the furled leaves of the lily pads peppering the surface of the glass calm lake. As he peered closer, he could discern ripples expanding from the leaves as their stems were being brushed by something of substance below the surface.

Despite the fact that he would not be able to cast a line for another twenty hours, Stan's pace increased as he neared the secluded swim at the edge of the wood. He silently uttered a prayer that he would repeat tens of thousands of times over the coming years. The prayer of 'Please, Lord, don't let anyone be in my swim!' What if there was? There was a whole lake to choose from so it wouldn't matter, would it? Of course it would, you fool, don't you know anything? But, this time, his prayer was answered and he gratefully lowered his rod bag and sun lounger to the ground before surveying all that he owned. The swim was not right in the middle of the pads but slightly off to the right, with thirty or forty yards of open water between them and the island to the right. The trees on the island hung over the lake a little more this year and offered a perfect forty yard cast to the shade beneath their branches. This would be where his right hand rod would go. The left hand rod, his new ten foot, glass fibre carp rod would be cast to the edge of the pads in a small bay created by the leaves and would be the one that, he fancied, would receive the most action. Due to its popularity over the past couple of seasons, this was the first opportunity that he had had to fish this swim. He was relishing the next couple of days in here, certain in the knowledge that he was soon to be cradling a double figure carp in his arms.

The day slowly moved on and it was with barely concealed smugness that he greeted three or four anglers who had obviously had the same ideas as him but, unfortunately for them, they either had no prayer or they found sleep too easy to come by. Whichever, they trudged away with less of a spring in their step than when they had arrived. One angler who seemed unperturbed by Stan's presence in the island swim was the guy who had caught the sixteen pounder the previous season. On his arrival at Stan's side, he merely said, "Stick the kettle on, mate. I'm gasping!" before shinning up a convenient tree to aid his view of the lake.

"Got a few fish out here, mate. Some good'uns as well. You wanna get some floaters out there, they're absolutely begging for one."

Stan looked up at the guy's legs and merely replied, "Sugar?" "Yes, honey," came the glib reply, but Stan did his best to ignore it. "Do you take sugar?" he repeated, less ambiguously.

"No thanks, mate. Got any biscuits?"

'This one's got some front,' thought Stan, but extracted his half empty packet of ginger nuts none the less, offering them to the now earthbound misfit.

Whilst they demolished the remainder of the biscuits, the newcomer suggested a few ways of extracting carp from the swim but Stan stoically declined, assuring the lad that his rods would not be cast out until midnight.

"Oh, I've gotta have a go at these. Thanks for the tea, mate, I'll see you later," and with that, he gathered up the rods and bag with which he had entered the swim and made his way further to Stan's right, appearing five minutes later on the far bank, eighty or so yards away. Stan watched intently as the guy fired out some small pieces of crust, dunking them in the lake to add weight and, therefore, distance, and within a few minutes Stan was aware of a slurping sound around the floating free offerings. Another few minutes passed with more hungry mouths arriving, then he saw another crust join the banquet, this time attached to hook and line. The take came almost instantly, catching the angler completely unawares, and he had little chance of stopping the carp's headlong rush into the sanctuary of the lily jungle, retrieving a bare hook a minute later. Unperturbed, he hooked on another square of crust whilst waiting for his replenished dining table to attract some more hungry diners. Within minutes, the swim was once again dotted with slurping lips and broken pieces of sodden bread crust. The tethered crust did not sail so far this time and the rapt onlooker could tell that the angler was giving himself more of a chance whilst still fishing as close as he dared to the pads. The take took a little longer this time but the angler was totally prepared and took little time in bullying the carp into the net, giving a little victory shout as he did. Stan was about to run round to see the fish when he spied, one hundred yards to the left of the successful angler, the park warden slowly making his way along the bank towards the unsuspecting law breaker. Both breaker and enforcer were oblivious of each other at that moment. Stan's wolf whistled warning soon alerted the angler who, looking across at Stan's waving arms, quickly assessed the situation and unhooked the carp, raising it up for Stan to see before releasing it back to join its slowly dispersing kin. Then he broke his rod down, threw it in the bushes behind him along with the dripping landing net and casually strolled in the direction of the approaching warden, passing a few pleasantries with the unsuspecting man before ambling off around the lake.

Stan couldn't help smiling at this bald-faced cheek, looking up at a similar whistle to his own and returning the thumbs up sign from across the water with a beaming smile. An hour or so later the guy returned for his hastily hidden tackle before strolling once again into Stan's swim.

"Cuppa?" Stan offered, smiling.

"Love one. Thanks for that, he's a right dodgy bastard. He would definitely have tried to nick my tackle."

"No problem. How big was the fish?"

"About six pounds, I suppose. Did you see that first one go? I nearly shit myself!" Stan laughed aloud at this. He liked this guy.

"Where are you fishing tonight?" he asked.

"Well, seeing as you're in the best swim I'll probably fish opposite," replied the other but, no sooner had the words left his lips than they spied two sets of tackle making their way into that very swim.

"Oh sod it!" he exclaimed. "Oh, well. Looks like I'm fishing in the rhodies, then. Thanks for the tea and the whistle, mate. Good luck tonight. My name's Chris, by the way."

"Nice to meet you, Chris-by-the-way, mine's Stan!" replied Stan, triumphantly.

"Never mind," retorted Chris "I suppose someone's has to be!" And with that he strolled out of the swim, leaving Stan open-mouthed but mildly amused.

Stan was still smiling to himself a couple of minutes later when Paddy walked into his swim. It was now mid-afternoon and the lake was beginning to fill up so Paddy's surprise was not unwarranted.

"How did you get in here? This is usually the first swim to go," he queried, stridently.

"It was," beamed Stan, "when I got here at four this morning, it was the first swim I chose!"

"Four! You said you'd get here in the evening," said Paddy, indignantly.

"Did I? Oh, my mistake, then!" replied the highly amused Stan.

"Oh, just put the kettle on, will you," huffed Paddy, feigning annoyance. "Was that Chris Rhodes I just saw leaving here?"

"His name was Chris, yeah. Nice bloke, he just poached a six pounder on crust from over there," Stan informed his mate whilst pointing across the lake.

"Nice one," replied Paddy, "he's a good angler y'know."

"Yeah, it certainly looked that way. Where are you fishing?" asked Stan, changing the subject to a more immediate one.

"Well, I was hoping to get down here somewhere, but it looks like it's all tied up so I'll probably see if I can find a swim in the rhodies. How long you down for?"

"Two nights, until Thursday afternoon. What about you?" replied Stan.

"The same, although I might stay until the weekend if things are happening. Have you seen anything out here?" enquired a progressively more restless Paddy.

Stan proceeded to recount the previous few hours' activity and this acted as a spur to his listener. Having finished the welcome brew, he picked up his tackle and bade his friend goodbye and good luck, casting a final comment over his rapidly disappearing shoulder, "Give me a shout if you have one, I'll come round and take some photos."

'Oh, I do hope so,' thought Stan, almost bringing his hands together in prayer. Evening drew in and, as the sun slowly sunk behind him, Stan revelled in the sights of Mother Nature pulling the blanket of sleep over her charges. Dipping, diving swifts and house martins gradually gave way to their leathery-winged counterparts and a million insects knew no difference, only that their fight for survival continued unabated. The lake, also, was alive with fish of all kinds enjoying the last of the daylight and they flopped and splashed on the mirror surface of the lake in front of Stan. He drank in the heady brew, and gasped at the crash of the occasional carp that made a mockery of the other, minor disturbers. Stan's night eyes allowed him to discern shapes for much longer than normal and it was not until he needed to use his torch to search through his tackle box that he realised, once the light was extinguished, how dark it really was. 'Ten to eleven,' he thought, and wondered if he should risk an early cast, but immediately dismissed the idea, despite hearing the distant 'plop' of leads cast by less disciplined anglers.

Then, cleaving the silence like an axe, he heard the first of twelve chimes from a distant church tower and, by the time the echoes from the twelfth toll were being swallowed by the night's stillness, his baits were both in position. One by the edge of the lily pads, the other a conservative distance from the island tree. After all the excitement and anticipation, Stan was suddenly overcome by an immense tiredness and was barely able to keep his eyes open long enough to attach the plastic monkey climbers. That done, however, he knew that he could fight off sleep no longer and, vowing only to doze for an hour, pulled his sleeping bag around his shoulders and was soon oblivious to anything.

The first he knew of the run was the insistent tap-tap-tapping of the monkey climber hitting the rod butt as he had not succumbed to the need for electronic bite alarms, as yet. Struggling to shrug off the shrouds of sleep and sleeping bag, he stumbled to the offending rod and lifted it high into the air. The resistance was solid but unmoving, the fish having transferred the hook into an unyielding lily stem during the twenty seconds prior to Stan's strike. All the luckless angler could do was point the rod tip at the lake and pull for a break. It took a few more minutes and a handful of lake water in the face to bring him to his senses, by which time he could discern the slowly brightening sky above the woods opposite - how long had he been asleep, he wondered. His watch displayed 03:51, over three hours was the answer. Rubbing the sleep from his eyes he bent to light the Calor Gas stove, lifting the kettle onto its yellow/blue flame before carefully retackling his rod.

By the time the dawn chorus was once again in full voice, he was satisfied with the position of both baits, having recast the right hand rod to within less than a foot of the overhanging branches. It would be a little while before he realised that that was still two feet shorter than was required in order to illicit a take from the island margin. The pads were, once again, being agitated from below. Ripple upon ripple emanating from the outermost leaves as Stan's trout pellet baits were creating a bit of a stir amongst the sub-surface diners. It was no surprise, then, when his hookbait was picked up by a fast moving carp. It was also no surprise that events followed the same pattern as an hour previously, for Stan could not cope with such power in such confined quarters, disconsolately winding in the limp, hookless line once again. Little did he know that fewer than fifty percent of the carp hooked in this swim were actually landed, not that that knowledge would have cheered him at all but it may have stopped him blaming himself so much. By the end of the day, however, that knowledge may have caused him to sling a noose over a nearby bough and insert his head into it as the fifth carp of the day followed its four predecessors through the lily stems to freedom. Stan held his head in his hands, the butt of his impotent rod protruding from a nearby hawthorn bush!

"Not having much luck then, mate?" enquired Paddy from a distance. Stan looked up forlornly and shook his head in defeat.

"I'm just crap, Pad," he replied. "Five I've lost. Five! Those kids over there have landed three, and I've lost five, what am I doing wrong?"

Paddy tried to explain that, although this was the most popular swim on the lake, it was also the worst for losing fish, but Stan was beyond hearing and was slowly beginning to pack his tackle away in preparation for an early exit.

"Tell you what," ventured Paddy in an effort to break Stan's dark mood, "why don't we swap swims? I've had two and there are a few fish moving along the rhodies. They obviously like your bait and you'll have a much better chance of landing a fish during the night. Go on, give it go, mate, and let me see how many I can lose in here!"

This last brought a smile to Stan's face and he nodded agreement to the suggested move. So it was that, as the sun painted the sky a thousand shades of red, Stan flicked his second bait along the margins, just off the trailing branches of the rhododendron bushes, throwing out a dozen or so small balls of trout pellet paste to accompany the hookbaits. Paddy had offered him an ingenious method of bite indication for the coming night, and it only cost two pence, for it was that coin that was balanced on the spool of the reel above a small, metal plate - nothing changes, he thought, only the change.

By the time Stan was ready to leave on Sunday morning the penny had dropped three times and the reward was a tench, a bream and a seven pound carp. This last was the most welcome capture that Stan could ever remember and was greeted with such delight that those fishing on the opposite bank thought that someone had broken the lake record! It mattered not to Stan. He could still catch carp and did not need to jeopardise the fish or his sanity by fishing the kamikaze swims in the pads, and this became even more apparent when he learnt that Paddy had landed only one of four carp that he had hooked. The carp he caught weighed less than Stan's. It became very evident to Stan that most of the larger fish were caught away from the pads, in the open water. Whether this was because that was where they fed or because they were too powerful to be landed in the pads was not readily obvious. Stan decided, there and then, that he would concentrate his efforts away from the pads and, although this would probably mean fewer runs he knew he would have a much greater chance of landing them.

Over the next few months, this theory proved to be amazingly accurate. By the end of the summer, he had accounted for a further seven carp, topped by his first double figure carp of eleven pounds and one ounce. This was taken on a hot, still night in the middle of August on a floating crust bait a yard from the edge of the rhodies - the fight in the moonlight being one of the most exciting he had encountered to date. The onset of autumn did not dull his enthusiasm and, as the leaves yellowed and bronzed, he girded himself for his first winter's carp angling. He had read as much as he could about this side of the sport but what he could find did not fill him with confidence - thermoclines, 39 degrees, wind chill, easterly winds, northerly winds, high pressure. It seemed that every possible weather condition was against him. Amongst this negativity he was able to find some crumbs of comfort and it was these that fed him and sustained him as the clocks changed and the days shortened - and catching a personal best carp at the end of October went some way as well.

"The low pressure area will persist over most of the country, bringing more rain and strong winds to most areas," decreed the weatherman, much to Stan's chagrin.

He had been hoping for a break in the almost constant rain, not because he was a fair weather fisherman but because he hated setting up in the rain, everything getting soaked and remaining that way for the rest of the session. But if that was how it was going to be, so be it. His confidence was high and, due to Jean's birthday the previous week, this was his first outing for a couple of weeks so his need was even greater.

Arriving just after sunrise on Saturday morning, he was pleased to see that the rain had abated for a while, although the wind was still a strong south westerly and would pose its own problems in setting up. Never mind that, he was fishing and all was fine with the world so, gathering up his bags and chairs he commenced the three hundred yard walk to the west bank rhodies. This area of the lake offered a number of things that Stan liked. The lake here was about eight or nine feet deep, sloping away to a depth of twelve feet off to his left. The sun, at this time of year, warmed that bank for most of the day prior to setting behind and to his right, and the rhodies offered suitable shelter from the harsh winds that blew down the lake from his right. By the time he reached the swim none of these points were at the forefront of his mind, having been over taken by the question 'am I still alive?' Dropping his luggage to the floor and then joining it in a sweating, gasping heap - surely there were some good points about the car park swim, weren't there? Within five lung-filling minutes, however, the swim took on a rosier hue and he began surveying the windswept waters in front of him. Having fished this particular swim on a few previous occasions his knowledge of it was quite good and he knew of two excellent spots to fish. The first, at sixty yards range, was a hard area, surrounded by soft mud or silt, which Paddy had pointed out to him and, although a bit tricky to hit in these conditions, offered him the best chance of a fish at this time of year, he thought. The second he was not so sure of. Just round to his right, in front of the trailing rhodie branches, was a small sandy patch which he had spied from a tree earlier in the year, and which had produced two carp and a number of tench for him in the ensuing months. However, he was uncertain if this three feet deep area would be as attractive to the fish in these colder conditions. Only one way to find out, he decided, and he put a bait along there amongst twenty free offerings before attempting to battle with the elements in positioning his second bait. Surprisingly, only three casts were required to achieve success and he was soon enjoying his first, hot brew of the day whilst listening to the sound of the rain pattering on his brolly camp, gradually succumbing to its soporific effect and nestling down on his camp bed for a doze.

A few hours had passed, he discovered later, when he was awoken by the squawking sound of one of his recently purchased Heron bite alarms. Totally disorientated, it took a few moments before he could shake the dream from his mind and drag himself back to reality and, on doing so, became aware that line was leaving the spool of the rhodie rod at an alarming rate. The usual mayhem ensued before angler and rod were as one. The swim resembled the scene of a small nuclear explosion, with sleeping bag and camp bed strewn across the mud. The non-struck rod lay on its side and a large streak of damp earth was missing from the swim, having been transferred to the seat of Stan's trousers as he skidded to the rod like a bobsleigher who had forgotten his bob! Once in contact, Stan attempted to steady his nerves in his normal manner - by talking to himself.

"Okay, take it easy, Peacock. Let it take line if it wants, there's no snags out there. Shit, I didn't think that rod would go, feels like a good fish too. Where's it going now? Easy, fella. Take it easy, there's loads of time."

This one-sided conversation went on for five minutes or so before it was interrupted by a burst of laughter from behind.

"Bloody hell! You look like you've just been mugged, mate!" came the amused comment. Stan thought he knew the voice and, on glancing over his shoulder, recognised the smiling face of Chris.

"Yeah, I was having a little doze and just got bored so I thought I would rearrange the furniture. What d'you reckon!" was his surprisingly casual reply.

"Like it," chortled Chris as he strode forward gingerly, "could do with a couple of throw cushions here and there, though. Need a hand?" he offered.

"Why, have you got some with you?"

Chris chuckled at this and bent to lift the landing net before getting down to the more serious business at hand.

"Good 'un?" he enquired, as he stood at Stan's side with the net.

"Feels alright. I picked it up along the rhodies to the right, there," replied Stan, motioning with a nod of his head to the relevant spot.

"What, off that sandy patch? Yeah, good little spot that. Not many people know about that," said Chris, impressed by this guy's knowledge. The same thought was also going through Stan's head and he was about to comment on it when, suddenly, the fished rolled on the surface ten yards out, a brilliant sweep of gold and bronze on the slate grey canvas of the lake.

"Whoa! Looks like a good 'un, mate, take it nice and steady and we'll have him straight into the net," advised the netsman, lowering the mesh into the wind chopped water. Stan steadily eased the fish closer, adjusting the clutch on his reel as he had learnt to do from his readings, and tried not to think about how big he thought this might be. Then, with barely a forward motion, Chris had the prize engulfed in the dripping mesh and the two victors let out a simultaneous roar of triumph.

Chris peering forward to glimpse the carp and then turned to Stan with a few simple words,

"How big's your p.b.?"

"Err. Eleven pounds," came the stuttered reply.

"Not any more it ain't!" beamed Chris. In his elation, Stan had little idea that these words would send him into paroxysms of ecstasy every time he heard them over the coming decades, for that same feeling was washing over him now.

The net was raised, then lowered onto the small piece of sponge that Stan used as an unhooking mat and the colours of the fish shone as though a beam of light was enveloping it. Stan was useless, and Chris did all that was necessary with the fish. He removed the hook, wetted the weigh sling, zeroed the scales and, finally, lifted sling and carp above the ground whilst reading the weight aloud.

"Fourteen ..." he grunted. "Fourteen ... six. Fourteen pounds six, mate. Well done, a new personal best I think. Got a camera?"

Stan thought that he would burst with joy. He felt so elated that he hugged Chris and just about stopped himself from kissing the man - valuing his front teeth! The camera clicked and Stan smiled, relishing the ache in his arms as he cradled his golden prize, and then smiled some more as he watched the gold fade back into the grey.

The pair chatted and joked and laughed for the rest of the day, only slightly aware of the bond of friendship they were forming in that short time. As Chris rose to leave in the dying light of the day, it was more than a little obvious to both of them that this was only the beginning of the road that they would walk together.

"Oh, by the way," said Chris just prior to leaving, "have you heard of the hair rig?"

Stan's blank expression was answer enough so he bade him farewell with one passing comment.

"Go and buy Carp Fever. You will be amazed. See you soon and ... bloody well done!"

'Carp Fever, I've heard of that,' he thought as his new friend departed into the growing gloom of evening. 'The Hair Rig, what's all that about then?' he asked himself, then pondered Chris's parting shot "... you will be amazed."

'Okay,' he thought, 'amaze me.' And he was....

"There, just there, see? By that scummy stuff in the corner, can't you see it? It's huge!"

The two young truants hung precariously from the branch of a lakeside tree and peered intently into the gin clear waters of Stanton's Pit, the younger of the two trying desperately to see the apparition that his older cousin was pointing out to him.

"Look, it's moving towards those lily pads. Can you see it now?" implored the older boy, but even though he willed the vision upon his young companion, he soon realised that some people just can't see for looking and so concentrated solely on drinking in the sight for himself.

His were not the first eyes to witness this sight since the turn of the decade but, in that first year of the eighties, only a handful of locals had ventured along the bumpy road to specimen carp country and fewer still had managed to land one of Stanton's increasingly desirable treasures - and that barely twenty pounds. But people were becoming more aware of the lake's potential as time went on and sightings like this one circulated the local fishing community, thus enticing a few would-be carp catchers to its banks.

Bream and tench anglers still fished the place and it was they who would, inadvertently, hook one of the few resident carp. Sometimes they would land one, but usually their tackle would prove inadequate and the carp would be left with a minor irritation in its lip, which it would soon rid itself of. Inevitably, The Scarred Mirror would fall for a succulent sweetcorn and maggot cocktail but the outcome was always the same, with the three or four pound line snapping like cotton and the angler shaking uncontrollably for the next few minutes, stunned by the power he had just felt. These stories, however, and the infrequent sighting of one or more of the huge trio soon helped to repopulate the banks with anglers better equipped to deal with the power - in tackle terms, at least. One of these, a local braggart called Joe East, was gradually drawn to the pit by the stories and the ever increasing need to be the next big carp fishing hero (the photo of Dean with the common kept in a bedside cabinet). He planned his campaign carefully, electing to tell nobody of his tactics until after his successful capture of the huge common which would launch him to the forefront of this increasingly popular branch of angling.

Carp Fever was his bible, also, and he read and re-read it over the winter months before embarking on his close season baiting campaign. As news of the sinking of the Belgrano made front page news, Joe was ever more certain that he would be holding his prize by the end of the first week of the season. Careful pre-baiting allowed him mind-boggling close-ups of the three huge carp and he began to wonder whether The Common or The Big-Scaled Mirror was the largest inhabitant of the pond. It was with great excitement, then, that he set up on the opening night, knowing that this small gravel patch in front of him had been the trio's dining table for the past fortnight - surely it would only be a matter of hours before his plan came to fruition.

A hundred miles east, Stan was ruing the loss of his second carp of the season. Whilst admiring a glorious sunrise, Joe's chance came and, as his hair-rigged paste bait was picked up by an, as yet, unseen quarry, his bite alarm sounded and the reel spun furiously as the fish attempted a prompt escape. But Joe's hook was strong, as was the twelve pound line, and he held hard as a huge be-scaled flank broke the surface twenty yards away - it was The Common and Joe suddenly felt the first twinges of doubt about his tackle. 'No need to worry,' he thought, 'this is the same stuff that Maddocks uses.' But that man had played many large carp on such tackle and was hugely competent. Not so, Joe East. With rod bent to its limit, Joe found himself suddenly flying backwards as the hook tore free of the small slither of flesh that it had hold of. The fish was gone and Joe was devastated, totally and utterly devastated. If there had been someone there to offer consolation, he would have cherished it. If there had been someone there to calm him and assure him that his tactics were good and that it was only a matter of time before they worked again, he might have listened and, eventually concurred. But there was nobody for Joe East but Joe East. He was unable to speak these things to himself, instead all he could feel was self-pity and injustice and so, rather than re-bait and recast, as Stan was doing, he grabbed his things and strode to his car, distraught. On his arrival home his tackle was thrown into the old cupboard in the garage where it stayed for a decade until his son found it...

If only Joe had persevered and not let his pride get in the way, he would have realised how successful the hair rig could have been and would surely have found his way into angling folklore. Never was the saying 'pride comes before a fall' more true than when referring to Joe. So, once again, The Common and his cronies were spared another season of distress and, despite the attentions of a small group of individuals, they wiled away the summer with barely a care. Naturally, The Scarred Mirror visited the bank on one occasion, its weight of thirty three pounds almost doubling the spellbound captor's personal best, but it spent more time ridding itself of unwanted ironware than having its photograph taken, such was the inadequacy of the anglers on the lake. The more elusive pair stayed well clear of any further close encounters, The Common's annual lapse of concentration once again strengthening its vigilance for the foreseeable future – if future it had.

The first couple of years of the new decade had hindered the trio not at all in their quest for food and immortality, but Man's greed and stupidity would soon provide the harshest test any of them had yet faced. Once a few anglers learned of Joe's experience, and the later landing of The Scarred Mirror, it took little time for them to obtain the necessary permits to fish the lake. However, few amongst them had the stomach for the long fight ahead of them and, with fewer than three carp per acre, their lack of success inevitably led to the usual moans about under-stocking that comes from people who think that more fish in a lake will make them a better angler. The committee could see little wrong with the proposal to restock Stanton's. In fact it would offer a perfect excuse to raise the fees a little if they could entice more anglers to fish there - they might even expand the required radius by another ten miles or so. And so, in the spring of '83, a consignment of small mirrors and commons was introduced into the lake from a fish farm a few miles away that was, apparently, supplying some of the more well-known lakes in the Southern counties with their fine strain of carp. The price was reasonable and this could be the first of two or three stockings over the next few years, depending on how these fish settled in. The time bomb was primed and the clock was ticking!

Chapter Eight - 1986

"Handball! That was handball! Are you bloody blind?" But Stan's protests, along with those of a few million television viewers and eleven England footballers went unheard by the referee and, as a diminutive Argentinean wheeled away in triumph, the bemused watchers realised that the Hand of God was pointing towards the exit.

After the dust had settled, Stan regained enough composure to reach for the telephone and call Chris. "What a bloody travesty," was his opening line.

"What was?" enquired Chris, totally bemused by the comment.

"That bloody handball. That was daylight robbery," expanded Stan, forgetting about his friend's total indifference to the game of football.

"Yeah, right. Was it a try, then, or L.B.W.?"

"Oh yeah, I forgot you were a heathen. Never mind, it'll mean nothing to you. Sorry I spoke," came Stan's pointless reply.

"Yeah. A heathen that's me. Not giving a toss about a bunch of blokes chasing a bit of inflated pig's skin around a lawn when they could be better employed getting very drunk. Oh yeah, I am definitely the heathen, aren't I?" replied Chris in his usual manner.

To argue was pointless indeed, Stan knew, so he switched straight to the usual topic of conversation, the one they had been having for the past three years.

"Okay! Okay! So, anyway, where are we fishing this weekend then?" and off they went, barely pausing for breath during the next ten minutes of intense discussion which was, as usual, punctuated with short bursts of hearty laughter.

Following Chris's assistance in the landing of Stan's fourteen pounder a few years earlier, it was a surprise that their paths had not crossed again until a month or so after Christmas. On that occasion, they arranged to fish together for the rest of the season and by the last weekend had decided to put a bit of time and effort in together, and fish in earnest the next season.

Stan had purchased Carp Fever and was, indeed, amazed. Not only by the hair rig but by the baits and the size of the fish that it was possible to catch and, so, he and Chris had elected to use some of the ideas in the book and incorporate them into their angling - thus they became chemists! All manner of powders and liquid flavourings were regularly to be found strewn about their respective kitchens, much to the consternation of their other halves, and a myriad of different coloured, shaped and flavoured balls were secreted in small, plastic containers in the fridge. They tried a number of strange and interesting combinations, taking them to the lake during the close season to try them out on the carp population. The problem was that the carp would eat almost anything so the pair of budding carpers had to rely on their own thoughts and ideas in order to narrow down the dozens of possibilities. Eventually, more by who shouted loudest than by general agreement, they settled on Maple crème as the flavour which was to be added to a milk protein base, coloured yellow. That decided, they spent the first couple of weeks in June rolling and boiling bait in readiness for the off, visiting the lake at least twice a week to tempt the carp into taking their offerings come the start of the season.

The beginning of the season was as exciting as the previous one, but this time Stan was better prepared and, knowing the carp's liking for the shallower water in these warm conditions, had once again made for the pads as a starting point for the coming three days. The lake was becoming more popular, though, and some brolly camps were erected two days prior to the start of the season, but not Stan's. He was unable to take that much holiday but, on his dawn arrival on the 15th he was happy to see that a swim on the periphery of the pads was still vacant. He and Chris had arrived together and had agreed that one of them would fish the pads, the other the rhodies, and if one or the other was having more action, they would double up in that swim. They need not have worried. Their bait was enticing, their swim choice adequate and their angling ability much improved and by the end of their first session they had accounted for nine carp between them. Chris had taken one more than Stan, the largest being a few ounces below his best of seventeen pounds and Stan's four fish had been topped by a double figure common of twelve pounds, a personal best common for him and one of the biggest in the lake at that time. The pair were obviously over the moon with their success and looked forward to a tremendous season together and, as the season went on they enjoyed mixed success - sometimes coming home with a three or four fish tally to relate, yet on other occasions blanking hopelessly.

There seemed no obvious reason for this disparity at first, but Stan soon realized that it was not just a case of turning up in any swim and chucking out their 'wonder bait' whilst readying the net for the arm-aching action to come. No, there was a lot more to this after all and so he started watching the few successful anglers on the lake. They were constantly looking, willing to change swims if they felt that the one they were in was devoid of fish, and they weren't just using boilies, either. Chris and Stan had pondered on the use of particles and had, indeed, been using hemp where it was viable, but their faith in their boiled baits following the early season success had put the particle idea to the back of their minds. Then something had happened to change their minds, and not just the obvious. The Carp Strikes Back had been published that year and, on buying and eagerly reading his copy, it was Stan who told Chris that he would be amazed at the content. Coupled with the revelations in Carp Fever, this opened their eyes to so many possibilities, not least the idea of a can or two on the bank! But the section that was most thumbed was the section on particles and soon they were visiting local health food shops and Indian supermarkets, coming out with bags of black-eyed beans, maples and chick peas.

With this new addition to their bait armoury their confidence was, once again, high and they approached the early part of September with renewed vigour and boiled nuts! The first session with this new bait attack produced a fish each for them but it was the next session that confirmed their belief in this new approach, and confirmed it in a way that neither of them could possibly have dreamed.

Chris, as usual, arrived at the lake first and on this particular occasion his arrival early on Friday morning proved even more beneficial than usual. During their numerous midweek telephone conversations they had come to the conclusion that their new bait and baiting approach would work best in amongst the dying lily pads. Not only were there still a lot of fish resident in that area but, because the pads were gradually withering away for another year, it should prove less of a problem to extract the better fish from there. How happy he was, then, when he found the double swim from which he had taken the 'poached' carp the previous year devoid of carp anglers, but not of carp. On climbing a nearby tree, Chris could just make-out the dark shapes of a number of fish cruising in and out of the lily jungle, the odd one occasionally rolling lazily on the surface as if to show its disdain for any angler present.

There was an angler fishing opposite and, it transpired, he had caught a couple of carp during the night but had then lost a good fish just prior to Chris's arrival, the lost fish seemingly moving the carp a little further away - to in front of Chris, in fact. This put Chris in a bit of a quandary. He had struggled to the swim with two buckets full of soaked and boiled particles to scatter liberally around the swim but, now that the fish were already present, he didn't know if that bait bombardment would move the fish away in search of peace and quiet. Erring on the side of caution, he put both hookbaits out by the edge of the receding water lilies, catapulting three or four pouches full of particles to the same area and adding a few Scopex flavoured boilies to the mixture around the right hand hookbait. This was baited with a similar flavoured bait, another revelation from 'the book'.

By the time that he was joined by Stan in the middle of the afternoon he had the capture of two carp to report and both of them just the right side of ten pounds to make the telling all the more sweet. Stan was buoyed by this encouraging news and he quizzed his pal as to bait, location and quantity of freebies. Stan was surprised to learn that, of the ten pounds that Chris had carried to the swim, only a tenth of that had gone into the lake.

"Fish already in the swim, Quill," he explained to his newly nicknamed friend, "didn't want to spook 'em, did I?"

"Well, what are we going to do with this lot, then?" asked Stan whilst gesturing to the three buckets, the last of which he had just dragged to the swim. "No. I'm up for it if you are. I mean, you've had a couple already haven't you, and this will probably be the last chance we get, this year, to pile the bait in. What d'you reckon, Rhodie?" Over a cup of tea, they pondered the whys and wherefores and finally decided to give it a go. Flexing their catapult elastic, they proceeded to bombard the swim with a bucket load of mixed particles. Half an hour later, after the water had stopped shaking, Chris climbed the tree to survey the swim, but all he could see was withering lilies and a slight foaming of the surface. 'That's buggered it,' he thought and descended to impart the news to Stan, who was in the throes of casting his baits into the melee of particles. He remained unperturbed, however, assuring his doubting friend that the carp would return in numbers and that, by morning, their arms would ache from the battles that would ensue.

By morning their arms did indeed ache, but not from landing carp. They must have missed the part in the book that informed the reader that tench and bream were also great lovers of a particle lunch, dinner and breakfast and awoke to find themselves and most of the swim covered in slime. Chris was less than happy about this turn of events and, as they washed down a bacon sandwich with the second cuppa of the day, was trying to convince Stan that a move was in order. Stan, however, had only just finished a chapter in the book about the 'baiting pyramid' and was doing his best to out-convince his mate by explaining that the tench and bream were a precursor to the arrival of the carp. Chris remained sceptical and was already working out where to move to when Stan's right hand rod ripped into action. Some of the runs from the tench had been of this ferocity so Stan was not overly panicked and gave himself just a few minor burns when he deposited the cup of tea over his leg! When he picked the rod up, however, the hooked fish shattered the early morning calm by crashing on the surface in front of them, before cleaving a path through the pads in a bid for freedom. The initial shock gave way to 'headless chicken mode.' Stan desperately held onto the raging bull on the other end of the line and tried to gain some semblance of control, whilst Chris scuttled back and forth behind him, offering advice in between asking where the net was and did he want the other rods wound in. Neither received a reply as the combatants tussled for superiority but soon the power of the rod and the eleven pound Sylcast began to gain supremacy and it was with great relief that Stan saw the fish roll his side of the pads. With the rediscovered net in hand Chris regained his composure and, standing in front of Stan, conceded,

"Well, maybe we'll give it another couple of hours then, eh?"

"No, it's alright mate, I'll give you a hand with your gear once I've landed this one," replied Stan, relishing the moment in more ways than one.

"No, no. You'll probably need a bit of a hand down here so I'll just hang around for a bit, just in case!" retorted Chris, tongue firmly in cheek.

On and on went the banter until, soon, the fish wallowed on the surface in front of the waiting net, Chris easing it forward to accept the beaten fish. Then, with no preamble, the hook flew over their heads and the carp hung motionless for a second, oblivious to its good fortune. Whilst the cry was making its way from Stan's larynx to his lips, Chris lunged forward with the net but succeeded only in nudging the carp back to reality with the net cord and watched, helpless, as it sped off to enjoy its newfound freedom.

"Bastard!" screamed a disbelieving Stan, before hurling the rod to the floor in rage, the pain of loss indescribable but understood just the same by Chris.

Ten minutes later, Chris wandered along with a fresh cup of tea and handed it to the silently staring Stan.

"You were right, Quill, they're back. I've just been up the tree and seen about seven or eight feeding on the edge of the pads. Better get' em back out there mate." Stan nodded and did his best to stop feeling sorry for himself, but that empty feeling would revisit him a few more times over the years and nothing anybody said would make it go away until it was good and ready. Maybe there has to be an opposite to the elation felt when a fish is landed, but right now Stan wasn't ready for that sort of philosophy, and indulged in the age old ritual of twisting the knife.

"How big d'you reckon it was then?" he asked Chris, despite the fact that he had seen it just as clearly as his mate, and had a perfectly good idea of the escapees size.

"Ten or eleven, I suppose," lied Chris, underestimating and knowing full well that they both knew that it was very close to Stan's personal best, if not bigger. "Too late now, Quill, you'll just have to catch his big brother, won't you? Come on, get that rod back out, there's carp feeding out there and time's a-wasting," he commanded, and the steadily improving Stan complied.

Stan had taken a fancy to the black-eyed beans as a hookbait, and it was those that had brought about the previous take. He had no qualms in putting another couple on a new hook and casting the tempting offering to the edge of the lily bed, spooking a feeding carp as his ounce lead hit the water above it.

"Yeah, they are still there, aren't they!" said Stan, nonchalantly, as he set the monkey climber on his rod.

Barely had he stood upright to turn on the alarm when there was a thunderous splash by the edge of the lilies, coinciding with the rod tip bending round and the clutch spinning. He looked on, bewildered for a second before he was wrenched from his reverie by Chris's shout.

"Strike, Stan, strike. You've got one on, man!"

Needing no further coaxing, Stan accepted the chance to right the wrong just done to him and once again the fish attempted to use the lily bed as a sanctuary. This time, however, Stan was not going to give it that chance. He ignored the desire to loosen the clutch as the line stretched to its limit, breathing a sigh of relief when the pressure told a few seconds later and the fish rolled on the surface no more than a yard from where it had picked up the bait. This time there was no amusing banter between Stan and his netsman, and they both offered a silent prayer that they would, on this occasion, be the victors. Once away from the danger of the pads, Stan felt that the fish was under his control. He still wanted to see it at the bottom of the net, so exerted as much pressure as he dared in order to bring the battle to a hasty conclusion. Within minutes he hoped for no déjà vu as the carp, now beaten, wallowed tantalisingly close to the net cord. Chris was not ready to accept a repeat performance, either, and strode confidently forward into the shallow margins, sweeping the net up around the carp in one swift movement. The journey from larynx to lips was much more pleasurable this time. The victory cry was joined by the same from Chris's throat.

"Yeesss!" echoed across the lake in duplicate and this time the rod was thrown to the floor in joy not anger. Hands were shaken and then grasped tightly as Stan helped his net-encumbered friend from the lake. Once again, Chris took control as Stan lost control, babbling, and the exertion was a little greater as he hoisted the carp-filled sack from the ground.

"What's your p.b.?" The ritual began, like a mantra chanted by Tibetan monks.

"Fourteen pounds," came Stan's expectant reply.

"Not anymore, Quill!" came the requisite response.

"How about, err …. Eighteen and a half!"

A full-throated scream met this latest addition to the ritual and Chris smiled widely at his friend's ecstatic reaction. The rest was, indeed, ritual - the smile, the lift, the photograph, the returning and the fists punching the sky in glorious victory.

The day was only eight hours old and it was apparent that the carp had returned, and not just the small ones. By midday a further three had followed the p.b. into the waiting net, although none of them neared that size. By early afternoon the pair had decided that it was time to get rid of the rest of their particles, so proceeded to pepper the swim with the tasty offerings. This time the carp knew what to expect and stayed for the free feast, unaware that there would soon be four offerings that had a price attached. These were soon winging their way out to join the rest of the ten pounds of bait and it was not long before Chris was once again doing battle with one of the greedy diners. This one was obviously a better fish than the previous couple he had landed that day, and he informed Stan of this fact. The fight seemed to last for an eternity, and Chris would not have been surprised to see the hook embedded in the fish's flank but as it rolled submissively a yard from the net, he could see the bait hanging from the fish's mouth on the long, two pound hair and, when it slipped into the waiting mesh, it was he who screamed the victory scream. Stan loved the next bit and, as he looked up from the enmeshed prize, took great pleasure in uttering the words,

"What's your p.b. then, Rhodie?" he enquired gleefully. "Err, seventeen," came Chris's disbelieving reply.

"Not anymore, mate. Not anymore!"

Chris's face was a picture, and Stan loved the role of informant, taking control as his friend had done a few hours earlier. They gazed down on the bronze flank of the lightly scaled mirror and Chris knew that his friend had not exaggerated the carp's size - this was definitely the largest carp he had ever landed. The next few minutes were, as usual, a bit of a blur to the captor but, finally, Stan hoisted the sling aloft and read off the numbers.

"Bloody hell!" he exclaimed, both at his exertion and also the weight that he was reading. "It's nearly twenty. Nineteen fourteen ... fifteen. I can't hold it still, grab the top as well, Chris."

Chris obeyed, numbly, and between them they held the scales steady enough for Stan to read the exact weight.

"That's it. Right. Nineteen fourteen. That's it, Rhodie, you've done me! Well done, son."

Snapshots and smiles followed, as usual, and then it was Chris who was punching the air with joy. But they had little time to sit back and celebrate because the carp were still in feeding mood and, over the next twenty four hours of the session they landed a further six carp between them, losing another three. No more of the fish surpassed their personal bests but that mattered not at all. They would remember this session for many years to come and, although they were unable to emulate this success over the rest of the season, they still enjoyed enough action to realise that what they were doing was acceptable to the carp.

One other thing that was significant about that session was the arrival of Paddy into the swim, drawn there by the commotion following the capture of Chris's personal best. Stan had only seen him on a few occasions since last winter and was pleased to see him now, but things seemed to have changed and, despite witnessing the largest fish he had ever seen, he was rather distant and did not stay long. A year or so later Stan saw him in a shopping centre and stopped him for a quick chat but it was soon evident that the carp bug had been exterminated and they found little to talk about. Stan a further ten years were to pass before Stan saw him again.

The next season continued in the same vein with the pair of them becoming increasingly confident in their abilities and, although they did not surpass their personal bests (if only by ounces) they enjoyed regular success, rarely recording a blank session. As winter arrived, however, it became apparent that the better fish that they sought were few and far between and repeat captures were becoming an almost weekly occurrence. So it was that, on a particularly cold and unpleasant January night that had been punctuated by Chris's third capture of the 'nineteen', they finally decided that it was time to move on. The subject had been mooted, half-heartedly, on a couple of recent sessions but now, the more they talked about it the more exciting an idea it became - the question was, 'where?'

A couple of lakes in the area seemed to present themselves as possible candidates so the pair did a bit of investigating in the ensuing weeks and it soon became apparent that one name kept cropping up – Winter's Farm. There were actually a string of three lakes there but the largest was reputed to hold a few fish in excess of twenty pounds and, although not easy, it would appear to be possible to land one or two of these larger prizes during a season. The lakes were situated about fifteen miles south of Guildford and less than ten miles from Stan's house. On closer investigation, he realised that this was the last of the three lakes that he had been told about on his visit to the tackle shop a couple of years previously.

A visit was planned before they attempted to obtain tickets, which were not too easy to come by, apparently, and so, on a bright, sunny day at the end of February, they made their way along the country lanes to the designated spot on the map. The walk from the car to the first of the three lakes was quite gruelling and the idea of repeating the journey laden down with tackle did not fill them with joy but once they arrived at the third lake all thought of that impending hardship was forgotten. The lakes were nestled in a lightly wooded valley and joined by a small stream that ran the length of the valley and beyond and, although the sides of the valley were wooded, the lakes seemed quite open in comparison to Manor Pond. Unfortunately, the largest lake was the last in the string and over half a mile from the car but, on seeing it, they both knew that the walk would be worth the effort. The West Bank was quite steep and the trees came within five yards of the bank in places, in amongst them were a number of lovely, secluded little swims. As they reached the far end and turned back along the east bank, the woodland thinned out and the rest of that bank was quite open and flat. The sloping sides of the valley were quite gentle here, dotted here and there with a few gorse bushes and the odd small copse of silver birch fairly close to the bank. Being winter, very little bankside vegetation was evident but the withered remains of sedges, rushes and sub-surface lily stems led the pair to believe that the lakes would be richly decorated come the onset of spring. It took little time for them to decide that this was to be their next fishing home for the foreseeable future and, during the slow walk back to the car, they were already planning their coming season on the lake. Deciding that there was no time like the present, they went straight to the farmhouse and quizzed the farmer as to the availability of tickets and were pleasantly surprised to learn that a cheque for £60 would secure them a place on the syndicate straight away.

Their assumption that the banks would be verdant and colourful was extremely accurate and when they made their next trip to the lake, just after Easter they could see the new growth bursting through and knew that it would not be long before the carp began showing themselves along the rich margins. They had taken a lot of what they had learnt in the past couple of seasons into consideration and concluded that this lake was ripe for a particle attack. The particles they had the utmost confidence in at the moment were tiger nuts, which they had used to good effect at the end of last summer on Manor. They began introducing these strangely enticing baits into the lake by the beginning of May, and with stunning effect. On the last weekend of the close season they had counted, from a tree on the West Bank, over forty fish in a feeding frenzy below them, rooting around in the silt for the last remaining nuts of the three kilos that had been fired into the swim by the now goggle-eyed pair.

"Look at that one. Blimey, it must be well over twenty. And that big grey one. How big is that, for chrissakes?"

And so it went for the next couple of hours before, with pins and needles coursing up and down their bodies, they eventually descended and, with one last handful of bait for good luck, left the feeding carp to enjoy their last free meal. Of the lake's reputed seventy carp, they had just counted more than half feeding on their baits and they felt so confident they thought they would burst!

The start of each new season seemed to be just that bit more exciting than the previous, and this year was no exception. When the pair arrived on Friday evening, thirty six hours prior to Saturday's midnight start, they were slightly deflated to find no less than eight cars already in the car park. The plan was to do a couple of trips from the car over the next twenty four hours so they grabbed a couple of manageable items and began the trek to the far lake with slightly hunched shoulders. However, by the time they reached that distant shore there was a definite spring in their step. On their journey past the other two lakes they had counted nine anglers and their confidence had soared once more. On reaching the nearest bank of Pit 3, as it was imaginatively named, it mattered not a jot to them that they could see a bivvy erected fifty yards along the West Bank. Their three preferred swims were all empty so it was just a matter of making the right choice, although they had no doubt that a move or two would be on the cards over the next three days. The weather was fine and was forecast to remain the same so they had only brought brollys with them, leaving the bivvy at home for at least three months. The lake was buzzing, not with anticipation but with insect life, and a major part of their tackle was taken up with sprays, before and after bite remedies, and sun tan lotion - just in case! The Saturday was hot and sticky and the fish were evident over most of the lake, cruising in fours and fives along the margins at their feet, seemingly oblivious to the anglers' presence, and it was with a slightly sinking feeling that it slowly dawned on the two watchers what this was a prelude to - and that night it became a prelude no longer.

The spawning ritual began just prior to midnight and continued well into the early sunlight hours. The warm, shallow water invited the carp to perform this yearly festival just a day too late, and Chris and Stan sat, bleary-eyed, as another egg-laden female was heaved above the surface by the amorous attentions of three or four smaller males. By the end of that first day not one fish had been banked by the six anglers on the lake and it was partly due to this lack of activity that Stan and Chris found that they had the whole lake to themselves by Monday morning. The thought had crossed their minds to exit as well, and return next week when the fish would be more co-operative, but then came the thunderstorm and the whole demeanour of the lake and its inhabitants changed. By midday, an hour after the raging storm had passed, the surface of the lake was alive with fish of all sizes, from the smallest gudgeon to the largest carp. The two anglers had seen some very large carp over the previous couple of fishless days - now it was time to start angling in earnest for them. If the fish activity was incredible for one reason over those two days, it was to be the same for a different reason over the next two and the pair enjoyed sport the like of which they had only daydreamed about in the past month. Tiger nuts were obviously a favourite post-coital snack amongst carp, and they were to be found in abundance for the weary revellers.

A dozen fish fell to their rods before it was time to pack up and leave and both anglers left with new personal bests. Stan's was an ounce or two below twenty pounds and Chris's an ounce or two over - and they looked forward to more of the same over the coming months.

The following month or so proved that, despite lowering their defences after their one night of passion, these carp were as wily as any others and it soon became apparent to the pair that they were fooling only themselves if they thought they were going to empty the lake before winter set in. They still caught fish. It was obvious that their pre-season baiting campaign had paid dividends for they were the only anglers receiving regular action from the lake's carp. But, by early August, the pair of them had decided that they needed a new plan in order to tempt the lake's larger denizens to pick up a bait. With a personal best carp apiece in their opening session, it seemed only a matter of time before Stan was holding his first twenty pound carp, and Chris his second and third. But these dreams had yet to become reality as a procession of low to mid-doubles had made their way to the bank, enticed by the never ending supply of tiger nuts - time to try out a few boilies.

They pored over the pages of recipes as recommended by Messrs. Maddocks and Hutchinson and were pretty soon slaving over a hot rolling pin in Stan's kitchen (much to Jean's distaste) trying to turn another ball of paste into 'the' bait. The odours emanating from there were a mixture of boudoir and abattoir. More often than not this resulted in one or both of them exiting very sharply, hand clutched over nose and mouth, but it was not long before they looked at each other with a sense of achievement. It would just need a little reassurance from the carp. Stan was sweet and Chris was savoury, if you get my meaning, and so it was a combination of the two that they eventually agreed upon to add to their bird food/protein base mix. A couple of drops of garlic, a hint of spearmint, a few mil of Scopex and a couple of additives from the local chemist that Chris had heard a whisper about were added. They rolled them all into little balls and threw them into the lake.

The results, although not immediately stunning were, nevertheless, encouraging and after a little tweaking here and there they soon had the utmost confidence in their new bait. They knew that it was just a matter of time before a really big hit came their way. How right they were. The third session with the new bait coincided with the August bank holiday and, as was usual with that time of year, the weather was set to change from the minor heatwave they had recently enjoyed to normal British summer weather - sunshine, showers, wind and rain.

Stan arrived, as usual, a few hours later than Chris and found him halfway along the West Bank and halfway up a tree. His rods were nowhere to be seen, but that in itself was not unusual, for Chris was rarely close to his rods if he felt he was in the wrong place, and would spend many restless hours pacing around the pool in search of his elusive quarry. This time, however, the quarry seemed to be no further than the tips of the branches that trailed into the water. Stan watched intently as a pair of tail lobes waved lazily on the surface, their owners' mouths a couple of feet below creating the cloud of silt and debris that was rising to the surface. It took little time for Stan to realise that these fish were feeding on some bait recently introduced by the tree bound watcher and he quickly began sizing up the area to see if there was room for two sets of rods. The overhanging branches of the tree formed a natural haven for the carp and it was not unusual to find a few fish here, especially as the water below the tree was a couple of feet deeper than that on the perimeter. It was possible from a couple of swims to carefully guide a lead below this barrier and feel confident of a take - and both of those swims were on the opposite bank. Little wonder, then, that when Stan arrived, breathless, in the obvious choice of swim, he found Chris's rods resting there - baits and rigs in butt rings. Taking no time to think, Stan hurried along to the next swim seconds before the other angler he had spied walking round the lake had a chance to drop his gear in there. With a muttered greeting and nod of the head the defeated angler traipsed on, shoulders drooping lower as he passed the next swim and spied Chris's rods in residence. Stan turned away from the disappearing back and gazed across the lake to the beckoning branches of the great yew tree opposite, gauging the cast at about sixty yards to the nearest branches, which were almost ten yards from the actual bank.

Although he had yet to fish this swim, he had fished Chris's swim on a couple of occasions. He knew that this one was a few yards closer, but the swim next door allowed the angler to cast into a depression in the branches and within two yards of the bank. As this area was unfishable from the West Bank, a well-placed bait was almost guaranteed action, but Stan was not so sure of his swim. The fact that he was a few yards closer was of no advantage because the wall of branches and leaves was almost unbroken in front of him, except for a small point on the right where the yew tree finished and the silver birches began. Here the bank came out a little and offered a small bay to cast at, and where the lead and bait would be no more than a yard from the bank. So it was this spot that Stan concentrated on, returning to his swim twenty minutes later after having crept stealthily along the bank and baited the margin with boilies and hemp. Much to his surprise, and great pleasure, his first cast was inch perfect and he smiled as Chris whistled his approval, Stan returning the compliment a few minutes later as Chris's lead inexorably found its target. Stan's other rod was cast to the centre of the overhanging branches and, although ploughing beneath them, he knew his lead was several yards from the marginal shelf and in with much less of a chance of enticing a carp. For this reason he had used a buoyant bait which, he knew, would remain a few inches above the silt and mud and, just maybe, tempt a browsing carp.

The threat of wind and rain had held off just long enough for Chris and Stan to perform these tasks. As they readied themselves for their first night of the long weekend, the weather began to change and it was not long before the steadily increasing south-westerly wind brought with it the first drops of rain. With the first cup of tea in his hand, it was obvious that now was the perfect time for Stan's first take and, sure enough, the margin rod was away in style. Within minutes he was soaked from tea and rain but it was not long before all that was forgotten as Chris slipped the net under a fine mid-double common; what a start to the session and, by the morning, the pair were both wet but happy having landed a further three carp of similar size. But where were the bigger fish? This question was being raised more and more but where was the answer - under the tree, where else? Due to the everincreasing wind it was becoming more difficult for the pair to recast to their desired spots. After putting two rigs into the tree, Stan opted for the safer approach and let the lead slide through the waves a few yards short of the branches, hoping that the angle of entry might take it close enough but, an hour later, he realised he needn't have worried. The take was much the same as the others but the fight was altogether different, not fast and darting but slow and ponderous, hugging the bottom but taking little line. Stan knew that this was something very different and when, ten minutes later, he saw a great, grey shape roll over in the waves his knees turned to jelly and he desperately craved a drink!

"Take it easy, fella," suggested Chris, needlessly, "this is all ours, just take it nice and easy." The fish rolled once more, closer now, and Stan's heart missed two beats as he felt the line 'ping' over the dorsal fin, the weight of the fish momentarily lost to his feel, but bringing his heart back to life a second later as he regained control. Swirl, splash, lift. Scream!

"Oh, my god. It's a monster!" bellowed Chris, peering into the net with eyes like saucers. "It's a bloody monster, Quill! You've landed the biggie!"

Stan ran around doing his usual headless chicken impression and it was only the fact that he was holding the net that prevented Chris from joining him. The next few minutes were, needless to say, mayhem, but they both knew what he had caught. The big, grey fish that they had seen at the beginning of the season had been spotted quite a few times since and was reputedly the largest fish in the lake and now it was lying on Stan's unhooking mat with his size six hook in its mouth. The scales told their usual story and, after the ritual telling, Stan gazed in wonder at his prize, then the camera.

"Twenty four and a half pounds," he muttered. "I've caught a bloody twenty four and a half pound carp!"

Not for the first time, the birds were scared from their trees, and not for the last either.

It mattered little whether another carp was caught for the rest of that session, but caught, they were. By dropping the baits just onto the edge of the tree-line and employing the six to eight inch pop-up that Stan had used, the pair managed to coax a further five carp to the net by the end of the session. This included a brace of nineteen pounders to Chris, an hour before they left. What a session! Nine carp including the biggie and two nineteen's. Whether it was the bait or the presentation or a combination of the two, neither of them cared. All they knew was that they had found a way to get amongst the larger inhabitants of the lake and they couldn't wait for the next session.

As usual, the anticipated emptying of the lake never transpired the next week, although they did manage three fish between them, with a seventeen and an eighteen amongst them. The upward trend in weight was encouraging.

This trend continued into the early months of winter. Then things slowed dramatically and, after their fourth blank trip in succession, they decided that something had to change. That something was the lake. They had noted, with interest, that a couple of guys were regularly fishing the first lake in the string. They seemed to be getting regular action, even in these colder months and so, despite the biggest carp in there reputed to be only sixteen pounds, both Chris and Stan agreed that a carp of any sort would be very welcome at the moment. It was no surprise, therefore, that the next week found them on the banks of Pit 1, armed with packs of Tutti-Frutti's (a bait they had seen the other anglers using, and one they had heard great things about). The lake was of a similar size to the third, but deeper and less sheltered, making a sturdy brolly camp a necessity, and it was with a modicum of confidence that they set up along the more sheltered West Bank. The weather was awful, with rain slanting down across the lake in great sheets, blown by the gusting south westerly wind and making brolly erection a two man job.

By the time they had cast out and settled into the relative warmth and dryness of Chris's brolly camp, it was almost dark and the pair silently craved the warmth of a sleeping bag. They could quite easily have foregone the luxury of a night-time carp, rationalising that daytime would be better for photos. By the time that Chris had slipped a small brandy into their third cup of coffee of the evening, the night was stygian black and the wind was buffeting the brolly from side to side and constantly extinguishing the jarred candle at the back of the brolly camp. Winter evenings always seemed to drag, because they started so early, and so it was no surprise to Stan that it was only eight o'clock when he braved the elements to return to his swim. The wind was picking up more by now, and he knew that he was in for a restless night's sleep so tested all the pegs and ropes before slipping into his sleeping bag. Despite the inclement weather, the night was not cold and his one piece suit was more than enough warmth when coupled with the sleeping bag. The steady sound of the rain and the cosiness of the sleeping bag soon had him drifting into a fitful sleep. Chris's call woke him suddenly and, for a few strange moments, he had no idea of who or where he was, then another demanding shout from his mate shook him closer to wakefulness.

"Yup," he acknowledged, as if he had been awake all along, slinging his legs over the side of the bedchair and feeling for his boots with his feet.

"Bloody hell, you can sleep for England, Quill. I've been calling you for ages!" came Chris's rejoinder.

"Sorry, mate, just having a little doze, y'know. What's happening?" replied Stan, trying to make himself heard above the noise of the rushing wind. Thankfully the rain had stopped, probably blown away by the force of the wind, thought the slowly rising Stan.

"I've got one on, and it feels quite good, fella. I need you to hold the net 'cos the wind keeps blowing it away from the water."

Stan thought about the term 'quite good' in relation to the lake that they were fishing and estimated a mid-double as the culprit, but any fish was welcome at this time of year, although maybe not at this time of night. A night that was inky black, and Stan's eyes took a little time before becoming accustomed to its darkness, but he still had to grope carefully along the bank before he came upon Chris and his fish. He managed to find the net but could barely see its mesh, let alone have any hope of seeing the fish to net it confidently, so told Chris of his predicament.

"Yeah, I know what you mean. I've missed it twice already. Look, it's real close, so I'll try to pull it right into the net. You just look for the light shape, if you can."

Stan concentrated as hard as possible on the spreader block of the net, willing himself to focus on the fish, all remnants of sleep long since blown away by the near gale-force wind. Chris's voice alerted him to the job in hand.

"It must be right in, Stan. Can you see it?" pleaded the battling angler.

Stan was just about to answer in the negative when he felt a shudder on the pole and saw a splash at his feet and, swiftly lifting the mesh, felt the fish surge against it in vain.

"Got it!" he cried, much to his partner's amazement.

"What! You've netted it? I can't even see you, let alone the fish! Well done, Quill, you are the man!" Chris pounded the netsman on the back and peered over his shoulder in the hope of some insight into what he had caught, but could discern hardly anything in the darkness.

"I'll get a sack, you do the unhooking. I think I'll sack this until the morning, what d'ya reckon?" asked the victor as he turned back to his brolly and searched for a torch to assist with the process.

"Yeah, good idea. What time is it then, about nine, or something?" Stan enquired whilst carefully laying the fish on the bank prior to unhooking it.

"Yeah, and the rest!" snorted Chris, emerging from the brolly with torchlight blazing. "It's about midnight, Rip Van Peacock! You've been snoring for hours, boy." Stan found this hard to believe and was just about to say so when the torch lit up the carp before him and he glimpsed its size for the first time. "Bloody hell, Rhodie, that's a bloody whacker!"

Chris stopped playing with the sack cord and his eyes followed the beam of the torch which, at its rainbows end, revealed a pot of gold and he realised that Stan was not lying; this was indeed a bloody whacker. A huge gust of wind shook him from his reverie and, whilst he readied the sack, Stan removed the hook and laid the rod against a tree. He wondered if he was, in fact, still on his bedchair and enjoying a rather whimsical dream, when another blast of cold air toppled the rod which landed squarely on the back of the would-be dreamer's head. Nope, this was reality, he decided! They sacked the fish and secured it in a tiny bay which was not being churned like the North Sea, then sought the shelter of Chris's brolly and the warmth of a cup of tea, before analysing the previous ten minutes.

"D'you think it was as big as I think it was?" asked Stan whilst rubbing his hands together in a bid to initiate some circulation in them. Chris, blowing on his own hands in an attempt to affect the same outcome, shook his head in bafflement.

"I dunno. I thought the biggest was about sixteen but that looks much bigger, doesn't it? I mean, it looks for all the world like a bloody twenty, don't you reckon?" came his puzzled, imploring reply. They talked through two cups of tea until both agreeing that the morning's weighing would reveal the truth and so, bidding his mate a hearty 'well done,' Stan braved the elements once again and returned to the relative security of his own brolly. The wind had not diminished in strength at all and they both spent the rest of the wild night dozing fitfully whilst hanging on to the spokes of their brollies, silently hoping that one of the huge 'high' gusts didn't materialise at ground level.

The day was a milky-grey when Stan was wrenched from his slumbers by a screaming buzzer and his swift exit from his bedchair almost rendered him fingerless, his hands still wedged between the spokes and the material. None the worse for their extraction, his hands were soon put to better use as he held rod and reel and commenced battle with the perpetrator of the early morning call. The fight lasted no time at all and he netted the four or five pound culprit at the first attempt, unhooking it in the net and watching it swim away in the remarkably calm waters. The wind had blown itself out during the night and the new day was dawning grey but calm - time for a cup of tea and a reassessment of the situation. Chris took some waking but, with a fresh brew wafted under his nose, he soon came around and listened to Stan's tale of the early morning capture, before saying, suddenly,

"Here, haven't I got one in the sack? I reckon we should weigh it, what do you say?"

They prepared weigh sling and scales before extracting the bulging sack from the margins and placed it on the mat. Stan unzipped it as Chris peeled back the nylon to reveal a golden mirror carp, which still looked as big as they had remembered.

"What's your p.b ...?"

The ritual began, but they were both amazed that this twenty two pound carp was residing in this alleged singles and doubles pool. No matter, it was Chris's personal best and made so much better for the fact that it was totally out of the blue.

By the end of the session they had both landed another single each, but were elated at the result that they had achieved. The rest of the winter was spent on the lake - well, that part of the winter that had not rendered the lakes unfishable due to a covering of ice, but in that time they only managed two more carp over ten pounds and were not to repeat their first success. The mystery of the twenty was solved at the end of the season when the pair were poring over their respective photo albums and Stan suddenly got 'Snap.'

"Look! It's the same fish as my nineteen, Chris," he exclaimed and, sure enough, it was indeed the same fish as the nineteen that Stan had caught at the very beginning of the season, after spawning. It had obviously been moved to add a little extra to the first lake - not entirely on its own, they pondered. But that was past, the new season beckoned and they were determined to get a few more twenties under their belts and, by the time that Maradonna was holding aloft a gleaming, gold trophy for all the world to see, they had indeed achieved their own goal.

Two twenties apiece was their tally by the end of July, but the only problem was that they were the same two fish they had caught last year. Both caught the biggie just shy of twenty five pounds, and both the very first twenty that Chris had caught, this time at twenty two, and a few ounces heavier. Where were the other half a dozen that people had talked of? They knew that one had gone walkies, was that the fate of the others or were they just the same fish being caught by different people without the benefit of photographic comparison?

Whatever the answer, the pair were becoming a little restless at catching the same fish, especially as the many doubles they were catching were also making reappearances for the second and third time. This was brought home even more when one of the other anglers asked them to take some photos of a twenty which turned out to be the biggie again, just two weeks after Stan's most recent capture of it. It was then that they realised they would not be renewing their ticket next season. The question was, of course, where next?

They had always kept an eye on the angling weeklies for any mention of lakes in their area and one name that had kept cropping up was Frensham, which appeared to hold some stunning carp to upper thirties. Not quite sure whether they were ready for this sort of leap they, nonetheless, began making enquiries but the news that came back was more depressing than if they had been unable to merely purchase a ticket. It appeared that about fifty small carp had been stocked into the lake to supplement the sixty or so big originals resident in there. Within a few short weeks, the first corpse was found, but this was just the tip of the iceberg and, by the time the 'mystery virus' had run its course a couple of months later, there were fewer than a dozen of the irreplaceable originals left alive. A lot of people were left devastated by these events, many of them never returning to the water again. As an addendum to this disaster, a few years later the same man stocked the same strain of fish into another lake in the vicinity with the same devastating effect. When will we learn?

With Frensham out of the picture, they began scouring the O.S. map of the area but, with so many lakes to choose from it was difficult to know where to start. After a number of futile visits to dried up puddles, fishless holes, trout lakes and private estate lakes it became necessary to enlist some local knowledge so Chris made a few discrete enquiries amongst the local carp fishing mafia and turned up a couple of prospective future venues. Both were a few miles further than they would have liked, but if they produced the goods then the travelling would be worth it. The first was a twenty acre pit near Farnham which reputedly held a fair head of twenties topped by four fish over thirty pounds. The second was a complex of lakes near Yateley, on the other side of the M3. This they had heard of and had already given a little thought to, concluding that they may not yet be ready for such a move. So it was that they visited Coates Pit in late October and, despite the bleakness of the day, could see the potential of the place, which was shaped like a love heart. As they walked its banks they could see that it was not overly busy. Then, as if to put the final seal on their decision a huge golden common carp rose from the depths not thirty yards from them, landing with a resounding crash as it re-entered its watery domain.

"That'll do for me, son," said Chris, emphatically, and Stan was in no mind to disagree.

The year ended with Chris's third and final capture of the 'spawny twenty' from Pit 3, and with Stan securing two tickets for Coates Pit for the following season. Their next big step was soon to be upon them and they couldn't wait.

The first casualty was found at the end of May, less than a month after the introduction of the stock fish. As very few people knew about the stocking at that time nobody put the two events together - least of all the two anglers who found the small, dead common in the margins. Because of this, they merely pulled it out of the lake and threw into the bushes for the foxes, rather than reporting the incident.

A few days later, three committee members were taking their usual pre-season stroll along the banks, making sure there was no last minute work required prior to the off. The day was warm, and the water looked marvellous with an abundance of waterfowl going about their usual mating and territory rituals. As the trio were watching a pair of grebes hunting along the margins, they spotted something floating in the edge beneath an overhanging willow and, on their arrival beneath the tree, were a little concerned to find the bloated corpse of a double figure carp bobbing about in the waves.

Their concern was heightened even more when they found four more carp in a similar condition. So, whilst two of them remained to search for further possible casualties, the third rushed off to inform the Club Secretary of their discoveries, returning an hour later with him and two more members. The remaining two had found another corpse of a much bigger carp and it was only the scar on its shoulder that gave away its identity - The Scarred Mirror, which had given so many people so much pleasure, had wolfed down its last free offering.

By the end of the weekend the death toll had reached well into double figures, but these were fish that had obviously been dead for a little while, and as the week went on, the bankside vigil would reveal carp with barely a breath left in their bodies. Not knowing what else to do, the Club Secretary called in the Southern Water Authority who promptly took away some corpses for autopsy and a couple of stressed but still living specimens, diagnosing the problem as a water-borne virus which fell under the heading of S.V.C.

What they really meant was that they did not know what was killing only the carp, but they had a good idea that it was related to the recent introduction of the stock fish. The water was closed until further notice, but that did not curb the carp deaths and a few club members wondered whether the virus would disappear as quickly as it had come, praying that it would be soon and that there would be some survivors.

Who knows what this disease is like for the carp? Is it like Asian Flu is to humans, affecting some more than others with the particularly virulent strains being fatal to many who contract it? Being in an enclosed environment, like a lake or pond, is it like a suffocating gas that attacks the nervous system of the healthy as well as the sick and aged? Who knows? Certainly not the people who should, that's for sure. Suffice to say that some do survive and it would appear that, within a couple of months of the first signs in a lake, S.V.C. is gone, leaving death and destruction in its wake.

The Common and The Big-Scaled Mirror were luckier than their scarred compatriot, but only just, although the disease took its toll on them as well, causing them to lose considerable weight in their fight to survive. But survive they did, along with a dozen of the original stocking and almost all of the new, harbingers of the disease. The problem, although not for the carp, was that amongst the corpses that had been dragged from the lake and burned were two or three large specimens in a poor state of decay, the only identification possible being that one was a big common and the other a mirror with large scales on its flanks. Thus, the conclusion was drawn that the three most desirable fish in the lake were history, nothing more. Once the last of the corpses had been cremated - and no more found over the next couple of months - the lake was left alone, being thought of as nothing more than a crematorium.

Within a few months, the eco-system began to rebuild and the surviving carp began, once again, to search out the necessary nourishment to help them through the coming winter. But would that alone be enough to enable them to regain enough strength for that long, cold vigil. For some, the winter was the final nail, and they did not wake to see another spring, their bloated corpses found by the occasional pike angler who would pass on the discovery to the committee. Strangely, no other fish were affected by the disease, but few anglers were aware of that, assuming that the smaller, dead fish had fallen victim to the pike and the herons, so the lake was deserted for most of the year. A few hopefuls trod the blossoming banks in the spring, but the natural casualties of that time of year (which would normally be ignored) seemed to confirm that the lake was dead as a carp fishery.

The disease did not return, however, and the surviving carp soon regained their normal vitality, feeding ravenously in the warming spring waters and patrolling the pit from end to end, lords of all they surveyed. No prying eyes were witness to this rejuvenation, as most of the carp angling fraternity in the area were fishing the other up and coming local lakes that had been previously ignored. The Common and Big-Scaled Mirror spent the long summer days completely unmolested and by the time the die-hard pike anglers arrived for their short, winter sessions, the lethargy of that season had slowed the carp's metabolism enough so that they very rarely showed themselves above the surface of the lake.

By the next spring, however, their joyous cavorting did not go totally unnoticed and, from his favourite old climbing tree, Dean watched elated as the two huge fish cruised below him, without a care. They had survived and they looked even more impressive than ever. If only he could stay and fish for them, but that was out of the question. He was home on shore leave before rejoining his ship, in a few short weeks, and sailing off to much sunnier climes in this, his third year in the Navy. How he would have loved to have had a rod with him at that moment, close season or not but it was not to be, so he contented himself with the wonderful sight before him. On returning to his mother's house he was sorely tempted to tell the committee members of his findings, but he had decided that this club, like many others, did not deserve fish like this and had no idea how to appreciate them. Instead, he phoned someone else, an old friend who had moved away and who, he seemed to recall, had been in the throes of buying his own lake a year or so ago. He had progressed greatly as a carp angler in the years that Dean had been away, and was well respected in angling circles, even though Dean knew he could pull as many strokes as the next man. Nonetheless, Dean was sure that if his old pal could repatriate these fine specimens not only would they be well cared for and greatly appreciated, but it would also go a long way to securing him a place on the exclusive syndicate in a couple of years' time.

The news was indeed of great interest to the joint owners of the new syndicate lake in Oxfordshire, and they took little time in arranging a meeting with their informant before he had to leave. Fortune was with them. Not only because they were able to see their potential quarry sunning themselves in a quiet corner of the Pit, but also because they bumped into the Club Secretary who was more than pleased to grant them a place in the club in order to fish for the large bream they had spied in the lake! False addresses were easily obtained and tickets purchased, it was now just a case of how to deal with the problem.

Due to their need for new stock they did two things. Firstly, they built a small stock pond as a quarantine area for new fish, keeping two or three small originals in there as a control, lest any new fish should be carrying disease. Secondly, they bought a second hand transit van and converted it for fish transportation, with two large, aerated tanks in the back, for the safety and comfort of their new guests.

Plans were hatched and they arranged to fish the lake a month or so into the season when they hoped it would be relatively quiet and the fish ready to accept their hookbaits, samples of which they would scatter around the lake on a couple of earlier visits. Everything worked to perfection and, by dawn of their second day on the lake, they were loading a twenty four pound common into the tanks, depositing it into the quarantine stock pond a couple of hours and a hundred miles later. They kept a close eye on the fish in the pond and whilst Chris Rhodes was celebrating the capture of an unexpected winter twenty, they were convinced that any trace of disease had disappeared from the carp and looked forward to transferring the larger fish to their new home in the new season.

They spent a lot of time on the road during the spring, usually taking in three lakes on their tour of Southern England, all with potential new inmates for their lake, and deposited a lot of bait in the respective lakes. The whole affair was handled with military precision and they made sure that they did not frequent each venue too often, fishing them on a three week rota. By the time that 'Handball!' was being screamed around England they were making their third trip to Stanton's Pit, the previous two having produced a total of nine carp. Of these, they returned four double figure carp to their home, but were happy to accept the other five twenty-plus carp into their new family, even though they were not the two which they most desired. That was to change, however, and in the space of two days they achieved their aim, banking both of the huge fish on their last night on the pit.

Being a midweek session, they encountered no one else on the bank so the transfer of the fish to the aeration tanks was simple and they were on their way before sunrise. The Big-Scaled Mirror had been the first to be caught and they weighed it at just over thirty five pounds in the dying rays of the sun. The temptation to leave there and then had been great but, finally, they agreed to wait until dawn but that departure time was amended when The Common also fell foul to the poachers' traps just after midnight. The decision was made to leave immediately and, despite their excitement and eagerness, they decided not to weigh the fish until they returned home, even though they could tell it was a good few pounds larger than its mirror companion.

Everything was secured and they were on the road and heading north within thirty minutes of The Common's capture. However, after only a couple of miles, the van began to behave very strangely and they quickly decided to pull over somewhere to perform some makeshift repairs. No sooner did they find a secluded field to use as a temporary garage than they heard nothing at all, complete silence. In other words, no noise from the aeration pumps. This was much more worrying than the van's mechanical hiccups and fairly soon they both came to the same conclusion - the pump was buggered! Desperate as they were to get the fish into their lake they were still carp anglers and had a deep respect for their quarry. It took little time for them to agree that they could not risk the hundred mile journey in summer heat with a dodgy motor. The fish would not survive. There was only one course of action - they must find a nearby lake to put them in until they could return and renew their acquaintance. The sun was slowly turning the sky a deep crimson and so, without further ado, they laid out the O. S. map of the area on the dashboard and scanned it for a possible retreat for the carp, but where were they? They knew that they were not far from Salisbury, but where on that route they had no idea, then one turned to the door and motioned for quiet.

"Listen, can you hear that?"

"What?"

"That. Hear it?"

And he did. It was the sound of the first coot waking on a nearby lake, quickly answered by another. Looking at each other without a word, they both leapt from the van and ran through the dew dampened grass to a distant copse of trees and there, forty yards away, they saw the wraiths of mist rising from the cooling waters of a lake. They had no idea of its size, but could see enough water to know that it would serve their purpose.

Returning quickly to the car, they each grabbed a wriggling, dripping sack from its dark confines and staggered manfully to the lakeside, arms aching from the weight they were carrying. Furtively glancing around, they lowered the sacks into the milk warm water before untying the cords and releasing their captives into an unexpected new home. Only then, as the daylight thickened, did they look up and fully take in their surroundings.

"Oh shit!" was all they could manage between them, as their eyes took in the full majesty of the fifty odd acres of water they had just released their charges into. "How do we get them back out of here?"

"We'll sort that out later. Let's just get the van sorted and get out of here before Farmer Giles wakes up!" came the blunt reply and so, ten minutes later, they coughed and spluttered out of the field and off, northwards, never to return.

The carp's new home was, in fact, a neglected gravel pit of just over fifty acres. A local club had the fishing rights to it but few people bothered other than a few tench and bream anglers in the summer, and the inevitable pike anglers in the winter. The lake was very rich and weedy and was home to the usual variety of freshwater fish, all of which had grown healthy with the abundance of natural food and the lack of angling attention. Amongst the lake's inhabitants were a small group of a couple of dozen carp and it was not long before the illegal immigrants joined up with the largest four fish in the lake - two mid-twenty *commons and two massive mirror carp, both at that time considerably larger than The Common. But that would soon change.*

Chapter Nine - 1990

'Maggie Quits!' blared the headline and so came the end of an era that had seen major changes for the British people.

Stan was not politically minded and took the news with a pinch of salt. Some people said she was the best thing that had happened to Britain, others said she was the worst, but Stan just sat in the middle. He had other things on his mind, like how he was going to pay for his nice new house after the mortgage rate had just gone through the ceiling.

Things had moved on apace for Stan, as another decade ended, and not just in fishing terms. A couple of years earlier, the firm he worked for had been forced to close down but before he had time to worry about where his next pay packet would come from, a couple of the managers decided to set up on their own. Stan was one of the people they asked to join them, confident in his ability to run the paperwork whilst they got on with the printing and although it would mean a more difficult journey to work, in Kingston, he was happy to accept and, before The Hurricane and the Stock Market Crash brought devastation of two different kinds to the country, the new company was up and running and all was right with the world.

His fishing had moved on as well with the move to Coates Pit near Farnham and it soon brought home to him and Chris how two dimensional their fishing had been over the past few years. Coates was a twenty acre gravel pit, roughly heart shaped with a point of land jutting out from the North Bank one hundred yards into the lake. Although its banks were quite well wooded, it was still a daunting expanse of water when the wind blew across it. Being an old gravel workings, the variance in depths were far in excess of those that the pair were used to, plummeting to over twenty feet in places then rising steeply to within four feet of the surface on top of the many gravel bars that contoured the bottom. These bars also brought home to the slightly worried new boys how little they knew about this sort of fishing; the sharp stones and mussels with which they were coated leaving anglers hookless and leadless on numerous occasions. But they had the tickets and, on a couple of close season sorties, they had seen the carp and impressive they were as well, so they greeted the new season with their usual enthusiasm.

By the end of June, however, they realised that they had a real task on their hands, neither of them having been in contact with anything bar a couple of dinner plate sized bream. When, after a month, Stan did eventually hook their first carp his elation was short lived as the razor sharp gravel bars treated his 12lb line with contempt and cut it like cotton. After the same thing had occurred a week later to Chris, they understood what people meant by 'snag leaders' and did the necessary research to find out the best line and method for tying these to their mainline. Once again, they relied on Mr. Hutchinson to provide the answers and were soon equipped with 30lb line in order to combat the mussels, and a week later this new ploy proved successful when Chris landed a low twenty from the warm North East Bay. Their first fish, and their confidence was sky high and, by the end of August, they had added a further three fish to that total, two of which were a similar size to the first. They were now much better equipped to deal with gravel pit angling, employing plumbing floats, Black Widow catapults and heavier test curve rods to aid them in their quest for the pit's bigger fish.

By mid-October they had added a couple of doubles to their tally but, even with the benefit of the heavy shock-leaders, they had not been able to prevent the gravel bars claiming another couple of victims. It became obvious to them, then, that some bars were much sharper than others and should be avoided at all costs and in accepting this they realised that the pit was becoming smaller and more manageable.

Stan had arranged to have the Friday off and would arrive at the lake early that morning, but Mother Nature had other ideas.

"It's getting a bit windy out there, love," murmured Jean. Stan didn't need her to tell him, though, as he had been lying awake for half an hour listening to the wind increase in strength. He was sure that he had heard a few branches crash to the ground but surely the wind wasn't that strong, was it? By the time he was ready to leave, just after dawn, the wind had disappeared but it left behind such devastation that it would take many years for some parts of the South of England to recover from it. As yet unaware of this destruction, Stan began the fifteen mile journey with his usual enthusiasm but, after taking almost an hour to travel a mere one mile from his house, the full picture was becoming apparent. Every road he went down seemed to have a wooded barrier across and, after the umpteenth U-turn, he realised that his day's fishing was looking less and less likely to happen so he finally admitted defeat and disconsolately returned home. The news reports revealed more eyebrow-raising stories, the television screen showing scenes that had never been witnessed in this country before and it slowly dawned on Stan how lucky it was that he had not gone to the lake the previous evening, as he had originally planned. Then, an horrendous thought struck him - what about Chris? He'd said that he might go on Thursday and Stan had taken no call from him during yesterday evening.

Quickly dialing the number, he prayed for it to be answered but after a minute of ringing tone he was just about to give up when the receiver was lifted and something vaguely human grunted down the phone line.

"Yerr."

"Chris, is that you?" gasped a puzzled Stan.

"Yerr."

"Bloody hell! You all right, son? You sound awful. I thought you might have gone to the lake and been out in that storm," babbled a now very relieved Stan.

"Nah. I was gonna but I went down the pub with Steve and John. What storm?" Stan just laughed and began telling his very hungover pal about the night's events, soon realising that he was wasting his breath speaking to someone with mushy peas for a brain.

"Give me a call later when you are able to walk upright once more. I'll explain it all then," said Stan before hanging up with a smile on his face.

Later that day the whole thing had become very apparent to both of them and they discussed the possibility of reaching the lake on Saturday morning. The emergency services had been doing a sterling job in clearing most of the main roads and the pair reasoned that if they stuck to those routes rather than the cross country route they normally took, they would have a good chance of reaching their destination, so they arranged to meet at Chris's house at dawn the following morning, he having promised not to go to the pub that night.

The journey to the lake was almost straightforward with only a couple of minor detours required, but the sight that greeted them was jaw-dropping. Most of their journey had been done in semi-darkness so that they were not really aware of the storm's effect, but once at the lake the sun was rising in the east and the full effect of the wind's power was there for all to see. As they reached the car park a huge, prostrate oak tree blocked their path and their view of the lake. They left the car and walked around its fallen bulk but if they thought that this was the only casualty along the banks of Coates Pit, their emergence from beneath the oak's trailing branches revealed the full extent of the damage. Looking across towards the Point and the Far Bay it appeared as if a giant finger had contemptuously flicked over a stand of matchsticks, leaving those on either side of the swathe untouched and vertical. What made this sight slightly surreal was the total lack of wind on the sun-dappled lake. They walked around, over and under numerous boughs that had succumbed to the awesome force of nature until they reached the Far Bay, still unable to fully take in what had occurred here just over twenty four hours earlier. The lake itself looked beautiful in amongst the devastation and the sight of a huge mirror carp leaving the water soon brought them to their senses. They were here to fish, and fish they would. The Point seemed an obvious choice at the moment as it had, amazingly, been spared from any deforestation, so they made the onerous journey to that area and set up for the session in brilliant sunshine, both casting back into the Far Bay where the fish had just shown itself.

They knew the area fairly well, having fished it on a few occasions in the summer, and Stan had taken his first twenty from the water in this swim a couple of months earlier. Baits were dispatched to the floats that marked a couple of previously productive bars, followed by a hundred boilies around each hookbait. They then spent the rest of the day discussing all aspects of hurricanes that they could, whilst watching coots and ducks diving around their baits in search of the free food dotted around them. Due to this activity, it was no surprise to Stan when he received a twitchy drop-back that had always preceded the capture of a flapping winged devil over the course of the season. He struck with some annoyance and saw a coot rise to the surface like an Exocet, flapping excitedly across the lake to the safety of the far margin but patently without Stan's hook in its beak. But something had hold of Stan's hook and was not ready to give it back, no matter how hard he pulled. After a few minutes of this impasse, it dawned on the bemused angler that he was in contact with a carp that was hugging the far side of the bar. .

"Give it a bit of slack," suggested Chris, so Stan grudgingly complied, holding the line between his fingers to feel for any movement on the other end. After a seemingly eternal minute, a sense of something living came throbbing down the line.

Curbing his initial urge to heave the rod over his shoulder once again, he waited a few more seconds in the hope that the fish would move away from the bar of its own accord. Unable to wait any longer, he lifted the rod steadily to the vertical, feeling the satisfying 'thump thump' of a good fish realizing its mistake. From then on, the fight was relatively straightforward, and within ten minutes of the initial take, Chris was sliding the net under a long, golden, common carp. Both men leapt for joy and Chris took little time in deciding that this was the largest common that either of them had landed, far exceeding the eighteen pound specimen he had taken the previous season.

"What's your personal best common, Quill?" he began.

"Fifteen pounds," replied Stan, expectantly.

"Not anymore, boy. Not anymore!"

The leaping and cavorting began in earnest, and continued even more after the scales revealed a weight of twenty four pounds six ounces. Stan grinned inanely for the camera then, as the fish swum strongly away, punched the air with delight whilst giving vent to his feelings only slightly less vociferously than Mother Nature had done a couple of days previously.

The day faded to evening and they broke out a few beers to celebrate this momentous event but no sooner had they begun supping the first brew than Chris's rod was demanding attention, which it got in a shower of amber liquid. This fish produced a less frantic fight than the previous but he could tell it was another good fish and when Stan netted it a few minutes later they both bellowed at the sight of another glorious common lying at the bottom of the net. They had fished the lake for four months and these were the first fully scaled carp they had seen, but now they had seen two and both of them over twenty pounds. Chris's fish was a couple of pound lighter than his friend's, but it mattered not a jot. Both personal bests were toasted royally that night, with the loss of another fish to Stan's rods doing little to dampen their elation, merely adding to the story of the 'hurricane session' they related to anyone who would listen over the next couple of years. The season ended with a total of nine carp between them, the largest being Stan's common. They had seen a couple of very large fish in the lake and had also witnessed the capture of a thirty three pound fish during the last week of the season and it was this, the largest fish either of them had ever seen on the bank, that spurred them on.

By the time that joyous date had arrived once again they had whipped themselves into a frenzy of enthusiasm, having seen most of the fish in the lake consuming their fishmeal baits over the previous month. They had changed bait just because. No real reason other than they wished to try something different but their experimentation with fishmeals, Shellfish Sense Appeal and garlic had proved very alluring to the lake's carp and the pair could not wait for the off. They were also anticipating using lots of hemp, a bait they had the utmost faith in.

On their arrival at the lake on the Wednesday afternoon prior to the midnight start, they spent the first couple of hours ferrying their mountain of bait and tackle to the far margin of the denuded East Bank. The lake was surprisingly quiet, angler wise, with only three cars present in the recently repaired car park but on the surface, and beneath, there was much activity with coots and grebes patrolling the herds of chicks that peppered the surface of the lake. The carp also seemed very active and Stan hoped that this start was not to be a repeat of the one on Pit 3 when they decided that now would be a good time to start spawning. By the evening, however, the steadily falling rain meant that there would be little chance of this annual ritual taking place in the immediate future and the eager pair sat beneath Stan's brolly with another couple of anglers, toasting the new season again and again.

By midnight, they were all a bit wobbly but still able to despatch their hookbaits to the required spots thanks to dental floss markers on their lines. The first morning dawned grey and damp but, after demolishing a very welcome fried breakfast, the world seemed a brighter place and they got down to executing the first of their preconceived plans. By the end of that day the weather had improved and they were both happier at their choice of swims in the shallower part of the lake. The water here had an average depth of eight feet but, running parallel to the bank at a distance of fifty to seventy yards, was a plateau of gravel less than four feet below the surface. It was this feature that had received the bulk of the ten kilos of hemp that they had dragged around to the swim. Also scattered across the area were a few hundred of the previously irresistible fishmeal boilies, however they seemed slightly more resistible at the present moment with very few fish showing in the vicinity. Due to the remoteness of their swims, they both decided to risk a well hidden stroke rod, Stan's flicked along the left hand margin amongst a few pounds of hemp and a handful of boilies, and Chris's likewise along the right hand margin. It was this stroke rod that produced the first carp of the new season - and what a carp. The run came just before dawn and the next fifteen minutes were a blur to the sleep-addled anglers but, somehow, they managed to bundle the carp into the net before they really realised what Chris had landed.

As the captor stood back to take in the result, Stan struggled to lift the prize from the margins, issuing that age old misinformed statement, "Give us a hand, Rhodie, I think the net's caught on a root. I can't lift the bloody thing!"

Neither of them were aware enough to realise what was occurring so, when the pair of them shared the weight it was not readily evident what was in the net. When they lay the carp on the mat, however, neither of them could believe how high the flank was from the floor. Chris hastily pulled back the mesh, and revealed the full, unbelievable length of the stunning, bronze mirror carp - the same flank they had seen at the end of the previous season.

"It's the thirty three!" screamed Stan, needlessly. Chris was already aware of this fact but the words attempting to leave his mouth could not decide which order they should be in and collided at the back of his teeth as if someone had stumbled on a busy, rush hour escalator.

"The .. err, it's ... wha ... how the f …. Bloody hell!" was the best he could manage. Stan understood every word and howled skywards, once more scaring the birds from the trees and sending the resident coots skittering off across the lake, complaining loudly. The pair ran around the swim like headless carp anglers before some semblance of sanity was regained and the weighing and photographing of the fish was completed. At thirty four pounds, the carp was a pound heavier than when they previously saw it on the bank and almost ten pounds larger than Chris's personal best. Once again, the air was rent with joyous screams. By the end of the four day session the pair had accounted for a further two carp apiece, the only one over twenty pounds also falling to Chris's rod. However, their plan was obviously working and Stan was sure that it was just a matter of time before he, too, was weighed down by more than thirty pound of glistening carp flesh. Due to the fact that he was self-employed, Chris was able to pick and choose when to be at the lake and, at the moment, he chose to be there as much as possible. So it was that Chris's capture of his second thirty pound carp in as many weeks was witnessed by no one but the local flora and fauna and a passing, bemused birdwatcher. The first that Stan knew of his friends capture was when he was summoned to the phone at work and greeted by,

"Yeaahh! I've had another one!"

"What? What have you had, boy?" asked Stan, frantically.

"A thirty. I've had another thirty. Whoooahah!" came the ear-splitting reply. Stan was soon able to discern that his mate had indeed caught another thirty in the shape of a thirty one pound mirror, along with a couple of upper doubles. Stan felt the first twinges of envy. He didn't begrudge his pal the fish at all, but he would have loved to have the chance to be at the lake at any time he wanted. Unfortunately, that decision was taken from him by the need to pay for house and family so the feeling lasted just a few moments before it was replaced by genuine joy for Chris and a stomach-churning anticipation for the coming weekend's session.

The next few sessions saw Stan land a few and lose a few but none came anywhere near the target that Chris had set and, by the end of August, despondency was beginning to set in. The larger fish had failed to make any more mistakes during the warmer weather, the largest they had heard of being a twenty eight pound common, and they had only managed a few carp to upper doubles in that time. With the arrival of autumn, however, there was a noticeable change in the weather and the cooler, fresher conditions heralded a change in the carp's feeding habits also.

By the end of September the fish had moved into deeper water and the necessity to cast accurately at distance became paramount, with the same required of their baiting. Initially, this caused them a few problems but, after persevering with the plumbing float and the catapult, the pair soon became happy with what they were doing and began to concentrate their efforts from the car park bank, the South Bank. In front of here a string of gravel bars ran parallel to the bank at distances of thirty, sixty and ninety yards. These were popular spots for any angler to fish on but, with a bit of concerted plumbing, they managed to find a couple of less obvious spots to cast to. Stan had found a small gravel hump between the second and third bars at about seventy yards distance from the bank, which rose to within seven feet of the surface in twelve feet of water. Due to the difficulty he had finding it with subsequent casts, he decided that it had probably been ignored by most anglers and so concentrated his efforts and baits in that area for the last couple of weekends of September. The first of these produced two fish to his rods, one of which was his first twenty for more than two months and, despite just beating that mark, gave him tremendous satisfaction in the knowledge that he was getting something right, at last. The second produced mayhem.

Stan arrived from work on the last day of the month, not at all surprised to find Chris's car in the car park, along with three others. He knew where his mate would be so, loading himself up with the necessary tackle and comforts for what was forecast as being a wet and windy weekend, he trudged the hundred yards along the bank to the first swim which was, indeed, occupied by Chris. Dropping his gear behind his pal's bivvy he entered the swim with his usual greeting, "Rhodie, old boy. How goes it and why isn't the kettle on?"

"It's on, it's on," came the inevitable retort. The kettle was always on in Chris's swim. "Good to see you, boy. How goes it? I've been here a couple of hours but I haven't seen anything yet. Baldrick's in The Point and had a small common this morning, and apparently Jilted John had a twenty six earlier in the week from your swim."

This last made Stan's heart skip a beat, "He's not in there now, is he?" almost pleading for the answer to be in the negative. Chris could tell in his voice his friend's concern, so toyed with him for a moment.

"John? Err, is his car still in the car park then?" he asked, mischievously. Stan searched his memory for recent makes of car,

"What, the white van? No. No, it's not. Is it? Oh, I don't know. Is he there, then?" he almost whined. Chris relented, chuckling.

"No, he went yesterday."

"You bastard, Rhodie! May all your toes turn into tree roots and you get a run to your far rod!" growled a relieved Stan, able now to relax and plan his session.

The wind, as predicted, was gaining strength and so, whilst Chris poured the boiling water onto the waiting tea bag, Stan strolled purposefully down to the next swim with his plumbing rod, in order to find the small feature before the cross-wind made that task too difficult. A couple of casts at a far, silver birch soon brought the desired tap-tap-tap on the rod tip, the orange tip of the plumbing float rising seven feet to the lake's surface to admirably mark the spot. Within half an hour both baited rigs had landed five yards either side of the float and the last of the freebies had splashed down in the vicinity. It was now just a matter of securing his sleeping quarters for the coming storm, the grey, scudding clouds looking more ominous by the minute. By early evening the sky was so dark and brooding that daylight had been ousted an hour earlier than usual, and soon the lake reverberated to the first, large splashes of rain. The only good thing about the coming storm was that the ravenous hordes of coots and tufties liked it less than the anglers so would leave the baited areas alone for the foreseeable future. The evening passed with the two anglers sheltered in Chris's bivvy, which was very sturdily pinned down, and thankful that they were set up in the comparative shelter of the South Bank. The night passed without any action to either of them but, in the middle of a wild night, Stan laid awake wondering if another hurricane was sweeping the countryside.

Although strong and, in some places, damaging, the storm was nowhere near as powerful as that of a year previously and they woke up to the normal wind ruffled surface of a brisk south-westerly. Looking across the lake from the comfort of his bedchair, Stan noticed two things. Firstly, Baldrick was no longer resident in The Point and Stan wondered if he had been blown away in the night. The second thing was much more pleasing, and that was the sight of a carp leaving the water in the general area of his hookbaits, then another. By the time that he had rubbed the sleep from his eyes and was peering through the steam from his first cup of tea, the increasingly excited watcher had seen six carp rolling and leaping over his baits. He thought to himself that it could only be a matter of time before one of them was picked up, when his right hand alarm bleeped once. Concentrating madly, he stared at the indicator, willing it to rise and, to further musical accompaniment it did just that, rising inch by inch before moving slowly forward and coming to halt against the alarm. What it would have done next is difficult to surmise because, by the time it had made this short journey, Stan had done the same and had struck firmly into a pleasing weight on the other end. Hearing the commotion, Chris was soon by his side but, before he had a chance to ready the net, his friend was cursing loudly and angrily winding in the limp, lifeless line which had cut on the closest bar. Chris turned and quietly walked away, knowing that it would be best to leave Stan for ten minutes or so, when he heard another buzzer scream behind him. Thinking that his distraught pal might have taken out his frustrations on the other rod, he was a little loath to turn round, but the screaming buzzer was replaced by a shouting Stan. He turned to see him with a very bent rod in his hands.

"What's going on, Quill?" he called as he ran back into the swim.

"The other rod just belted off and I've got one on," came the incredulous reply. The usual banter followed about how big, whereabouts, what rig and who shone his nether regions for him! But soon the banter stopped as the serious business of landing the fish became imminent and, as it cruised slowly along the deep margins in front of them, Chris caught a glimpse of the flank and recognised it straight away.

"Oh, shit, don't lose this one mate!" came his worrying command.

"What! Oh, don't say things like that, Rhodie. What is it? What fish is it, Rhodie?"

"Just shut up and get it in the net, boy, then you can find out for yourself," replied the nervous netsman. The usual dorsal clipping caused palpitations for both of them - but, a few minutes after Chris's original exclamation, he let fly another as he slid the net under a huge mirror carp.

"Yesss! Well done, Quill, you've just joined the thirties club!"

Chris's words were like a right hook from Mike Tyson and Stan was momentarily stunned whilst his mind reeled at their impact. Then that moment was surpassed. By one, two, three and more of unadulterated bliss! Thirty pounds! How often had he daydreamed of this moment? Now that it had finally arrived it was a thousand times better than any dream. He helped Chris lift the bulging net from the lake and lower it onto the waiting mat, all in a daze. As Chris revealed the carp he understood his mate's remark - it was the thirty three that Chris had caught at the beginning of the season and it dazzled him with the brightness of its golden scales. Chris took over proceedings but needed a hand to lift the scales, reading from them aloud.

"Bloody hell, it's put on a bit! Thirty five.... six. Bloody well done, Quill, you've beat me mate."

Stan could barely take in this latest piece of news, content to grin inanely at the fish, stroking its flank and cooing over it like an auntie over a newborn baby. Photos were graphed and throats were tortured as the great beast was once again returned, and Stan turned to face Chris's grinning visage and shake his outstretched hand.

"Rhodie, it don't get better than this," he said, smiling back. "Methinks we will get very drunk tonight, my son." And they did, especially as Chris also managed to sneak out a twenty five pound mirror in the middle of a terrific afternoon downpour, giving them even more cause to celebrate.

The next few sessions became progressively harder as winter's fingers began to stretch out towards them and they managed one carp apiece before December's foggy freeze brought proceedings to a temporary halt. Christmas, however, brought with it a thaw and, after a couple of tentative pike fishing excursions on Manor Pool, they elected to spend the last six weeks of the season at Coates in the unlikely event of a last gasp carp. Time was tight for Stan as he and Jean had decided the time had come for them to move to a larger place. With Jean working full time now, they felt they could just about afford the extra outgoings and, at the end of the year, they had found the perfect house just outside Farnham. It was close to the M3 making Stan's journey to work much easier and, more importantly to Stan, only five minutes from the lake! It appeared that, if all went well, they would be moving in the close season, which was fine by Stan and he vowed to make the most of the fishing time he had available to him.

February, as usual, was a real ball-buster but after Stan's birthday the weather began to change for the better and spring beckoned in the distance. The carp seemed to realise this as well and, as the close season moved ever closer, Stan and Chris began to see encouraging signs like tench rolling and the occasional loud splash just out of view that might just have been a carp. The rest of Mother Nature's children were waking up from their winter slumbers as well, with the wildfowl beginning their mating rituals and the invertebrate life in the weed beginning to noticeably increase. The first fish was, inevitably, a tench, as were the second, third, and fourth, all falling to Stan's rods in one weekend and he and Chris were confident that this was just a prelude to the big boys starting to feed. But, then, winter flicked out one last icy blast and it seemed that the final weekend of the season would be a huge anti-climax. Saturday dawned bright and frosty, the rods lying like horizontal icicles on the rests, a light mist hanging over the water, undisturbed by breeze or leaping carp. Stan ventured a peek from beneath the comfort of his lovely, warm sleeping bag but, seeing nothing moving, elected to stay put until such time as his bladder or a steaming cup of tea made it necessary for him to rise. Snuggling back down, he thought he heard a shout so, peeling back an ears worth of quilted cover, he listened intently in case it was repeated. Sure enough, and to his great dismay, it was indeed repeated, and moreover, it was his name being shouted by Chris.

"What?" he called, allowing another micro-therm of heat to leave past his reddening nose.

"Quill! I'm in!" came the call again, easily heard without the sleeping bag muffler.

"Okay, I'm on my way," he replied and, grudgingly leaving the tropical confines of his bed, he quickly slipped on his thermal boots and jacket before crunching along to his neighbour, muttering under his breath, "This'd better be a bloody carp or he's had it." On reaching his swim, he found Chris with a sleeping bag wrapped around his legs and a twelve foot icicle in his hands!

"Is it a carp?" asked Stan, ready to make a hasty return to his rapidly cooling bed if he got the wrong answer.

"Certainly feels like it. Do us a favour, get my boots from over there, will you, my feet are bloody freezing."

Stan obeyed and held Chris steady as he carefully put first one leg then the other into the boots.

"Good man," he said, by way of thanks. Then, "'fraid you're gonna have to pick that up," nodding at the frosty white handle of the landing net.

"Cheers, mate. This'd better be a whacker or you're in real trouble," replied Stan, feigning annoyance, but Chris knew him too well to know that he didn't really mean it - well, not all of it! As the fish rolled on the bright, still surface of the lake the onlookers saw a flash of scaled flank and simultaneously chorused, "common!"

They knew there were very few commons in the lake with all, bar two, in excess of twenty pounds and this knowledge brought a modicum of seriousness to the next few minutes. Stan had got a good view of the fish and he was certain that this was no double so picked up the frosted landing net handle and dipped the frozen mesh into the lake in readiness for his part of the proceedings. The fish rolled once again, revealing even more of its frame to the two anglers, who both realised that this could be a bit special. When it rolled for a third time it was to be its last as the now thawed mesh engulfed their scaled prize. Rather than the usual shouting and hollering, Chris immediately dropped the rod and wrapped his freezing hands about his body, rubbing them furiously in order to return some heat to them. Stan attempted to do the same with one hand whilst keeping hold of the landing net handle with the other, peering down onto the scaled back of a very long common carp.

"This is a good 'un, Rhodie. I'll allow you to make me a cup of tea after this, mate," he said, switching hands to warm the other one. The unhooking and weighing was a bitter-sweet affair, with the ice that clung onto their hands screaming agony, but the scales spinning around to twenty eight and a half pounds countering that with a beautiful aria. The contrast of golden brown against white served to enhance the stunning beauty of the fish and, as it slipped back into the icy waters, Chris, then Stan sang their own unique aria. 'Oh no, they're back,' squawked the coots and moorhens, performing their usual rapid exit of the offending area.

So ended a momentous session that ended a momentous season and the pair had no doubts that they would go on from here to attain even better things next season.

During the close season, Stan and Jean completed their house move. Stan was able to 'pop down the road' on a few June evenings to keep an eye on the lake, dropping the odd pound of bait here and there along with the same amount of tiger nuts that they had decided to use as well.

Close season baiting is so deceptive, for the anglers that is, and even after seeing the carp's pre-season feeding frenzy dozens of times, Stan and Chris could not help but get excited at the prospect of another opening day bonanza.

They arrived on the morning before the off, brimming with as much confidence as the buckets they carried were brimming with tiger nuts. It transpired that the particle had been used on the lake to good effect a few years earlier, but this was the first time since then that anybody had baited so heavily with anything like this and the carp's weakness for this delicacy was irresistible. So it was that the opening session was, indeed, a bonanza with no less than twelve fish falling to their rods and, although seven of these were over twenty pounds, none exceeded mid-twenties. This minor fact did not enter the minds of the pair of tired but happy anglers at the end of their remarkable opening session, they just couldn't wait to get back to the lake with as many tiger nuts as it was possible to carry. Like déjà vu, the first session turned out to be the exception and, despite pouring over a hundredweight of hot, steaming carp sweets into the lake over the next month, they managed only to double their tally during that time. This in itself was remarkable and showed that they were, once again, doing something right. However, the bigger fish were proving elusive and although half the fish they had landed were over twenty pounds the largest was only twenty six pounds. The fact that they were even thinking like this failed to register at the time but, once again, another step on the ladder was being left behind as the pair subconsciously raised their level of expectancy, constantly striving to catch the biggest carp they possibly could.

In what was becoming their favourite month, September, Stan thought he had achieved that goal when he landed a huge mirror from what had become known as Peacock's Swim. This was the swim that he had caught the thirty five from the previous September and which had produced over half of the twenty carp he had caught so far that season. The weather was very different from a year ago with the south of England enjoying a brief Indian summer so rather than fish his normal gravel hump, Stan had elected to put both baits on the shallowest points of the second and third bars, which were no less than three feet below the surface. Due to the distance involved, he had reverted back to the successful boilie mix of last season which enabled him to accurately bait the bars and, thus, attract as much bird life as was humanly possible! As soon as he had put down the catapult he regretted ever picking it up as everything that flew, swam and squawked homed in on the bounty set before them. Within five minutes, Stan began getting lifts and bleeps as the hungry beaks sought out every last morsel - even the gulls were dive-bombing the swim in an effort to get to the very visible bait just below the surface. Two hours and three snapping, flapping, angry coots later he had

had enough and furiously wound both rods in, retrieving the lead so fast that it was skimming across the surface, like a film of a stone in reverse. Night was quickly drawing in by now and he had no idea where to put his baits. He daren't put any more free offerings out, no matter what depth, as he had no wish to be unhooking a demented coot in the middle of the night, so reverted to the thing he knew best in this swim and fished the 'hump.'

Not wanting the baits to be totally on their own he tied a couple of five bait stringers to the hooks and cast them to the spots he knew so well. The first landed perfectly and a slight tug on the lead produced the desired tap-tap-tap, the second, however, went a little too far and he felt the lead nestle into the silt bed just behind the 'hump.' He was in no mood to retie the P.V.A. stringer so disconsolately laid the rod on the rest and clipped on the bobbin before wandering along to Chris's swim for some solace. His dark mood soon lifted with the banter that flowed between them, accepting the biting sarcasm flung at him by his ruthless partner. This was enhanced tenfold when, an hour after the sun had set so spectacularly, he heard his buzzer sound three or four times. He rapidly returned to his swim to see the bobbin on the rod that had successfully landed on the 'hump' a few inches lower than a few hours earlier. Not sure what to do, his hand hovered over the rod in readiness whilst Chris urged him to strike. Then, as the bobbin began a slow return to its previous position, he heeded his friend's advice and swept the tip high into the air. Although he felt a resistance it gave him a sickening feeling in his stomach because he knew what had disturbed his only well placed bait and, three minutes later, his fears were confirmed as he unhooked a tench in the margins before turning to tie on another bait. The night was very dark and he had trouble lining up the marker he used on the far tree-line, but he had cast to the spot many times that season so hurled his new offering in the required direction, hoping he had the distance right. Pulling back a fraction revealed no tap-tap but he knew he would be lucky to hit the feature in the dark so put the rod back down and reset the bobbin.

By four in the morning he had repeated the whole process three times, his clothes stinking of tench slime and his mind fuzzy from lack of sleep. He had long since dispensed with the stringers and, in a bid to avoid another lime-green alarm call, flung his single pop up into the margins to his right, throwing a handful of tiger nuts after it. He fell back into bed and pulled the sleeping bag over his head, hoping never to see another tench for as long as he lived.

He was being molested by a large bumble-bee which kept prodding him with its sting, but it did not sting rather than tickle. Then it slapped his face!

"Quill! Quill! Wake up you berk, you've got a run. Come on, it's been going for ages, are you deaf?" came Chris's insistent voice, cutting through his dreamy sleep like a feather through jelly!

"Wha... whayasay? Wassat bloody noise, Rhodie?" he attempted to enquire but all that came out was a strange burbling sound.

"Come on get up you *******," screamed Chris this time, and the effect was like a shower of cold water in the face. Stan sat bolt upright and suddenly knew exactly what to do. He rolled from his bed and stood up by his rods before picking up the offending wand which he struck firmly over his left shoulder. It was the hastily cast margin bait, and the perpetrator of the early morning raid had made off with its booty a long way along the tree-line. However, all that pre-breakfast exercise had obviously not agreed with it because, once Stan had stemmed its initial run, it seemed to have little fight left and was soon wallowing close in and waiting for Chris to oblige with the net, which he did with aplomb. There was none of the usual caterwauling by the jubilant pair because they were both in different states of consciousness - Stan's semi, and Chris bewildered! Stan was still not fully coherent, but made himself sufficiently understood to Chris who turned and replied, "Bit of a lump I think, Quill. Oh, yep. We know you don't we, fella?"

Stan looked at the large expanse of flank and, recognising it as the one belonging to his thirty five, let out a half hearted victory shout. This time it weighed six ounces less than a year previously, but after a season where neither of them had seen a fish of this size, it was most welcome. The preceding set of circumstances made the taste even sweeter for a rapidly awakening Stan. By the time they were watching it swim away, everything was back to normal and they shouted and shook hands as they had done many times before, Stan chuckling to himself at the thought of the banter they would have later.

This capture, as fortunate as it was, acted like a cork from a bottle, and the contents that came flowing forth was a succession of the lake's larger specimens. The next half dozen sessions, up to and including the first couple of winter sessions, saw the two of them land nine carp but, unlike earlier in the season, over half of them were in excess of twenty eight pounds including another thirty pound mirror to Chris. This fish came as part of a brace with a twenty nine pound linear and was later recognised as the second thirty Chris had caught the previous season, this time turning the scales to a little under thirty two pounds. Happiness was unconfined and their confidence soared, so much so that they decided to persevere on the lake for the rest of the winter in the vain hope of catching some big, cold weather carp. The first two weekends in November seemed to indicate that their decision was a good one, both sessions producing a twenty pound carp to Chris, with Stan chipping in with a mid-double on the first weekend. Then the weather became very wintry and the first frosts of the season curtailed their run of good fortune. With Christmas looming and no end in sight to the cold weather the pair relented and decided to revisit Winters Farm, fishing the first lake in the hope of a few runs. The weather was in total contrast to their last visit when Chris had landed the surprise twenty and instead of gale force winds and driving rain, the skies were bright blue and cloudless with the low winter sun making sunglasses a necessity. The forecast was for conditions to remain steady for the next few days and both anglers had brought an extra sleeping bag to combat the frosty night ahead.

They arrived on Saturday morning and crunched across the frosted ground to the sunny North Bank, not too concerned about fish location but more about picking the bank that would receive the most sun during the day!

They had taken to cooking a few meals to take with them rather than rely on tinned food or take-aways, and it was no surprise that the menu tonight was very curried! With a couple of bottles of wine to wash it down and a small hip flask of brandy to cheer up the coffee, there was very little fear of them actually needing a second sleeping bag - more likely was that they may spontaneously combust! Despite the maximum sunlight to their bank, the frost still remained in the shade and the few puddles around had a thin layer of ice over them and prospects for the night looked decidedly chilly. Little thought had been put into bait placement on their initial arrival but, once warmed by the sun and a couple of cups of tea, it was soon out with the plumbing float and do the thing properly. In the early afternoon, Stan landed their first fish of the session - a common of just over ten pounds. The fish felt freezing cold and Stan took little time in returning it to the ominously still lake, looking across at the rapidly sinking sun and realising that daylight was soon to be replaced by a very long, cold, dark night. The prospect did not fill him with joy but they were there, now, so they had to make the most of it and that they did. Within a couple of hours of dark they had consumed a huge curry and were washing it down with the second bottle of red wine when Chris's buzzer squawked into life. On lifting the rod Chris could tell something wasn't quite right but, not being in the best of conditions, he continued to reel the patently small fish towards the net. Then the problem made itself apparent when, on trying to net the fish, Stan came across an interesting problem - he couldn't sink the net below the lake's surface! A minute or so later, after pushing and cursing, it suddenly dawned on them what the problem was - the lake had frozen! Sure enough, on shining a torch out across the lake, they could see the beam bouncing off the icy blanket that now covered two thirds of the lake. At their feet Chris's line disappeared through a hole in the ice whilst being tugged hither and yon by a very bored carp. Almost as if the torch had been a candle, once the beam lit upon the tethered line they saw it chafe against the ice for the final time and flap limply from the rod tip. The loss of the fish was of less concern than the possibility that they might get another bite, with no visible way of landing the victim, and they pondered the options before them. Wind in and go home - no chance! Wind in and go to sleep - some chance! Wind in, get drunk and go to sleep - every chance! The decision made, they wound the three remaining leads to the edge of the ice and then returned to Chris's bivvy to finish off the wine and cheer up a few cups of coffee. Pretty soon, at a frighteningly early hour on a Saturday night, they were both snuggling up in their respective duvet mountains.

Despite dropping five degrees below zero, the temperature had very little chance of penetrating the central heating surrounding the recumbent anglers and the sun was steadily rising in the eastern sky when the first stirrings were seen within the multi-coloured sleeping quarters. Once awake, it was a battle of wills between angler and bladder but, inevitably, bladder won and soon the only cloud in the sky was a steamy one as both of them tried to complete the necessary ablutions as quickly as possible in order to warm their gradually chilling extremities! Stan peeked from beneath his cover over the solid and unmoving lake, and glancing at his rods he could see that ice was forming on the tips of his rings. There was nothing else for it so, pulling the bag over his head, he dozed back off into a fitful sleep. Eventually, both of them rose and after a couple of cups of very warming tea, began the agonising process of packing the still freezing tackle away, stopping frequently to hug their frost-bitten fingers to their sides in order to transfer a little warmth to the numbed digits. Needless to say there were no foolhardy carp hanging on the end of their lines, all three of which had to be broken in order to get the line back.

That session was the last of the year and, as a new decade dawned, they spent the next few, fishless weeks discussing the season past and that to come. It was evident that they were, once again, recapturing the same fish and when, a month or so later, they were to compare photos with a couple of the lake's regulars it became glaringly obvious that there were only three different thirties in the lake. Or at least three that got caught regularly. The other thirty, which they had not caught, gave itself up very infrequently but, at between thirty one and thirty two pounds, was not enough reason to continue fishing the lake and, so, with a few weeks of the season left they once again made the decision to move on.

This next move was a difficult one because they now knew that they could fish for nothing less than mid-thirties and so the obvious choice seemed to be Yateley. The problem was that, due to its 'circuit water' status, it did not really appeal to either of them and they desperately wanted to find another water that could offer them the same pedigree of carp, but that seemed unlikely in the immediate vicinity. As with all of these things, the first they heard of their future venue was merely a hint, a whisper, a passing comment, but when all these were added together over a few weeks a pattern began to emerge and an idea to form. So it was that, a fortnight into the close season, they were making their way across the M4 to Burghfield on the outskirts of Reading.

As the M4 skirts the south of Reading it is flanked by a number of mature gravel pits that were dug in the mid '50's to provide the necessary raw material to build the motorway, the pits quickly filling with water and becoming a haven for all forms of wildlife. Many species of waterfowl and water-dependent birds were to be found along their banks and surrounding woodland, and mammals from the smallest vole to the largest badger also used these oases as breeding and feeding grounds. And then there were the fish. All freshwater species thrived in the nutrient rich waters and, following the drought of fifteen years earlier when a lot of normally submerged bank side was left dry and fallow for almost a year, the natural larder had bloomed and all the fish species had benefited, as had their predators. It seemed that many pits in the south of England were reaching a stage in their lives that was akin to adulthood in humans, when they were able to put to good use the bounty laid before them, and the more adventurous anglers could also benefit from the riches therein.

"It's pretty big" had been the normal description of the pit they were visiting so, when they found The Botley Arms and drove two hundred yards further, as described, they thought that the huge inland sea in front of them must have been another water entirely. They retraced their steps, popping into the pub to quench their thirst and enquire of the landlord where they could find the pit.

"Oh, yep. That's him just up the road a piece. Can't miss him, gurt lump a water he is." Oh, bugger!

They went back for another look and their senses reeled. Surely the far bank must be home to Frenchmen, it was so far away, and it would take a ferry or something equally as sturdy to navigate these wind-tossed waters. 'But, here there be monsters,' thought Stan, remembering the stories they had been told of carp in excess of forty pounds captured from these very same windswept waters less than a year ago. They walked for a mile and lost sight of their car, another mile and they expected to see a strangely dressed cyclist shouldering onions ride by! At this end of the lake in the lee of the wind, however, they began to see beauty where before they had seen horror and, as they wandered along a thin point of land they marvelled at the profusion of bays and islands which were invisible from the car. By the time they had returned to that vehicle they had half convinced themselves that it could be worth a go. All they needed to do was see some fish, so a return was planned in a month or so when the weather was more clement and the carp more mobile.

So they did, and it was, and they were. The bays and islands were like a small piece of heaven. They spent the whole of an early May day wandering the banks and climbing its trees, spotting a few average specimens here and there until, in the early afternoon, Stan heard a whistle from Chris who had moved on a few hundred yards. Stan dropped from his perch and hustled quickly along the thickly wooded bank looking for some sign of his pal. Another whistle, this time from behind him, caused him to stop and look upwards; spotting Chris high in a tree that he had just passed. The elevated angler was becoming highly animated, giving the appearance of a gibbon on some performance enhancing drug, and Stan feared that he would be crushed by a falling Rhodie.

"Calm down," he whispered as loud as he could, "what have you seen you mad fool?"

"Come up here," Chris demanded and beckoned. "Come up here quick, Quill. You won't believe it!"

Stan couldn't resist an invitation like that and was soon shinning up the tree to join his high flying buddy. Once aloft, Stan found himself the most comfortable perch and, settling himself back against the trunk, adjusted his sunglasses on his nose and peered down into the gin clear water. At first he could see very little to excite him, apart from a couple of tench rooting around on the bottom then, from beneath the very tree in which he was sitting, the bulk of a large carp slowly emerged, followed shortly by another, then another. In all, six carp meandered around beneath the two intense onlookers but, although these were good fish, Stan estimated them at about mid-twenties and not really anything to get agitated about. He looked up towards Chris, about to mention this point, only to see him staring back down and frantically pointing further out.

"Over there, by the willow. See it, just coming out from under the willow now."

Stan looked where he was bade and nearly fell out of the tree! There, just coming from beneath the fronds of the willow branches, was the biggest carp he had ever seen and as it slowly swam towards them, the group of six turned to meet it. This allowed the watchers a chance to compare the size of the carp and it was obvious that the big fish was at least ten pounds heavier than the others. They continued to watch the group for another ten minutes until, as if at a hidden signal, the carp turned and swam purposefully away, leaving the anglers gawping at the empty lake. That was enough. They made the necessary enquiries and were readily furnished with tickets for the coming season. The rest of the close season was spent making plans, making baits, and making the odd thirty mile trip to the lake in the hope of a repeat performance but, despite seeing a number of twenty plus carp, they never set eyes on the bigger fish again before the off.

So they prepared for the first session of the first season of a new decade. A decade that would see them raise their sights higher than they could possibly have imagined at that moment - and Burghfield was just the first step.

It took little time for The Common and The Big-Scaled Mirror to acclimatise themselves to their new surroundings, just the time it took to circumnavigate a fifty acre lake a few times. Felcham Mere was a well-established lake on the northern perimeter of the New Forest, whose inhabitants thrived in the rich waters.

Being stream fed it suffered little variance in depth, with an average of eight to ten feet of water covering three quarters of the lake-bed. The newcomers soon found that, not only was there an abundance of invertebrate life for them to dine on but, most important for their increased growth and good health, a wealth of protein-in-a-shell food. Assorted mussels. There were masses of small pea mussels up to huge swan mussels, and snails of every kind and even some small crayfish. With this variety of food in their diet it was no wonder that all the fish in the lake were doing so well. As the decade neared its close, the wealth of protein and lack of angling pressure enabled all the carp to increase their size dramatically. As the last decade of the twentieth century began, the lake was home to four carp in excess of forty pounds and none of them seemed likely to slow their growth rate. Fish of this size could not go unnoticed, though, and every now and then rumours would circulate the local angling community of the two huge fish in Felcham Mere.

The main rumour-mongers were the infrequent bream and tench anglers who tried to outwit the huge specimens of their favoured species to whom the Mere was also home. But there had always been stories about the place - huge pike that swallowed goslings, isolated cottages haunted by ghosts, big cats roaming the woods and ravaging local poultry farms and, of course, uncaught monster commons. Little did the locals realise that one of their rumours was becoming truer by the day.

Part Three

The Common Bond

Chapter Ten - Burghfield

"...And Pearce has missed it!"

The first of a decade of endless penalty misses and jubilant German faces had Stan holding his head in his hands, a gesture that was being emulated by millions of his fellow countrymen. He watched almost dispassionately as Chris Waddle's kick sailed high into the crowd to end England's last, faint hopes of progressing to the World Cup Final.

The football had been a welcome distraction over the previous couple of weeks as the anticipated flood of huge mirror carp into his landing net had failed to materialise. The initial burst of opening day fever on a new water had gradually given way to a nagging fear that he was suddenly out of his depth. With the season just over a month old Stan had not even had a run on the new water. It was only the previous weekend that Chris had landed their first carp from the water, a twenty two pound common, and gave them a glimmer of hope that they may be starting to get to grips with the huge lake. How different his present feelings were in comparison to those of a month previously.

The last week of the close season was spent kneading, rolling, boiling and generally dusting down fishing tackle and, of course, discussing tactics during endless telephone conversations. With the start of the season falling at the weekend, it was no problem for Stan to blag an extra day from work. Chris had long since dispensed with that necessity by being very self-employed.

It was with ill-contained enthusiasm that the pair of thirty-something children giggled their way across the sleeping countryside on the Friday morning, arriving at a mist wreathed lake as the first rays of the sun shafted through the trees, turning them to gold on the far bank. The pair had come to the conclusion that the northern end of the lake would be their first port of call, this being the area where they had seen most fish in their infrequent pre-season visits, and they had earmarked three or four possible swims as potential starting points. Only one other car was evident on their arrival but, despite walking the banks for half an hour or so, they had no idea where the occupant might be or even if he was an angler at all. In fact, they saw no one else on the bank until early afternoon and were able to ready themselves for the coming night in an almost civilised fashion.

The fish were evident in amongst a small group of islands which were situated a quarter of a mile from the car park and a hundred yards from one bank. As this was one of the spots they had already pinpointed, it took little to persuade them to set up in the two obvious swims. Chris had brought a lilo with him and they spent the next couple of hours pouring tiger nuts onto the inflatable catapult, before lying on top of them and swimming out to the bars that ran off the islands, where they would up-end the whole lot before swimming back and repeating the whole process again. This worked admirably for the most part but, on one occasion, Stan got a bit carried away and thought he was Mark Spitz, attempting to reach his destination in record time but merely succeeding in depositing the whole lot just four strokes and five yards into his journey. Chris was not amused but Stan assured him that he was intending to fish a stroke rod in the margins and the whole thing had been pre planned! Chris just snorted derisively whilst pouring another bucket of particles onto the lilo and fixing his grinning mate with his best baleful stare. All that achieved was a wider grin and a hearty chuckle.

"Don't spill this lot or you're not having any more," he commanded, sternly.

"Sorry, Dad. I promise I won't do it again," came Stan's muffled reply as he eased himself most carefully onto his heavy load.

"Piss off!" retorted Chris before sitting back down and putting the kettle on once more.

No more mishaps were forthcoming and, by early afternoon, the pair were lying back in the warming sun with a beer in one hand and a very welcome bacon and mushroom sandwich in the other, toasting their bodies and a job well done. The only cloud on the horizon, in fact, wasn't. That is, it wasn't a cloud nor was it on the horizon. It was, in fact, a speedboat with skier attached and was very much in their faces. Then it was four hundred yards away. Then it was in their faces again, and so on for the best part of an hour. Obviously, they really hoped that the guy didn't fall off or ski into an island or something like that - heaven forbid! Unfortunately, he did nothing other than cling on for dear life and create the sort of waves a tsunami would be proud of, the water crashing over their rod tips every few minutes until, mercifully, he got bored or tired or had his arms pulled out. Whatever the reason, the water torture ended by three in the afternoon and within the time it took to boil another kettle, and drown another couple of teabags, the lake's surface was ruffled by nothing more than the light southerly breeze. The pair had been joined by a couple of young anglers, Rick and Dave, who were also fishing the lake for the first time and they spent the next few hours sharing their limited knowledge of the lake and generally getting to know each other. The newcomers were from Andover, thirty miles or so further down the M3 from where Stan and Chris lived, and had spent the past couple of seasons fishing at Yateley, but with little success barring a couple of low twenties from the Match Lake. They, too, had heard rumours of a couple of big fish from the lake in front of them and had, in fact, seen a photograph of a forty three pound mirror carp that had been caught from these very waters a year previously. This news was like a flame to a blue touch paper and it was all

Stan and Chris could do to stop themselves exploding like a pair of Roman candles on hearing it!

"Forty three! Who caught it? I mean, d'you know ...?" blurted Stan.

"What did it look like? Did it have a big scale on one side ...?" babbled Chris, almost tripping over the words.

"The left side. On the left side, just up from the tail..."

"You sure it was from here? I mean, could you see anything like ...?"

"Who did you say caught it? Did you recognise him ...?"

And so it went on for the next five minutes, like a pair of Gattling guns having a tennis match and with Rick and Dave alternating between crowd, umpire and ball boys! Eventually, the rallies slowed and the pair of stunned young anglers were able to intercede with comments of their own until normal service was, once again, restored.

With the sun gradually losing its ferocity, the younger anglers bade their hosts farewell and bon chance before making their way back to their chosen swims, a further three hundred yards along the bank from the car park.

"Nice guys. Not sure about that Rick, though, he looked a bit of a left footer with his ponytail, didn't he?" commented Stan.

"Nah, he was alright. I thought the other one was a bit quiet, though. Not giving much away, was he?" replied Chris.

"Yeah, I noticed that. Anyway, what the hell? By the morning we'll be able to identify that fish ourselves, won't we!" chuckled Stan.

Chris joined in the chuckling contest and off they went, into the land of carp-dreams, where every fish is a monster and you land three or four before breakfast. The rest of the evening was spent toasting the new season in fine style until, with very little left in the way of conversation, the pair sat back in a purple haze and awaited the midnight hour. As a distant church bell tolled in the new season, the lake was peppered with lead and a chorus of strange bleeps and whistles echoed along the bankside, fading gradually to an eerie silence. Stan lay down on his bedchair, smiling in anticipation of the great things to come, both in the immediate future and also in the forthcoming months, and was woken from his semi-comatose state by a series of bleeps from his right that rent the still, night air. He lay there silently for a minute, waiting for a call from his friend but none was forthcoming then, just as he began to relax back into his dream state, he heard some splashing along to his right that caused him to rise quickly and hurry along to Chris's swim.

"You in, Rhodie?" he enquired in his loudest stage whisper.

"Yeah. Bloody tench!" came the less than joyous reply.

"Oh. Right. It's a start though, mate," he ventured, by way of consolation.

"Yeah. Right!" growled Chris, and Stan made his way quietly back to his swim, hoping desperately that he wouldn't get a 'start' until the morning!

His wishes were granted but, once awake, he quite fancied the idea of sharing one of his friend's four night-time tench, especially as none of them weighed less than five pounds. Chris was less than happy about the whole affair and would have willingly swapped every one of the 'slimy-green bastards' for a few hours' kip, spurning Stan's offer of an early morning cuppa in order to return to that sacred realm.

By the time Chris had returned to the land of the fully awake the sun was high in the sky but Stan had nothing to report, having seen no carp in their immediate vicinity, nor knowing whether any had been caught at all. Rick and Dave had enjoyed a fish-free night and had little to report from further along the bank. Once again, the carp's calendar was working perfectly, although, with the sudden bombardment of lead it was probably not necessary for them to discern the angle of the sun to work out that the fishing season was once more upon them.

It didn't take a rocket scientist, either, to work out that the islands in front of Stan and Chris were not only lovely spots to put a few kilos of bait but, also, a perfect roundabout for the speedboats and water skiers. Saturday was also their favourite day for circumnavigating the lake at a bucketful of knots. So, by mid-afternoon on what was supposed to be their favourite day of the year, the pair were slowly cooking in the relentless sun whilst their baits rocked in the wave battered margins. They'd been despondently cast there after first Stan and then Chris had suffered cut-offs by the rapidly spinning propeller blades of the speedboats. All the cursing, screamed threats, arm waving and general air of discontent did nothing to stop the bombardment and the pair had finally admitted defeat and brought their baits into the margins until such time as the lake was once again safe for them to cast into. Rick and Dave had suffered just as badly and had decided to curtail their session a day early. It was obvious that Rick was less than happy at this decision, suggesting that they take a look in the back bays where the boats were unable to go. Dave, whose car they had arrived in, was adamant and the pair disappeared down the bank whilst the sun was still high in the sky.

"Hmmm," mused Stan, "the back bays."

"Yeah, just what I was thinking," concurred Chris.

So, before Dave's car had left the car park they were packed up and on their way along the bank to the car park, only to turn back along the opposite bank that led to the back bay. On their arrival, ten minutes later, they were both dripping with sweat and flung their tackle to the floor. Chris picked up one of the water containers and poured half the contents over his head before passing it to his dripping companion, who repeated the act over his own, steaming cranium. Refreshed, they left the tackle where it was and strolled along the pleasantly shaded banks until they came to a peninsula of land that separated the main lake from the back bays. They knew that a swim at the far end looked out on an island some forty yards distant and that two people could fish it comfortably. As they rounded the last bush they came to a sudden halt and their hearts sank as they saw the bright green of an umbrella through the last few branches. So this was where the missing car owner had hidden himself. They wandered into the swim and made a few pre-emptive enquiries as to his fortune but got little in reply so left within a few minutes, not before both noticing the drying weigh sling and unhooking mat.

"He's had one, hasn't he?" blurted Stan as they left the swim.

"Yeah, certainly looked like it. Happy bugger, weren't he?" replied Chris.

"So, where to now, Keemo Sabi?"

"Hmmm, right round to the river bank, I suppose. What d'you reckon?" suggested Chris.

"S'pose so, mate. Not a lot else to go on and I don't fancy another day with those bloody boats. "

"Yeah, right," said Chris, and led the way back along the peninsula before turning left towards the river.

Once away from the main part of the lake it was like entering a different world, with back bays, small spits of land and small islands that could barely support one tree. The speedboats were a distant memory and the increasing power of the sun's rays was diffused by the verdant tree growth, and carp were here, too. Beneath the fronds of a huge weeping willow, whose drooping branches delicately flicked the lake's surface, they spied two small carp lazily cruising towards them. Standing stock-still, the pair of wide eyed onlookers held their breath as the carp, both commons, swam casually by almost within touching distance. Just as Stan turned to Chris with a smile, he glimpsed another movement out of the corner of his eye and once again held his breath as another fish hove into view. This time, however, he couldn't help but gasp as, ever so slowly, the full expanse of the fish was revealed to them. They stared, open-mouthed, as a huge scaly mirror carp ambled along the marginal shelf in front of them before suddenly sensing their presence and, with a flick of its huge tail, spooked from the area whilst leaving an impressive bow wave in its wake.

"Jesus! Did you see that?" gasped Stan, rhetorically.

"Oh yes, I saw it mate. That was a monster," replied Chris, excitedly. "Did you see those huge scales along its back, they looked like bloody dinner plates!"

"Yep, and I reckon it's time for dinner, Rhodie. Hungry?"

There was no need for a reply and so, without a further word, they turned on their heels and swiftly retraced their footsteps to the pile of tackle they had deposited fifteen minutes earlier. Chris grabbed as much as he could and began a staggered trot back to the fancied spot lest someone else should decide on a move but, of that, there was little chance and the only other soul who was as intent as him was the swiftly following Stan. As they neared the willow, they slowed to a crawl and carefully laid down their tackle as far from the lake as possible before quickly returning for the remainder of the gear. Their return journey was suddenly halted by a distant but piercing and familiar sound - the scream of a tortured bite alarm. Glancing quickly at Stan, Chris nodded in the direction of the peninsula and the less than talkative angler at the end of it, before heading off along that spit of land and the possible recipient of the mid-afternoon run. As they neared the swim, Chris slowed and continued more stealthily, stopping by the final tree lest they were mistaken. As he peered around the trunk he could see the twelve foot length of carbon attempting to point at the sun, but unable to raise itself above forty five degrees due to the weight at the other end of the line. Chris motioned for Stan to follow and they casually sauntered into the swim, making enough noise so as not to give the guy a heart attack.

"Well, you've either hooked a motor boat or that's a big old carp, mate," ventured Chris in a 'break the ice' sort of fashion. The approach obviously worked, or else the angler was welcome of some support, either way his words flowed more freely than before.

"Feels like a bloody motor boat," he began "but I can assure you it's not. I only hooked it down there."

With a nod of his head to the right, he indicated a small channel that joined this area of the lake to the back bay where Chris and Stan had just deposited their tackle, and it was this knowledge that caused them to look at each other with eyebrows raised. After five minutes of patient line retrieval, the combatant seemed to have things under control and smiled raggedly when the fish rolled fifteen yards from the bank, revealing huge, plate-like scales that caused the two onlookers to gasp and groan at the same time.

"D'you want a hand with the net?" offered Chris more out of politeness than willingness.

He had never even seen a fish of this size on the bank, let alone been called upon to land one, and he would have felt little effrontery if his offer had been declined. This relief was not forthcoming, however, and the angler nodded his acceptance in the knowledge that he was playing a carp many pounds bigger than anything he had previously landed, and wanted to have as much control as possible during the last, vital seconds. The next minute seemed to pass in slow motion for all three men, and all for differing reasons, but the one moment they all shared was when, with the carp's head just sliding over the net cord, the hook pulled free and the lead shot up into an overhanging branch.

The next three seconds passed as if dipped in treacle. The anguished angler and astonished Stan watched in horror, then delirium, as Chris dropped the net cord down into the water, pushed the handle forward as if he were sweeping the floor with an industrial yard broom, then scooped the net back up out of the water. It was brought to a halt by the weight of the carp within its mesh. It would have been difficult for an onlooker to discern who the captor was in the next few manic, ear splitting, arm waving, back-slapping seconds as all three anglers celebrated a phenomenal capture. Eventually, they calmed down and set about the task of weighing the huge fish. Chris had trouble lifting its bulk from the water, requesting a bit of help from Stan, who was more than willing to lend a hand in this momentous capture. They both grunted and strained during the five-yard journey to the unhooking mat, reverently laying down the massive fish and allowing the victor the pleasure of peeling back the mesh to reveal his prize. As they had guessed, here lay the big, plate-scaled mirror they had spied only minutes earlier and obviously less spooked than had appeared, but they had never thought it would look this big and this beautiful, nor that they would be gazing down upon it so soon. The angler (Tom, they found out later) slid his prize into the dampened sling and watched intently as both Stan and Chris eased it off the mat with the zeroed scales, all three of them watching the needle on its seemingly endless rotation of the dial.

"Shit!" was all that Chris could muster as the pointer finally rested a few ounces above the thirty eight pound mark. All agreed, they lowered the great fish back down before heartily shaking Tom's hand and banging him on the back. Stan ran off to get their cameras whilst Tom held the fish in the lake, a look of bemused contentment upon his face. They all gasped at the size and beauty of the fish and then repeated the handshakes after Tom had returned the fish and punched the air in triumph.

They stayed in the swim for an hour or so, very welcome now, and learnt that this was Tom's third season on the lake and only his sixth fish. He had, indeed, caught a fish that morning, a common of twenty one pounds, but this was what he was here for. The previous year he had caught three carp, topped by a mirror of thirty one pounds, but he had also lost a big fish at the net when the hook had pulled out and he had been unable to perform the manoeuvre that Chris had executed so successfully. In that hour they learnt much about the lake, and not all of it encouraging, with stories of car break-ins, tackle theft, Sunday morning regattas and winds that could make matchwood out of brollys and bivvies. But, they also learnt that the lake held at least six carp over thirty pounds including the forty-three that Ricky and Dave had shown them the photo of. There was every possibility of a few uncaught whackers in this vast, inland sea - including, according to Tom, a massive common carp that had been seen many times in the company of the forty three pound mirror and dwarfed it by at least five pounds!

This knowledge diluted the other, more unsavoury points that Tom had brought up and on their journey home the next day, following an uneventful night, all their talk was of the monster carp they had witnessed and of uncaught common carp as big as caravans!

The next few sessions followed a similar course to the first with more altercations with water skiers, more green alarm calls in the wee, small hours and further sightings of a few small commons, but no actual close encounters. Then, a month into the season, Chris hooked a carp and all hell broke loose.

Stan's wife, Jean, had been unable to join him at the lakeside much over the previous few years due to the child minding duties of motherhood, and on the few occasions she did make it, it was invariably with children and, therefore, only for a few hours. Now, however, Stevie was old enough to entertain himself - and that was normally with a fishing rod, like his father. Laura and her friends took it in turns to stay round each other's house on most weekends, which at last left Jean with some free time which she filled easily. She still enjoyed her time by the lake and it took little for Stan to convince her to join him for the weekend, with the promise of her own bedchair, a huge sleeping bag and as much sleep as she could cope with. There was also the lure of a float rod and the chance of a few roach and perch and, although not her primary reason for going, she had learnt to enjoy this style of fishing and would certainly give it a go over the weekend. Not to be left out, Chris talked his girlfriend, Sam, into joining them and by Friday they were set fair for a weekend of barbecues, beer and big fat mirror carp.

The weather had been settled for most of the week and looked to be staying that way, with light clouds and bright sunshine during the day and a light north easterly to tone down the heat of the sun. Due to these conditions, the anglers decided to set up at the southern end of the lake for the first time. They knew just the spot that would allow them all to fish in close proximity whilst still having plenty of water to share, and also little shade to disturb the girls' sunbathing. This was a point of land thrust almost one hundred and fifty yards into the lake, forming a bay on either side. At its tip it was possible for two anglers to set up back to back and fish out into separate bays, whilst in between them was a nice area of grass the size of a large dining room - perfect for sunbathing and barbecuing. The wind was rippling more into the right hand bay so, when Stan won the spoof, he naturally chose that side - the fact that he had spied, from a tree, several carp lazily sunning themselves near a distant weed bed may have helped a little in his choice as well.

After the ritual of casting, cursing, recasting and catapulting, the four of them gathered on their lawn and began the other ritual of chicken and sausage cremation, mosquito crushing and thirst quenching. So it was that, by the time that the only light in the area was the slowly dwindling glow from the dying embers of the barbecue coals, everybody was very ready for bed, the space between conversation and subsequent bursts of laughter becoming ever greater. Tottering unsteadily to his feet, Chris held his can aloft and bade his good friends farewell before turning, treading on his own shoelace and toppling flat on his face. Stan thought that his lungs were about to burst, his laughter gushing forth like a raging torrent, and the sound of Chris's own, manic guffawing did little to stem the flow. Eventually, after many minutes, the two of them lay there clutching their sides lest their broken ribs should pierce flesh, gasping for breath and manfully trying to stop another burst of laughter, much the same as you try to stop hiccups by holding your breath. The two girls, although amused, just shook their heads in confusion and carried on chatting inanely, attempting to ignore the quivering heaps on the floor. After many minutes everything had returned to normal and Chris was carefully repeating the manoeuvre that brought about the breakdown in communication when a piercing scream shattered the relative silence. At first nobody could work out what was happening but, with the scream carrying on at the same pitch, it took Jean to point out the obvious.

"That's a bite alarm, isn't it?" came her sobering observation, and with it a scene even more amusing than the previous one, only this time nobody was looking. Stan and Chris both jumped unsteadily to their feet and performed brilliant parodies of the proverbial headless chicken as they ran around each other trying to work out whose swim was whose.

Jean's further observation of "It's coming from over there," served only to enhance the growing confusion and panic in the two de-stringed marionettes. Where the hell was there? And how did you get there? Almost bored by the farce, Sam grabbed hold of Chris and shoved him in the direction of his swim and this impetus was like a slap to the face. Chris immediately weaved his way successfully between the brolly and the bush to his rods and lifted the offending wand to give respite to the tortured alarm. The whole episode had seemed to last for hours but, in fact, the alarm had been singing for little more than ten seconds and the fish had made little headway from its original pick up point. The next few minutes could have been disastrous but sanity and sobriety soon held sway and Stan took little time in netting the party pooper. All through the short fight Chris was cursing yet another tench but, as Stan lifted the net he knew that assumption to be very wrong and took little time in putting Chris right.

"Some tench mate! If it is, it's a bloody record, that's for sure!" came another verbal face slapping for Chris.

"What? Let me see. Is it a carp then?" he demanded, peering over his friend's shoulder as he hoisted the net from the water. "Bloody hell, it is! It's a bloody carp! Hah, ha!"

Stan lowered the prize onto the unhooking mat whilst Chris found a torch to light proceedings and the wavering beam revealed his declaration to be true as, there on the mat lay a fine, lightly scaled mirror carp. Chris continued chortling away to himself whilst getting the sling and scales and, shortly, he was peering at them a little out of focus as Stan held them aloft.

"How big is it?" enquired Jean, curiously.

"Nearly twenty three, I think. Have a look, Quill," said Chris, whilst taking the scales from his friend and hoisting them for his perusal.

"Yep. Twenty two fourteen I would say," confirmed Stan. "Well done, son, the first of many I reckon. What's the time?"

"Just gone one o'clock. Why?" queried Jean whilst looking at her watch.

"What we gonna do, Rhodie? Sack it or photo it?" asked Stan.

"Sack it, I reckon," came his mate's reply from out of the darkness of his brolly, "it'll be light by four, half four. We can do the photos pretty early and be ready for a bit of breakfast!"

With that, he emerged, grinning, from beneath the brolly grasping a green carp sack and proceeded to dunk it into the lake before holding it open for Stan to gently slip the fish into. Then, with Stan steadying him, he carefully lowered the bulging sack into the margins, securing the cord tightly to a bankside tree. Suddenly, the excitement seemed to take its toll, a wave of lethargy swept over them and within minutes there was no one to be seen as they all retired to their respective beds.

The rest of the session followed much the same pattern as previous ones. Stan and Chris spent a fruitless afternoon firing Chum Mixers at any passing dorsal fin and climbing numerous trees in a bid to ensnare an unsuspecting carp but the weather meant that the carp were intent on the same thing as the women. Unfortunately for the blokes on both counts, it was sunbathing!

The night also followed a similar pattern but there was no final, one-legged clog dancing nor bite alarm hunt and the session ended with no further carp to either of them. Jean had dabbled a little on both mornings and had succeeded in not only fooling a few small perch, but also an unwary male tench of just over three pounds - her largest fish to date and one worthy of celebration.

But they had caught their first carp from this huge expanse of water and their confidence was once again on the up. The next couple of sessions were spent in the same area, as the weather remained settled and the carp continued to sun themselves in the shallower waters. They could not repeat Chris's success so, by early August, their confidence cup had once again sprung a leak and they knew that they must go in search of some different fish to see if they were feeding elsewhere.

So, once again, they found themselves at the north end of the lake in the hope that they could find some more fish than the south end held. Chris had arrived early on Thursday morning and, by later that day, had found a few fish in front of Tom's Swim, so had decided to set up there, and was in extremely confident mood on Stan's arrival later the next day.

The swim looked out on an island, some forty yards distant, and this allowed both anglers to fish an island margin, the left hand one already being attended to by Chris which left Stan custody of the equally inviting right hand side. After some extensive plumbing, Stan found a couple of likely looking spots and dispatched his pop-up rigs to them. One was cast to a small bar that extended from the right hand side of the island for a few yards and was covered by four feet of water, the other was cast straight at the middle of the island under the drooping branches of a weeping willow. This was a spot so inviting that all that was missing was a big neon sign saying Cast Here! Chris had also seen the sign and had put a bait to the left side of the tree where it formed a small bay with a smaller overhanging bush and, for the first time in many weeks, their confidence cup was filling up again.

By early evening they were sitting back and enjoying the sights and sounds of summer by the lake, attempting to identify as many wildfowl as possible from the throngs that frequented the lake when, shaking them from their reverie, a voice from behind alerted them to a visitor.

"Hello, guys. Is one of those cold ones for me?"

On turning, they spied the familiar, sinewy figure of Rick smiling down at them. With his long, dead straight black hair normally kept in a ponytail, much like the one Rodney donned in 'Only Fools and Horses.' Coupled with a pronounced widow's peak, it gave him the appearance of a young, modern day Dracula but nothing could be further from the truth. Whilst

Stan extracted a can of cold lager from the cool box, Chris enquired as to his whereabouts over the past few weeks and also to the absence of Dave.

"Well, I was beginning to wonder where you two had got to. Me and Dave have fished up here a bit but he's knocked it on the head, now," came the reply.

"Why's that then?" asked Stan, passing the very welcome cold offering into Rick's outstretched hand.

"Cheers," said Rick and, quickly pulling the ring, poured half of the contents down his throat in one gulp, sighing ecstatically as the liquid lifesaver performed its task.

"Bloody hell, I needed that!" he exclaimed, and then continued to answer Stan's question. "Car got done a couple of weeks ago, didn't it? Up in the car park. Smashed the side window and nicked the stereo and all his tools. He was bloody fuming, especially when the insurance said they would only pay out two hundred quid. I mean, the tools were probably worth near on a grand. So, that was the final nail in the coffin. He'd really struggled to get to grips with it and I think he was just looking for an excuse to get out of it."

"What about you then, Rick, have you had any, or what?" asked Chris.

"Nah! Well, sort of. I had a couple of tench one night then, first thing in the morning, the same rod goes off, same sort of fight so I heaved it in and there on the end is a bloody common carp! Seven pounds it weighed. Not really what I came here for but I suppose I can only go up from there. What about you guys, you had any?" They related the tale of Chris's twenty, and of the netting of Tom's thirty eight, and brought him up to date with events, prior to asking where he planned to fish that evening.

"Well, I had planned on fishing here, but that looks like it's out of the question," he chuckled, "so I may fish round on the river bank in the swim where I had the common from. But first, I'd better have another lager 'cos this one seems to have evaporated!" he said, smirking whilst returning the empty can to Stan.

Handing the extremely personable young angler another can, Stan posed another question,

"Why don't you set up just back there?" indicating a small swim forty yards back down the peninsula. "You can still fish across the back bay and I won't have so far to walk when your lager keeps evaporating, will I?"

Gentle laughter spilled out from the trio, and Rick seemed to ponder the idea for a few seconds before posing the obvious question,

"Have you got enough food, though?" he asked, smiling, whilst eyeing the other contents of the cool box.

"You've got some front for someone with a ponytail, ain't ya?" retorted Chris, but his beaming smile and twinkling eyes betrayed the total lack of malice in the remark. "Yeah, we've got loads, as long as you like curry, fella."

"Like curry! I bathe in Biryani and have Korma cornflakes for breakfast! Just call me Abdul, sahib!"

That was good enough for all of them so, whilst Rick left to get his gear set up, Chris and Stan began preparing for the coming night.

"He's alright really, ain't he?" conceded Stan.

"You said he was a left footer before!" squawked Chris in reply.

"Yeah, well maybe he is, but he ain't a bad one, is he?" joked Stan, whilst peeling the skin from an onion and waving the knife about like a baton. The subject of their discussion soon returned to their swim and they settled down for an evening of curry, lager and humorous repartee.

The sun had long since departed when, totally out of the blue, Rick piped up, "On the way here, this afternoon, I was following one of those horse boxes and it had 'CAUTION HORSES' on the side. What are they, then?" he asked, dryly.

Quick on the uptake, Stan expanded on the strange theme, "Oh yeah, you know. You've heard of dray horses and race horses, well Caution horses are similar but they're really paranoid. You can spot them easily, though, they're the ones that tend to have one hoof to their lips whilst looking around furtively."

Equally sharp, Chris carried on the bizarre description,

"Yeah, and you can always tell them at Kempton and Aintree and that. When all the other horses jump the fence, the Caution horse stops, looks left and right then carefully climbs over the fence - they normally come last!"

"Sort of a Green Horse Code, then," added Stan, as the heights of the ridiculous were being scaled, and then Rick took them into orbit.

"Of course, you know why there are so few of them, don't you?" he began. "Well, the one's before these horses were even more paranoid and cautious, and the mares used to insist that the stallions wore contraceptives."

He stopped and smiled at the two puzzled listeners who had the sort of looks on their faces that said 'What are you talking about?' so, after a few seconds of silence, he added, "you know, pre-caution horses!"

A mixture of groans, laughter and various missiles greeted this revelation and proceedings deteriorated rapidly, as they are wont to do in the dark hours after midnight, the night echoing with laughter until tiredness dictated the end to a fine evening's entertainment.

Bright sunlight dazzled Stan's eyes and he wondered why on earth they were open - sleep and lowered lids seeming to be a much more preferable condition to be in.

"Quill! Quill! Are you awake?" came Chris's insistent call, and the answer for Stan's wakeful state.

"Yep, coming," replied a temporarily blinded Stan, groping underneath his bedchair for the respite of sunglasses, then naturally enquired, "got one on, fella?"

"Yeah. The one next to the willow," explained Chris. "It dropped back and I thought it was a tench at first, then it charged off to the left and I had to backwind for about twenty yards. Now it's coming in real slow, covered in weed I think."

As Rick wandered slowly into the swim to see what all the commotion was, Chris implored Stan, "Get my shades for me, Quill, I can't see a bloody thing at the moment."

Whilst Stan dodged into Chris's bivvy as he was bade, Rick tried to ask all his questions at once, "You got one on then, Chris? What time is it, anyway? Why 'Quill', Stan?"

"Yep," came Chris's reply to the first question and, whilst putting the sunglasses over his friend's tearful eyes, Stan answered the other two.

"About six, I suppose. My second name is Peacock, y'know - peacock quill. Chris's name is Rhodes so I call him Rhodie, what about you?"

"My surname's Powell, some people call me Spud!" replied Rick, straight-faced. Stan was just about to ask the obvious question when Chris interjected.

"Hello! Man playing carp here!"

"I'll call you Rick then," said Stan whilst bending to pick up the landing net.

The fish and its wreath of weed was no more than five yards out but it was difficult to gauge the carp's size and Stan knew he had to make very sure with the net. Dropping to one knee, he lowered the mesh into the margins and waited for Chris to ease the whole lot over the net cord and, just as the captor was about to say 'Now!' Stan lifted the net and felt the satisfying surge of the fish vainly attempting to escape its tether.

"Yerrrs!" screamed an elated Chris, whilst Rick lent forward and patted him heartily on the back. "Well done, mate. Any chance of a cuppa?" he asked, smiling and raising his eyebrows, indicating the humour in the question.

"Very soon, Spud. Very soon," retorted Chris, with a similar arching of the eyebrows.

"Hello!" mimicked Stan. "Man holding a carp in the net!"

The other two went about the normal procedure for unhooking and weighing a carp before Chris went over to help Stan to heave the netful of weed and carp onto the unhooking mat. As they gradually removed the weed, the familiar fully scaled flank of a common carp was revealed. It was obviously in excess of twenty pounds - four pounds in excess the scales revealed, and it was smiles all round before Chris let the fish swim strongly away, his victory cry echoing in the early morning air.

"Any chance of that cuppa, now, Rhodie?" repeated Rick as he heaved the smiling captor from the lake.

"No problem, Spud. Got any biscuits?" replied Chris, whilst shaking the young angler's hand.

The day was one of muted celebration and much tree climbing, but no further carp were seen nor caught and Stan began to understand how Dave must have felt. With two months of the season gone, he had not even had a run from a tench or a bream, let alone a carp, and his confidence was taking a bit of a beating.

The next few weeks were a struggle for all of them, with the carp utilising the vastness of the lake to make good their escape from prying eyes but, with Rick tending to join them on a Friday evening, they worked hard to track down their quarry. At the beginning of September, this continued graft paid off when Stan spied two or three leaping carp on one of his many walks around the lake. The three anglers had continued fishing the north end of the lake but it was in the huge middle section that Stan had tracked down the carp. The knowledge induced a swift move by the trio and, by mid-morning on the first Saturday in September, they had spread themselves out along a lawn-like bank to the left of the sailing club. The fish had shown just within casting distance and, as three separate marker floats were peeking above the mild swell, Chris shouted to the other two and pointed to a flat spot to the left of his marker.

"Big, fat mirror!" he bellowed, and the others joined in as the fish repeated its antics for all to see.

They all agreed that there was a gravel bar at the distance the fish had jumped and that feature was soon peppered with leads and flying boilies. The waves of the final baiting onslaught had barely died when Stan's left hand rod tip was wrenched down and line flew from the spool, the alarm not even turned on yet. It took some moments for an astonished Stan to realise what was happening but, when he did he lifted the rod high in the air and felt the satisfying power of a rapidly moving carp on the end. His fellow anglers were soon at his side and offering the usual advice, but Stan was just concentrating on not letting his first carp in six months fall off. After the initial burst of power, the fish came slowly towards the bank, zigzagging from left to right on its journey and, soon, it was Chris who was kneeling with net in hand and preparing to slip it under Stan's prize. The last few moments of the fight were, as usual, much better when viewed in hindsight and it was as much with relief as joy that Stan screamed on seeing the fish slip into the net.

The usual backslapping and congratulations followed, and a small crowd of sailing types gathered to witness the photographing of a very welcome twenty one pound mirror carp and captor. The sailing types then returned to their craft and proceeded to cleave up and down in front of the trio of very frustrated anglers, picking up Chris's lines on a couple of occasions but seemingly oblivious to his rantings. By the time they had finished tacking and tocking, or whatever it is they do, the day was near to its close and of the carp there was no further sign. What had begun as an inspired move had turned into nothing less than a disaster, totally detracting from Stan's success. By the time that the jolly jack tars emerged for their Sunday morning jaunt the anglers were long gone, having spent the night in semi serious discussion over their future on the lake.

What had really fuelled this discussion was Rick's revelation that he had heard of a smaller pit nearby that, although private for the past few years, had been purchased by a fairly wealthy angler who had formed a small syndicate on there. Rumour had it that the lake had produced a few thirty pound carp over the past few seasons, and also that the owner had had difficulty in filling the syndicate places. This knowledge had the three of them agreeing to find out as much about the lake as they could over the coming months with a view to applying for a syndicate ticket for the next season.

The next few sessions did little to dissuade them from this course of action, especially when an out of control wind surfer had clattered into Rick's line whilst he was playing his first decent carp of the year. The fifteen pound nylon being no match for a few hundred pounds of speeding idiot and snapping like cotton, much to Rick's displeasure and he aired his feelings in tones something like, "I say old chap. Dashed unfortunate that my line got in your way. Didn't harm you in any way, I hope!" Well, something like that!

The final straw came at the end of October when, after a session of bivvy-wrecking winds and driving rain, Stan returned to his car to find all four of his tyres slashed - no theft, just vandalism. Enough was enough, and when he eventually returned home - six hours later and a few hundred pounds the poorer - he immediately phoned Chris and told him, in no uncertain terms, that he had fished his last session on 'that shithole!' Chris found no reason to disagree, and a few phone calls later had Rick agreeing to join them on Coates for the winter, where they could plan for next season.

They had all made enquiries about the mysterious syndicate lake and had found out that it did, indeed, exist and had been a syndicate for a couple of years. Tickets were limited but rumour had it that they were not exactly selling like hot cakes and that a few words in the right ears could well secure them a place for the next season. They spent the weeks before Christmas trying to find out who the right ears belonged to - and the left ones, come to that!

The winter was hugely enjoyable, with the three anglers forming a strong friendship, and landing a couple of carp along the way, but the most important occasion came a week into the New Year when Rick came loping along the path in his familiar manner.

"What ho, chaps. How goes it my bonny lads?" came his cheerful greeting.

The others looked at each other in bewilderment at his hugely beaming smile and pondered the reason for it.

"Just got your leg over, or something, Ricky boy?" enquired Chris, subtlely.

"No, my old mate, Rhodie, much better than that," he replied, still beaming widely.

"Come on then, Spud, give it up, boy. What's with the grinning fool look?" joined in Stan, eager to learn the secret.

"These, my friends," he answered, whilst holding aloft some pieces of paper, a la Neville Chamberlain.

"What's that, a writ?" came Chris's impatient, snapping reply.

"Nope. Even better than that. It's us for the next few years." With that puzzling statement, he handed an A4 sheet of paper to each of the equally puzzled anglers and, at the top of each sheet was typed:

APPLICATION FOR MEMBERSHIP- KINGFISHERLAKE 1991/92

Incredulous at first, it took only a few seconds for the pair to start leaping and shouting and assailing their smiling benefactor with a thousand questions.

"How did you get these? I mean where from?"

"What's in there? Do you know?"

"How much is it?"

"Did you speak to the owner, or what?"

"What's the biggest fish? When can we go and have a look? Whereabouts is it ..?"

"Enough, already!" screamed Rick, holding his hands to his ears in a bid to blot out the avalanche of sound. "Enough boys. Calm yourselves down, get your good buddy Rick a nice cup of tea and I'll tell you a story."

That stemmed the tide of questions enough for him to relate all that he knew. Rather than carry on chasing rumours and suppositions, he had decided to take the bull by the horns so had popped into a tackle shop in Reading to ask if they knew anything about Kingfisher Lake. As luck would have it, one of the guys had just joined the lake and gave Rick a telephone number to call. Not one to shirk a challenge, he went straight to a phone box and called the number, getting straight through to the owner, a guy named Les Morgan. He couldn't have been more helpful and was soon giving Rick directions to the lake where he would meet him, show him round and hand over the all-important application forms. Rick found the lake quite easily and was immediately impressed by the tall, locked gates that barred the way to the lake and car park. Les turned up shortly after and spent the next hour walking Rick around the lake whilst filling him in on all the main information.

The lake had been two small gravel pits that had been joined together a couple of years ago, when Les had bought the land. They were both about forty years old and, by now, very mature and even in their winter shrouds, Rick could see that the banks would be lush and green in a few short months.

"What about the fish?" Stan blurted out, unable to contain himself.

"I'm coming to that, have patience, my son," replied Rick, calmly.

When the two separate lakes were drained as much as they could be, the extensive gravel bars limited the extent that they could be netted. They had caught a lot of small stunted commons, which were subsequently removed. However, there were also a dozen or so commons in excess of eighteen pounds which were later returned to the new, larger lake. Along with these, thirty mirrors ranging from fifteen pounds to thirty-two pounds were also put back into the lake but, and here was the interesting part, not all of the fish were netted from the lakes prior to the digging.

Rick paused for a sip of tea, relishing the steadily bulging eyeballs in the reddening faces of his two, rapt listeners, then carried on as if he were a presenter on Jackanory.

The larger lake was about twelve to fourteen acres with an average depth of twelve feet, however one corner was considerably deeper and it had proved impossible to lower the water level enough to give the netsman a chance of extracting anything from this deeper area. A month or so after the netting and digging had been completed, and the new lake had begun to refill naturally, a work party of eight men saw five fish just below the surface in the remaining acre of four feet deep water. All present agreed that at least three of the fish were larger than anything that had been netted. Within a few more weeks, the pit had filled up enough to allow the re-introduction of the original tenants, along with another dozen or so fish between sixteen and twenty-four pounds in weight that Les had acquired. Along with a few large tench and bream and the ever-present roach and perch, these fish made up the stock of the new twenty acre lake. Les had dubbed it Kingfisher, following his sighting of one of those magnificent birds which dived into a quiet corner one morning and reappeared with a beakful of fish.

This all took place over the winter two years previously, so this was the second season it had been fished. Les finished Rick's tour by showing him some photos that were kept in an album in a workman's shed that the bailiffs had seconded to keep a few nets and the like in. In the album were some impressive photos, mainly of twenties, but there were a couple of low thirties as well. However, Les was saving the best until last and handed over a second album once Rick had finished the first.

"These are this year's fish, the biggun's that is," he said with a smile.

There were sixteen photos, two of each fish, and Rick's eyes bulged as he took in the manna set before him and read the inscriptions beneath each photo. Three of the fish were long, lean mirror carp with big plated scales and weighed between thirty-three and thirty-five pounds, two of which had been caught twice. The fourth was a glorious common carp of thirty-two pounds, but it was the last two that blew him away. The first was a huge, grey almost leather carp that had the legend 'Dean, 37.12. 16/7/90' written beneath it. The second fish couldn't have been more different, being a long, dark linear with huge pectoral fins and a tail like two dinner plates welded together. Beneath the photo was a lovingly typed label that had been stuck to the page, which read: 'Don Leach with The Linear at 38lb 7oz. Caught 24th September 1990 P.B.'

Rick could feel the pride pouring out of the picture and couldn't wait to meet Don and warmly shake him by the hand. The final coup de grace came when Les casually said, whilst closing the album,

"Of course, they're only two of the three biggies we saw that day. The other one hasn't been caught yet, but it has been seen."

He left the last statement hanging in mid air and Rick snapped it up like a swallow snatching a crane fly.

"How big d'you reckon it is then, Les?"

Les smiled and completed the entrapment like a man who had done it many times before, which he had.

"It's been seen with The Linear on more than one occasion and rough estimates are that it's about three to four inches longer. If it's any deeper, I'm not sure, but it's a dark, almost black common carp and is unlike anything else in the pool. So, do you and your mates fancy it, then?" the last being said with a huge smile.

Forms were handed over, hands shaken and Rick was on his way like a man in a drunken dream.

Silence reigned once his story was complete, his two mesmerised companions digesting this wealth of information before looking, once again, at the forms that were the key to this Utopia.

"How much, then, boy?" asked Chris, breaking the spell.

"One eighty. Needed by the first of April," came the reply.

"Phew. That's a bit steep, innit?" came Stan's initial comment. "Suppose I'll have to knock that new carpet on the head then!"

With that, Chris and Rick both smiled and their nodding heads were enough acknowledgment. They were all in agreement, this was their next move and while they saw out the season on Coates, all their thoughts and discussions were of the coming season. When, three months later, the membership cards dropped on their respective doormats the time had come for their first serious look at the lake that, they hoped, held their dreams in its cool, clear waters.

Time passed. The carp enjoyed the wide open spaces of the mere, and the larder they had to offer, and were, by and large, left unmolested. Occasionally, a half-hearted attempt would be made to fish for the carp by a hopeful angler, but it would invariably end after a couple of fruitless sessions. Still they fed, still they grew and, very occasionally, still they picked up an angler's bait.

Ted was making his perennial visit to the lake, as he had done for the past few years and, as normal, was fishing his usual swim on the North Bank, near to the car. It was summer, so he used worms fished along the right hand margin (he had hooked a fish on worms from there six years ago, losing it after a couple of minutes, so he always fished the same tactic). After a few hours his silver paper indicator lifted slowly to the butt, then moved steadily towards the ring. Ted waited the required time before lifting the rod into the air, the tip pulling over and the ancient reel squealing as the fish tore off along the margins. Ted was totally unprepared to handle a fish of such power, as was his six pound line, and it was no surprise when the nylon snapped just above the split shot a few minutes later. Ted stood shaking for a minute or two before slowly packing away his tackle and walking to his car, the story that would keep him well lubricated at The Fox running over in his head.

The Common sulked in the branches of the snag tree for many hours, occasionally rubbing its mouth against the rotting wood in a bid to rid itself of the irritation there. Once again it had dropped its guard, but its immense size and power had proven enough to avoid capture and the lesson was, once again, well learnt. The knowledge held it in good stead for a couple more years.

Chapter Eleven - Kingfisher

"Chris! Chris!"

Stan's insistent calls alerted Chris to his whereabouts and he was soon joining his friend twenty feet above the ground in a less than sturdy willow tree. Their perch afforded them an excellent view of a secluded corner of the Main Lake, and in that corner Chris could see the objects of his friend's affections drifting in and out of some lily stems.

"Bloody hell, Quill, how many are there?" came his urgent enquiry.

"I've counted about fifteen different fish, and half of them are bloody huge!" Stan replied excitedly.

The season was little more than twenty four hours away and they had spent most of the day aloft, in search of just this sort of treasure trove. The previous month had been spent similarly and with moderate results as far as fish spotting was concerned, but they had been encouraged firstly by the lack of people they had seen on their weekend visits and, secondly, by the carp's instant attraction to their free offerings. They had decided to start on the bird food bait as well as the usual particle mix. It seemed that most of the carp, and the tench and bream, had been in total agreement with this decision, hoovering up everything that the three of them could fire into the lake.

They had also, with Les's permission, spent a considerable amount of time with plumbing rods trying to find out as much as possible about the make-up of the lakebed. The fact that Les had quite a few photos of the lake when it was drained helped no end as well. The two original lakes were quite different in composition as they had been used for different purposes - the larger lake (known as the Main Lake and originally about 12 to 14 acres in size) had been dug solely for the purpose of gravel extraction and, so, had its fair share of gravel bars, humps and plateaux, with an average depth of about ten to twelve feet. The smaller lake (the Back Lake, which was originally about five acres in size) was used as a 'wash down' pool for diggers and dredgers and, although there were a couple of small features, it was mostly a uniform seven feet deep and covered mainly in soft sand and silt. The spit of land that had divided them had been about thirty feet wide and when that had been excavated it had left a hard strip of lake bed that wide and a foot shallower than the Back Lake.

This feature had proved to be very productive during the previous couple of seasons and the two swims at either end of The Bar were by far the most popular on the lake. Being only one hundred yards apart, the anglers occupying them had to be very tolerant and courteous. A lot of the bait that Stan and his cohorts had introduced had been onto The Bar and, due to the carp's regular visits to and from the Back Lake, the bait had not remained there for long. The swims were known, inventively, as East Point and West Point and were two that the trio had earmarked as high on the list of starters. But they were a little unsure as to the etiquette of the opening day draw for swims. Was it first come first served and, so, a walk off, or was there an actual draw? The answer was unclear as Les had said that it had been different on both previous occasions and, as the start this year was on a Sunday, he expected a fair few to turn up. The number of members was supposed to be sixty but it seemed unlikely that all the tickets had been sold and also that all of the members would bother to turn up. Nonetheless, Chris and Stan still felt it unnecessary to take any chances and arrived early on Friday morning.

Rick worked in a motor repair business in Andover and Friday and Saturday tended to be his busiest time. With as much grovelling as possible without compromising his honour, he had managed to get the Saturday off work and would arrive on Friday evening (he had to work every fourth Saturday and fate had dictated that it fell on June 15th this year -some guys have all the luck!).

The tree in which Stan and Chris were doing their gibbon impressions was in the south west corner of the Main Lake and at the opposite end to The Bar and The Back Lake, but it overlooked the shallowest part of the Main Lake, a ten foot wide marginal shelf that ran three quarters the length of the south bank and a few yards around the south west corner. In the height of summer this bar would be covered with four feet of water and eight foot high reeds and, in the corner, one of two lily beds (the other, larger one being in the south west corner of the Back Lake.) At the moment the reeds were a couple of feet shorter and the lilies not quite extending over the full width of the shelf. The southerly breeze was barely rippling the water below them, so the two wide eyed anglers had an excellent view of all that was laid before them and could identify each of the larger fish which they had so recently examined in Les's photo albums.

"There, Rhodie. Just coming out of the pads now. That's the Big Linear, isn't it?"

"Where? Oh, yeah. Jeez, it looks massive, I wonder if they've spawned?"

"Les doesn't think so, but if this weather keeps up they'll probably start on Sunday midnight, knowing our luck," observed Stan. "Remember the off at Winter's when they spawned? Bloody hell we hauled after that, didn't we. Maybe it'll be the same here," he said, turning to Chris with a twinkle in his eye and a smile creasing his face.

"Oh yes, my son. That would be a stroke, wouldn't it? I wonder. ..... Bloody Hell!" Stan looked round sharply at his friend, expecting a boa constrictor to be enveloping him or a herd of tarantulas to be making a nest in his hair! The look on Chris's face indicated that both could have been a possibility but the look was directed at the lake and Stan immediately followed its direction. His gaze fell on the object of Chris's outburst and a similar one formed on his own lips. Following the Big Linear out from under the shade of the pads was a long, black carp and it kept coming. And coming. And coming. It was a common and it looked huge!

The pair of them dared not speak and sat in their own little worlds of wonder, silently fantasising the capture of such a carp. Then, as if it had been aware of its audience all the time, the great fish turned its flank to one side, shimmied along the edge of the shelf for a yard and then launched itself into the air, re-entering the lake with a sound like a thunderclap, before disappearing into the depths. Just like a great whale sounding.

"I think we need a bigger boat!" said Stan, tonelessly and looked round to see if Chris's expression was anything like his own. It was like looking in a mirror. After a minute's silence they descended the tree and sat at its base, shaded from the sun, and eventually the words spilled forth. How big? What a fish! Never seen anything so big. Could they ever land it? Did you see that kingfisher?

The halcyon bird broke the spell and the pair of them made their way back to the car park to await Rick's arrival and to tell him, in a babbling rush, of the awesome sight they had been privilege to. As is always the way, the weather changed the next day and the fish were not to be found beneath the pads but mainly in the shallower waters of the Back Lake and, because of this, they all decided that this was the place to start. If there was to be a walk off, Stan and Chris would set up in each point swim with Rick doubling up with either one of them as there was ample room in both swims.

There was a draw! Stan came out third, Chris seventh and Rick eighth out of the twelve anglers present and, at four on Saturday afternoon, they made their way to their selected swims. Amazingly, only the West Point was taken when Stan came to choose, so he immediately opted for the East Point with Chris joining him, whilst Rick was able to setup in the first swim in the Back Lake, thirty yards to their right.

Of the other anglers, they had recognised no one from the photos, especially Dean and Don, who they had dearly wanted to talk to. One guy seemed to ooze charm, charisma and lager from every pore and it was not long before they all realised that they had found a kindred spirit. Brad Busby ('just call me Buzz, everybody does') stood six foot four tall and his sixteen stone frame was topped with a mane of golden brown hair. A beard that could house a family of small rodents gave him the appearance of a modern day Grizzly

Adams - without the pet grizzly - and, coupled with a pair of blazing blue eyes, the whole effect was dazzling and caused great consternation in any passing group of females. Fortunately, his temper was more like a lamb's than a bear's, although you wouldn't want to find out how far you had to push it before the mass reached critical! His enthusiasm was infectious and having him around for any length of time left you with the certainty in your mind that you were going to catch carp, it was just a case of how big and how many.

This was his first season on the lake, also, so there was a lot for all of them to learn from the lake and each other. He had come second out of the bag and, rather than fish The Point had opted for a swim close to the pads that had recently housed a couple of monster carp. Chris and Stan thought this was a bit of a mistake but weren't about to be telling Giant Haystacks' big brother that he was wrong! Especially as he was nearly so right…

The last few hours of the close season were spent as they always had been - plumbing the area in front and to the sides, deciding on the spots for the first two casts of the new season. Then baiting up, tackling up and, finally, settling back for a few cold lagers and some food as the last rays of the sun signalled a mere two hours to go. Not surprisingly, the fish had become less evident as the day had worn on and, by the time that the three anglers were settling down for a late evening toast to the new season, the only evidence of any fish was the occasional swirl by a tench or bream. The conversation was, obviously, all about the fish they were going to catch and especially the Black Common that they had witnessed earlier in the day, and it was as this subject was being discussed that a deep, booming voice interrupted their chat.

"Don't you be worrying about that old fella," came the command, "I'll be dealing with him in the morning, boys. Any more of those lagers around, then?"

In unison, three heads turned to see the beaming smile of Buzz, lit up by the slowly setting sun, and Chris proffered a cold can as requested, watching it disappear into a huge paw of a hand before its contents disappeared into the seemingly bottomless throat.

"Aaaahhh! That hit the spot. Cheers mate. What was your name, by the way?"

They re-introduced themselves, first with their normal names and then possible alternatives, then proceeded to interrogate their guest as to the contents of his swim. It seemed that he had spent most of the afternoon aloft in the same tree that Chris and Stan had occupied a few hours earlier. He had watched with growing amazement as one carp after another sought the sanctuary of the lily pads whilst the rest of the lake resembled a time bite from the Battle of the Somme. By early evening, he feared he would shake the leaves from the trees, such was his excitement, and so, when the sun had sunk behind the West Bank trees thus making the lake like a mirror once more, he had decided to calm his nerves by taking a stroll around the lake to visit Stan and his mates and join them in a pre-season ale. He regaled them with tales of the huge fish that were at present readying themselves for his hookbaits and was convinced that, by first light, he would require some photographers to take shots of a monster common and a slightly smaller mirror!

They chortled and teased for an hour, eventually all agreeing that a group shot would be necessary in the morning to record their results. Then, with half an hour left of the evening, Buzz rose and bade them all the best of fortune whilst warmly shaking all of their hands. As he disappeared through the bushes, all three of them were trying to massage some life back into their crushed digits and vowing that they would practice crushing apples in their bare hands before attempting another handshake with Buzz! But what he also left them with, as well as dodgy circulation was an overwhelming sense of confidence and when, a few minutes later, their first leads broke the calm, surface film, they were all convinced that they were only hours away from the fish of a lifetime.

The quiet of the night was soon shattered by a few dozen beeps and chirps before silence reigned once again and the anglers fell into differing states of fitful sleep. A couple of times in the small hours an alarm would call out, followed by the 'swish' of carbon, but it was impossible to discern the outcome of the encounter and the realm of half sleep was soon entered once more.

The day was no more than minutes old, the first birds clearing their throats for the coming arias, when Stan's alarm issued forth three or four bleeps. Immediately awake, Stan sat bolt upright and readied himself for the lunge forward to his right hand rod. This had been cast a mere five yards out on the downward slope of The Bar and was surrounded with a liberal scattering of hemp and tiger nuts, the hook bearing a tiger nut and cork sandwich as offering for any curious carp. Peering intently at the alarm, he willed its red light to ignite once more but when, a few seconds later, it did just that he nearly jumped out of his skin. Though not screaming out a single tone as he would have hoped, it was never the less very insistent and then silent as the offending rod was whisked into the air. After the third 'thump,' Stan knew this was not the early morning call he had hoped for and was soon unhooking a slab of a bream in the margins. He then wiped the glutinous slime from his hands onto the grass before sitting back and taking in the full glory of the morning.

Rising behind him, the sun was hidden, its presence given away only by the deep orange glow on the trees opposite and slowly brightening sky. Turning to fill his kettle for the first cuppa of the season he heard a distant, single tone which seemed to ring like a bell in the still, morning air before being cut suddenly short. A muffled commotion followed before everything once again fell silent and Stan wondered if the recipient of the run had been more fortunate than he with the outcome. This time he managed to get the kettle onto the camping stove before his attention was once again distracted, this time by a distant shout, and then another. Was that someone calling for help? Slipping on his trainers, he made his way out of the swim and round towards the source of the commotion, following the direction from another shout until, rounding the corner onto the South Bank, he realised that the caller was Buzz.

"Okay, boy. I'm coming," he called as he neared the Pads Swim, his trousers now soaked with early morning dew from the knee high grass.

On entering Buzz's swim, he assumed that a party had been going on but the guests had all recently left! There was a bedchair on its side and a trail of sleeping bag leading into some bushes. An umbrella was upside down to the right, like a communication satellite hoping for signs of extra-terrestrial life, and the sole remaining rod was lying next to the rod rests as if it were having a little doze before recommencing its hectic existence twelve inches above the ground. Of Buzz, there was no immediate evidence, but a splash and a muttered curse soon gave away his hiding place and, moving carefully forward, Stan crept to the water's edge and peered around a bush. There, to his left and in amongst some lily pads, was the top half of the angler with his arms held high, and rod even higher.

"Morning. Any joy?" asked Stan, casually. The semi-submerged angler's reply was unprintable but very audible and ended with, "... but now it's stuck on the other side of the bloody pads and I can't shift it!"

Stan pondered the problem and could see that wading out from the far corner with a landing net was probably the only option, so made the suggestion to the increasingly more agitated Buzz.

"Yeah, you're probably right, Quill. Do you fancy giving it a go, mate?" The last was almost pleading, but Stan had thought of doing nothing else and was already making his way through the bushes with net in hand whilst running the next few minutes through his head.

On reaching the lakeside, he stripped down to his pants and stepped gingerly into the surprisingly cold water, gasping through gritted teeth as he sank lower into the lake, then stopping for a second as those most precious of jewels were submerged in shrinkingly cold water! He gasped once more, then looked across at Buzz who, despite his predicament, was grinning widely,

"Watch out for that step, it's a real lulu!" he chuckled, before replacing the grin with a grimace of concentration.

The rod was still arced over and Stan could see the line entering the water five yards in front of him so began slowly edging forward. He was now on the marginal shelf so the depth remained relatively constant, but for how long? A few more careful steps took him within the landing net's reach but he had no idea whether the fish was beneath the line or twenty yards further away, so knew he had to edge even closer. Buzz was giving him a running commentary about events on the end of the line, but they were quite predictable and changeless, with everything remaining solid. Stan inched forward until, suddenly, his outstretched foot could feel the ground sloping steeply away and he knew that he could advance no further.

"I might be able to reach the line, Buzz, and try to hand-line it. What do you reckon?" His teeth were starting to chatter as the cold was gradually seeping into his bones and he hoped that the end would soon be reached, whatever it may be.

Buzz was just about to concur with Stan's suggestion when the rod tip was pulled down viciously and the line sang with the sudden increase in pressure. Desperately fumbling with the clutch, Buzz felt a sudden, sickening lack of tension and knew immediately what had occurred. Cursing aloud once more, he began winding slowly whilst silently hoping that he was wrong. But he was not. The fish was gone. The final, desperate bid for freedom bringing just that, as the line had cut on the edge of the gravelly, marginal shelf.

Stan waded forcefully back to the shore and attempted to dry himself enough to stop his shivering before running back to his swim and leaving the despondent Buzz to his sorrow. He had to get back into his sleeping bag to warm himself up again, and lay there shivering for many minutes until Rick poked his head round the corner of the brolly, smiling.

"Still in bed, boy? Come on, I've just had one and I need some photos taken!"

Stan stared out, speechless, and watched the gleeful captor disappear into Chris's swim to pass on the news.

Ten minutes later, they were gathered in Rick's swim drinking tea and discussing the merits of the twenty four pound mirror they had just weighed and sacked up until the sun was higher. Stan was in the throes of explaining his early morning antics when the hulking subject of the conversation entered the swim, his normally sparkling eyes dull and downcast.

"That was a whacker, boys. A real whacker. I am absolutely gutted," came his sullen comment. Then he seemed to become aware of little things - a wet weigh sling on the unhooking mat, an equally wet landing net propped in a tree, a scattering of rods and reels on the ground, and a huge grin splitting Rick's face. He suddenly put two and two together and came up with 'carp'. His demeanour immediately changed and his eyes once again shone like blue beacons, his smile mirroring Rick's.

"You've had one, Sid, haven't you?" he blurted.

"I have indeed, boy. A twenty four pound mirror, but I'm sorry to hear you lost one, mate."

"Oh, don't worry about that. You've caught a carp, boy, and that is all that matters at the moment. Well done," and with that last, he extended a huge paw for Rick to bury his own puny hand into, which he grudgingly did whilst girding himself for the finger crushing power to come. When a nice firm handshake was forthcoming, he looked at the grinning, bearded face opposite in puzzlement and Buzz let forth a hearty chuckle.

"Sorry, boys. My first handshake with anyone is always the 'Crusher', just to see what they're made of. You lot were okay, but we'll soon make real men out of you, eh, Sid!" he explained, smiling.

"Yeah, nice one big fella. But why do you keep calling him Sid?" asked Stan.

"That's what you said his nickname was, didn't you? And when I saw his van with BARRETT'S on the side, and the ponytail and all that, I thought 'Oh, Sid Barrett, I see'!" explained a slightly confused Buzz.

As the laughter began to roll, Chris chuckled and said, "No. Spud, not Sid, you fool. But, I tell you what, you're probably closer to the truth. He looks a bit like a Sid, don't he, Quill?"

"Oh, yeah. Definitely. What d'you reckon, Sid?" came Stan's equally chucklesome reply, and the three of them started laughing uncontrollably, spurred on by 'Sid's' feigned look of indignation and verbal rebuttals.

"Sid, my arse! I don't look like a Sid! What about you then, Rhodie, you look more like a daffodil!"

This outburst not only fuelled the fire of amusement, but also doused the flames of Buzz's disappointment, if only for a short while, and they were soon all toasting Sid's fish and new name with cups of tea and Chocolate Hobnobs.

The inquest into Buzz's lost fish followed later that morning. It transpired that, following a sleepless night due to huge fish leaping in front of him, he had finally dozed off just before dawn, only to be woken minutes later by a screaming take to the rod that had been dropped in the margin between the pads and the bank. When he struck, the fish had crashed on the surface before diving into the pads and Buzz had seen a huge, grey flank flash in the early morning light. The rest they knew, and could only offer their consolations whilst assuring him that his chance would soon come round again. Later that day they were proved right but although he was elated with the eighteen pound common that accepted his floating Mixers, Buzz knew that this was merely the grandchild of the fish he had lost earlier and just hoped he would have a chance to redress the balance.

The weather that had caused Buzz to use floaters also had another, major effect on his session - it heated the water to the perfect temperature for carp to spawn, and they did. In earnest.

By Sunday evening, Chris and Stan had seen a number of fish cruise past them into the shallow water of the Back Lake and, despite leaving out a couple of anchored floaters for most of the afternoon, they had been only successful in landing a coot and missing two possible takes by carp. From a tree to the left of Sid's swim they had watched the fish cruise aimlessly around the Back Lake in groups of four or more and it took little to realise what this was a prelude to. Buzz had moved to a small swim to Sid's right and it was from there that he landed the eighteen pounder, but as the sun sank lower in the sky the anglers stopped their futile thrashing of the water with crusts and controllers. They accepted the inevitable, congregating in Sid's swim (making sure to use his new nomme de plume as many times as possible, lest he should forget it!) for an impromptu barbecue where they were joined by Les, the lake owner. He accepted their offer of a tepid lager and apologised for the lack of action, for which they assured him there really was no need. After he left as darkness fell, they were all refreshed at his attitude towards the fish and the anglers.

He had asked how they felt about the possibility of a temporary closure of the lake whilst the fish recovered from their rigours, to which they had all been in agreement, but Les said he would see how the night went before making a decision.

The margins opposite Sid and Buzz were the largest area of shallows in the lake, with a huge reed bed stretching over half the length of the bank. It was in these three foot deep waters that the carp crashed and thrashed all night long, almost decimating a small bed of lily pads in the process. To Buzz's right was a fallen willow tree that the fish had frequented regularly during the close season, and it was amongst these leafless branches that the anglers found a number of recovering carp early the next morning. It was obvious that these fish would be doing little but resting for the rest of the day, probably as a prelude to a repeat performance the following night, and so, by midday, the four anglers bade each other farewell until the next time, whenever that might be.

By later that day there were only two anglers left on the lake so Les decided not to close the water but asked that the anglers did not fish the Back Lake for the next couple of days. The fish spawned, on and off, for the next three days so when Chris and Stan arrived on the following Friday they were not surprised to learn that nothing had been caught since Buzz's fish. This they learnt from Buzz himself, who had been at the lake a few hours prior to their four o'clock arrival and had been watching the fish cruising lazily below the surface.

"They certainly don't look like they fancy feeding at the moment," he said from atop a lakeside alder. "Les reckons they stopped spawning yesterday morning, but a few of them look a bit beat up. I don't know what to do."

"What d'you mean, Buzz?" asked Stan, whilst peering across the still surface of the Back Lake.

"I don't know whether to fish or not. You know. Whether it will be worth the effort or whether the fish will be up to it," he explained.

"What does Les reckon then?" asked Chris from an adjacent tree he had just climbed. "Does he think they're up to it or does he want us to leave it alone for a while?"

"I want you to decide for me, lads," came a voice from below and Chris looked down to see the stocky figure of Les ambling along the bank towards them, his voluminous shorts giving his thin, white legs the appearance of two pieces of string dangling down from them.

"Blimey, Les, you've got lucky legs," came Stan's greeting, to which Les gave a long, puzzled look.

"Lucky they don't break," explained Buzz from above, which caused Les to let out a short bark of laughter before retorting.

"You cheeky bastard, Buzz. You better not stay up there too long unless you want a squirrel to make a nest in your face!"

"Touche!" came Buzz's reply, and he dropped to the ground next to Les and gave him a huge bear hug which engulfed most of his body, before extending his hand to shake Stan's. "Good to see you boys. So what decision have we got to make then, Les?" he asked of the owner.

"Well, I put a temporary closure on the Back Lake area earlier in the week, whilst the carp were spawning, but I'm not sure whether to continue it for the next couple of days, or not. What do you boys think?"

For the next ten minutes or so, the three anglers discussed the pros and cons of this dilemma before coming up with a possible working idea, voiced by Stan.

"So, we leave the Back Lake out of bounds at the moment, unless too many anglers arrive to fish, then we select certain swims that can be fished. What about the two Point swims? I reckon we should leave them empty at the moment. What do you think?"

Once again they debated the subject, having also been joined by two more anglers, until all were happy with the arrangement. Sid was to be absent for this weekend and they all thought it unlikely that there would be the same amount of anglers as on opening night, which proved to be a correct assumption, and so they set about choosing swims for the night. After another circuit of the lake they all decided to fish along the South Bank of the lake, the left hand end of which was the scene of Buzz's opening day disappointment.

The shallow marginal shelf extended from the left hand corner to three quarters of the way along the South Bank so they spaced themselves along the bank accordingly. Buzz in the Pads Corner, Chris forty yards to his right, and Stan a further eighty yards away at the end of the shelf and its resident reed bed which separated him from Chris. The weather had been forecast to change, and the change in wind direction from mild southerlies to stronger north-easterlies was evidence of this, the new wind blowing encouragingly into the faces of the anglers on the south bank.

After what seemed like hours, they were all settled in their respective plots and oozing different levels of confidence. As if his normal level of confidence was not enough, Buzz was almost bursting at the feel of the warm wind in his face and, coupled with the sight of two or three carp rolling in the ever increasing waves, he almost felt like screaming! Chris and Stan were equally as elated, if only for the reprieve that Les had given them, and were both very happy with their bait placement. Chris's choice was simple, for his swim was bordered by an overhanging tree to the left and the reed bed to the right, and a bait plus free offerings was carefully placed in each spot. The left hand one had been walked under the branches of the tree and dropped on a small area of sand in amongst the thin layer of silkweed that covered most of the shelf. A scattering of hemp and tiger nuts poured straight from the bucket to accompany the popped up tiger nut rig. The right hand bait was flicked to the front of the reeds on the downward slope of the shelf and a few handfuls of broken birdfood boilies were thrown into the waves that lapped against the reed stems.

At the other end of the reeds, the same waves were lapping against Stan's thighs as he too walked his bait along the shelf to his left. Observation from a small tree had allowed him to find a small bay in the front of the reeds and it was here that he was placing his birdfood boilie, carefully kicking the mud with his foot so that it covered most of the line and the lead, hemp and boilies scattered around being the final act of enticement. The margins shelved away steeply to his right but he knew, following their pre-season observations, that there was a 'step' at about six feet in depth that a bait could be lowered onto. So he did just that, dropping a dozen broken boilies around it before putting back leads on both lines in a bid to disguise them more.

A small clearing at the back of Chris's swim lent itself perfectly to a dining area and the three very confident anglers gathered there to discuss their swims, the lake, Les, and anything else that sprung up, whilst lubricating their larynx with some well-earned lagers. They chatted for a couple of hours, rejoicing at the strengthening wind and at the occasional crash of a carp in the waves just the other side of the reeds. It was suddenly a matter not of 'will we catch?' but 'what will we catch, and who will catch first?' They retired to their respective swims, an hour after dark, each hoping that they would be the one to receive the first action of the weekend.

Stan's bladder woke him, as usual, just as the black of night was turning to the grey of pre-dawn. Although he had yet to receive any action, he was still encouraged by the light breeze that caressed his face, and slipped back into his bag still confident of that early morning call.

He was awoken a little later by the strident call of a coot as she ushered her brood through the reed stems, reminiscent of a school ma'am chivvying her young charges across a busy main road. The morning was now bright and he assumed that he had slept for a couple of hours but, on peering up at the travel clock wedged in the spokes of his brolly, he was surprised to see that it was just a few minutes past four o'clock. Then he remembered that today was Midsummer's Day, the longest day of the year, and so he weighed up his options. Get up now, put the kettle on and enjoy the serenity of a glorious summer dawn or nestle back beneath the sleeping bag and grab a couple more hours' sleep. There was no contest but, no sooner had he snuggled down into the folds of his bag than another strident call wrested him from his bedchair. It was the lilting call of the Optonic bird and was accompanied by the buzz of the baitrunner on his right hand rod as an early morning raider made off with its breakfast.

Stan managed to compose himself enough to stop himself striking the fish's head off, but the need for a firm strike was superfluous and he was soon holding on for dear life as the fish, obviously now a carp, made a bid to reach the right hand margin. Stan managed to halt the fish a few yards short of the winning post in its fifty yard dash for freedom, then gradually coaxed it back towards him, realising with some relief that the carp had expended most of its energy in that initial run. Pretty soon, it was wallowing ten yards out and he lowered the net ready to accept its prize. For one awful moment the line pinged sharply off the carp's dorsal and he thought that the hook had pulled, cursing aloud more in relief than anything else when he realised the fish was still attached, and as he slipped the carp into the net, he let out a roar of triumph causing the mother coot to squawk loudly and skitter across the lake with her young once more.

It was only evident now that he had walked straight out into the lake, and the lapping waters cooled his belly as he drew the net towards him, having thrown the rod behind him onto the bank.

"What you had, Quill? What is it, man?" came Chris's insistent enquiry.

"Big fat mirror, I think, boy," replied the wet but happy captor, and he accepted Chris's proffered hand to heave himself out of the lake, handing the net over to his mate whilst he returned to his brolly to dry himself off. As Chris laid the fish on the mat, Buzz excitedly entered the swim and squealed with delight at the sight of the ample mirror carp that was covering quite a lot of the unhooking mat.

"Well done, boy!" he exclaimed, whilst offering a plate-sized hand to be shaken. Stan gave him a crusher of his own and Buzz smiled back his approval.

"See. I told you I'd make a man of you, Quill," he beamed, before bending to offer some assistance to Chris. The big man hoisted the scales effortlessly above his head which gave the impression of a relatively small carp below them, but nothing could be further from the truth as Chris read the weight aloud, once more.

"Ooh, this is close. Twenty nine.....fourteen. Yes, Quill?" he said, by way of confirmation. The happy captor didn't even look, knowing his friend too well to need to verify his verdict.

"Yep, that'll do me boys. Yeeeessss!" he screamed. The coots were not amused! They sacked the fish for an hour or so until the light was better for photos and wiled away the time drinking tea and listening to Stan's first telling of the fight. They all anticipated more action as the wind steadily began to strengthen, however, by the time Stan was beaming his final smile for the cameras whilst watching the fish swim strongly away, they had yet to see a fish in front of them and wondered if Stan's capture had spooked them away.

Breakfast followed the photos, which was in turn followed by an early afternoon snack. Still no more carp made a mistake and, despite all three of them spending the time between meals up various trees, they saw no sign of any fish. Early afternoon found the hooks in the butt rings of three sets of rods as the anglers strolled around the lake in search of their quarry. It did not take too long to find them.

"Look, over there," pointed Chris from above, and Stan and Buzz followed his finger to the far reeds in the Back Lake. There they could see, in the calm, windless water, first two, then three, then a dozen or more dorsals creasing the lake's surface. But Chris could see more.

"Bloody hell! There must be about fifty fish out there!" he exclaimed.

Buzz and Stan were soon on a similar level to Chris and immediately saw what he was talking about. Practically the whole of the lake's population was in front of them, and they had agreed not to fish for them there! They debated whether to ask Les to change his decision but soon realised that they would be little more than cattle rustlers, so resigned themselves to just looking. They thought about moving as close to the entrance to the Back Lake as possible, but the two other anglers on the lake were fishing the two best swims for that, on the East Bank. Another angler had just turned up and was eyeing the equivalent swim on the West Bank, so they resigned themselves to staying put and hoping that one or two more fish might be enticed to feed by the steady breeze blowing into their shallow margins.

Once settled, they spoofed for a trip to the off licence and the Chinese take-away, and soon Chris was grudgingly taking their orders before disappearing for half an hour. On his return, they ate heartily and toasted Stan's capture with extremely cold lagers and began interrogating Buzz as to his line of work and previous fishing experiences. After much leg pulling and false leads, it transpired that he was a professional diver, and had travelled the globe visiting possible drilling sites for oil rigs, assisting in salvage operations and, less often but more gruesomely, helping in discovering the cause of shipping disasters. His rapt listeners were mightily impressed by the new found knowledge. Even more so when he told them that, wherever he went he took his fishing rods and had used them to great effect in all the oceans of the world, and many lakes and rivers on almost every continent. He had, however, retired as a full time diver last year, after twelve years in the job, and was now involved in training and instruction for a number of companies.

Despite having caught marlin, shark, tuna, arctic trout and fresh run salmon, his first love had always been carp yet, amazingly, he was still awaiting his first thirty - an event both Stan and Chris dearly wanted to be present at.

He related a tale, however, that he said was the most harrowing dive of his career and it soon became evident that all three of them had been moving in the same circles but slightly different orbits. He told of a dive he and a group of his lads did into Pit Five in Farnham in the depths of winter and there, beneath a covering of ice, they found the first of the many dead carp that littered the bottom of this most prolific lake.

"I had tears in my eyes when I realised what I was seeing," said Buzz with emotion in his voice, brought on by the memory of that day almost five years earlier, and they told him of their plans to fish Frensham at the same time.

After that episode, he accepted a four month posting in the Azores and sated his fishing needs by catching sand sharks and sting rays before returning to England and opting for the banks of Yateley as his next carp fishing step. So, whilst Stan and Chris were at Coates Pit, Buzz was the other side of the M3, no more than ten miles away, but his luck was not as great as theirs and he contrived to lose two good carp in amongst a smattering of fish to mid-twenties. The talk meandered from one carp lake to another after that, until Stan rose unsteadily to his feet and bade his companions farewell, assuring them that he would call them to do the photos once again in the morning!

They both chuckled at this remark but, less than eight hours later, they were indeed doing that very thing. The same rod had wrenched Stan awake at a slightly more civilised seven o'clock, but this time the carp had succumbed quite easily and soon a double figure common was lying in the mesh whilst Stan called for assistance. The fish weighed a little over nineteen pounds and it was a very happy Stan that posed for the cameras once more.

"Them golden balls are glowing this weekend aren't they, Quill?" japed Chris whilst taking one more shot.

"You know what they say, Rhodie. If you've got 'em, flaunt 'em!" came the retort, and he then lowered the carp back into the lake before punching the air with glee.

A few hours after Stan's joyous display, they left for home, looking forward to the next session when they hoped that the whole lake would be available to fish.

That benefit was bestowed the next morning when Les decided that the fish were looking much healthier and, by the time that Buzz returned on Thursday, a further six fish had been caught including two different thirties. The first was a stunning double row linear which they had seen photos of from last year, and it had been caught at the same weight as previously - thirty one pounds twelve ounces. Buzz had not witnessed that capture but arrived at six in the morning just as a guy called Dean was landing a stunning leather carp. The fish weighed a dozen ounces over the thirty pound mark but that mattered little for this was a superb specimen and, barring two small scales by the tail root, was totally bald. Fired by this, Buzz spent most of the morning looking for feeding fish, eventually finding some in the snag corner of the Back Lake and was rewarded twenty four hours later by the capture of a mirror carp of twenty four pounds.

On their arrival, later that day, Stan and Chris were regaled with the full story of the capture, as was Sid an hour later. The weekend was busier than previous ones, so the opportunity to move onto fish did not readily present itself. By the time of their departure, on Sunday morning, their only successes were a fifteen pound common to Buzz - one of six carp to be caught in the weekend - and a plague of tench and bream to the other three. To rub salt into the wound, they found out a day or so later that someone had moved into the swim recently vacated by Sid and, after a few hours, had bagged the Big Linear at a weight of just over thirty seven and a half pounds.

Over the next couple of weeks the action slowed, as the post spawning 'munchies' were replaced by the carp's usual wariness and guile. During this time each member of the band managed to open their account but, despite six carp between them, they managed only three fish in excess of twenty pounds, the largest of those a twenty four pound common as part of a brace of commons to Buzz. During this time, however, the lake gave up another four thirties, the largest of which weighed just under thirty five pounds. It was distinguishable by three large scales on one flank - a fish they had watched closely during the close season and one that Chris and Stan had both pinpointed as one of their target fish. Buzz was once again present at this carp's capture and was equally as desperate to make its intimate acquaintance.

So, by the end of the first month, Stan and Chris sat down and assessed their results thus far. Actually, they were in Chris's car on their way to the lake, but it seemed a logical topic of conversation and would wile away the next fifty minutes admirably. Between them they had caught four carp, the largest being Stan's twenty nine, which they had nicknamed 'Double D' for the two huge scales, one on either flank. What was interesting was that they had found out that the fish had been out twice since that capture, and both times a few ounces over thirty pounds, obviously a carp that loved its grub. They were both a bit surprised at how busy the lake was and surmised that this was one of the reasons they had been unable to get on the fish. This situation would soon be rectified, however, because Chris had secured a sub-contracting job with the local council that would last for the rest of the year. This would allow him to cram the work up until Thursday, thus giving him the freedom to arrive at the lake that same evening, ahead of the weekend crowds and, where possible, secure a good area for himself and Stan. Stan himself was working on a similar ploy that would allow him to leave work at midday on Friday, giving that vital extra couple of hours to avoid the nightmare traffic and the Friday afternoon arrivals at the lake. They were happy with the bait and rigs and were convinced that it was only a matter of time before they got amongst the better fish.

The day, however, was a normal Friday for them so they were pleasantly surprised by the sight that greeted them on their arrival, just after five o'clock, as they cruised into a virtually empty car park. There were two other cars present, and neither was Buzz's, which was a greater surprise, but they took little time getting over the shock and were soon marching along the East Bank, water bottles in hand.

It came as no surprise to them that two anglers were occupying both Point swims and, after a brief chat with a guy they had dubbed Fat Bob who was in the East Point, they carried on towards the snag corner of the Back Lake. The forecast was for some fierce thunderstorms later that evening accompanied by strong southerly winds which would blow straight up the lake into the shallows of the Back Lake, so they hoped that they might get a chance to fish the reeds on the West Bank. The obvious choice would have been for either of The Point swims but, as they had been unable to get in there since the start of the season, they had discounted them from their plans on their earlier journey to the lake. The West Bank of the Back Lake, although over one hundred and fifty yards long, had only two easily fishable swims. The first was a few yards from the North West corner, at the end of the reeds, and was only used as a stalking swim when the fish were in close. The other was halfway along the bank and was flanked on the left by a wall of reeds that extended thirty feet out into the lake, and on the right by a smaller bed of reeds and a larger bed of lilies. The swim was easily fishable by two anglers and so it was with some considerable confidence that the pair placed their swim-securing water bottles down and peered out across the lake. Ripples expanding from the lily pads betrayed the presence of something fishy, be it tench or carp, but twenty yards out into the lake an explosion of water left them with little doubt as to the perpetrator's identity and, with merely a glance and a nod, they turned on their heels and hightailed it back to the car.

An hour later they were angling. Stan had lost the spoof and watched with some envy as Chris set up to the right and flicked a bait alongside the lily pads, a dozen leaves twitching on the surface as his two ounce lead startled something beneath. Unperturbed, Chris threw out a dozen handfuls of hemp, maples and tiger nuts to accompany his delicately balanced tiger nut offering. His other rod was cast fifteen yards past the pads onto a hard, sandy patch amongst the soft silt that his studious plumbing had revealed. This rod was baited with a bird food boilie and thirty or so similar free offerings were catapulted out to join it. The southerly wind was starting to pick up and the reeds to Stan's left were swaying ever more vigorously. It was to the far edge of these stems that Stan cast his first bait, wading carefully along the edge of the reeds, where the ground was firmer, and deposited half a bucket of hemp and maples over his birdfood hookbait. His right hand rod was cast a few yards further where the lake bed sloped down from three to five feet quite rapidly and, as with Chris's further bait, was liberally surrounded by boilies. Once settled, they set about changing the swim from a refuse dump into something fishable, as there were bits of tackle, bait, cans of drink and assorted rucksack contents strewn across the grass behind them like the aftermath from a plane crash!

Stan was just putting the final peg into the ground to secure his brolly when a familiar voice greeted him.

"Well, boys, you certainly listen to the weather reports, don't you?" commented Sid as he strolled into the swim, his eyes scanning the ground for an errant can of lager.

"Siddy, boy. How the devil are you?" replied Stan as he emerged from his brolly.

"Good to see you, mate, where you thinking of angling?" he asked whilst shaking the newcomer firmly by the hand before handing him the usual peace offering. Quickly pulling the ring, Sid took a long gulp of lager before gasping aloud and smiling.

"Quill, you are a god! Don't you believe any of the things they say about you, mate!"

Stan smiled back, and shook his head. Oh, how I love this repartee, he thought.

"So, where are you fishing, Sid?" came Chris's repeat to Stan's question.

"Well, I was going to fish here, wasn't I? But, seeing as you two poachers got here first, I'll have to go in the corner, won't I?" came his feigned indignant reply, which was followed by another pull on the can.

"Oh, well. Shit happens, Sid!" said Chris.

"Yeah, and then you go fishing with 'em!" to which Stan and Chris both raised their cans in mock salute.

The wind was slowly gaining in strength and, in the distance, they could hear the delicate sound of thunder.

"Be here pretty soon, I reckon," said Stan, "d'you want a hand with your gear, son?" he asked Sid.

"No, I dropped it in the corner on the way round. But thanks anyway."

"No problem, mate. Rhodie needs the exercise, anyway, don't he!" replied Stan, whilst Chris looked at him as if to say that there would have been more chance of him flying to the moon.

With that, Sid strolled off and began preparing himself for a bumpy ride. The wind was pushing practically straight into the Corner Swim and the reeds to the right were bending over at almost ninety degrees, making casting very difficult. Eventually, he enlisted Stan's help to hold the reeds back with a landing net pole whilst he flicked out his tiger nut offering to the far edge of the reeds, fifteen yards out. His left hand bait was cast along the bank to his left beneath a very inviting willow tree whose drooping branches were being bustled by the strengthening wind. By the time he had completed this operation, the sound of thunder was not so delicate, and the darkening skies were a perfect canvas for the lightning to paint bright streaks across.

Barely had Stan and Sid returned to the former's brolly, when the first huge drops of rain splattered down on the ground and splashed audibly on the lake's ruffled surface. Chris called out to tell them that he had seen three fish in front of them whilst they had been away. Without warning, the heavens opened and the rain crashed down with such violence that the surface of the lake was flattened by the force, the skies reflection turning it black. Barely had this happened then the whole sky was lit by an almost blinding flash of light, which was accompanied, seconds later, by a deafening crack of thunder.

"Whooo-haaa!!" screamed Sid at the top of his voice, but his cry was barely audible to Chris, five yards away, whose brolly was being pounded by a thousand raindrops a second!

Another flash and crack followed. Then another, and it was obvious that the eye of the storm was right above them. But this was no hurricane and there was no respite in this eye, just pure, natural violence. The brolly offered little in the way of shelter as all the leaks and imperfections were sought out by the driving rain, and a fine spray covered the anglers, the sleeping bag and the bedchair. They felt the full force of the storm for twenty minutes and marvelled at the spectacle, Stan trying, unsuccessfully, to capture it on film. Then, just as suddenly as it had begun, it ended, and the final drops of rain splattered onto the sodden ground, trying to catch up with the rest of them like stragglers in a marathon. The anglers emerged into the gloom of the evening and, although it was barely eight thirty, it seemed that night had arrived very early. On looking up, however, they could see a great swathe of blue sky growing ever nearer as the dark clouds moved on, the thunder rumbling in the distance and the odd flash of lightning marking the storm's exit route.

They were soon sitting by the lake enjoying the last hour of the summer evening, drinking tea and discussing the vagaries of Mother Nature, when a huge carp slid out of the lake and seemed to hover half in, half out of the water. The sinking sun picked out every scale before it slid back into the lake like a leathery Excalibur.

"That's about two feet from my bloody bait!" exclaimed Chris.

"What about that one, then?" asked Sid whilst pointing at another airborne carp. "And that one." Suddenly, the surface of the lake was alive with rolling and leaping carp and, equally as suddenly, a screaming alarm split the cool evening air just as startlingly as any thunderclap. The trio leapt up and looked at the alarms in front of them before turning and looking in the direction of Sid's swim. But the noise was not emanating from there. Then Stan pointed to their right.

"Look. Fat Bob's in," he declared, and they all saw the angler opposite with rod held high, and probably thankful that the storm had passed. The battle lasted five minutes before he slipped the net under his prize and lifted it out of their sight and into his swim. A few minutes later, a camera flashed four times and then they saw him carry the fish to the water's edge and release it.

"How big?" shouted Chris, to which the muted reply came that it was twenty three pounds. Whilst the battle had raged, the carp were still making themselves evident in the Back Lake and each angler was silently hoping that his buzzer would be the next to break the silence. The sun was below the horizon and the lake was lit by the last, residual light of the day. Another carp flopped over in front of them and sent large ripples towards the watchers, jostling the lily pads as they reached the bank, and all three sighed at the sight of it.

"Wassatt?" whispered Sid, as if a louder question would have scared all the carp.

"What?" asked Stan, peering into the gloom in search of revelation.

"Shit!" squealed Sid, and leapt to his feet, knocking the chair over and skidding onto his side in the slippery grass. He dallied no longer to hear the burst of laughter from his two compatriots, but was straight back on his feet and running along the edge of the reeds towards his swim. Stan and Chris took a more leisurely stroll and arrived in the muddied Sid's swim to see him battling with the test curve of his rod.

"I thought I could hear a buzzer. It's these Stevie Neville's, they're really quiet sometimes. Picked a bait up under the willow, Quill."

"Nice one. Wassit feel like?" asked Stan whilst seeking out the landing net in the dark of the swim.

"Dunno. Not very big, I don't think. Might even be a tench or something," came Sid's evaluation. Then, just off the edge of the reeds, they saw an oily swirl and Stan readied himself with the net. Three more such swirls and the fish was in the net and, although not huge, was the first carp of the session for them. Chris took two flash photos of the thirteen pound common for a smiling Sid.

"We'll have to call you the Common Man, Sid," commented Stan, in recognition of the fact that this was his third double figure common of the season so far.

"Oh, yeah, Quill. You can do that when I have the Black Common, mate. And that'll be in the morning!"

Chris and Stan left him to recast whilst chuckling away to themselves but, eight hours later they though t his prediction had come true when they were dragged from their slumbers by a screaming Sid. The sun was painting the first wash of colour on the world when they peered into his landing net and saw a huge, black common carp lying there. Their first impressions were the same as Sid's - this was the big fella - but, once they carried the net from the gloom of the swim and laid it on the mat at the back of the reeds, the fish glowed bronze and gold in the early morning light.

"Jeez. What a fish!" gasped Chris, whilst holding the carp down as Sid removed the size eight hook from the fish's lip. Stan was on hand with the dampened weigh sling and it was he who uttered a well-known phrase.

"What's your p.b., Sid?"

"Twenty seven twelve," came the reply, and Stan and Chris looked at each other before chorusing, "Not anymore!" and smiling hugely at the stunned captor.

The huge common weighed thirty one pounds exactly and was the largest any of them had ever seen on the bank, and it would be known as Sid's Common forever more.

Once the fish was photographed and returned, they adjourned to the middle swim for a celebratory cuppa, almost needing to guide the bemused Sid by the hand. As they sat silently drinking their brew, Stan noticed the far reeds twitching, and tried to assess where exactly that was in relation to his bait when his left hand rod jumped in the rests and the alarm screamed. His strike met with firm resistance before his cup had had a chance to reach the ground and deposit its contents on the grass. The clutch buzzed as the fish left for the middle of the lake, followed by a huge wake of bubbles, and Stan bent the rod to the right to stop the fish from kiting back along the reeds. This, however, only seemed to make it more determined to do that and, shortly, Stan found himself waist deep in water at the end of the reeds whilst attempting to bully the carp back along the reed line towards an equally submerged Chris and net. For a moment, it seemed that the carp would win, but then the steady pressure told and it rolled on its back in submission before Chris scooped it into the net. Backs were slapped and whoops were hollered before a relatively dry Sid helped them back out of the lake, and over to the waiting unhooking mat. The carp was an almost perfect linear which weighed a few ounces over twenty seven pounds and it was a smiling Stan who now posed for the photos.

Amazingly, after all the disturbance, it was Stan again who was having his photo taken a couple of hours later with a carp six ounces larger, and with far fewer scales.

The storm had obviously stirred things up but Chris could not believe that he had yet to receive any action, from carp that is, because he had landed three tench from the edge of the pads during the night. The weather had changed, now, and the wind had swung round to a steady south-westerly, blowing over their heads and into the snags in the opposite corner, and it was there that Chris saw a good carp leave the water, just after midday. On taking a stroll round to the Snag Tree, he climbed into its branches and saw, below him, at least six carp. The tree was normally a refuge to a few carp but, after an hour, Chris had counted eight different fish meandering in and out of the sunken branches and he was soon devising a plan that might help entice one or two of them from their sanctuary and, hopefully, onto his baited hook.

He had trickled a few baits onto a clear, gravel mound to the left of the tree and had watched with growing confidence as one or two carp cruised over and sampled some of the free offerings. With patience, and a certain amount of numbness to his buttocks, he was soon watching five or six carp feeding confidently on the spot. Gingerly lowering himself from his perch he made his way back to his swim, stamping his feet as he went in order to regain some circulation to his legs. Stan was happy to remain where he was, still confident that carp were visiting the area, and helped Chris move his tackle to the new swim. Setting up five or six yards from the lake, Chris carefully lowered two baits onto the spot and slackened the line off so as not to spook the carp. Stan was in the tree directing operations and letting his friend know when the coast was clear and, fifteen minutes later, was wishing him the best of luck before returning to his swim.

Chris was expecting action immediately but as the sun set opposite him, he was still fish-less and a previous visit to the tree had shown the swim to be devoid of everything except two tench. Despondently climbing down, he returned to his bedchair and wondered whether to attempt a move back to his first swim before nightfall. As he was pondering this, a skinny pair of booted legs poking out from a pair of voluminous shorts hove into view. He gazed up at a large, balding figure grasping a can of nuclear strength cider in one paw whilst the other hand was busy investigating the contents of his head via one nostril!

"Seen any fin'?" it demanded of everybody in a three mile radius. This sort of person was depriving a village somewhere of a prize winning idiot, thought Chris, before attempting a reply.

"Well, I had done until you jack-booted into the swim, mate!" he said, venomously, but the inference was totally lost on the wavering individual.

"I'm Kirk. Kirk Byron. I seen 'em down the other end. In the pads," he bellowed, as if his name would make the situation any better.

"Well, why don't you go and fish for them then, Kirk?" enquired Chris, through gritted teeth, almost spitting the guy's name on the floor.

"Yeah, I am. Jus' thought I'd come an' see what else was going on, didn't I," came the reply, followed by a medal winning belch. He then raised his can to take another swig and proceeded to pour half the contents over his copious belly.

"Oops. Missed again. Herr! Herr! Herr!" and with that he turned unsteadily and tottered back the way he had come, shouting "See yer, mate," over his shoulder in a strange, non-London accent that Chris couldn't quite place, but hoped was very far away and making his departed visitor very homesick!

After this close encounter of the nerd kind, Chris gave up all hope of any fish being left in the swim and, as the light had all but faded from the sky, he resigned himself to a blank night in the swim and settled into his sleeping bag, suddenly feeling very weary.

Sleep came easily and lasted well into the small hours until, in the blackest of nights, he was scrabbling across the grass towards the rod that was demanding screaming attention. The run seemed to go on forever before he was able to fumble around and find the offending item and lifted into a very fast and angry carp. The fish powered away strongly, but fortunately out into the main part of the lake and away from the snags and it was out there that the majority of the battle was fought. The wind was still pushing into the corner so Chris was unable to see any swirls to indicate whether the fish was on the surface or not and it was with great relief, and a small heart attack, that he felt Sid's hand on his shoulder.

"Bloody hell, Rhodie, I can't even see you, man," came his urgent whisper.

"That's okay, mate. You should be able to smell me after that!" came Chris's breathless reply. "Can you see the net, Sid? It's just over to the right. There's an L.E.D. on the handle."

"Yeah, got it. Nice touch that, Rhodie. Now, how we doing with that carp?" he asked from Chris's side.

"Nearly there, I think," came the reply. "But I can't see a bloody thing. You get the net in the water and I'll do my best to guide it in."

The next couple of minutes were strange and dark, then there was a swirl on the surface and Sid instinctively lifted the net, which was nearly wrenched from his hand.

"Gott 'im!" he declared, and Chris lowered the rod and massaged his aching shoulder before bending to give Sid a hand with the bulging net.

"It's a bit of a whacker I think, Rhodie," he assessed, and the two of them grunted under the strain before lowering the prize onto the unhooking mat that Chris had searched out with an outstretched foot.

After unhooking the fish, Chris grabbed a torch and shone the beam along the carp's flank, picking out three large scales that were as identifiable as a fingerprint.

"Bloody hell, it's Three Scale!" he shouted, and immediately let out a whoop of joy. They decided to sack the fish for the remaining couple of hours of darkness, as to attempt a weighing in the stygian blackness would have been extremely difficult, so Chris lowered the full sack into the margins and securely tied the cord to a tree.

"Well done, Rhodie. I'll be back in a couple of hours with Quill and the cameras." With that, Sid crept off into the darkness, leaving an elated Chris to his thoughts. How big would it be? It was only out a couple of weeks ago at thirty four twelve, but that was after spawning, so would it be heavier? These thoughts and many like them rushed through Chris's head until, like leaping sheep, they eventually sent him to sleep.

The sun was quite high in the sky when he was woken by the sound of voices from behind his swim and he blearily peered out to be greeted by two smiling faces and a mug of tea. After all the pleasantries, they readied the cameras before heaving the fish onto the mat and hoisting it up on the scales.

"What's your p.b., Rhodie?" asked Sid, with a twinkle in his eye. This came as no surprise to Chris, but he went through with the rest of the ritual just the same.

"Thirty four pounds," he replied, smiling from ear to ear.

"Not anymore, mate. It's thirty four twelve now! Bloody well done!" exclaimed Sid gleefully and extended his hand to congratulate the grinning captor. Stan did likewise before they laid the carp down and proceeded to take the photos, and then it was Chris's turn to watch in reverence as the huge fish glided away.

"Oh. You had 'un, then."

The trio turned to see Kirk standing there in all his glory, can in hand, and Stan looked at Chris in astonishment as if to say 'you know this man?' Chris just shrugged, being beyond caring, and merely looked at the newcomer before saying,

"Yep. Personal best mate. What about you?"

"Oh, I lost one in the night and had a couple of little 'uns just before dawn," came the reply, which was swiftly washed down by 8.6% cider. "Anyway, well done, see yer later." With that he turned and left the swim, only slightly steadier than the night before.

Looking at his companions' gaping mouths, he simply said, "Don't ask. Just don't ask, okay."

They looked at the departing figure, at each other, at Chris and back at Kirk's back before shaking their heads and swiftly searching out the kettle and tea bags.

What a session it had been. Two personal bests, a brace of stunning mirrors and a world class arsehole! What more could they ask for?

Chapter Twelve - Thirties Galore!

The news of their session soon reached Buzz's ears and, with only three days work a week planned for the next month, he was seriously fired up.

Chris was also ready to put his four day week into action and over the next fortnight it was this duo that took advantage of the lack of midweek pressure on the lake. Invariably, they had tales to tell Stan and Sid of their conquests prior to the others' Friday arrival, and by the beginning of August had accounted for a further five carp between them to twenty eight pounds.

The weekenders had also had a modicum of success, with Stan landing a couple of double figure commons and Sid a twenty-plus mirror but, despite their supreme confidence, none of them had managed to repeat the successes of the thunderstorm weekend. The lake, however, had given up some of its riches in that time with three further carp in excess of thirty-four pounds visiting the bank, and all different fish. The largest, a plate-scaled mirror of thirty five ten, was landed a couple of days after Chris's thirty four by Don Leach, the guy who had so lovingly inscribed the card in the photo album. Unfortunately, none of them were there to witness the capture but, a few weeks later, Buzz and Chris were shown the pictures by the proud captor and could not stop talking about them afterwards. Don was one of four bailiffs on the lake but, unlike most, was a lovely man who would do anything he could to help someone catch a carp - a far cry from a couple of the others who aided Les in controlling the water. Over the coming months, Don was to be a great help to all four anglers and they, in return, would help in his greatest triumph.

The other two thirties were both witnessed by the mid-weekers. The first a stunning common carp four ounces shy of thirty five pounds - and not the Black Common - caught by a young lad who was making only his third visit to the lake and which almost doubled his previous best. Although pleased for the angler, both Chris and Buzz could tell that this would do him no good at all and, sure enough, after suffering half a dozen blanks on the trot he left the lake with head bowed, never to return. The final capture was a bit galling for, at five thirty on a Friday morning, Chris was greeted by the now familiar sight of Kirk 'The Can' ambling into his swim. But this time he had news that proved not to be the usual fabrication and it was with stunned silence that the pair watched him heave the magnificent Double Linear out of the water, weighing thirty four and a half pounds.

"Talk about beauty and the beast!" commented Buzz later that day, but jealousy, he knew, would get him nowhere and the event was soon put to the back of his mind.

More than a month had passed since Chris's capture of Three Scale and, as was usual for the weekend preceding the August Bank Holiday, the weather forecast was not encouraging. Well, not for sun worshippers, that is, but for carp anglers conditions sounded ideal - south westerly winds, a chance of rain, relative low pressure and temperatures in the mid 60's - all in all perfect fishing conditions, if there is such a thing.

Stan had talked Jean into coming along for the weekend and had even managed to get permission from Les for her to use a float rod if she desired. She had eventually agreed to arrive on Saturday, and had even agreed to bring fresh supplies of cold lager and hot chilli and, with her presence in mind, Stan was hopeful of getting into either one of The Point swims. To this end he had seconded the help of Chris, who would be at the lake at least a day earlier and who had agreed, if the swims were free, to set up in one of the larger swims until Stan arrived - the best laid plans...!

Stan managed to leave work a little before three on Friday afternoon and was confident of reaching the lake by no later than four. Then Sod decided to intervene and, as he left Slough behind him, he saw a trail of brake lights snaking along the M4 in front of him. With less than twenty miles to his destination he was stranded in a classic Bank Holiday jam and arrived at the lake, steaming, almost two hours later than expected.

Chris was none too happy, either, because two of the swims that he had earmarked as worth a move into were now occupied and he was left with two options. Stay put for the night in the East Point with Stan, or choose a swim for the night and rise early in the morning on the lookout for carp. Stan's black mood made his mind up for him but, just as he was about to leave, he had a take to his left hand rod and proceeded to land a nineteen pound mirror. Suddenly, larks were singing, roses bloomed and laughter was unconfined and the pair of them forgot their cares and woe and, after the photos, prepared for the night in the double swim.

Buzz was a couple of swims away to their left, in the Main Lake, and was still licking his wounds after suffering yet another beating from one of the lake's more powerful denizens. This was his third loss of a substantial fish and he was beginning to wonder if he would ever break the thirty barrier and, despite his happiness for Chris, he could not hide the hurt in his eyes.

"Here y'are, big fella. Get this lot down your neck before you have me in tears," said Stan, handing him a can of soothing lager to ease away the pain, whilst preparing himself for the weekend. Buzz gratefully accepted the offering and downed the contents in one, absentmindedly crushing the can as if it were someone's neck, before reaching out for another. Chris and Stan looked at each other with raised eyebrows, and wordlessly said, 'I don't ever want to piss him off!'

By the time that they were both fishing, Buzz was into his fourth can and his dark mood had brightened with the constant badinage between the three of them and, soon, the pain was just a dull ache that gave a slight twinge every now and then. The skies were beginning to darken and threaten rain when the last member of their merry band arrived with his usual hearty welcome.

"Ah, my good fellows. Is there, perchance, a casket of your finest mead with my name upon it!" haled Sid from afar.

Buzz, as usual, was the first to greet him with a huge handshake, to which Sid looked at their clasped hands and said, with a twinkle,

"I'll make a man of you yet, Chewbacca!" but was careful to have removed his hand from the bear-like grasp before that last comment. Buzz laughed hugely and handed a can to Sid, before snaking an arm round him and crushing him like a bear,

"Yep, I reckon you will, Dracool, my friend," he replied to the steadily reddening face in the crook of his arm.

"Put him down, Buzz. You don't know where he's been," remarked Stan, and Buzz obeyed, Sid rubbing his neck and feigning loss of breath, before pulling the ring of the can in Buzz's face and bounding backwards out of arm's reach.

"Boys will be boys, won't they?" said Stan, but laughed just the same.

Things settled down after that and they went through the remaining swims to see where Sid should settle himself. For the time being, the small swim between Buzz and the East Point seemed an obvious choice and, within half an hour, he was back, having decided to drop both of his baits close in on his return. The weed growth had blossomed over the last month and there were very few areas that were fishable more than twenty yards from the bank. Buzz, however, had utilised his profession to the full and, after convincing Les that it would also turn up any dead fish that may be trapped in the weed, had obtained permission from the owner to dive in the lake.

So it was that, the previous Wednesday when only one other angler was present, Buzz had donned his full Scuba gear and had spent two tanks of oxygen and an hour and a half below the lake's surface. His escapade had revealed no corpses, but had opened his eyes greatly to the small areas that the carp fed on. After a number of visits to the surface to triangulate his position, he was extremely happy with four small, clean gravel spots he had found that appeared to have been regularly and recently visited by fish of some sort. He had also marked these spots with small polystyrene markers attached to light line and light leads and was able to cast his own marker to them and pinpoint their position very accurately from a few different swims. It was one of these spots that he had lost the earlier fish from and he was still confident of further action, but he told Sid of a clear area in front of his swim which Sid vowed to investigate in the morning.

The night had drawn in by now, and Buzz had his talking head on so they prepared themselves for some more of his wonderful stories from his travels far and wide. Tonight was to be no exception and taught them a valuable lesson - never let the boat go!

"We were out in the Azores" it began, "and had to try to salvage this wreck that had gone down a few years earlier. Radar had picked out what they thought was the spot. It was up to me and my crew to dive down and investigate, and bring up anything that might verify its identity. Anyway, we'd been booked for a six week stay - there's loads of preparation goes into this sort of op and the actual diving only constitutes about twenty percent of the time spent out there, so, as you can imagine, we had a bit of spare time on our hands. We'd spend it drinking, sunbathing, swimming, trying to pull any bird that was silly enough to come within striking distance, and fishing. Now, the fishing where we were was good, but it was a bit busy, especially with the young local kids constantly asking for fags, beer and any fish you might catch. So, anyway, me and this guy - Jock Peters (great bloke, drank like a bloody fish and could drop a man with one short right) - we decided on a little trip to one of the tiny little atolls just off shore. We knew we wouldn't be diving again for about four or five days so decided to take enough supplies and stay out there for a couple of days. The supplies, as you can imagine, consisted mainly of alcohol in one form or another and the next morning this little launch was dropping us on our own tropical island, about two miles out. It was bloody heaven! We cracked open the first case of beer for breakfast and by lunchtime the second was half empty! I was well into the fishing and was catching all sorts. Bonefish, amazingly coloured rays, little sand sharks, it was brilliant! Then, early evening, this fantastic yacht came chugging past. You know the sort of thing, forty foot long, gleaming white and gold and draped with half a dozen of the most beautiful, scantily clad honeys you could ever wish to see. It was like a bloody Bounty advert. Well, my eyes were out on stalks, and they weren't the only thing! I was just standing there, mouth open, watching these goddesses waving at us, when from above me, I could hear Jock hallooing and yelling and I look up and the silly bastard was about thirty feet up a palm tree, screaming and waving. Pissed as a potato! Then, all of a sudden, he thought he was a bloody coconut and just dropped out of the tree and landed with an almighty thump. I ran over thinking the worst but he was so pissed he couldn't feel a thing and just lay there laughing his stupid head off. I got the giggles then, didn't I, and we were just lying there pissing ourselves when I heard a voice behind me and this blond bombshell was asking in some Swedish accented English "Is he alright?" Well, I thought I'd died and gone to heaven.

Jock just said, "Och, aim fain, lassy. Dinny fret yerself!"

I could have throttled him there and then, but all I could do was watch this gorgeous pair of buttocks wobble off towards the rowboat, and wave back as she waved and smiled. Then, when the yacht's just setting off, the stupid Scottish bastard only goes and tells me he thinks he's broken his leg. I nearly broke his bloody neck!"

"So how did you get back, then?" asked a highly amused Sid.

"We stayed for two days until the boat arrived of course. We had another four crates of beer, a case of whisky and a bucket of bait to get through, mate. No way were we going back early!"

"Had he broken his leg, then?" asked Stan, already dreading the answer.

"Oh, yeah. But I set it for him and put a splint on it, and he just finished the case of whisky off over the next couple of days! Next day I caught a bloody great barracuda and we cooked it on the beach, it was brilliant!"

The three listeners didn't know whether to laugh or cry, but Buzz just took another swig from his can and ended with,

"I never went fishing with him again. That was the one and only chance I've had of landing a mermaid and he let it slip the hook, silly bastard." With that, he finished his drink, rose to his feet and said, "Right, I'm off to me plot to catch me a real sea monster. I'll see you chaps in the morning," disappearing through the trees with a final farewell.

The others chuckled and surmised for a further ten minute before it was Sid saying farewell, and the remaining two cleared everything away before retiring to their beds.

The night was punctuated with tench for both Stan and Chris so they rose much later than dawn, the sun quite high in the sky when Buzz wandered into their swim demanding tea. Nothing had been out during the night, although Buzz had heard one screaming alarm, but was soon assured that all that was attached was another tench. The green devils had become a bit of a pest, and barely a day went by without at least one falling to each angler's rods. They had quizzed Les as to the possible removal of some of them, but he was a little reticent to do that and so the problem remained.

Chris was unsure what to do now, especially as Buzz had seen three or four carp in the vicinity of Chris's baits, and it took little for Stan to persuade him to stay put for the rest of the day. Jean arrived just after midday and Buzz made some comment about coconuts which was totally misconstrued - or maybe not. Whatever the meaning, it brought a chuckle from all present and was repeated a few more times over the course of the weekend.

Buzz had divulged one of the secret spots in front of Sid's swim and assisted the said angler by climbing a nearby tree to watch the lead enter the water perfectly above the clear gravel spot. All the clear areas that Buzz had found were on the top or sides of the three or four bars that ran at right angles to the bank, away from the anglers. Accuracy was paramount and a few hours later it was obvious that Sid had been extremely accurate in his casting when a twenty seven pound mirror picked up his hookbait and was soon nestling in the folds of the net Buzz was brandishing.

After the photos and usual congratulations, Sid returned the favour and watched Buzz's entry! The spot he was casting to was very narrow and close to the edge of the bar but, being only five feet deep and twenty yards out, was easily seen from the tree, which was just as well for Buzz. On three occasions he had to recast as Sid called down that he had missed the spot and had slid down the side of the bar into the weed below but, on the fourth cast Sid shouted, "Perfect!" and watched as a kilo of bait peppered the spot. Buzz knew that a lot would miss or roll off into the weed, but was confident that fifty or sixty baits would find their mark and, hopefully, entice any passing carp to stop and sample his wares.

The evening followed a similar pattern as the previous, and Jean was highly entertained by Buzz's story-telling and the constant barrage of friendly abuse that accompanied them. At one point, and completely out of the blue as was his wont, Sid had a momentary lapse of reason and said to Buzz,

"Maybe we should call you Muff."

It took a second for the penny to drop before the others howled with laughter.

"You know, what with all that hair round your chops and everything!" he concluded, to which the howling increased tenfold. Buzz just sat there quietly, sipping his beer before calmly replying,

"Yep. A few people have called me that - but only once! "

The three of them looked at the huge man, looked at each other, then, with a wink and a nod from Stan, they leapt on Buzz and proceeded to lick his face, his eyes, stick their tongues in his ears and generally abuse him until he was totally disabled. His and Jean's manic laughter echoed across the lake!

"Don't make us do that again, sonny, or there'll be tears!" warned Sid, after he had regained his breath. Buzz wiped every orifice dry, uttering the word, "Mad!" over and over again between bouts of giggles. The evening deteriorated rapidly after that and, pretty soon, they all retired for the night.

The next morning was bright and very early, and brought with it a certain amount of fragility. That was soon forgotten when a buzzer screamed and they heard Buzz calling for assistance. On arriving, breathlessly, in his swim, they saw the rod bent and Sid by the big man's side offering needless advice. The take had come from the previous evening's careful cast and the fish had doubled the distance between itself and the angler in a very short space of time. Now, it had become weeded, and they went through the usual debate as to the next move. Put the rod down and let the fish swim out, keep a constant pressure on and hope that the weed starts to give, 'saw' the line back and forward in a bid to cut through the weed, or just give it the big heave and hope for the best. Whilst they pondered their options, Buzz replaced the rod in the rests and stared intently at the water, oblivious to the debate going on around him.

"I'm gonna swim out there," he declared. Stan looked at Chris and frowned.

"It's pretty deep there, Buzz. And weedy. How you gonna net the fish when you get out there?" he asked, but before Buzz could reply, a bleary-eyed Jean strolled into the swim and said, "Haven't you got a boat?"

They looked at her, then at each other, as if someone had just slapped them across the face. Of course there was a boat. Les had installed one only last month because of the heavy weed growth and had told them that it was only to be used in an emergency. And this, as far as they could tell, was one hell of an emergency!

"I'll go," declared Chris, and was off like a jack-rabbit, leaving the others to work out the tactics. They came to the decision that three of them should be in the boat - one to row, one with the net, and Buzz - and obviously Chris had been of the same mind because, on his arrival, he had brought two spare life jackets with him. Buzz donned his, as did Sid before grabbing the net, and Stan handed Buzz the rod before scurrying back to his swim to grab his camera. It took little time for them to reach the point where the line disappeared vertically into the lake, Sid gingerly holding the nylon in his hand and gradually easing it towards him. He could feel a presence on the other end and informed all that the fish was still on, then leant further over the side of the boat and began peeling the clinging weed fronds from the line. All the time Buzz was keeping up a continuous commentary of how he was going to lose this one as well and it took a determined Chris to tell him to, "Shut the **** up!"

After ten patient minutes, Sid had removed an impressive amount of weed and, suddenly, felt the fish surge strongly on the end of the line, letting it slip easily through his fingers before saying,

"Okay, Buzz, it's all yours boy."

The increasingly paranoid angler felt the rod tip pull over, the boat swinging round as the fish made another bid for freedom. The clutch clicked a little, then he eased the tip up and felt the fish wallowing beneath the boat. Peering over the side, Sid saw the sunlight glint off of a huge flank and forced himself to say nothing, praying that he would need only one chance with the net. As the boat turned, the sun picked out the twisting and turning form of a large fish just feet below the boat. It mattered not what Sid said, because all was very clear to Buzz now and he groaned, "Oh, my God," under his breath as he saw what he was attached to.

The next few minutes lasted a lifetime and were etched forever more in the minds of all concerned. Then, at last, rising from the deep like one of Buzz's salvaged wrecks, a huge, grey flank rolled a yard from the boat and was scooped up first time by the grateful Sid. Then all hell broke loose, as all of Buzz's pent up emotions burst forth like a breached dam and, with a deafening scream, he launched himself into the lake, landing with a sound like a killer whale at Sea World in the throes of drenching the audience.

Drench them, he did, but they cared little as they were also in the throes of joyful celebration, as were the watchers from dry land - Stan hoping that he had just snapped the best mid air shot ever. (It wasn't to be, but the content was good enough to bring back marvellous memories whenever they looked at it.)

Once back in his swim, Buzz left the others in charge whilst he dried himself and changed into some dry clothes. A small crowd had gathered by now, amongst them Dean, the angler who had caught the Grey Mirror at thirty seven plus last year, and it was he who immediately recognised Buzz's fish as one and the same. This time, however, it was a pound heavier and had just broken the lake record. Buzz's elation was unbounded and he couldn't stop shaking his head in disbelief, at one point squatting down and shielding his eyes from view, until Jean went over and kissed his forehead and congratulated him once more. The fish was huge, even against a huge man, and he stood in the water up to his chest cradling the great carp, gently stroking it as it lazily swam out of his arms. His arms then shot aloft and he howled at the moon before declaring to all, "I think it's time to get very, very drunk!"

The rest of the session was one of celebration, drinking, Buzz's continual reminder to anyone who would listen that he had caught a, "Thirty eight pound twelve ounce mirror carp, which I believe is bigger than anything anyone else here has caught!" The sun shone and once again the weather men had got it wrong and most of southern England enjoyed a warm and sunny Bank Holiday. The weather enticed the fish to move into the shallower waters of the Back Lake which, in turn, gave Chris and Stan some action with both of them hooking a couple of carp but landing only one each. Both mirrors, they barely added up to the size of Buzz's monster and Stan's eighteen pound linear was his fourth double figure carp in over a month and he was beginning to wonder if he was going to join the thirties club that all of his friends had recently formed. The weekend ended with Jean landing a six pound tench on float tackle and barely avoiding a ducking from the others.

As summer gradually gave way to autumn, the carp's habits seemed to change and the Back Lake became frequented less and less by them. This made location difficult on the one hand because they were invariably in deeper water, but easier on the other hand because there was less area of water to worry about. The first evidence of this change came a couple of weeks after Buzz's success. After spending the weekend in and around the Back Lake with only a couple of small tench to show for their troubles, news reached the band's ears of a stupendous catch a couple of days later. Two anglers, who they knew by sight but not really to talk to, had set up in the same swims that Buzz and Sid had fished on the Bank Holiday weekend and, over a forty eight hour period, hooked ten carp between them, landing seven. Although they lost a couple of very good fish - one, a big, orange leather coming off within inches of the net - they did, however, set a new lake record when one of them, Micky Charles, landed the increasingly awesome Big Linear just two ounces shy of the forty pound mark. Unfortunately, none of them were there to witness it but, a week later, they gawped at the stunning photos in the angling press.

Just after the publication, Chris met the pair and congratulated them roundly, especially Micky. It transpired that they had only obtained a ticket a month or so earlier and that this was their fourth session on the lake, and their first success! Chris wondered whether it had just been luck but, on chatting longer it was obvious that these boys were very competent anglers, having spent a season or two on Harefield and accounted for a number of fish to low thirties.

"What were they like then?" Stan had asked, the next day.

"Well, Micky is a really nice bloke. Easy to talk to and obviously a good angler. But the other guy, George Glasman I think his name was, well I'm not too sure about him. He didn't really say much but I'm not sure if he could, y'know," replied Chris, strangely.

"What d'yer mean, Rhodie?" asked a puzzled Sid.

"Well, he's a big fella. Rugby player I would think. Shaven head, couple of scars over his eyes and talks real slow. Doesn't elaborate on anything, just the bare bones, but he was still friendly. He looked like the sort of bloke who would do anything for you but, if you asked him to fetch something for you, you'd better make sure it wasn't attached to a wall, a tree or another person or he'd probably bring back bits of one of them as well. Intellectual capacity of an Abyssinian Ferris Slug, I reckon!"

Two fountains of lager shot from the mouths of the listeners as they tried to gargle and laugh at the same time, and it was a few minutes before they were capable of coherent speech. Over the next few months they met the pair on a few occasions and found Chris's assessment to be perfectly correct - Micky was a nice bloke and a very good angler and George (a.k.a. 'Ferris' from then on) did indeed have the intelligence of an Abyssinian Ferris Slug, whatever it may be!

Much to Stan's chagrin, Jean had booked a holiday for them at the end of September, for a week, and he was less than happy at the prospect of missing two weekends at his favourite time of year. His hope was, therefore, that he could bag himself a whacker before departing for foreign climes but, with only one session remaining before that departure, he had managed to catch only two carp a few ounces either side of the twenty pound mark.

With much grovelling and a couple of late nights, he had been able to elicit an early arrival at the lake on Friday, pulling into the relatively deserted car park just after one o'clock. Of the three cars present, two belonged to Chris and Buzz, the other was Dean's and it was in his swim that Stan found all three anglers drinking tea and discussing the moods of the lake.

"Quill, you sneaky ol' dog! What you doing here so early, boy?" exclaimed Buzz whilst vigourously shaking the newcomer's hand.

Stan smiled and, with a wink, replied, "It's amazing what you can achieve from beneath the boss's desk, boys!" With that, they all guffawed and Dean put the kettle on.

Stan was brought up to speed with recent events, of which there were very few. Dean had arrived a day earlier than the other two and had caught a twenty five pound mirror on Thursday evening from the swim he now occupied. The others had been less successful and were in the throes of moving swims but, as yet, they had seen nothing else to take their fancy. Dean was in a small swim a third of the way along the west bank of the Main Lake and had taken his fish from the marginal shelf to his right. Since then, no fish had been evident close in although a couple had shown themselves at range earlier on. He was due to leave in a short while and Stan could tell that Buzz was seriously thinking about moving into the swim after Dean. Stan had a couple of swims in mind but knew that he only had a couple of hours to make a decision before the Friday rush that he was normally an integral part of began in earnest. It had become increasingly evident that the carp were less affected by wind direction than the anglers were and, after half a day of a new wind, the fish could be found anywhere on the lake, not necessarily on the windward bank. To this end, Stan was not too concerned by the south-westerly breeze blowing over his shoulder and into the far corners of the Main Lake and the Back Lake, and was, instead, concentrating his thoughts and attention on the Pads Corner to the right. The surface of the lake was barely being ruffled here, and although the last remnants of the pads were not a patch on their former, summer glory, Stan was still convinced that the fish would visit the area a few more times. Dean's fish had come from the very same shelf, but seventy yards away from that which the dying leaves clung to. Finishing his tea, he took a stroll along to the corner, accompanied by Chris, and they both climbed the tree from which they had seen their memorable pre-season sights. The day was quite bright and still relatively warm for the time of year but, away from the shelter of the trees and bushes below, the wind had that certain nip that was a foretaste of what was soon to be common. The water clarity was good, the weed growth assisting in this, and the pair of watchers could clearly see the gravel shelf and its sloping sides that disappeared into the green jungle fifteen yards from the bank. A couple of small clearings in the weed were evident from this height and it was from one of these, ten minutes after first ascending the tree, that the pair saw a carp slowly emerge, shortly followed by two more.

The anglers whispered and pointed excitedly, eyeing the bank below for possible spots to fish from, then Stan glanced to his right and saw a sight that would stay with him forever. Cruising slowly along the front of the reeds to their right, he and Chris gazed down on four carp that, from the height of the tree, looked to be of considerable size. Then, as they gradually moved closer, Stan suddenly realised what he was looking at and gasped, "It's the Black Common!"

Chris was nodding silently, having come to the same conclusion seconds earlier, and was greedily drinking in the sight before him. As the fish cruised beneath the tree, the anglers above shifted position so as to get a better view through the branches and this helped them identify the three other carp accompanying the mythical common. Two were very obvious, the first being the Big Linear which they knew to be around forty pounds, the other was a huge orange fish which, they assumed, was the one that Micky had lost at the net recently. This looked comparable in size to the linear, but both of these were dwarfed by the common and they struggled to accept how big it could possibly be. The fourth fish was not much smaller than the other two and, when it rolled on its side to rub against the gravel shelf, it revealed two distinctive rows of scales.

"Double Linear," declared Stan, needlessly, before returning to his daydreams.

What he would give to catch any one of these magnificent carp but, oh my, that Black Common. He was shaken from his reverie by Chris's sudden descent and realized that he had better hustle along if he was to get in a good position to fish for these dream makers. Once down, they sat beneath the tree and tried to collect their thoughts. From above, they had seen at least two small, clear holes in the weed and they were in such a position that one could be fished from the swim they were sitting in, where Buzz had lost his fish at the start of the season. The other could be fished from the swim to their left, on the West Bank. That way, they could both place a bait next to the pads, if desired, and also fish a clear, deeper area. Both agreed, and they were soon back with their tackle, Chris beneath the Climbing Tree and Stan at right angles to him to his left. They spent the next couple of hours assisting each other in finding the clear spots with a minimum of disturbance, one directing the other from a tree. By the time that Stan would usually be arriving at the lake, he was sitting in his swim drinking tea and discussing a job well done with Chris.

Chris had opted to fish his other rod to his right, in front of the reeds and along the route that the four carp had recently taken, whilst Stan had dropped his right hand rod on the edge of the withering lily bed. The carp had still been evident on their final visit to the tree, although they were now a little further out and in amongst a jungle of Canadian pondweed, but their continued presence filled the anglers' confidence cups to overflowing.

The nights were drawing in much earlier now and it was as the sun slowly sank behind them that Stan, Chris and Buzz were joined by a panting Sid.

"Bloody hell, this is really getting to be a rush," he gasped, as he dropped his tackle at the back of Buzz's swim and sank to the floor. "Is that kettle on, boy?" he enquired, whilst sticking a cigarette into his mouth.

"Oh yes, your Highness! Could I possibly blow it for you until it reaches the desired temperature?" came Buzz's sarcastic reply, but it was like water off a rhino's hide to Sid, who smiled back and said,

"That would be very acceptable, my good man. And while you're at it, could you set my rods up in a swim that is brimming with carp so large it looks like their mother has been rogered by an omnibus?" Buzz's reply was unprintable, and the gathered throng chortled heartily at the verbal tennis.

Sid opted to fish to Buzz's left for the night. As darkness descended, the four of them were gathered around a bubbling pot of curry that Stan had concocted the previous evening, washing it down with a few bottles of ale and a liberal smattering of good humour and repartee. They were about to be regaled with another of Buzz's tales when the softly playing radio behind them issued forth the first notes of a favourite tune and they paused to take in the full majesty of Pink Floyd performing Shine On You Crazy Diamond.

"They're playing your tune, Sid" commented Stan, to which Sid frowned quizzically. "This song. It was written about Sid Barrett," Stan explained and Sid nodded in acknowledgment, all four falling quiet in readiness for the opening verse. Then, a few minutes later, the Kingfisher Male Voice Choir offered vocal accompaniment to the band.

"Remember when you were young? You shone like the sun. Shi.."

Bleep!

The chorus ended abruptly as another of their favourite tunes issued from Stan's swim.

Bleeeeeeeeeeep!

Stan had already covered half of the forty yards to his rods when the buzzer issued a continuous tone as the perpetrator of the interruption made off with Stan's bait at speed.

On reaching his swim, very few seconds after the initial indication, Stan saw the L.E.D. on his right hand buzzer, the rod next to the pads, glowing brightly, and could hear the baitrunner fizzing as line was being removed at an alarming rate. He lifted the rod and clicked the baitrunner off, but the line still hissed through the rings as the lightly set clutch came into play. He had now been joined by the other three, and also by Pink Floyd, as Sid had thought it highly appropriate to bring the radio along. As the final notes of the tune drifted across the lake five minutes later, they heard the fish roll on the surface for the first time, ten yards out. Stan had no concept of how big the carp might be as it had picked up quite a bit of weed on its travels but, when it went into the net minutes later, he howled with joy, certain that this was no mid-double.

Buzz and Chris lifted the net onto the waiting mat, grunting under the strain, and they were also fairly certain that this was going to be a very pleasing moment for Stan. All that was to be discerned was how much of the weight was weed, and how much carp. The answer was very much in the carp's favour and, as the weed was removed, Sid's torch beam revealed a double row of linear scales and Stan went into paroxysms of ecstasy, his gleeful cries echoing across the lake and bringing the inevitable response from the resident coots. The standard procedure took over, as did the not so standard question and answer session.

"What's your p.b., Quill?" asked Sid.

"Thirty five pounds. Has it changed then?" the ecstatic Stan queried.

"Oh, yes, boy. Oh, yes! It is now, ooh, just under .... Err, yep. Just one ounce under thirty six pounds!"

Stan's elation continued through the sacking of the fish and subsequent retrieval, ten minutes later once all the cameras were ready. They had decided that it was too early in the evening to sack the fish until morning and, although the photos would not be as good as in daylight, the welfare of the fish came first and Stan still smiled brightly as the flashes lit up the night.

They retired to bed hours later and Stan's head buzzed, not only with the alcohol but also that feeling of contentment that comes on such an occasion.

The session could have been even more memorable when Chris hooked a good fish from the clearing in the weed in the early hours of the morning but, after doing battle for ten minutes or so, the line suddenly parted and the fish was gone. Chris's dismayed cry woke many sleeping individuals around the lake.

Chris did manage to redress the balance a fortnight later when, whilst Stan was sunning himself on a foreign beach in the Mediterranean, he repeated Stan's success and landed the very same fish from the same swim but, this time, a couple of ounces over the thirty six pound mark.

On the day of his return, Stan also missed the capture of the Grey Mirror at a lake record equalling weight of thirty nine twelve, a pound heavier than Buzz's capture of the fish. It was becoming very evident that the forty pound mark could soon be breached by at least two of the lake's carp - and that didn't include the Black Common.

Stan's return to the lake, early in October, coincided with the capture of another thirty in the shape of the increasingly desirable 'Plates' at thirty seven twelve to Dean. He was steadily becoming the most successful angler on the lake, this being his third thirty pound carp of the season. As if to confirm his status, he landed a personal best common just short of thirty pounds and went home a very happy man.

The weather had changed noticeably since the end of September, and the drop in temperature seemed to curb the carp's natural instinct to feed at this time of year, the next few weeks producing just a couple of small doubles to Buzz and Sid. The four began thinking ahead to the winter and possible venues for the colder months. Nobody really knew how the lake would fish over the next few months as there had been hardly any anglers on the lake at this time during the previous couple of seasons, so they elected to stay put until Christmas to see what transpired. Dean had been one of the few anglers to sit out the previous winter on Kingfisher, but his rewards had been few and he was unsure whether to repeat the tactic this year. However, when he learnt of their plans, he decided to do the same and would arrange his sessions accordingly, trying to be at the lake at the same time as at least one of them.

Their decision was further reinforced on the first weekend in November. Stan arrived an hour before dark to be greeted by a beaming Buzz and it was obvious that he had more than a double figure common to talk about. It transpired that he had seen a couple of fish on his arrival, the previous morning, and so had set up in the West Point, casting to his right into the deeper water off The Bar. It was from there that he had received a take in the early hours of the morning. The fight was dogged rather than spectacular, but resulted in his second thirty pound carp of the season. The fish was 'Double D', the same one that Stan had caught at the beginning of the season just short of thirty pounds and, on this, its fourth visit to the bank that year, it had recorded its heaviest weight of thirty two and a half pounds. Buzz was, naturally, overjoyed and had been joined in the swim by Chris, who was fishing to the left into the Back Lake. Stan found this puzzling until he was informed that they had both seen carp in there over the past few hours, as had Don Leach who was fishing in the middle of the reeds to their left.

Stan was unsure how to proceed as the Back Lake had not even entered his thoughts over the past few weeks, but the knowledge that Buzz's fish had come from the deeper water of the Main Lake convinced him to go with his original feelings. So he set up further round to Buzz's right in a swim that looked straight down the lake towards the South Bank. This was the only swim that faced in that direction and, so, had the gravel bars running diagonally across from right to left, making them much easier to locate with a marker float. In the summer months, when the lake was busier, this swim was not a viable proposition due to the anglers normally fishing to the right on the West Bank but, with that area free it became a very good choice, especially with a brisk south-westerly blowing up the lake.

Stan had little time to prepare for the night, so cast his marker float twice, once to the close bar and then to the seventy yard bar, dropping a small pop-up next to each amongst a small scattering of boilies. He then adjourned to the larger swim behind him to join the others for the evening. Sid was working this weekend so would not be present, but their number was made up for a few hours by Don who regaled them with a few stories of his own. He knew a great deal about the lakes in the area, having lived in Reading for most of his life, and was convinced that the lakes hereabouts contained some massive carp. He then told them of some rumours he had heard recently of a very large gravel pit nearby that had, this season, produced a carp in excess of fifty pounds, and when he saw the doubt in their eyes, decided to come clean and reveal the whole truth.

The lake was to the east of Reading and was in excess of two hundred acres. As with most lakes of this size it was home to a couple of sailing and wind surfing clubs, as well as a couple of angling societies. There was also an out of bounds area that was deemed a Sight of Special Scientific Interest (SSSI), so the whole thing proved a difficult prospect to fish. But, as with all lakes, there are always a few hardy individuals willing to suffer for their sport and it was one of these who had caught a fifty one pound mirror carp earlier in the season. This expansion on the story had really caught the attention of the other three and they were soon asking the usual questions like how to join, who to speak to, what other fish? The answers were encouraging, especially as Don knew of another carp over forty pounds being caught plus a few upper thirties. The fishing rights were owned by a couple of clubs, one of which would be easy to get into, so the three of them set themselves a target of two years on Kingfisher before a possible move to the bigger pond. In the meantime, they would have a walk round whenever possible to get a feel for the place.

Having whet their appetite sufficiently, Don bade them goodnight and good luck and returned to his swim, leaving them with their tongues wagging. Not long after, Stan made the fifteen yard trip to his bivvy to dream of monster carp, the wind still pushing down the lake towards him and filling him with confidence. Barely had he nestled into the folds of his sleeping bag when he heard a huge splash to his right and was immediately on his feet and peering along the margins. There were no birds present and he could just make out the ripples emanating from a spot fifteen yards along the bank from where the disturbance had occurred. Unsure of what to do, he turned back to his bivvy when an equally loud splash had him spinning on his heels just in time to see the water rocking from the fish's re-entry. Quickly picking up the rod cast to the far bar, he rapidly wound in his rig. He checked to see that the boilie still floated, and then he side-armed the lead along the margins, watching it enter the water fifteen yards away, feeling the satisfying thump as the lead hit lakebed instead of weed. He had, in fact, sprinkled some hemp and maples in the spot a little earlier so was quite happy to fish a single hookbait in the area, and returned to bed glowing with anticipation.

He was awoken a few hours later, not by a fish but by a shout, and it took him a few seconds to realise what was happening. The shout seemed to come from far away, yet he could hear a commotion behind him in the West Point so staggered sleepily from his bed and, donning a jacket, made his way to the swim. On seeing Chris and Buzz standing there, he asked with a yawn,

"Wass happening, chaps?" to which they both answered with a shrug and a 'dunno.' Then the shout came again and Chris said, "That's Don, innit?"

In total agreement, they walked through the bushes and along the reed line to Don's swim where they saw him silhouetted against the sky, rod pointing high.

"Someone's cut his legs off," observed Stan in a puzzled tone.

"No, you fool," replied Chris, "he's standing in the water."

"What on earth for? Has he lost his mind?" retorted Stan, pensively.

"No, I just don't want to lose this fish," explained Don, "it's kited along the reeds and I think it's buried itself halfway along. I haven't been able to move it for the last five minutes and the water level along the front of the reeds is pretty deep, now."

His teeth chattered as he spoke and it was obvious that they had to do something quickly. Buzz immediately started stripping off and when asked what he thought he was going to do, replied, "I'm going in, boys. Man's got a carp on. Can't let him lose it now, can we?"

After a minute's conversation, they came up with a possible plan. Stan and Chris would take it in turns to hold the rod whilst Don came ashore to dry and warm himself. Then Buzz would take a torch with him into the reeds to see if he could follow the line to the fish. Once there, he would attempt to free the carp or spook it out so that Don could play it out in open water. This seemed the best idea to all of them, and they made Don vow that he would buy them all a very large curry if they were successful.

First Stan, then Chris shivered and squealed as the surprisingly cold water froze their nether regions. Then Buzz did the same, only further along the bank. He gave them a running commentary, not only about which part of his body the water had reached, but also the lack of line above the surface. To this end, Chris raised the rod as high as he could before handing it over to Don, who was warmed enough and eager to regain control.

"Right, I can see the line," Buzz called. "I'm going to get hold of it and follow it along. Right I've got hold of it, can you feel that, Don?"

Don nodded, then realised what he was doing and called, "Yes, I can feel it. Can you see the fish?"

"Not yet, mate," replied the talking reed bed, "but I can see the route it's taken. It's wound its way along the reeds about five or six yards, I would think. Just felt it move. It's still on, mate."

Don was shivering again but the knowledge that the fish was still on made him stay where he was until the bitter end. A few mutterings came from the reed bed, then, as quietly as he could, Buzz instructed, "Somebody bring me a landing net. Quick!"

Stan had the net already in hand, so quickly ran to the point of Buzz's entry, wading a couple of feet into the reeds before he could make out Buzz's outstretched hand.

"Can you see it?" he whispered.

"Yeah. It's just about a yard away, but the line's well tangled. If it spooks I think the line might go. I'm going to try to put the net the other side of it and then move forward and coax it in there," Buzz replied.

"Will that work, then?" asked Stan, sceptically.

"Dunno, but I'm freezing my nuts off here, and I can't think of what else to do," came the muffled reply, and before Stan could suggest a better idea, not that he had one, he saw the net disappear below the line of the reeds. There was a bit of movement, then a violent commotion, followed by a sound like a gunshot as the nylon parted. This was followed by a wail from Don and a defeated, "It's gone!" from the freezing angler.

"No it bloody hasn't!" bellowed Buzz. "It's in the bloody net, boys! Yesssss!"

Stan waded further forward to assist the grinning netsman with his bounty, and Buzz greeted him with, "This is a bloody whacker, Quill!"

Back ashore they were greeted by Don and Chris, who were both still totally bemused by recent events. Once on the mat, Chris took charge of the fish whilst the others dried themselves off and got the blood coursing through their bodies again. On removing the hook and peeling back the mesh, Chris let out a gasp, "Bloody hell! It's massive!"

"Turn it over," instructed Buzz, and, on seeing the other flank, he declared, "It's the Grey Mirror. I recognise that scale by the gill cover. Well done, Don, I think you've just beaten your personal best."

With that he held out his hand and shook the bemused captor's warmly, before searching out a weigh sling and a set of scales.

They zeroed the forty pound Avon's and hoisted the fish up, gazing intently at the dial, before Stan uttered those immortal words, "I think we need some bigger scales!" They did indeed need bigger scales and minutes later they stared, mouths open, at the first forty pound carp they had ever seen, Although only six ounces heavier than that mark, it was a momentous milestone, and they were all speechless for a few seconds before the quiet of the night was rent with the sounds of anglers howling at the moon.

The night had only a few more hours before its shift ended, so they decided to sack the fish until first light to better take the photos, and they left Don to gaze at the heavens for the next few hours, marvelling at how wonderful life could be.

On another occasion, Stan's subsequent capture of a personal best twenty seven pound common an hour or so later would have been the main talking point of the weekend, and many blank weeks to come, but he cared little that it wasn't. It still filled him with pleasure and was just reward for the midnight move to the margins, and the brace shot of his and Don's fish would be seen by thousands in the papers a week or so later.

Their hopes of a productive winter, following such a successful start, were ill founded and by the middle of December no further fish had fallen to their rods. The only fish to be caught being a mid-twenty at the end of November to Micky Charles, so as the weather deteriorated and the year ended, they decided to leave the lake alone for a month or two.

Buzz was fortunate that he could choose certain jobs at certain times of the year and was soon bidding them farewell for six weeks, prior to leaving for New Zealand. The others were much less fortunate and had to suffer the British winter, come what may, and they all decided that there was only one thing to do at this time of year and that was to fish for something with teeth. That decided, they spent the next few weeks throwing dead fish around in a bid to bag some impressive predators but, although they caught quite a few pike, none of them were in excess of ten pounds and the trio's thoughts soon turned to carp once more.

Their plans for a mid-February return were put on hold, however, or more to the point, temporarily frozen as Jack Frost and his chilling friends came out to play for a couple of weeks. During this time, the phone lines sang but there was little they could do apart from pray for some low pressure, and a swift thaw.

Their prayers were eventually answered with just two weeks of the season remaining and the four of them made plans for a staggering finale to their season. Unfortunately, the carp had not seen the plans and remained in their winter hiding places until the very last weekend of the season. The temperatures had gradually risen over the previous fortnight and, finally, this better weather had made an impression on the carp and in the final two days of the season, four were caught. Three were low twenties, one of which fell to Sid's rods on the last morning. These were overshadowed in the final afternoon of the season when Dean, fishing a clear area he had found sixty yards from the west bank, had hooked and landed the Big Linear at a lake record weight of forty one pounds, crowning his brilliant season spectacularly.

It was the first time that the four of them had seen the fish on the bank and they were, for once, absolutely speechless. Dean was totally blown away by the capture and welcomed their assistance with the weighing and photographs, repaying those deeds with a huge curry and a crate of lager later that evening. What a way to end the season. They had caught more than thirty carp between them with seven being in excess of thirty pounds, all beating their previous bests in the process, and had formed strong friendships along the way. Thoughts now moved to the next season and, over the next couple of months, the phone lines were red hot, especially on the subject of bait.

In their final night conversations with Dean they had discovered that many of his fish had fallen to tiger nuts, including the most recent, and it was this topic that was high on the list of telephone discussions over the following month. Once agreed on the use of tigers with their usual mix of hemp and maples, they decided on a pre-baiting campaign over the last six weeks of the close season and so, in that time, steadily but carefully introduced the bait into the lake. By the first week of June the fish were becoming very accustomed to their free meals and it was with the usual amnesia that the four anglers marvelled at the carp's confident feeding habits, forgetting, as usual, about the lack of lines and end tackle in the lake. Nonetheless, they felt amazingly confident as the season drew nearer, having seen all of the larger inhabitants (including the seemingly uncatchable Black Common) partaking of their regular free meals. One black cloud crept into view on the horizon, and that was that Buzz had been offered a four week assignment in Dubai which would last for the whole of June. Although loathe to miss what could be a memorable start to the season, he could ill afford to turn down the obscene amount of money being offered and, so, could only witness the final few frenzied feeding sessions through Sid's eyes, whom he phoned on an almost daily basis.

On his final pre-season trip to the lake, days before the off, Chris bumped into lake owner, Les Morgan, who seemed far from his usual effusive self, so Chris enquired as to the problem.

"I'm glad I bumped into you, Chris," began Les. "I'm afraid I've got a major problem so I won't be around much this year. I've handed over the general running of the lake to Rod Jones so if you've got any problems you need to talk to him."

Rod was the head bailiff and not one of life's charmers, either. They'd had a couple of run-ins with him during the previous season and so the idea of him being in total control left Chris with a tight feeling in his stomach. But first he needed to know why this course of action was necessary.

"What's the problem then, Les? I thought you loved the place."

"Oh, I do, believe me Chris. But I love my wife more and I'm afraid she's just been diagnosed with cancer and she needs all the help I can give her. Hopefully she'll be fine in a few months, after the treatment, but in the meantime I intend to be at her beck and call twenty four hours a day."

Chris didn't know what to say to this news, so just mumbled some apologies and tried desperately to think of a change of subject. Les had seen the same reaction many times in recent weeks and knew how uncomfortable people felt in Chris's position so had become well versed in changing the subject himself.

"Anyway mate, you going to slay 'em this year, then?" he asked with a smile. Chris was still thinking of the previous conversation so stumbled a little at the change of direction.

"What? Oh. Yeah. Err, yeah, I reckon we'll have a few whackers out this year. So, Rod's the main man, is he?" he managed. Les knew of their differences so did his best to reassure Chris.

"Yeah, he's the main man at the moment but don't you worry. As long as you boys keep your noses clean you probably won't even know he's there."

With that, he bade Chris farewell and they both wished each other different sorts of luck.

As Chris was preparing to impart the news of Les's wife to his mates, Felcham Mere was under the influence of a huge daphnia explosion, certain parts of the lake appearing pink. This explosion of food benefited not only the carp, but the myriad of invertebrates that made up the bulk of their diet, and in that respect they benefited even more. The long days of summer flowed into one another and the sight of one or more of the huge carp lazily cruising the margins left the occasional tench or bream angler shaking their heads in disbelief.

All four carp were of comparable size by now, but The Common was steadily becoming the largest carp in the lake and, at that moment in time, had very few betters swimming in English waters. By the turn of the year that number had decreased, and the wealth of highly nutritious food was put to only one purpose - growth.

Chapter Thirteen - Green-Eyed Monsters

"Chris Rhodes," announced Rod Jones as he pulled the first name from the hat, to the usual accompaniment of catcalls and cries of 'Fix!'

"Yes!"exclaimed Chris, able to relax, now, and watch the faces of the other fifteen anglers as they anticipated the next name to be drawn. Despite the season starting on Monday midnight, Chris was surprised that there were so few of the sixty strong membership present for the start and was pleased that he and Stan had decided to take the week off. His mind buzzed with the prospect of first choice of swim and he suddenly realised that the position was an unenviable one, the possibility of a cock-up of mammoth proportions looming large in his mind. The mention of Stan's name shook him from his reverie and he had to ask what number they were at.

"Ten," mouthed Stan, and Chris felt a twinge of envy at his friend's position in the running order, he would have only two or three good swims to choose from so would have less chance of making a mistake. Suddenly, the sixteenth and last name was pulled from the hat, which meant it was decision time for everybody. Chris's mind was a blur as he tried to remember what the weather forecast was, where the fish came from at the beginning of last season and what his and Stan's game plan had been for this eventuality.

"Down to you then Chris," called Rod, "where's it to be, then?"

He could feel all eyes on him and suddenly realised he had lost all power of speech! Stan was staring intently at him, willing him to say the words he obviously knew but seemed incapable of repeating. Then, in a torrent, they burst forth, "Crazy Diamond!"

The assembled throng looked extremely puzzled, but Stan's smile beamed through the surrounding frowns and he realised that he had made the correct decision.

"Where?" queried Kirk, asking the question for most of the anglers present.

"Crazy Diamond," repeated Chris, as if he was talking to a three year old child. "South west corner, by the pads. Crazy Diamond!"

With that, he nonchalantly turned away and let the proceedings continue, glowing at his good fortune and certain, now, that his choice had been the right one. He, Stan and Sid had fed the fish on numerous occasions in this corner, as they had in two other corners of the lake but they were keeping them up their sleeves until required. If Stan could not get in the swim on the other side of the pads - The Paddling Pool they had dubbed it after Buzz's antics in there - then he would probably choose one of these areas. Just as Chris was finishing his can of lager in readiness for the walk to the swims, he heard the words, 'Paddling Pool' and knew that only Stan would call it that at the moment. Looking up, he returned Stan's beaming smile and soon they were making the first of many sweltering treks to their chosen homes for the next few days.

Chris and Stan had banked all their hopes on the weather forecast for the coming week being correct for once, and that was for the wind to change from its present south westerly to a north easterly, which would blow straight into the Pads Corner. With six hours to go there seemed little chance of a change in the warm, sunny conditions and, by ten in the evening, they wondered whether they had blown it. Isn't it strange that, with a whole nine months in front of them, anglers put so much faith in their choices for the first couple of days of the season which, invariably, turn out to be a complete anti-climax?

As a distant bell tolled midnight, a faint cheer went up and, once again, the lake was peppered with lead and the night rang to the annual chorus of bite alarms. Stan and Chris had kept things simple, having baited the pads only two days earlier, and the straightforward hooklinks and tiger nut baits were flicked along the marginal shelf amongst a small handful of free offerings. As the electronic chorus slowly faded to silence, the anglers settled back to dream of gargantuan carp and, soon, the air was filled with soft, snoring sounds.

The sun was barely a pink glow on the horizon when the first fish of the season became just that statistic, but what a fish and what a way to start your first session on a lake! The angler, a young guy they knew only as Ken, had previously only caught a handful of twenty pound carp and so was completely unprepared for what the lake had in store for him. It was he who was to be the captor of the first carp of the season, the first forty and a new lake record, when he caught the Grey Mirror from the West Point at forty two pounds six ounces. Not being too sure what to do with such a fish, he enlisted the help of the angler to his right in the Looking Back swim who happened to be the head bailiff, Rod Jones. He took it upon himself to photograph the fish straight away without alerting any other anglers. Fortunately, Dean was fishing in the Middle Reeds to Ken's left and heard the commotion, so was able to offer his assistance and also take some shots, as well. Rod found out later that he had no film in his camera so was greatly relieved when Dean's photographs came out superbly.

Whilst all this was going on, Fat Bob, fishing opposite in the East Point, went quietly about his business and landed a new thirty, a mirror with distinctively large pectoral fins, the fish weighing thirty two pounds twelve ounces.

Stan and Chris were oblivious to this burst of activity further up the lake, their heads still cocooned in sleeping bags to cut out the glare of the rising sun. It wasn't until mid-morning that the news filtered down to them of the dawn surprise, and they quickly reeled in so that they could congratulate the still stupefied captor. Stan whistled across to Fat Bob and gave him the thumbs up, which Bob acknowledged with a smile and a wave. Then the two wanderers returned to their padded corner, a corner that was becoming increasingly more animated by the strengthening northeasterly breeze - for once the weathermen had got it right! By mid-afternoon the reeds along the South Bank, to Stan's right, were being bent alarmingly by the increasing wind and it was not too long before they began to see the odd carp frolicking in the waves but, as yet, they had received no action. Chris was in the throes of tying up a pop-up tiger nut rig when his right hand rod wrenched round like a quiver tip, the buzzer screamed and the baitrunner sang. In a blur of flying tackle, Chris grabbed the rod and held on as the fish made off into the deeper water to the left but, by the time Stan was by his side, the line was flapping wildly in the air with nothing to tether it. Stan did the usual reversal and left Chris to his cursing, hoping that it had not been a big fish but also that his turn would soon come. He was wrong on both counts. The fish was caught a week later with Chris's rig still in its mouth and was the Big Common at just over thirty six pounds. This fact would normally have left anyone devastated but Chris was inured to the news by the fact that it was his turn again, the following morning, and the same rod (this time with the pop-up rig attached) produced the fight of his life. Despite calling at the top of his voice for Stan's assistance, Chris was left to net the carp himself as his friend slept on oblivious, and it was with tonsils akimbo that he woke the whole avian population of the lake and, eventually, Rip Van Peacock!

The fish was familiar to both of them as it had been Chris's first thirty from the lake - Three Scale - but it looked even more stunning than before and, once on the scales, it was obvious why as it had increased to a weight of thirty eight and three quarter pounds - by far Chris's personal best.

They hoorahed and hollered for England then, after the photographs and the return, they did it some more! Some people seemed less than happy at their show of exuberance but it mattered little to them, especially when Dean turned up a little later with a carrier bag of cold lagers as a toast to their success. Dean had also bagged a carp that morning but, at almost fifteen pounds smaller than Chris's, he dismissed it with a shrug and cajoled the elated captor into relating the story again, bringing a theatrical groan from Stan.

"Don't you worry, Quill," he prophesied, "you'll get your turn soon enough, you mark my words."

Stan hoped that he was right and, with the wind still pushing into the corner, he had every confidence. Later that evening he thought that Dean's prediction was going to be fulfilled sooner rather than later when he hooked a fish that, quite simply, beat him up. It took him almost fifty minutes to bring the hardest fighting fish he had ever hooked to the net and, at one point, he asked Chris if Les had stocked any marlin in the lake during the close season! When the fish finally went into the net they both let out a roar but, on parting the mesh, Stan thought that it must have been the steadily fading light playing tricks with his eyes. Throughout the fight he had visions of a huge, black common carp nestling in the folds of his net but, instead, he peered down on a mirror carp of no more than twenty five pounds. Chris looked at the fish, then at Stan, then back at the fish, before saying,

"Maybe you need to eat more Shredded Wheat, mate!"

Stan grimaced, but the ache in his shoulder reminded him that he had just had the fight of his life and size mattered little after that. The carp was built like a torpedo with a huge tail, and they were sure that half of its twenty seven pounds came from that power house, they just wondered what would happen if it got angry!

By the time that Sid arrived later the next day the wind had lost not only its strength but also its holding power and, following Chris's post-midnight capture of a double figure common, they had seen no further sign of carp. Though not overly busy, there were few places to move to so they had to stay put for the time being, which proved a little frustrating when Rod, the head bailiff, landed Double D at a little over thirty six pounds a few hours prior to Sid's arrival. The reason for the frustration was that he was fishing a corner of the lake that they had baited regularly during the close season, and had regularly seen carp hungrily accepting the bait. To compound this frustration, he had said only a couple of hours earlier that he was thinking of leaving but, on catching the carp, elected to stay put for at least another day. They had dubbed the area Nutty Corner and it was at the far end of the West Bank from the Pads Corner. Some studious plumbing in the close season had revealed a hard, clay area twenty five yards from each bank which could be fished from two swims - much the same as the Crazy Diamond and the Paddling Pool. It was to the left of one of these swims that Rod had caught the carp. The problem was that the area was so tight it would be impossible to fit another two anglers in there, so Stan and Chris decided to stay where they were for the time being. Sid, however, could go where he wanted and elected to fish the West Bank of Nutty Corner. This choice proved to be very rewarding and, with the careful introduction of the tiger nut mix, he managed to winkle out four carp to mid-twenties over the next three days.

The lack of carp in their vicinity was causing Stan and Chris much consternation and, with Friday afternoon looming, they knew a new influx of anglers would soon make a move impossible so they had to take a chance. It seemed that Rod would be leaving on Saturday morning, so that area would be viable. But where else?

"Well, what options have we got then, Quill?" asked Chris, rhetorically. "There's Dean's, The Top Corner, middle of the Top Bank, the far side of the Back Lake, the Car Park swims, The Bottom Corner and The Step."

He had gone clockwise around the lake, starting with the swim next to his, and they sat running the mental map over in their minds.

"Well, you wouldn't think that The Step and the Bottom Corner would do much," began Stan. "I've been having a look down there a couple of times a day and I haven't seen squat!"

"Yeah, and the Top Corner and the Top Bank are pretty much covered by The Snags and the Middle Reeds," continued Chris, "so what does that leave us?"

Again, the question was rhetorical and they both mused over the remaining possibilities. After a few minutes' pensive silence, Stan gave a sigh and said, "I suppose we'll just have to wait until Rod leaves, then, and we can go in the Looking Back and Nutty Corner."

Chris nodded slowly at the suggestion and Stan could see the same thought going through his friend's mind as was going through his own - 'who fishes where?' They looked at each other and, with one mind, spoke one word, "Spoof!"

Collecting three coins each they put their hands behind their backs and commenced the same ritual for settling arguments and disputes that they had used for years.

"Whose call?" asked Stan.

"Dunno. Let's spoof for it!" replied Chris, smiling.

Stan looked hard into his friends eyes and began the mental evaluation of how his friend would think he was thinking. And, in thinking that, the changes he would make to his original thought process! Complicated stuff, this spoofing game!

"I'll call," he declared, then looked even harder into Chris's intense stare. "Two." His decision met with the usual face dancing and squinting before Chris went through the same, elaborate process, eventually declaring, "Four."

Stan winced at the call and awaited the outcome of Chris's outstretched clenched fist which, when opened, revealed all three coins.

"Bastard!" cursed Stan and Chris did not need to see the contents of Stan's hand to know that, this time, he had out-spoofed his friend.

"Nutty Corner for me then, Quill," he beamed, triumphantly, and rose from his chair to relieve his bladder.

Their decision made, they strolled up to the corner in time to see Sid returning a small common, for which they congratulated him and then told him of their spoof and its result.

"What you gonna do tonight, then?" he asked whilst wiping his hands on a towel.

"Just going to have a quick word with Rod to see what time he's off," explained Stan, "then Quill's going to drop in over there for the night. Just drop 'em in the edge until Rod leaves."

Sid nodded at this but looked a little sceptical, and his scepticism was well founded because the head bailiff was his usual, non-committal self.

"What did he say, Quill?" asked Chris as his friend strolled disconsolately back into Sid's swim.

"Oh, you know. The usual 'don't know if I'm going yet' scenario, with that stupid smirk on his face. God, he's a slimy git. I'm gonna move round into Dean's for the night, I think. Then I'll just have to wait and see what occurs."

Chris was about to offer the swim to Stan, then thought better of it, knowing he would turn it down but worried just in case he didn't!

By early Friday evening they were all established in their new swims, and just in time, as another four anglers turned up to occupy the remaining few swims. The night was quiet for most, apart from Sid who had a slightly larger common to deal with in the dark, then the morning brought young Ken more rewards when he landed a personal best common of just over thirty pounds. Another new thirty but plain for all to see that, after spawning, it would probably weigh no more than twenty five pounds. Nonetheless, Ken was suitably elated, this being his fourth fish of the week - a start he could never have dreamed of.

The wind had changed back to a southerly now, and the Nutty Corner was looking good for a few more fish. When Stan went round to see what time Rod was moving out he was stunned to see another angler setting up in there whilst Rod moved his tackle out. Stupefied, Stan blurted out, "I was moving in after you, Rod, we sorted it out last night!"

The head bailiff looked at him with the same smirk on his face that made you want to wipe it off with the back of a shovel and said, "Oh, sorry, Quill, I didn't realise. When I saw you move I thought that was you for the rest of the session!"

Stan glared at him and said, "Don't call me 'Quill', only my friends call me that," and, with that, he spun on his heel and stomped out of the swim, cursing loudly.

Seeing his friend's face, Chris stood wide-eyed and asked, "Shit! What's up mate?" Stan's reply was unprintable and he walked purposefully past Chris and Sid and on down the bank to his swim, where he stomped around and swore for ten minutes before calming down.

Resigned to his fate, he decided to make the best of a bad thing so set about finding out a bit more about his swim with the aid of a marker rod and float. A few casts later he was pulling the float off a close in bar when a voice from behind said, "No, you want to be further than that, Quill."

On turning, he saw Dean standing there, cigarette in hand. The swim was named after him following the exceptional results he had achieved in there last year and it was obvious that he knew a lot about the swim. With this in mind, and still aggrieved by recent events, Stan was more direct than normal and said, "Really? Where should it be then, Dean?"

Dean smiled and pointed towards the far bank. "See the right hand side of the shed and the big silver birch to its right?" He waited until Stan acknowledged the sight markers, then continued. "That's the left and right of a hard area at seventy yards. The lake doesn't really vary in depth but there's a big, sandy area out there. I reckon it's about the size of a couple of brollys."

With this knowledge, Stan hurled his marker the required distance and, on his second cast, felt the lead land with a satisfying thud. The marker quickly ascended the twelve feet to the surface and Dean murmured appreciatively, "Yep, that's bang on it. You could put a bait two yards either side of that and still be on the money."

Stan was suddenly flying and, picking up a rod, he let fly a lead and rig, glowing with boyish pride as the waves from its entry rocked the red float from the right.

"Yeah, I suppose that'll do!" said Dean, smiling. Stan slid the lead across the lake bed until he felt it pull into weed after a couple of yards, nodding to himself as he made up a mental picture of what was happening beneath the float. Happy with this, he recast his pop-up tiger rig the same distance, this time landing just to the left of the float. He was unsure about fishing a tiger nut on its own at that distance, but it was the distance that precluded the use of any free offerings and, anyway, there were enough tiger nuts scattered around the lake for the fish to know what they were. He toyed with the idea of putting the other bait out there, as well, but decided that he wanted to fish one bait amongst a bed of the same so put that one fifteen yards out at the edge of a weed bed.

Earlier that day, Micky and Ferris had moved in either side of him. Micky to his left and Ferris in the recently vacated Crazy Diamond so, after completing the baiting of his closer rod, Stan wandered along to see how Micky was faring. He was in the throes of putting out his second rod and was eyeing his plumbing float, sixty yards away.

"How's it going, Micky?" enquired Stan. "What you got out there?"

Pointing to his float, Micky explained, "Where the float is, it's eight foot deep. Then, a yard or so to the left it drops down to twelve feet and is pretty weedy."

Stan knew that the float was on the bar to the left of the hard area that Dean had shown him, and hoped that his neighbour didn't stray too far to the right. Micky then gained his attention again by holding out his rod, "What d'yer think? I just got these from a mate at work. Brand new, twelve foot two and a halves for two hundred quid. Not bad, eh?"

He seemed genuinely pleased with his bargain, and Stan showed equal enthusiasm, "Bloody hell, that's a good deal. What they like?"

Micky shrugged and replied, "Dunno really. I've had a couple of casts with 'em but haven't actually fished with them yet. S'pose I'd better christen 'em with a thirty, eh!" They both smiled at this and Stan stood to one side to allow Micky to cast at the marker. One second there was silence, the next a 'crack' like a gunshot shattered the calm and they both watched with a mixture of consternation and disbelief as six foot of splintered carbon flew down the line and into the lake, twenty feet out. For one brief moment they were both open mouthed and silent, then Stan's laughter burst forth like a dam breaking whilst all that Micky could do was stare intently at the splintered remnants in his hand and utter the same expletive over and over again, compounding Stan's humour tenfold. Eventually, Stan calmed down enough to commence breathing again, while Chris and Sid joined them in the swim to see what all the commotion was. Stan did his best to relate the events but, after a few sentences, broke down again and had to be led away to a shady corner to recover.

A semblance of sanity was soon restored and Micky, very tentatively, used one of his old rods to cast to the required spot, happy to hear just a plop as the lead hit the water, rather than the earlier, sickening sound. Later that evening, when Micky and Ferris joined him in his swim, Stan couldn't help smiling whenever he looked across at Micky, as he would whenever he saw him in the future.

A couple of fish had shown themselves in front of Stan and Micky and they mused on their chances for the remainder of the session, both feeling they had a good case for righting recent wrongs. The evening was a pleasant one and, after an hour or so of darkness, Stan was left to clear up the swim and prepare for his last night of the session. Sid had run down earlier on to declare that he had caught a twenty two pound common but that they had seen few fish since the afternoon and assumed that they had moved out.

Stan woke with the sun melting his retinas and pulled his sleeping bag over his head to blank out the glare. When would he learn to orient his bivvy better when fishing on the West Bank? These thoughts drifted aimlessly around his semi dormant mind until he was wrested from his slumbers by a single bleep to one of his rods. He rose on one arm while looking at the two rods and gazed, in amazement and wonder, at the sight of a kingfisher perched on the left hand one. He sat stock still whilst the bird bobbed its head up and down, searching hither and yon for an unsuspecting fry to dimple the surface. After what seemed like ages, but was only a few seconds, the bird was just ... gone. With a flick of the azure blue wings and a piping call, it flashed across the lake and was out of sight in a blink, its departure causing the rod to bounce and the buzzer to utter a couple more notes.

"That has made my session," thought Stan, "now, if only that buzzer would continue!"

With that wish, he lay back down and stared at the spokes of his brolly, trying to decide whether to rise or to grab a few more minutes sleep. Another bleep made him glance to the left in the hope of seeing the halcyon returned, but his rods were bird-less and before he had a chance to ponder the single bleep it was joined by another dozen, all clamouring to be heard first! The left hand baitrunner was a whirr and, in a split second and a tumble of sleeping bag and bedchair, Stan was on the rod and waiting for the run to slow so that he could engage the clutch. After twenty yards or so, the fish slowed enough for Stan to do just that and he watched in wonder as the line rose up in the water whilst cutting steadily to the right.

"Good 'un Quill?" came Micky's opening remark as he rushed into the swim. This was followed by a snort of laughter as he took in the full disaster that was Stan's swim. "Bloody hell, it looks like a bad night in Beirut!" he chuckled, whilst picking his way through the debris to Stan's side. "Need a hand, mate?"

This last came as he bent to pick up the net, knowing full well that his services would be much appreciated. By now, the fish was thirty yards out and meandering back and forth, just below the surface, throwing up huge whirls and vortices as its tail pushed once more towards freedom. But, today, it would not be successful and it was not too long before Stan saw the impressive frame of a large mirror carp slide into the outstretched net. He vocalised his delight, as usual, then bent to help Micky with the net.

"It's a good 'un, Quill. Definitely a thirty."

This news was imparted just as Sid ran into the swim, followed shortly by the contrast in size of Ferris and Chris. The usual 'how big', 'what fish', 'where from' questions ensued, but these were answered once the net was pulled back to reveal a huge, almost scaleless flank.

"Bloody hell! It's a whacker," exclaimed Chris. "Well done, my son!"

The others echoed these sentiments, and even more so when the scales revealed a massive weight of thirty eight and a half pounds. After the hollering, handshakes and back patting, Stan calmed enough to say, "Oh, I can't wait to see Rod. I must thank him for putting me in this swim!"

He smiled at the assembled admirers and roared "Yeeeessss! You beauty!" whilst punching the air in triumph. Even more pleasing was the fact that the fish was unknown to them and, after perusing the photographs a week later, they came to the conclusion that the fish had last been caught three years previously at twenty eight pounds and had, since then, managed to avoid a recapture. What was bizarre was that, despite being seen on a number of subsequent occasions, the carp remained uncaught for the rest of their time on the lake.

So came to an end the first, amazing session of the season. One forty (a new lake record), five thirties (including personal bests to Chris and Stan), and eight fish between them in total. After their departure, Micky and Ferris managed a fish apiece, Ferris moving in after Stan to land a personal best common of twenty six pounds. All in all, the best possible start they could have wished for, they just wondered if it would continue or, like the previous year, slow up considerably. Unfortunately, the latter proved to be true, at least for a couple of weeks and especially as the fish spawned after a fortnight of the season. However, in that time, another four thirties were caught including Sid's recapture of the eponymously named Sid's Common, ten ounces bigger than last year.

All of this news made Buzz's stay in Dubai torturous and it was with some joy that he learnt that he would be returning to England a week early. His arrival at the lake, just hours after stepping off the plane, coincided with a change in the weather; the warm, high pressure being replaced with a run of low pressure, strong winds and intermittent bursts of rain - carp weather!

The news that the Big Linear had yet to succumb to anyone's tackle filled his normally brimming confidence tanks to overflowing and he told the other three that it was not a matter of if, just of how big! Once again, his confidence and ability were found to be perfectly warranted and on a windy Saturday morning it appeared that his prophecy was about to come true. Fishing the East Point with Sid, Buzz had hooked a fish close in and commenced taking a twenty minute beating from the extremely angry carp. Fishing almost opposite, in the Middle Reeds, Stan and Chris heard the take and saw the commotion, so ran round to witness the fight. After half an hour Buzz had gained the upper hand and was slowly guiding the fish towards the outstretched arms of the net. From a tree next to the swim, Chris could see perfectly and, as the fish rolled five yards from the net, saw the huge, linear scales glowing like gold doubloons on the huge flank of the fish. Just in time, he stopped himself from declaring the fish's identity and was just making his way down from his perch when he heard the wail of anguish.

As the fish rolled five yards from the net, Stan caught sight of the scales along the carp's flank and gasped in recognition. He looked at Sid's expression and knew, from his wide, staring eyes, that he had come to the same conclusion. Looking back at the beaten carp, he prepared himself for the chorus that would shortly echo across the lake, then watched in horror as the lead sailed, in slow motion, over Buzz's shoulder and into the grasping branches behind. The sound issuing from Buzz's mouth was a chilling one and was, indeed, chorused by the other three, thus forming a baleful quartet. The hook had simply slipped loose and the great fish was gone.

No one uttered a word until, at the top of his voice, Buzz screamed one four letter word at the dismal skies before hurling his rod to the ground in despair. The others faded from the swim in silence, Sid wandering back with the others to leave Buzz to his emotions.

"It was the Big Linear wasn't it?" asked Stan, although he needed no confirmation from the others and they just nodded silently as they trudged along through the damp grass. "Bastard!" he concluded, which brought further nodding.

Half an hour later, Buzz entered their swim with the same word on his lips and it was many, many days before the sparkle once again returned to those blue eyes.

The return of the sparkle was brought about by the capture of Big Pec's, the fish that Fat Bob had caught at the beginning of the season. This time it weighed just under thirty two and half and was taken on a floater by Buzz whilst the other three were at work. They were entertained regally by the captor on Friday evening and were greatly relieved to see the big man back to his bubbly, storytelling best. After a further reliving of the carp's capture, all were treated to another of his repertoire of international incidents. His latest tale revolved around his recent visit to Dubai, but neither fish nor Sheiks were involved.

"Just a little way from where we were staying there was an American army base, and a few of them would regularly come down to the complex for a beer and a game of pool or tennis or whatever. Anyway, this particular evening, me and a few of the guys were farting around with a basketball, you know, three defenders, three attackers, one hoop, when half a dozen Yanks saunter up and one of them pipes up 'Hey, Limey's! Who's your best man?' We all looked at each other a bit puzzled and Simm asks 'Is someone getting married or something?' which we all laughed at. Then matey says, 'Who's gonna take on Johnson?' and with that this monster strolls forward. Have you seen Heartbreak Ridge with Clint Eastwood?"

The enthralled listeners all looked at each other, and Sid nodded. "Well, you know that huge guy that Clint had to fight?" continued Buzz.

"Yeah, Swede weren't it?" offered Stan.

"That's the one. Well he looked like a bleedin' runner bean compared to this Johnson, and I thought, 'Oh, shit, it's gonna be me!' and so I was just preparing to get a good pummelling when this little weedy voice from behind yaps, 'I'll fight 'im. Let me through, I'll have 'im.' And with that this scrawny little geezer we called Clyde came barging between us. Now, the reason we called him Clyde was that he looked like the orangutan out of Every Which Way But Loose – five foot tall, covered in hair, and knuckles that nearly dragged on the ground. Anyway, without another word he whipped across the ground in a blur, clambered up matey and, grabbed him by the ears, pulled his head forward and bit the end of his nose off. He then dropped to the ground and spat it out and, whilst he was squealing like a stuck pig and clutching his face with both hands, Clyde kicked him in the balls with all his might. He then turned around and trotted back over to us. Stoney chucked him the ball and we continued our game as if nothing had happened."

The listeners were crying with laughter by now and Stan managed, "So what happened to the big fella?"

"Well, they just stood there looking stunned while the big guy's writhing on the ground not knowing whether to hold his re-shaped nose that was gushing like Old Faithful, or try to push his balls back down from next to his tonsils, Clyde's kicked 'em so hard! Then they just all grabbed a limb and dragged him away as quietly as they could. We continued playing until they were well out of sight, then we just fell about. I haven't laughed so much in all my life. God, did we get drunk that night!"

Sid was openly weeping by now, clutching his sides and begging for Buzz to stop, and the sight of that made the other two almost as bad. The sound echoed across the lake, and it was the sound of people enjoying themselves. Strange how some people don't like that.

The next morning, Rod strolled into Buzz's swim and told him to keep the noise down in future. Buzz merely looked deep into his shifty eyes and smiled his hugest smile whilst saying, "How kind of you to ask. Thirty two pounds six ounces, actually," before turning away to talk to Sid.

The irony was totally lost on the head bailiff and he blurted, "I mean it, you know!" whilst backing out of the swim and nearly tripping over his dog.

"Yeah, and so do I," replied Buzz, slowly. This is how it begins thought Stan, later. August came and went in a blaze of sunshine but little carp activity, especially for the four lads, but the Big Linear did make its first appearance of the season on one of the few rainy days in that month. The weight of forty two pounds fourteen ounces once again increased the lake record by half a pound and also captor Paul James's personal best by almost ten pounds. A couple of other thirty pound carp were caught during the month, notably the Big Common at thirty six and a half pounds to Micky Charles. Suitably elated he was as well but, as September arrived, Stan and Chris's daily phone calls were of the total lack of action to their rods and possible ways of ending the drought. The end of the drought came with the end of the drought and, as the south of England was washed clean for the first time in many weeks, the influx of fresh water and oxygen to the lakes and rivers stirred the fish to feed feverishly.

The first week in September saw Buzz repeat his capture of Big Pec's, this time six ounces larger than before and the following weekend brought action to all of their rods with six carp from fifteen to twenty six pounds between them.

The next weekend brought a major change to all the anglers on the lake when they were told, without ceremony, that tiger nuts were banned.

Rod called everybody together in the car park on Saturday and announced the news, explaining that the decision had been brought about by the excess use of the bait and the possible detrimental effects on the carp. When asked what Les had said about the decision, Stan was told that he was in full agreement, and that was final.

Though this came as a bit of a blow to them, the four anglers had taken to baiting with boilies over the past few sessions as they thought that the fish would move further out over the coming months which would hamper their use of particles. Still, they felt that the whole affair was ludicrous and all doubted that Les would have taken this course of action without discussing it with the anglers first. The problem was that none of them really knew how his wife was doing, so they decided against contacting him. Instead, they vowed that they would do just as Buzz said, "We'll just have to catch 'em all on boilies instead, boys. That'll stick right in Jones's throat!"

And they commenced straight away when, two hours after the car park meeting, Sid caught the first post-tiger carp and, although it weighed barely more than twenty pounds, it was cheered and revered as if it were twice that size. Over the weekend they caught another four of similar size and applauded each one with gusto, which soon began achieving the desired results, and they smiled with satisfaction at Rod's increasing agitation on the opposite bank. He walked like a man who had been born with three legs and who had, recently, had the right one removed, giving him the semblance of someone permanently on the verge of toppling over. This strange ambulation was enhanced tenfold when he was stressed, and more so when viewed from afar - like the opposite bank. To further exacerbate the comic aspect, he owned a cocker spaniel called Ted that was as daft as a brush. Constantly chasing invisible rabbits, it then suddenly went regularly into a frenzy of leaping, spinning and yapping as the occasional butterfly lazily floated by, totally oblivious to the dementia its casually flapping wings were causing in the almost rabid cur. Yep, this was the Head Bailiff and his dog.

The next weekend brought them similar results, and similar enjoyment, and they were cheered even more to learn that Don had captured the Big Linear at yet another lake record weight, this time at a few ounces under forty four pounds. Don was still a bailiff but definitely did not see eye to eye with Rod so the capture meant even more, if not to the captor then at least to the other four. Don was one of life's gentlemen and would never use the capture of a carp as any sort of medal to shove in someone else's face, but he did not need to because the bitterness in Rod's heart had malice enough for all.

They spent a couple of hours in Don's company later that weekend and listened, enthralled, to tales of his recent angling endeavours. He belonged to a number of Colne Valley pits, most of which had publicity bans and strict rules, but he had quietly gone about his business over the past few years and this year had proved very bountiful indeed. His audience were surprised to learn that this was his third forty pound carp of the season, and not his largest, and listened in awe as he quietly spoke of lakes they would probably never get to see. He then brought up a subject they had all but forgotten about.

"You remember the fifty I told you about last season?" he began. Buzz nodded, saying, "Yeah, the one from the big yachting lake?"

"Yes, that's the one. Well it came out again last month. Fifty one twelve. And three different forties have also been out this year," continued Don.

This news brought murmurs of interest and they spent the rest of the afternoon interrogating their host as best they could, vowing to look at the lake sooner rather than later. As much as they were enjoying their game with the Head Bailiff, they all knew, subconsciously, that it could end with only one winner so were mentally preparing for a move. In the meantime they aimed to catch as much as they possibly could and glean as much information from guys like Don before the move became a necessity.

"What time are you getting there, then, Rhodie?" It was Wednesday afternoon and Stan looked out of his office window at the trees opposite being buffeted by the strengthening south-westerly wind. He was desperately trying to wangle the next couple of days off work and Chris's call had made that imperative.

"Probably about three tomorrow afternoon. Depends how long it takes me to finish this bloody alcove."

Stan had played the double bluff game many times with Chris, but since his friend had been getting to the lake on Thursdays, it had become unnecessary - until now. With the wind predicted to increase to almost gale force by Saturday, Stan knew exactly where he wanted to be and that was in either the Middle Bar or Sid's to the right of that. Chris was oblivious of his plans to leave work tomorrow lunchtime, so that just left Buzz to contend with, but either of the swims would do and he looked forward to seeing Chris's face the following afternoon.

He left work at a little after midday and, forty minutes later, was pulling into the fishery car park. He had not expected it to be empty but, of the five cars present, the last he had expected to see was Chris's white van and he realised he had been out-spoofed again. In five short minutes his mood had changed from glad to sadness when he saw a brolly set up in both of his favoured swims and it surprised him not at all that they belonged to Buzz and Chris. They were both genuinely pleased to see him but he could not hide the play of emotions on his face and, pretty soon, Chris was grinning widely as he worked out his friend's intended ploy.

"Never kid a kidder, Quill. You'll never get away with it." Stan grimaced, then sat down on Chris's bedchair to evaluate recent events, and future ones as well.

"The Double Linear's been out," Buzz informed him.

"Oh, right. Who had it?" asked Stan whilst sipping a welcome cup of tea.

"Ferris had it on Sunday afternoon from 'The Crack-off.' Thirty six six - personal best," explained Buzz. "Apparently he was so happy he nearly fractured an eyebrow!"

Stan nearly choked on his tea at this and had tears in his eyes from the coughing fit that ensued.

"Yeah. And he completed a sentence of more than four words without the aid of a safety net. It was 'Micky, pass me the monkey wrench'!" added Chris.

They chuckled away for a couple of minutes at Ferris's expense but were still happy for the man, despite his lack of any emotion.

Once he had calmed down a little, Stan gazed out at the white horses galloping across the lake and tried to decide on a swim for the weekend. The two he fancied were taken, as were the other obvious ones - The East Point, Dean's and The Crack off - so he pondered other possibilities in this weather. The Kingfisher Corner to his right should have been the obvious choice in a south-westerly but had never really produced the goods. However, as he and Chris stood in there a few minutes later neither of them could deny that it really did look the business. The trees were being pummelled by the strengthening wind, and the waves were crashing over the defunct landing stage to the right. Chris was just about to comment on how good it looked when a carp head and shouldered no more than ten yards out and all he could manage was, "Shit! Did you see that?"

His words were snatched away on the wind, which was fortunate because the ears that they were meant for were heading purposefully back to the car park and, minutes later, Stan was surveying the waves in front of him, having deposited all of his gear just behind the swim. The sight of another carp ten yards further out spurred him into action and, pretty soon, two single pop-ups were winging their way into the turbulent waters. The swim was renowned for being deep and featureless and his initial casts seemed to validate that supposition as the lead seemed to take an age to reach the bottom, indicating a depth well in excess of twelve feet, he thought. Half an hour later, however, it seemed to matter little how deep it was because the carp were obviously quite comfortable here as one of them sped off with his bait and, minutes later, he was calling for his partners to help photograph a twenty four pound common. By now the wind was accompanied by squally rain showers, and it was evident that they were going to be in for a rough night. After recasting the rod, Stan erected his brolly behind a wind battered copse of trees in a bid to gain as much shelter as possible whilst still being able to see the lake.

Buzz and Chris had yet to receive any action but the sight of a carp leaving the water sixty yards away gave Buzz cause to cheer at the top of his booming voice. Night came early and, by seven o'clock, the three of them were huddling beneath Chris's sorry excuse for a shelter whilst consuming a fine curry and washing it down with the odd glass of wine. All these factors soon took their toll on the anglers and a couple of hours later they were all nestling down in anticipation of a wild and restless night.

Buzzers bleeped all night long as the wind, waves and errant branches beat upon the rods and it was three bleary-eyed anglers who gathered in the same swim ten hours later to relate their night's events. Stan had suffered the loss of a carp in the early hours and had been woken twice after that by tench. Buzz had fared little better other than the fact that he had landed an eighteen pounder, to go with his early morning tench. Chris, however, was tired but happy and, on dragging the sack from the froth-lined margins he revealed why in the shape of a glorious, chestnut brown mirror carp of twenty seven pounds, so after the photographs they all agreed that there was only one thing that could follow this, and that was a full fried breakfast.

Twenty minutes later, three cookers were ablaze and had woks and saucepans liberally and treacherously balanced upon them and the smell that permeated the swim was accompanied by the gurgling of three cavernous stomachs. With the steam rising from the utensils, the scene resembled that of the three witches at the beginning of Macbeth, and Stan was very aware of this when he viewed the laboured gait of the Head Bailiff sloping towards them. Without looking up, he carried on stirring the contents of his cauldron-like wok and intoned, "Something evil this way comes!"

Buzz glanced up and guffawed at the analogy. Stan never ceased to amuse him. On entering the swim, Rod tried to make pleasant conversation, "Something smells good, boys. Got enough for me?"

Stan and Chris glanced up at him, then back to their cooking without a single word and it was left to Buzz to reply in his own subtle way, "Only if you want to eat it with no teeth!"

Rod laughed, falsely, but realising that Buzz's remark held more than an element of truth, ignored that course of conversation and continued instead with, "Right. Well, any good in the night?" Stan gave him a quick resume of events before turning away to get the necessary plates for their feast and, when he turned back, he saw Rod's back through the trees as he made his way to the next swim.

"Arsehole!" spat Buzz, venomously. Then he picked up the kettle and made the tea.

Ten minutes later the swim echoed to a championship belch, and the three of them sat back and waited for their cholesterol level to return to normal.

"That was the dog's dangly bits!" commented Buzz, and the others nodded in agreement. The weather had got no worse but the forecast had warned of gale conditions later that day and it was because of this that they all returned to their swims to ensure that their brollies were firmly pegged down for the beating to come. Stan was in the throes of taking all unnecessary tackle and clothing back to the car, fifty yards away, when he thought he heard a shout but after listening for a few seconds put it down to the wind. Then, on his return from the car, he glanced along and saw Chris standing behind Buzz's swim so walked down to investigate. On his arrival, he saw Buzz holding an alarmingly bent rod and tried to glean the necessary information from Chris,

"I thought I heard a shout. How long's it been on, Rhodie?"

"Couple of minutes. He just got back into his swim and saw the indicator was a bit low so was just about to level it up when it was ripped from his hand. Didn't you hear the run? It was a bloody screamer!"

Stan shook his head then asked Buzz, "What's it feel like, boy? Any good?"

Buzz shook his head and replied, "I can't really tell, Quill. This wind is really putting a bow in the line and I can't feel much at all. It's kiting to the left at the moment and at least it's clear out there."

The next ten minutes passed with little change in the proceedings, and Buzz began to lose patience. "Oh, this is bloody silly. I'm not gaining any line at all, it's just kiting from left to right. I'm gonna give it the big'un in a minute," he growled.

Stan and Chris managed to dissuade him from that course of action and, soon, they began to see the odd swirl in the waves that indicated that the fish was tiring. Stan looked at Buzz's face and, on seeing the look in his eyes, realised what must be going through his friend's tortured mind and tried his best to calm him, "Take it nice and easy, big fella. This one's in the bag, boy, no problem."

"I hope so, Quill, I really hope so. This feels like a good fish," he replied in a pained tone.

Suddenly, the fish rolled dramatically on the surface and revealed a huge, orange flank before disappearing once again beneath the waves, and Chris felt like a harpoonist aboard Ahab's ship, only this whale wasn't white!

"Oh, shit!" groaned Buzz, and he wished that, at that precise moment, he could be somewhere else. Once again the fish rolled, this time five yards closer, and Buzz could appreciate the finer points of gaffing at that moment! Again. And again. And again. And all Buzz could see was the lead flying over his shoulder and his recent breakfast making a sudden reappearance.

By now, Chris was waist deep in not very warm water, the spray from the waves occasionally covering his head, and he knew that, for his sake as well as Buzz's, this had to go in first time.

Then it was in. No hook pull. No last minute dive into a snag. No gunshot report of snapping nylon. Just a whole netful of huge mirror carp and three sets of tonsils screaming so loud that their owners couldn't talk properly for two days!

Buzz's ecstacy was unbounded and his huge arms engulfed Stan in a bear-hug, whilst the pair screamed over each other's shoulders. Then they both heard Chris's plaintive cry and assisted in heaving him from the waves with his very welcome bounty. He ran off to get dry whilst Stan and Buzz unwrapped the prize like a mystery Christmas present, revealing the most stunning, scale-free orange flank belonging to a very large carp.

'Jeez, what one is it, Buzz?" asked Stan, agog.

"Who knows and, quite frankly, who bloody cares!" he replied, breathlessly.

They removed the hook that was firmly embedded in the huge, bottom lip and then Stan laid a steadying hand over its eye whilst Buzz retrieved his weigh sling from a nearby tree. At that point, Chris returned and enquired as to the fish's identity, receiving a similar reply to Stan, then they watched as the pointer on the scales swung round perilously close to the forty pound mark, finally settling just eight ounces short of that target. Their tonsils were, once again, tested to the utmost before the carp was sacked in preparation for the photographs.

The noise had, naturally, attracted some attention and pretty soon the swim was full with one extremely happy captor and five envious photographers. Nobody recognised the huge, orange leather carp and they concluded that this must have been the fish that Micky had lost from this very swim a year previously. Buzz punched both arms into the air as the carp swam away, and screamed at the leaden sky, but this time in ecstasy, not agony - his wrong had been very much righted.

Sid arrived as the skies darkened and found it difficult to get much sense out of the three, very happy anglers, so set up between Chris and Stan and prepared to join the celebrations. They went on for many hours and, by the time the anglers left to return to their brollys, the wind was reaching the strength that the weathermen had predicted and they were all thankful for the extra nightcaps and bivvy pegs that they had taken.

At some time in the night, Stan was wrested from his slumbers by a crazed double figure common and he had to stand at almost forty five degrees to play the fish, the wind was so fierce. By morning it had abated a little but, on creeping delicately into Sid's swim, he was surprised to find a noticeable lack of said angler. The puzzle was too complex for him in his fragile state, so he returned to bed for an hour, only to return and find Sid sitting behind his rods. Speech came with difficulty but, after stringing a few syllables together, he discovered that Sid had returned to his swim after the celebrations to find his brolly in the trees behind him and his sleeping bag on the path. After ten painful minutes trying to erect his brolly in the gale, he gave up and, reeling his rods in, retired to his car for the rest of the night.

Everybody else survived, barely, and another fried lifesaver was soon settling decidedly unsettled stomachs. The rest of the session was relatively uneventful, although Stan did find a small, shallow hump along the right hand margin of his swim that produced another double figure common and a couple of tench. This was enough to ensure his return to the swim in the near future. Like the next weekend!

Conditions had remained the same for the past week and the first weekend in October found them back in the same swims as last. The wind had lessened in strength since its brolly-wrecking power of the previous week but was still strong enough to cause a decent swell on the lake and Stan set up on Friday afternoon confident of further action. Buzz and Chris had been on the lake for twenty four hours and had seen a number of fish jumping in front of them. Both received action, Buzz taking a twenty three pound mirror from the spot that had produced his orange leather and Chris a common of half that size. They were not the only ones on the lake to catch, as Fat Bob had snared the Double D Mirror earlier that day at just under thirty four pounds from his favourite swim, the East Point. Bob was consistently successful and had, only three weeks earlier, beaten his personal best by a few pounds when he caught the stunning Three Scale at thirty eight ten from the same swim.

Bob had always been treated well by the four of them and he regarded them as friends, which was why he tended to shrug off things that others might have found annoying. On one of the long, hot afternoons in August, Chris and Stan had reeled in and gone to join the other two on West Point for a couple of very welcome beers. The conversation was light-hearted and amusing and, after a couple of hours, Buzz glanced along the path and noticed a figure ambling towards them.

"Here comes old Fat Bob," he announced.

"He come grooving up slowly.... !" sang Stan, which brought a smattering of laughter from the others.

"He certainly has got choo-choo eyeballs, that's for sure," added Chris, bringing hoots and guffaws from the other three and, as is the way of these things, once they started they were unable to stop and the arrival of the poor, unsuspecting stooge in their swim only made matters worse.

"Blimey, what's tickled your funny bones, then?" he asked innocently. "Oh, we've just Come Together, Bob!" Sid replied.

Tears were running down grinning faces by now and Buzz had fallen over backwards in his lowchair, his arms tightly clutching his aching sides and his legs kicking the air like that old 'Smash' advert.

"Stop it! Stop it!" begged Chris, gasping for breath, and it was left to a stomach clutching Stan to utter the final coup de grace.

"It's alright, Bob, it's just something in the way you walk!"

They didn't even notice the confused target of their humour leave, shaking his head, and it was many minutes before any semblance of sanity returned to the scene, the odd chuckle issuing from one or another of them as they replayed the whole thing over in their heads.

Now, however, when he walked into Stan's swim he was greeted by a warm handshake and hearty congratulations for vanquishing another of the lake's good 'uns.

"Thanks, Quill. You've had that one, haven't you?" he asked whilst eyeing the water in front of Stan.

"Yeah. First one I had from here, just under thirty. It's a real honey, isn't it?" he replied.

"Oh, yeah. And that one didn't look bad either," he said whilst pointing to a spot thirty yards distant. Stan looked up instantly and followed Bob's finger.

"Where, Bob?" he pressed. Bob indicated an area on the edge of a shadow thrown by the far tree line and, as Stan was attempting to pinpoint it, a large, golden fish slid out of the swell and fell sideways with an audible splash.

"Ah hah. So, they're here, then," he mused and, putting his hand to his chin in the classic thinker's pose, he ran the possibilities through his head. He definitely wanted a bait on the small gravel hump he had found the previous week and that was the same distance out that the fish had shown, only thirty yards to the right along the tree draped margin that was so favoured by the lake's kingfishers. His other bait was, at present, ten yards further out than the fish amongst a hundred or so bird food boilies. After a few minutes pensive silence, he declared, "Well, I'm happy with where my baits are at the moment, but can you just keep an eye on the rods for a sec, Bob. I'm just going to run round and put some hemp over the margin bait."

Seeing Bob's nodded agreement, he grabbed a white bucket full with hemp and maples and rushed around the corner to the bush that overhung the small, gravel spot he had found. This corner of the lake was, indeed, very deep and his plumbing last week had revealed depths of seventeen feet no more than three rod lengths out. Further investigation had revealed the gravel hump along the margin which was about three yards square and rose to within ten feet of the surface - at this time of year and in these conditions, Stan was convinced that it would produce more than last week's double. A liberal amount of particles peppered the water above his bait, followed by a couple of handfuls of boilies, and he returned to his swim with renewed confidence.

The early onset of evening meant an eventual early retirement, so it was barely midnight when Stan was dragged from a deep sleep by a screaming bite alarm. The right hand margin rod was suffering severe abuse, as did the angler's arm as he hung on for dear life whilst the carp (for that was obviously the identity of the midnight raider) tried to pull his shoulder from its socket! As is the way with night-time battles, Stan just pulled and reeled, pulled and reeled and, in a relatively short time, he saw a flash of light in the dark water just out from his landing net. The fish kicked a little and caused Stan some concern when it darted along the left hand margin and under some overhanging branches. A deft lowering of the rod tip beneath the waves soon negated that problem and it was with a howl of delight that he netted the carp a minute later.

Everybody else slept on oblivious as Stan's torch beam revealed his prize, then they were all awake as his scream of delight shattered the silence. The huge, plate like scales made identification simple and Stan knew that his personal best had, once again, been raised a notch or two with the capture of 'Plates.' He was soon joined by four disheveled and bumbling anglers, and it took Fat Bob to bring some sanity to the situation as he handed Stan the sack, whilst zeroing the weigh sling on the scales.

"What's your p.b., Rhodie?" asked Stan as he gazed at the faintly flickering pointer. "Err, thirty eight twelve. Why?" replied Chris, somewhat baffled. Stan smiled a beaming smile and extended his hand, "So's mine, now!" he declared, then howled at the moon.

Once the fish was safely sacked in the deep margin, they bade him goodnight and well done and melted into the night, to return in the light. An hour before they returned, Stan was woken once again from a strange dream of carp and caravans by another take, this time to his left hand rod and the subsequent twenty five pound fully scaled mirror made a fine partner for the big mirror in the photographs.

Another two fish fell to their rods that weekend - one to Sid of twenty four pounds, and another double figure common to Chris - but, despite no further action, Stan could not have been happier with his session.

Autumn was rapidly packing its bags for warmer climes and they all knew that time was running out for the chance of one more whacker. A sudden, early frost over the next week seemed to confirm this and they wondered whether it would be worth staying on the lake once winter officially began, a fortnight hence.

Mother Nature, however, had other ideas and the last week of October saw her relent a little as temperatures reached unseasonably high levels and it was with a modicum of confidence that they approached the last weekend of summer. The days were warm with a light, southerly breeze blowing up the lake and any sign of frost was long since faded, so they decided to switch banks and fish on the west side where the depth was not as great and the water there received more sunlight. Buzz had taken on another short term appointment overseas, due to the sudden frosts, and was unable to take advantage of this brief, Indian summer, so the only person present on Stan's usual Friday afternoon arrival was Chris and it was no surprise to find him in Dean's. They had seen little of Dean this year as he, like Don, belonged to a couple of very desirable waters in the Colne Valley and was taking advantage of the surprisingly unpressured fishing on there. He would return just prior to Christmas, he had told them earlier in the season, and hoped to fish there for a couple of months in the hope of fooling an unsuspecting whacker. Whether they would join him was uncertain, as yet, but with little else on offer there was every possibility that they would.

Stan, naturally, moved into The Crack-off to Chris's left but knew that Chris had the perfect feature in front of him and there was little chance that Stan could poach it. One fish had shown earlier in the day, according to Chris, but it was at least a hundred and twenty yards away and Chris had chosen to ignore it for the moment. This knowledge, however, spurred Stan to cast as far as possible and it was with some satisfaction that he saw his lead land over a hundred yards distant, feeling it land with a thud in the weed free centre of the lake. He tried to fire out some baits but the ones that weren't snapped up by the gulls landed woefully short so he convinced himself, instead, that a single hookbait at this time of year was the perfect ploy. Chris had been able to outwit the gulls earlier in the day, but was watching with growing frustration as the herd of tufted ducks camped above his hookbait was gradually reducing the number of freebies around it. Every now and then a single bleep would indicate the presence of a beak around his hookbait and it was unsurprising, although very annoying, when the single bleeps continued and the indicator fell to the floor, announcing the arrival of the unluckiest duck of the flock. Winching it in, he cursed and threatened it with all manner of torture, however, once it was unhooked, he merely swore loudly at it and threw it high into the air, watching it flap manically before regaining its balance and flying back out to its brethren to nurse its punctured tongue.

In the fading light, Chris was just able to recast to the spot but, uncertain how much bait was left out there, he decided to cast his other rod to the same area. As the lead sailed out, a sudden gust of wind rushed by on its way to its night-time resting place, and it succeeded in pushing Chris's lead a little too far left. Unhappy with the result, he commenced reeling it back in, only to look, in horror, at the indicator on the other rod dancing silently up and down - he had snagged his other lead! The air was blue with expletives and, from the next swim, it took Stan no time to realise what had transpired, so he elected to stay put for another ten minutes or so until all was well.

It took more than ten minutes for Chris to untangle the bird's nest of line and, by the time both baits were balanced and ready to be recast, the daylight had all but disappeared. The silhouette of the tree on the far margin showed him the direction he had to cast, but the distance was purely down to touch and feel and he was unsure if his first cast was near the mark or not. Knowing that he had as much chance with any further casts, he settled the rod on the rests and attached the indicator then, aiming a little further left, he hurled the second lead into the darkness and prayed that it was far enough left. He tightened the line up and tried to line it up by sight to a marker on the far tree line. Fairly happy that they had not crossed, he adjusted both lines before flicking the switch on the alarms, then strolled along to Stan to relate the whole torrid affair.

Sid, once again, turned up well after dark and was regaled with the story also, whilst he cast his baits out in the Nutty Corner. This time they were birds not tigers, and it was with gusto that he put out a couple of hundred boilies tight to his two hookbaits, assuring his slightly doubting pals that this was the last big feed of the year for the carp.

Stan had the photographs of Plates with him, so they sat in his swim and oohed and aahed in the torchlight at the stunning fish.

"I've sent a couple off to the papers, they're probably the best ones," he told them, and Chris nodded appreciatively.

"Yeah, well they would be. I took 'em!" Stan smiled and nodded in agreement. They had all become adept with a camera over the past few years and were confident of each other's ability to capture the quality of the fish of a lifetime perfectly on camera.

"You didn't mention the lake, did you?" asked Sid, knowing full well the answer.

"Oh yeah. I gave 'em the address, post code and grid reference as well! No, of course I didn't," replied Stan.

There had always been a publicity ban on the lake, but Les had made it clear that, as long as they didn't mention the name of the lake and its whereabouts, he didn't mind pictures of the fish appearing in the weeklies. This year, however, they had to be extra careful as Rod was looking for any way he could to trip people up. Fortunately, he had been one of the first to publicise a fish after his capture of the thirty six at the beginning of the season and had, therefore, set a precedent that everyone was careful to follow.

The eastern sky was beginning to turn a milky-grey when Chris was woken by a single bleep to his right hand rod. On peering into the murk he could make out the faint outlines of the dreaded tufties and cursed quietly to himself, pulling his sleeping bag over his head and hoping they would go away. Another bleep, seconds later, told him that they would not and he slowly raised himself to a sitting position in preparation of the flapping fight to come. Yet another bleep echoed forth, but the indicator had not dropped a millimetre and it was with a sense of wonder that he watched the rod tip gradually pulling round to the left, accompanied by another bleep. Then another. Frowning, he picked up the rod, clicked the baitrunner off, and struck as hard as he could, expecting to see the culprit exit the lake like a feathered Exocet. The culprit, however, stayed exactly where it was for a second and the rod hooped over, holding the curve for a second, also, before slowly easing upwards as the unseen perpetrator rose up through the water. The fight that ensued was slow and deliberate and at no time did the fish take any line. Despite this, Chris felt sure that it was a good fish due to the weight he was forced to heave in and, after six or seven minutes, he was proved correct as a large grey flank emerged from the depths and turned in front of him, five yards out. It was the Grey Mirror and Chris suddenly felt very scared and very alone. The fish hadn't been out since the start of the season and speculation was that it could be huge, and this fact alone forced him to call for Stan's assistance. Stan, as usual, slept on for a few minutes until Sid came running past and called to him loudly, Chris's shouts having alerted him.

As Sid entered the swim, Chris was bending down with the rod held high in one hand whilst the other was extending the landing net as far as possible to a large bulk wallowing just out of reach.

"Here you are, Rhodie, I'll do that, mate," called Sid, and he strode forward to grab the net but, just as he did, he saw Chris raise it and drop the rod, uttering one word - very loudly, "Yesss!"

Stan had just entered the swim, and they all clamoured forward to get a look at the net and its cargo.

"Yesss!" he repeated, "it's the Grey Mirror! Yes! Yes! Yes!"

The others looked down and could see that he was not wrong and it slowly dawned on them that, at last, one of their merry band had caught a forty, and all hell let loose!

The carp weighed forty one pounds twelve ounces, many pounds less than the fantasy figures that are always bandied around when a big fish evades capture for a while, but that meant nothing to the three elated anglers. They simply enjoyed the momentous milestone and couldn't wait to see the contrasting looks on Rod and Buzz's faces when they learned the news.

Hours later they were still all blown away, and took it in turns to say 'forty one and three quarters', followed by a suitable silence, which was followed by equally suitable laughter. Strangely, they drank tea all day, wanting to savour the moment without the dulling of senses that drink eventually brought. There would be time enough for drink and they thought it only fitting that all four of them should be present when that took place. The umpteenth kettle of water was coming to the boil when they heard a buzzer screaming and it took a few seconds for Sid to realise that it was coming from his swim, to which he returned at great speed. The fight was as different from Chris's as the run had been and it was half an hour later before they caught a glimpse of row upon row of golden scales.

"Not another bloody common!" growled Sid, but when, a minute later, it rolled again, he realised that this was not just another common, it was the Big Common and he roared along with the others as it finally rolled into the net. It was, indeed, the Big Common and its weight of thirty five and a half pounds increased Sid's best by almost four pounds. The colours were dazzling, and Sid smiled without abandon for the cameras.

"You really are the Common Man, Sid!" remarked Chris whilst taking another shot, before the grinning captor finally lowered the great fish back into the lake and punched the air with joy. Hands were shaken and, as Sid was re-baiting, Stan said, "What we need in this swim, now, is some dodgems, coconut shy's, a big wheel and loads of candy floss stalls!"

The others stared at him open mouthed until Chris voiced their sentiments.

"What on earth are you talking about, Quill!"

Stan smiled, content that his friend had taken the bait perfectly, before replying, "You know - a Funfare for the Common Man!"

Groans of derision and 'Oh, no's!' filled the air and Stan laughed maniacally at his jape. It got no better after that.

Stan did, indeed, have the last laugh when he landed a fine twenty two pound mirror from very far out in the pond but little did they realise that this would be their last carp for almost four months.

The weather took its usual pre-Christmas turn for the worse and, despite their presence at the lake for all bar two of the winter weekends leading up to the festivities, they received action only from the tufties and a couple of incredibly stupid pike. What to do next?

Over the Christmas break, Stan and Chris met on a couple of occasions for a few beers and their respective better halves were happy to disappear into another room, leaving their men to discuss all matters carpy. This they did with the aid of the telephone and regular calls to Sid and Buzz until they eventually all agreed that the thing to do would be to join Dean on his winter campaign at Kingfisher until such time as the lake should freeze.

So it was that they were huddled together in Stan's voluminous bivvy on the first weekend in January, gazing across a grey and wind tossed lake. Seagulls wheeled across the sky, their raucous calls lending an eerie quality to the dull vista before the anglers. With the absence of reeds and marginal vegetation, it was possible for all of them to set up along the South Bank and cast up the lake, thus giving them all a gravel bar to fish on or behind. This feature ran parallel to that bank at seventy yards distance.

Dean was already present in his swim on the West Bank, having amazingly caught a thirty three pound common from there the previous day. He had wound in and popped round for some very welcome company and hot turkey broth, courtesy of Stan's mum, and been congratulated warmly on his success.

The conversation meandered around, as it is wont to do on these occasions and eventually, brought on by Dean's fish, settled momentarily on the subject of the Black Common, and all the other monster common carp that seemed to reside in lakes, ponds and meres the length and breadth of England. Dean looked pensive for a second or two and, spotting this, Sid said, "What's up, Dean? Don't tell me you've actually caught one, or something."

The others laughed, but then fell silent as he gazed deeply at each of them in turn, before starting, "I've never really told anyone about this."

"You're not a transvestite are you?" said Sid, "'cos if you are, I'm desperate for some sheer nylon stockings. I've laddered mine!"

They all chortled at that and Dean retorted, "Yeah, that as well. I'll see if I've got any," to which the laughter swelled, then he continued. "No, this is something much more interesting. I used to live near the New Forest about ten years ago, before I joined the Navy, and I used to fish on a carp lake with a couple of huge fish in. One of which was a common which I caught at thirty four pounds in the early eighties."

This brought some impressive grunts and groans from his audience.

"When I left the services I moved up to Slough and began fishing the Colne Valley and, so, pretty much forgot about those fish back home. Anyway, a few months ago I was fishing at The Cons and I met a guy called John who used to fish at Stanton's with me and it all came back to me. Just before I joined the Navy, the lake had been hit by S.V.C. because of some stupid stocking policy the club had embarked on. A lot of fish died and they closed the lake and, eventually, everyone assumed that all the biguns had died. But I knew different because, a year or so later, before I went abroad again, I had seen the two big fish - a common and a mirror - as large as life. I knew a guy who was thinking about buying a lake with Ken Sankey, you know the one I mean. Anyway, I phoned him and told him about the fish and suggested that they might fare better in another lake. After that, I went round the world and pretty much forgot about 'em. John also moved out of the area and, a few years later, joined that lake owned by Ken Sankey.

"Well, one night last year, John's fishing with Ken's mate, Bill, the guy I told about the lake, and they're having a few ales and telling a few tales when Bill looks around all furtively and ushers John closer. 'You know where some of these carp in here are from, don't you?' to which John says, 'No,' so Bill proceeds to tell him. He didn't mention my name, fortunately, but just said that they heard rumours of a few good fish in a very unfished water down south, so went down to have a look and found a few good fish swimming around, totally unmolested, in Stanton's. Well, they got a ticket as easy as pie and started fishing it the next season and caught a small common straight away, which they transferred to a holding pond for the next few months to make sure there was no sign of disease. Happy with this, they returned the next season to get what they could, especially the two biggies. They'd got this big old transit van all kitted out with aeration chambers and tanks and, over a couple of months, they transferred a few fish from there up to Ken's lake. Then, on the last session they planned to do, they hit the jackpot. In one night, they caught the two biggies. A mirror of thirty five pounds and a common a few pounds bigger."

This story had their full, undivided attention and not a word was uttered whilst Dean stopped to lubricate his larynx with a fresh cup of tea.

"So, they crept away at the crack of dawn with these two whackers in the back of the van and made their way back to Oxford, but about ten miles down the road the van started playing up and, not only that, one of the aeration pumps packed up. They tried to fix the van but it was having none of it, then the other pump packed up and they were really in trouble. By now it was getting light and they knew there would soon be a few people on the road so they could do only one thing and that was to drop the fish in a lake or pond somewhere. It just so happened that, when the sun got up, they were parked in a field that had a lake at the far end of it so they grabbed a sack each and carried the fish to the water. But, just as the fish swam away, they looked past an island in front of them and realised that it was bloody huge and that they would probably never see the fish again. Now, two things are important here. The first is this - you know the biggie in Ken's lake, the forty two?"

Once again, his silent listeners nodded their answer.

"Well, that is one of the fish from Stanton's and it went into Ken's lake about six years ago at twenty four pounds!"

This brought exclamations and raised eyebrows from the others, and then he produced the punch line.

"The second is that I know the exact location of the lake the other two went into!"

Silence reigned for a nanosecond, then all hell broke loose as they each tried to get a question in first, like a press conference held by a President or Prime Minister. The general theme was, obviously, where was it, was it fishable and could they get a ticket but, before he answered those he answered the last question that Buzz asked, "So, why aren't you fishing it then, Dean?"

Dean nodded at that and calmly replied, "My mum moved to Salisbury whilst I was in the Navy, so whenever I visit her I tend to have a little dabble on the local lakes and river. The problem is that I am pretty well known down there and a few people are less than friendly towards me, especially most of the members of a certain angling club. They own a couple of lakes in the area, including a lake called Felcham Mere. They have made it patently clear that I will never get a ticket for their waters, which is a pity really because I know of a couple of huge fish that are presently swimming around in Felcham Mere!"

This last brought smiles from the enthralled listeners and they spent the next hour or so discussing the how's and whys of getting a ticket for the lake. It transpired that few people bothered about fishing the lake for carp because, although there had always been carp in the lake, it had been considered too large to fish with any chance of ensnaring one of the small head of carp resident there. The only anglers were the odd tench and bream hunters. Getting a ticket could prove difficult but, with Sid living not too far away in Andover, they decided it worthwhile him applying for a ticket. This decided, and with plenty left for them to discuss, Dean made his way back to his swim before darkness fell for another sixteen hours. Discuss it they did and all agreed that, along with the yachting lake just down the road, Felcham should be investigated in the close season to see if the rumours were true.

The next morning was as grey as the previous, but it was brightened up greatly when Dean yelled across from his swim and bade them all come see. On their arrival in his swim they were greeted with the sight of him preparing to slip a huge, orange leather carp into the weigh sling. He had caught the same fish as Buzz, only this time the needle stopped the right side of forty by four ounces, and they congratulated him hugely. The fish shone like a beacon in the grey, morning light as did Dean's beaming smile and they all felt it fitting that, after imparting last night's news to them, he should be rewarded so grandly.

Following Dean's success, they anticipated an action packed few weeks whilst having the lake to themselves. However, despite all five of them fishing for the next six weeks, no further carp came to the bank and it was with little enthusiasm that Stan set out in the cold and rain of a late February morning to join his friends once more.

He had planned to arrive after work as usual, but Jean had other plans for them and it was well after nine o'clock on Saturday morning when he eventually eased his aching head into the car and made the thirty minute journey to Reading. The other three were already there, along the East Bank in front of the car park, and they greeted him with the news that Buzz had caught a double figure common in the night - the first carp for six weeks. This went a little way towards easing Stan's aching head, but he still needed some assistance with his tackle and it was just after midday when he was finally settled in the Car Park Swim. Buzz and Sid were in the East Point, with Chris to their left in The Kingfisher. Just to be sociable and nothing at all to do with the fact that Buzz had caught his fish by casting way out into the lake in front of the Car Park swim, Stan set up there. He put both baits out towards a clear, shallower area that they had found at ninety yards or so. This area was actually in front of Sid's, to his left, but as that swim was unoccupied he felt it a shame to waste such a nice spot.

By early evening, Stan was feeling a little better and joined the others in the East Point but, by nine in the evening he was all washed up, and strolled off into the night with his friends' catcalls and derisive remarks ringing in his ears. He cared not a jot, and merely waved one arm high in the air as he left the swim and, within minutes, was snoring loudly on his bedchair.

At first he thought it must be one of those waking dreams. The ones that seem so real that you convince yourself it can't be a dream. He was standing by the lake with his rod in his hand, and the wind blowing into his face, making his eyes water.

Every now and then the carbon would creak and the clutch on the reel would click a couple of times but, apart from that, he had no sensation that he was actually playing a fish at all. The dreamlike state was gradually falling from him like so many veils of silk and when the rod bucked again he was sure that this must really be happening. A splash in front of him alerted him to the fact that he had, in fact, been doing quite a bit of work whilst semi-conscious, and it was with not a little confusion that he eased the net forward for it to accept whatever had woken him from his deep slumber. Lowering the rod to the ground, he searched around for the unhooking mat, then tried to lift the net onto it but it seemed to be stuck.

"I really don't need all this," he growled, and bent to remove whatever was obstructing the net's passage.

It was as his hand brushed against the bottom of the net that it first dawned on him that the thing doing the obstructing was actually in the net, and it was purely weight that had caused the hold up. Grimacing, he heaved hard and carefully laid the fish on the mat before removing the mesh to reveal a whole lot of carp! Suddenly, he was wide awake, and let the rest of the lake know about it, as well. It was the Grey Mirror, of that he was certain, and that he had caught his first forty was without question as well. The next few minutes were as much of a blur as most of the fight had been, but they must have been quite vocal because he was soon joined by the other three, all of them rubbing sleep from their eyes and mumbling incoherently. Stan was suddenly the most lucid of all and manned the scales himself, grunting with the pleasurable pain of holding the great fish aloft. Eventually, all were agreed, "Forty two, exactly. Bloody well done, Quill!" declared Chris, and they all joined in the congratulations.

The carp was sacked until morning, and it was with some satisfaction that Stan peered past the cameras pointed at him and saw the sullen face of the Head Bailiff watching the proceedings. For his benefit, Stan strained every tonsil as the fish swam strongly away and, maybe because of that, was spoken to by Rod a minute or so later when the others had returned to their swims.

"Be careful how you report that, won't you Peacock?" he warned. Stan frowned at him before smiling and replying,

"Don't worry, Jonesy, I won't mention anything different to anyone else who sends their photographs to the papers."

As he was about to walk away Rod added, "You know tigers are banned still, don't you?"

This stopped Stan in his tracks, and he spun on his heels and confronted the now smiling bailiff, face to face.

"What the bloody hell's that supposed to mean?" he snarled, glaring straight at Rod. "Nobody's used tigers for nearly six months, now, and you know it."

"I'm only saying, you know, that if you thought it was alright now…well, it's not."

Stan stared a little harder, then turned and walked away, scared that he might say one thing too much.

On seeing the look on his face, Chris asked what was wrong and, once he had digested the explanation, replied, "Green-eyed monster, Quill, that's all it is. Pure jealousy. Don't worry, mate, if he tries anything we'll get hold of Les and get it all straightened out."

"Yeah. And you gotta remember one important thing," added Buzz. Stan looked puzzled until the big man continued at the top of his voice, "you've caught a forty two pound carp!"

This brought smiles and cheers from all present and, very shortly, the incident with Rod was forgotten and Stan looked forward to seeing a much more pleasing look on the faces of his family when he told them the news.

The news of Stan's capture soon permeated down to the other members so it was unsurprising that the next weekend found as many anglers at the lake as had attended the draw at the start of the season. This influx, however, served only to put the fish down and, with less than two weeks before the season ended, no further fish had been caught. One of the thirties had been netted, however, but it was with great sadness because the extremely desirable Double Linear was found, washed up and bloated, in the Snag Corner. The carcass was too far gone to do anything with, like stuffing and mounting, so it was buried in the corner near where it was found, and greatly missed.

Stan had been unsure what to do with the pictures of his fish, having taken Rod's words more to heart than he had originally thought. The decision was made for him a week before the end of the season when young Ken ended his season as well as he had begun it by catching the increasingly awesome Big Linear at forty three pounds six ounces. He was, obviously, over the moon with the capture, and the subsequent photographs, and took little time sending them to the papers. On hearing this, Stan sent his own pictures away and both fish appeared in the same issue of Angling Times, a few days after the end of the season, although the paper made no reference to the fact that they were from the same lake.

One thing that all present at the photographing of the Big Linear had noticed was the crushed tiger nuts in the carp sack. Ken was quizzed about this by Rod, but a search of his bait box and rucksack produced none of the offending particle so no more was said.

With three days of the season remaining, Chris had a stunning finale when, whilst fishing the Middle Reeds in the Back Lake, he landed a thirty two and a thirty five in one hectic night. These were the last of the biggies to come out, although another five fish to twenty four pounds did pose for the camera in the last couple of days. The four anglers celebrated Chris's angling good fortune in fine style. Once again, crushed tiger nuts were found in the sack that had housed the larger of the two, the Little Linear, and although Rod was not present, Chris showed everybody else the bait he was using and the lack of tiger nuts amongst it.

So ended a stupendous season, culminating in a last night party in the car park where stories were told, friendships strengthened, and many an ale consumed until the final stragglers staggered off to bed in the early hours of the final morning.

Stan, Chris, Buzz and Sid had spoken at length about their next step and all were in agreement that the next season would be their last on Kingfisher and, with that in mind, they would look seriously at the yachting lake, whose actual name was, strangely, Shiplake Pit. Another venue that would also require close scrutiny would be Felcham Mere, but this would be very dependent on whether Sid could obtain membership for the club. In the meantime they planned their final year at Kingfisher. Chris had been doing some investigating and had found one of the many small bait companies that were springing up who would be willing to provide them with ready rolled bait, made to their specification, at a very reasonable price. This was the final piece to their puzzle and they planned to prebait with the new bait as soon as it arrived, in the spring.

Then it all went very pear shaped.

The phone rang, and Stan answered with his usual, "Good morning, Halcyon Printing. Stan speaking."

"Bastards!" came the vehement reply.

"I'm sorry?" said Stan, quite stunned.

"The bastards!" came Chris's confirmation of the first statement. "They've only bloody banned me!"

"What! Who? What d'you mean? Who's banned you?" came Stan's very confused reply.

"That bastard Jones, that's who. I've been banned for using tigers!"

Over the next, expletive punctuated, five minutes Chris explained the whole thing. He had received a letter that morning saying that it had come to the attention of the owners that he had broken the 'no tiger nuts' rule and, therefore, would be banned for one year. The worst of it was that the letter was signed by Les Morgan, himself.

This news was very distressing and they both knew that Chris had been set up but, with Rod getting to Les first, they doubted that they had little chance of an appeal. Chris informed both Sid and Buzz during the day and it was obvious that the phone lines would be humming that evening, but little did they realise what else fate had in store for them.

Chris answered the ringing phone with his usual, "Yup!"

"Bastards!" came Stan's vehement reply.

"Oh no! What now?" winced Chris.

"They've banned me as well, the bastards!" came Stan's angry reply.

Once again the story was told, this time of how he had been banned for breaking the no-publicity rule on more than one occasion, and after having been warned not to. The ban was, once again, for a year and was, once again, signed by Les. The next few hours were spent on the phone to Bracknell and Andover and they all agreed that a face to face discussion was required, which was planned for that Friday in a pub near Yateley.

The conversation was long and the air very blue but, eventually, all were agreed. Goodbye Kingfisher, hello Shiplake or Felcham, whichever was the more alluring. There was no doubt that they had been stitched up but they all knew that there was little point in taking the matter further, nor contemplating a return in a year's time - that old, green-eyed monster had an extremely long life span! So, bigger plans had to be made and put into action immediately. With just over two months to the start of the season they had to move fast in order to decide where to fish and so agreed that they would meet on Sunday at Shiplake, to have their first serious look at the place.

The three of them were waiting at their agreed meeting point when they saw the familiar 'Barrett' van pull into the car park. The door burst open and a grinning Sid strode purposefully across the gravel towards them.

"Shake the hand of a winner, boys!" he demanded, beaming from ear to ear. Doing as he was bade, Buzz then enquired for all of them, "What have you done, Siddy boy? Why the Cheshire Cat impression?"

With that, Sid put his hand into his pocket and produced a small, blue booklet and held it out for them to see. 'Wilton Angling Society', it read. They looked puzzled and Sid could hold out no longer.

"Here, my good friends, is the Holy Grail. Turn, if you will, to page six of this small but impressive tome," he instructed, expansively.

Stan took the proffered booklet and turned to the required page and, at the top, he read aloud the words, "Felcham Mere. Sid, you old dog, you're in!"

Pushing out his pigeon chest and polishing his finger nails on his shirt front, Sid smiled his hugest smile before confirming, "I am, indeed, 'in' my dear Quill. After parting with the princely sum of thirty of your earth pounds, I was handed this ticket to dreamland. You, too, can become an illustrious member of the Wilton Angling Society if you can find an address within the required catchment area. I was just on the limits, which is nothing new!"

This news buoyed them greatly and, with the knowledge that Dean had the required addresses if they should need them, they looked forward to joining Sid on the membership list. So, it was with a spring in their step that they began their first, four hour long walk around Shiplake. It was a huge expanse of water and Stan had memories of the days he had spent on Burghfield in a vain search for carp in its windswept waters. But this could be different. There were four of them, now, and they had learnt a great deal over the past couple of years, not least about themselves. And they had firsthand knowledge of a fish of huge proportions swimming in these waters.

The day was quite mild for the time of year and the wind, although quite brisk, did not give the lake an impression of limitless size and depth. By the end of their tour, therefore, they were all enthused by the prospect of fishing there and set about, over the next week, obtaining the necessary licences.

The purchasing of the Wilton A.S. tickets were less simple because the phone number that they had for Dean had been cut off and they were left in limbo for a few weeks. This time was spent, mainly, at Shiplake and they soon started becoming familiar with one or two areas that they thought might produce carp.

This conviction was made certain on one visit when, whilst staring into the south westerly wind that was whipping the water to a foam, Buzz and Chris saw several carp cavorting in the waves. Two of these were of an impressive stature and this knowledge was gleefully received by the absent Stan and Sid.

By now they had all obtained tickets for the lake and had learnt that the use of boats was allowed, pending certain rules being adhered to, so Buzz set about seconding a couple of sturdy inflatables so that they could better explore the lake. As the days lengthened and warmed they took to the water most weekends and, on one Saturday in May, they were treated to a rare but impressive sight.

The wind was light, the day warm and the possibility of spotting carp quite high. They paired off into the boats, as usual, and rowed leisurely out to one of the large islands on the far side of the lake. The islands, like most of the bankside, were very overgrown and it was beneath the overhanging marginal trees that they had found some carp lazily cruising around a week earlier. As they neared the island, Stan and Chris headed to the left and the others to the right, planning to meet up on the other side. Stan peered intently over the side into the deep, blue water whilst Chris rowed them closer to the trees. After ten minutes or so their quest was still fruitless and, as they rounded the left hand side of the island, they saw Buzz and Sid sitting in their vessel and staring intently, not at the island but at the near shore of the lake. The grass was high, there, and Stan and Chris were unable to see what the attraction was but, just as Chris was about to signal to the other two, he saw a movement in the grass.

Edging slowly nearer, they both saw what appeared to be a pair of buttocks and, as they drifted within fifty yards of the bank, sure enough, there was a pair of buttocks going up and down like pistons! Not that they needed any confirmation of what Buzz and Sid had found so enthralling, but the grunts and groans from the bank left them in little doubt as to what was occurring. Sid turned to them smiling and put a finger to his lips, bidding silence, and they watched the final completion of the act with amusement and a certain envy! His amorous task completed, the bankside lothario rolled over onto his back to catch his breath and it was at that point that Buzz applauded rapturously, immediately accompanied by Sid with piercing wolf whistles. Before the bemused couple could work out what was happening, Stan and Chris had joined in and the air rang with appreciative applause and cries of, "Author! Author!"

The young lady suddenly squealed with horror as she realised what had happened and quickly gathered her clothes about her in order to best hide her charms, shuffling backwards through the long grass in the hope that it would shield her from the audience's view. The young man was, initially, equally abashed but then realised the futility of it all and, to even louder applause and whistles, stood up and faced the floating revellers. He then took a deep bow, before turning to walk away and taking another! They laughed and whooped for many minutes before continuing on their search - you see so many wonderful things when you go fishing!

By the end of May, Buzz had gained permission to use his scuba gear on the lake and it was on the last weekend of that month that he made his first sub-surface sortie into the lake. They had found carp sunning themselves under the branches of the Rumpy-Pumpy Island a week previously and, with conditions very similar, decided that here was a good place for Buzz to start his explorations. Fifteen minutes after disappearing below the waves, he emerged thirty feet along the shore from where they were waiting. His beard and hair were hanging damply, both adorned with small strands of weed.

"Bloody hell! Where's your trident, Neptune?" exclaimed Sid.

Buzz shipped his mask and tank and stared at them intently before uttering his first words.

"Oh my God!"

"What? What have you seen, boy?"

The question could have come from anyone of them and it was to all of them that the answer was directed.

"Oh my bloody God!" he repeated, before continuing. "There's about twelve carp down there, under those trees."

With this, he pointed at the nearside of the island. "They're all about mid-twenties, I suppose. But then I swam round the side of the island and, under that willow to the right there. Well, there are four fish there, and I doubt if any of them are under forty pounds!" This revelation brought squeals and shouts and blurted questions, before he held up his hand for silence.

"Then, out of the deep water I could just make out another fish moving towards me. At first I thought it was a pike, 'cos of its length, but then it just slowly cruised up to me before swimming past and joining the other four. I could have reached out and touched it, it was so close."

His wild, staring eyes told them that he was not exaggerating and they waited, breathlessly, for the finale.

"How big?" asked Stan.

Buzz looked at him thoughtfully before carefully replying.

"Well, if there is a fifty in here I reckon I've just been swimming with it!"

This brought even more commotion before he, once again, motioned for quiet. "If we could get hold of a photo I could tell you for definite. I saw every scale along its left flank and, if you've got a piece of paper, I can draw them now."

None of them had the required drawing equipment, but they had no doubt that Buzz was confident in his assessment. This was the final confirmation they needed, and the news acted like a cork from a bottle, all of them trying to talk at once with their ideas for the coming season on Shiplake.

Felcham Mere was temporarily forgotten and all of their energies were put into preparing for June 16th. They had thought about pre-baiting with their wonderful new bait, but decided that this would be a waste of bait if they were unable to find the fish in future. Instead, they spent their last couple of visits subtly crafting two or three new swims in the area of the Rumpy-Pumpy Island. These were in the north eastern corner of the lake and would benefit, also, from the prevailing winds. They had found a couple of swims in the vicinity which, they assumed, were the most frequently inhabited, so tried their best to stay clear of these and, with so much bank at their disposal, this did not prove to be a problem.

If the start of the season the previous year had been their best in living memory, then the one at Shiplake could well have been the worst. As he was preparing to leave work on the 15th, Stan received a phone call from Chris to say that he had broken down ten miles from the lake.

He had tried, unsuccessfully, to reach Buzz and Sid, who would both have had to practically drive past him on their way to the lake, so Stan was his last hope. With his own car full of fishing tackle, Stan knew that the only thing they could do would be to tow Chris to the lake, so he made his way to the rendezvous, somewhat peeved but also certain that the same favour would be returned if necessary - and had been on many an occasion. The ten-mile journey was, quite simply, a nightmare as the Friday evening traffic built up, forcing Stan to stop and start on numerous occasions which, in turn, caused their makeshift tow rope to snap seven times! By the time they had completed the torturous journey, over an hour had passed and their tempers were as frayed as the rope. To compound matters, rain had begun to fall steadily, which not only made driving more interesting, but would also not help when they arrived at the lake.

Sid had, for once, been able to get a couple of days off work and he and Buzz greeted the weary travellers at the lake with the news that there was to be a yacht race tomorrow. No anglers' boats would be allowed on the water during that time. They gave the new arrivals a hand with their tackle and made the long, wet trek from the car to the swims, four hundred yards distant. The wind was picking up and, as Stan peered out across the vast, windswept expanse of water in front of him he was quite glad to have an excuse not to go out on the water tomorrow.

Being last at the lake, Chris and he obviously had to accept the swims left by their friends and found themselves a few hundred yards south of the Rumpy-Pumpy Island. Plumbing the water in front of him was becoming increasingly difficult, with the strong side wind creating a great bow in the line and making the task of feeling for clear spots and features nigh on impossible. Then, when he did find what felt like a clear, gravel hump, his subsequent casts with a lead and a rig produced ball after ball of weed. By seven in the evening he was wet, tired, hungry and very pissed off! Chris seemed to have fared little better and, having found a clear area, proceeded to tow his marker float in with his rig, the wind getting up much stronger after that and making plumbing impossible. Eventually they both opted for a night in the edge, and strolled disconsolately down to join the other pair for a pre-season drink. Half an hour before midnight, they returned a little happier, only to find that the wind had swung around, unnoticed from the shelter of Buzz's swim, and had blown straight into their swims. The result was a soaking wet bed for both of them, and an inside-out brolly for Chris!

After a night in their cars, they returned to their swims to find that one of the buoys marking the course of the yacht race was floating thirty yards out from their swims, so nothing other than a margin rod could be risked for the duration of the race. Sid and Buzz were also chagrined to learn that their island served as a roundabout for the yachts and they would have to fish similarly to the others until evening. As the race progressed, they all gathered in Sid's swim for the day and watched, frustrated, as a number of carp showed themselves in the island margins. The wind still made boating very tricky but, after much help and a couple of tangling disasters, Sid and

Buzz both managed to get their baits where they wanted them after the race had finished. Stan and Chris were less happy and still found it difficult to find any clear spots in front of them so did, as they had planned for the previous evening, drop them in the edge.

The darkness produced a take to one of Sid's rods, but whatever it was came adrift after a matter of seconds, but not before it had kited to the right and picked up his other line! The final nail came when they woke to see that the wind had changed completely and was blowing into the opposite corner, the one area on the lake that was out of bounds. They moved as close as they could to that area later in the day but, even with the aid of the boats, were unable to get near enough to where the odd fish had shown. They sat out the remaining thirty six hours of their first, disastrous session gazing sullenly across this 'hell water.'

To say that they approached the next session with a mood of trepidation would have been a gross understatement, but it was as different from the first as the weather was. When Buzz arrived on Wednesday morning, he was greeted by glorious sunshine and a light southerly breeze barely rippling the surface of the water. By the time that Chris arrived a day later, Buzz had once again been sub-aquatic and had plenty to tell.

He had seen some carp on the surface in the large North Bay and donned his scuba gear to join them. It was his firm opinion that carp, like all other fish he had encountered, found the sight of a human being swimming amongst them far less alarming than the upright versions they saw stalking the margins of their homes. With this in mind, he was much happier viewing them from below than from a boat. His second twenty minute supply of air still had eighteen minutes to run when he came across the fish, sunning themselves on a lightly weeded plateau, and he was able to manoeuvre to within a few yards before they showed any signs of unrest. He had counted twelve fish in all, as well as a few bream on the periphery of the shoal, and had then spent the next quarter of an hour scouring the area for likely places to put a few baits. The plateau they were above was twinned by another of similar size about fifty yards away and, after dropping a couple of polystyrene markers, he returned to the bank to see where both plateaux were in relation to any fishable swims nearby. They were within one hundred yards of the bank and could easily be fished from three or four different areas and, by the time that Chris arrived, Buzz had set up with the left hand plateau eighty yards out from his swim and with a bait positioned on either end of it.

Further investigation from the boat revealed three or four small, clear areas and, by Friday evening, all four of them were fishing with confidence and renewed vigour. The fish had been spotted again just prior to the arrival of Stan and Sid, and were still well within range of the baited areas and the three of them spent the evening quizzing Buzz as to the size of the fish he had seen. Though none of the bigger fish were present, he was confident that at least three of them were in excess of thirty pounds, including two commons. With this knowledge they all went to sleep anticipating some midnight action.

'Picked the wrong swim again,' thought Stan as he covered his eyes with his pillow to shield them from the rising sun. He had woken an hour earlier, as the first birds were also beginning to wake, and wondered why they had to be so bloody vocal! Why couldn't they just spread their wings the way men stretched their arms?

They were even noisier now, and he lay there mesmerised by the intricate song of the wren in the reeds to his right, then listened to the call repeated almost perfectly from a further reed bed. This went on for ten minutes before he realised that he was fully awake, so slowly rose and stretched expansively. The clock showed a few minutes after five and on went the first kettle of the day. Buzz was seventy yards to his left so, once the water had boiled, he made two cuppa's and wandered through the dew-damp grass and nettles to the big man's swim. He took a little waking but, soon, they were sitting together, gazing out across a mist wreathed lake.

"This is just the nuts!" sighed Buzz, and Stan nodded in silent acknowledgement. The silence remained as they drank in the tea and the atmosphere, then it was shattered by the sight of a carp sliding silently upwards through the surface, then backwards without a sound. Two jaws dropped open and the watchers stared in disbelief.

"That's about ten yards from my right hand bait," explained Buzz, and they both glanced down at the rod in question, willing the buzzer to burst into life. Five minutes later, another fish declared itself somewhat more noisily than the first, and the anglers squealed like two five year olds who had been told that they were going to see Father Christmas. Still the alarm remained stubbornly silent, as it did for the next hour whilst the carp casually slipped out of and back into the water. This caused Buzz and Stan to skip from foot to foot and take it in turns to run naked through the surrounding woods to douse the flames that were intermittently bursting from them! Amazingly, not one single bleep was uttered by the alarm and it was with a tinge of sadness that they realised that the spectacle was over, two hours after it had begun.

Sid strolled into the swim half an hour after the last carp had shown itself and asked, quite innocently, "Alright boys, seen anything?"

They looked at him, then at each other, before slowly shaking their heads and smiling.

"Sid, you'll never know mate. You will never know," said Buzz, before Stan gave the bemused Sid the full story.

By the end of it, Buzz had only one thing to add, "And people say, 'What! You didn't catch anything? Blimey, I bet that was boring!' If only they knew. God, I love carp fishing!"

The spectacle was not repeated that day, nor the next, and they received no action but packed away much happier than the week before. Then, just as Chris was winding in the last of his rods, he heard a shout to his left. All of the others were fishing to his right, so he assumed that it was one of the recently arrived yachtsmen. Then he heard it again so went along to investigate. After a couple of hundred yards he could clearly hear someone calling for assistance so shouted back to let them know he was coming and, on rounding a small point of land, was confronted by an angler waist deep in the water with his rod bent at an alarming angle.

"Alright mate?" called Chris. "Need a hand?" The anguished angler looked round and gave a relieved nod.

"Oh boy, do I need a hand!" he called back. "Can you grab the landing net for me? This fish has got a bloody weedbed attached to it and I can't seem to get it any closer," the frustrated angler explained. At that point the other three, having heard Chris's shout, had also come to investigate and arrived in the swim en masse.

"Have you got a boat, mate?" asked Stan.

"No. But I don't know if that will help. The fish is about ten yards out and not moving," came the reply. With that, Buzz stripped down to his boxer shorts and strode straight into the lake. For a moment, the water-bound angler wondered what this semi naked giant was about to do, then sighed when Buzz said, "Right, young fella, whereabouts is this bloody carp?"

The angler pointed to a point where the line entered the water and said, "About five yards behind tha ...!" and was unable to finish the sentence before Buzz dived below the surface like some hirsute mermaid!

Two strokes of his long arms brought him to within feet of the weed bed and he could just make out the shape of a slowly twisting carp amongst its fronds. He surfaced, dripping, and trod water whilst shouting, "Net!"

Chris passed it to the angler, Steve, who then passed it on to Buzz, unsure if this was the correct course of action but in no position to question it. Buzz took the handle then kicked himself a further yard or so before disappearing below the surface once more. Steve looked around at the others and was about to voice his concern when Sid said, with the utmost sincerity, "It's alright sir, he's a carp angler." Before Steve could fathom this remark out, he felt the line slacken and assumed that the foolhardy venture had ended in disaster.

Instead, the water exploded two yards from him as Buzz exited like a Polaris missile. Spitting water from his moustache, he wiped a hand across his eyes, before declaring through grinning teeth, "Gottit!"

'Deja vu,' thought Stan, while assisting the sodden anglers from the lake. The net was bulging with weed, and through the green they could discern the odd flash of golden brown.

"I wonder what it is?" pondered a disbelieving Steve.

"Oh, I know which one it is, fella. Don't you worry about that," declared Buzz, and with that, they all scrabbled at the weed to reveal more and more carp. By the time that there was simply carp on the mat, the only noise was the odd gasp and expletive. Even Buzz, who had had eye contact with the fish a few weeks earlier, could do little but stare, slack jawed.

What a fish it was. Obviously the fifty, that was beyond doubt, but its size was nothing without its shape and the fat, bloated carp they had all expected was, in fact, the most handsome beast they had ever laid eyes on. The weight really was irrelevant, but fifty one pounds was a pretty impressive statistic to have on your C.V.!

Steve could not stop thanking them and then saying, 'I don't believe it' after every sentence, like a budding Victor Meldrew. With one final handshake, they left him to his impressive thoughts.

They each had thoughts of their own on the journey home and were all filled with a certain knowledge that, pretty soon, one of them would be feeling like Steve. One of them would, in the very near future, get to hold the great fish, but his thoughts and those of his friends would be very different from today.

On arriving home, Jean saw Stan's smiling face and assumed that he had been successful,

"No love, not me. But what a great weekend."

He went on to explain events, knowing that she was one of the few non fishermen who would understand how he felt.

"Oh, well. It'll soon be you, dear. Then you'll really have something to smile about."

She put the kettle on, then said, "Oh, by the way. Dean phoned just now. He left a number." This was good news also and, after a shower, he returned the call.

"What's all this about you getting banned?" began Dean, and Stan proceeded to tell him of the incidents that led to their ban, before relating the most recent events. Dean was suitably impressed and asked Stan if they would mind him going along for a look in the near future.

"Bloody hell, you don't have to ask, mate. Just tell us when you're coming and we'll get a few beers in. However, we could do with a favour from you, mate." He then went on to tell Dean of Sid's Wilton ticket and their need for some local addresses. Dean assured him that there would be no problem, in fact he would make a few phone calls that very day.

Stan was just digesting a huge roast dinner when the telephone sprung him awake from his dozing, "Hi, Stan? It's Dean," came the voice. Stan wiped his eyes in a bid to get himself more alert before replying. "Hello, mate. What's happening?"

"Grab a pen and paper, I've got those addresses for you," came the surprising reply and, within a few minutes, Stan had the required information that would obtain them three Wilton tickets. For the moment, though, he had other things on his mind, and put the information to one side whilst he day-dreamed of fifty pound carp.

Time still passed and, despite a small but steady flow of anglers to the mere, the fish remained uncaught. Sightings of them were infrequent and when they did occur, the description of the fish was hardly believable, especially when being told over the fourth pint of ale of the night. The problem was that the witnesses were totally unprepared for what they saw and, invariably, had only seen dolphins or sharks that came anywhere near the scale of the carp they glimpsed. Hardly surprising, then, that their descriptions sounded incredulous and born of fantasy.

Heavy with spawn, the four great carp meandered slowly through the burgeoning weed beds, only days away from the release of the pressure inside them and, at that point in time, the locals had no idea that the mere contained four carp in excess of fifty pounds; some exceeding that mark by far more than others.

Chapter Fourteen - Felcham Mere

"Right, that's the lot. Come on, if we push it we might catch the earlier ferry."

Stevo closed the van doors on the dripping cargo before jumping into the passenger side and preparing for the four hour journey to Calais. The trip had been quite successful, with the four of them catching more than thirty fish in the five day stay by the huge, French lake. More importantly, twenty of these had been in excess of thirty pounds, including seven forties, and it was these carp that they had just loaded into the two specially equipped transit vans for transportation back to England, and a very lucrative pay day.

Everything was going to plan when, suddenly, the leading van coughed, spluttered then came to a staggering halt in a cloud of smoke and grinding metal. After an hour of sweating and cursing over the stricken engine, it became very apparent that this was an ex-van. With that came the knowledge that they would have to ditch most of the cargo, there being no room in the other van for any more than two extra sacks and the rest of the tackle.

They argued over which fish to transfer, having previously decided to separate the forties between the two vans. Eventually they realised that there was no way that they could transfer the fish by the side of a busy road, opting instead to leave them where they were and hoping that they would be found before the aeration pumps packed up. Being the beginning of May, the temperatures were far from sweltering but, by the time that a local gendarme happened by and chose to investigate the breakdown, three quarters of the gasping passengers were beyond help and were eventually left to die and become fertiliser on a local farmer's field.

The other van did not make the earlier ferry, nor the one it was booked on, and so it was almost eighteen hours after leaving the lake that they eventually arrived at their rendezvous point outside Reading. The recipient of the shipment was less than pleased at the delay and demanded to see that the fish were alright, but on opening the first two sacks he was even less pleased to find two dying carp inside. The ensuing exchange was curt, succinct and terminal and, as the taillights of the truck left the secluded car park, the smugglers looked at each other for a clue as to what to do.

"Well, we can't keep 'em, can we? We passed a big lake back there, let's see which ones are still alive and just dump 'em in there. Then let's go home."

"But what about the money? We was s'posed to be taking a couple of long ones each. I can't go home broke, my missus'll kill me!"

"Sod the bloody money! We've blown it! Let's just dump the fish and piss off, like Johnnie said."

With that, they squeezed back into the van and drove the couple of miles to the shores of the large lake, where they backed the van up to its windswept shore before ditching their useless cargo. Of the sixteen sacks remaining, only ten were filled with living carp and these were slipped into the oxygen rich water in the hope that they would survive. By morning, eight were left swimming this foreign water, the others going the way of their recent co-passengers who had been unceremoniously dumped in a nearby rubbish skip.

Amazingly, amongst the survivors were four of the forties. None of them were very well and they spent their first few days in their new home huddled together in the margins of one of the lake's islands, being occasionally investigated by the lake's resident carp and the odd, passing scuba diver!

A week after witnessing one of the biggest carp in the country, they were to catch their first from the lake and, although less than half the size, Sid's twenty three pound common was received grandly. Not only because it was their first fish from the lake, but mainly because it proved that they could catch fish from this inland sea and, suddenly, size meant nothing. This was just the fillip they needed and, over the ensuing couple of weeks, another three fish of similar size fell to their rods, with yet another falling off Buzz's hook. With this renewed confidence, they arrived on the penultimate weekend in July knowing that, if they could only find where the bigger fish were feeding, they would be in with a great chance of catching one of them.

Buzz, as usual, was already present and, when Stan strolled into his swim he spied the discarded mask and air tanks that told of his recent investigation of the depths.

"Yo, Buzz boy. How you doing, mate? Been canoodling with any whackers under there?" asked Stan, prior to lowering himself onto the low chair next to Buzz's brolly. Buzz was strangely quiet, and Stan assumed that he must have been having a little afternoon siesta, so sat back for a second to take in the view of the lake before him.

"I thought I'd never see it again," Buzz mumbled.

Stan barely heard him so asked him to repeat it. "Just like Pit Five all over again," came the equally puzzling reply, and Stan shook his head and asked, "What are you on about, mate?"

"Dead carp, Quill! Bloody dead carp, that's what I'm on about," came the strident reply and Stan felt like he had been slapped. Over the next few minutes he managed to piece together the story from Buzz's fragmented tale.

On his arrival, earlier that morning, he had spied a couple of cruising carp in this area so elected to set up camp before having a closer look. What he saw, however, was not encouraging at all. The two cruising carp, on closer inspection, were swimming very strangely and did not attempt to move away, even when Buzz got so close that he could touch one of them. This immediately sent warning signals through his troubled mind, and they were well founded for, over the course of two tanks of air and forty minutes, he discovered the corpses of four carp tangled in the surrounding weed. Stan's stomach was tight and he felt a little dizzy and it was a few minutes before he could work out what to say.

"What are we gonna do? Do we, err, y'know, do we tell anyone? I mean, like, the club. Do we tell the club? Maybe it's just a few, y'know, sick ones."

Buzz let him ramble on for a few minutes before putting his hand on Stan's arm.

"It's just like Pit Five and Frensham. Just like it. There'll be more, quite a few more I would guess, but it's such a big water we probably won't know until they float to the surface."

He then stopped and sat with his brow deeply furrowed as a thought process ran its course, before continuing.

"However, I know some guys at a diving club near Woking who would be up for going in to have a look. I wonder if we can get permission?"

They mulled the idea over for a while before Buzz stood up, purposefully, and declared, "You stay here with the gear. I'm going to ring the club secretary. What's his name?"

"Jim Greenhough, I think," replied Stan, then watched as the big man strode away.

Chris was away in Spain this week, and Sid would not be down for another couple of hours, so he sat there, alone, and stared at what had been a marvellous vista only minutes earlier. Now all he could see were corpses scattered hither and thither.

Within an hour, Buzz returned with the news that the secretary had okayed the dive for tomorrow, if Buzz could arrange it, and would phone the water authority in the hope that they could get someone to the lake as well. On his grinning arrival, they updated Sid with the events of the afternoon, but it took many minutes before he was convinced that this was not an elaborate spoof. They did not know what to do that evening, none of them wanting to put a rod out lest they should hook a sick and dying fish. Instead, they sat by the lake, rod-less, and talked away the night.

By ten thirty the next morning, a team of ten divers was preparing to systematically search the lake for signs of sick or dead fish. Buzz had been out earlier and had found another two dead carp in the margins, one of which was a very big fish, possibly a forty. The scrape lines on its flanks led the water authority representative to believe that it had recently been in an enclosed environment, but they could also have been caused by spawning, so that line of thought was inconclusive.

Stan and Sid stood on the bank like wives awaiting the return of their whaling husbands but when, twenty minutes later, the men returned from the deep they were not greeted with cheers and kisses. Eight corpses were recovered in this first sweep and, from afar, they could tell Buzz's frame and, from that, discern that the fish he was cradling was no mid-twenty. The huge carp was still, intermittently, moving its gills but it was obvious that this was just a nervous reaction and that the life had sadly gone from this, one of the biggest carp in England.

By the end of the day they had barely covered half of the lake, but the tally of twenty seven corpses told its gruesome tale and the lake was shut down until further notice.

Four months earlier they had been toasting their best ever season. Now their world lay shattered and directionless.

Chris returned three days later and simply did not believe what Stan told him, needing to phone Buzz, Sid and Jim Greenhough before he would accept the tragic truth. However, due to his lack of direct involvement, he was sharper and more aware of the situation they were in, so said to Stan, "So, have you sent off to Wilton Angling Society for tickets yet?"

"What?" asked Stan. "Shit, I didn't even think of it!"

"Well start bloody thinking of it, Quill. I want to go fishing this weekend, so we need to hustle a bit."

Phone calls were rapidly made, cheques raised and application forms sent and, with much grovelling and a few white lies, they were able to pick up their permits on the following Saturday. Sid was the only one of the four who had actually seen the lake, so it was with a mixture of trepidation and excitement that they rolled down the dirt track just before midday on Saturday and first set eyes on Felcham Mere.

Parking the cars on a small hard standing, they skipped over the five bar gate and strolled through a small copse of trees that hid the lake from view. The familiar sound of coots squabbling drifted to them on the warm, summer breeze and they followed Sid through the trees until they came to the northern shore of the lake. A light southerly gently caressed the surface of the lake and, as they parted some tall reeds, a huge explosion of water announced the departure of a startled pike from its usually undisturbed daytime resting place. Gazing down the full length of the lake, all four of them drank in the almost palpable atmosphere.

'This,' they all thought, 'is a carp lake.'

Buzz broke the silence with a huge gulp of air before sighing,

"Oh, yes. Oh, I like this. I like this a lot."

The others nodded their agreement whilst their eyes darted wildly about, gathering information as quickly as possible.

A shoal of small fish, possibly perch, flipped and flopped excitedly on the surface, trying desperately not to become dinner for some unseen predator, and the movement caught Stan's eye and dragged his gaze to the right. There, a hundred yards or so into the lake, was what Sid had described as the 'Banana Island'. From his present vantage point, it was difficult to see why his friend had named it so, but it was, apparently, banana shaped so he supposed that might have something to do with it!

They spent the next few hours slowly and meticulously walking the banks and investigating as many swims and trees as was possible. The far, southern end was split into two shallow bays by a wide point of land, and it was in these bays that they saw the most activity. The bay to the right of the point was semi-covered in lily pads and it was these, initially, that gave away the presence of something beneath as ripples constantly emanated from the leaves after their stems had been knocked or rubbed. Whether there were tench, carp or conger eels below was uncertain. It mattered not, though, and they sat watching the area intently for ten minutes in the hope that the invisible rippler would show itself, until Chris lost patience and moved off toward the other bay, the others slowly following.

This bay was larger by half again and was fringed almost entirely by reeds. The tall, green fronds extended at least a couple of yards into the lake and it seemed, on first sight, were almost impenetrable. Once again, the anglers' passage around the perimeter of the bay stirred fish of unknown origin to bolt from the refuge of the reeds, one such leaving a long line of bubbles behind it as it bow-waved across the shallow bay.

By the time that they had reached the top of the West Bank, and the Banana Island, they were hot and sweaty and in need of sustenance but, as they passed the island and came to the top corner, they were confronted by a large fallen tree in the margins. Knowing the carp's natural instinct was to use these snags for a hiding and resting place, they slowed in their journey and watched whilst Chris lithely climbed the most sturdy limb before easing himself over the water. Peering into the black depths below, he thought that he could discern a couple of large shapes slowly moving between the branches, but the light was poor and, after a couple of minutes, his thirst got the better of him and he returned to dry land.

Sitting in a swim in the middle of the North Bank, they supped a tepid lager each and surveyed the lake's other island. This was in the bay at the north eastern end of the lake and was three times the size of the Banana Island. The swim they were sitting in offered a good cast to the right hand side of the island, but it could also be fished from a swim at the top of the bay, as well as two or three swims on the east bank. These all allowed a cast of about sixty yards to the left bank of the island. As the wind was still pushing lightly in this direction, they decided to fish around the Top Bay, as they dubbed it, which would allow each of them at least one rod in the island margins if they wished. It was also very close to the cars and tonight was not a night for lugging tackle around a fifty acre lake!

Happy with their decision, they spent the next couple of hours exploring their swims, discovering a pleasant amount of gravel spots and humps as well as prolific weed growth. What they all noticed, and commented on in length later that evening, was the proliferation of shelled creatures. Mussels of every size and shape. Small, medium and very large snails. And loads of creeping, slithering and wriggling creatures in every ball of weed that they retrieved. It was obvious that, if the story of the immigrant carp was true, then they had not gone hungry for the past decade and the four anglers began fantasising about what size they may have achieved. They went to bed to dream of monster commons and hoped that one might pull their strings during the night, but this night they just caught forty winks or so.

At some dark point in the small hours, Stan was awakened by a huge splash and stared into the dark until the ripples eventually reached the shore in front of him. He lay awake for a time in the hope that the great fish would repeat the act but, barring the muffled call of a dozing goose, the night remained silent and he drifted back to sleep. Buzz had also been awoken by the sound and stood by the lakeside for the time it took to smoke a cigarette, before also returning to the land of dreams. In the morning, they both spoke of their wake up call and were surprised that such a noise had not stirred the other two, before working out that the island must have muffled the sound (Sid and Chris being almost on the opposite side to the others.)

The dawn passed them by, and it was not until well after seven that they were all fully awake and having the conversation. Despite this tardy start to the day, they did see a couple of disturbances further down the lake that appeared to be larger than tench or bream, and so chose to spend the remainder of their stay walking the banks of the lake with a rod each. So it was that their first sighting of a carp was witnessed by only one pair of eyes, but the story that was told of it fired all of them up.

With the heat of the midday sun burning down, Buzz moved from the pads, next to which he had spent the last hour float fishing, and made his way over the outlet stream and up the east bank towards the small wood that encroached to the lake's shore along there. Just before he reached the first of the trees, he sat on the grass and enjoyed a peaceful smoke behind some marginal reeds. As he sat there, gazing through the thin stalks, he noticed half a dozen of them twitch then, just to the left, the same again only more violently. Stubbing out his cigarette on the ground, he crept stealthily to the water's edge and peered carefully through the reeds. At the far edge of the stems he could see a small vortex in the surface film, like a tail pattern, so adjusted his sunglasses a little better before bending a little closer. The change in angle made the water almost transparent and there, not three yards away, was a carp of huge proportions. For a moment all was still - the carp, the reeds, Buzz's pulse, Buzz's breathing - then someone flicked a switch and they all started up at once!

The reeds rustled in a sudden breeze, Buzz gasped at the sight before him, and the carp decided that it had posed for long enough and, with one flick of its huge tail, made off into deeper water. Buzz looked all around him, hoping that someone had seen what he had just witnessed, but he was all alone and had no idea what to do. In a desperate but very late bid to ensnare the carp, he flicked his float at the spot it had just vacated but, other than a heart-stopping knock from a passing perch, the red tip remained motionless and he soon wound it in and strolled off in search of someone to tell his story to. His was the only sighting any of them had been privy to, but that alone was enough and they left an hour or so later much happier and ready for a serious campaign on this untapped paradise.

The phone lines hummed, as usual, and Buzz arrived at the lake on Thursday, as usual. He then spent a good deal of time looking around the lake before choosing to fish on The Point for the night and it was here that he received two strange but very different visitors. He had been settled for less than an hour when he saw a figure appear from the cover of the East Woods and move slowly along the bank towards the Pad Bay. A few minutes later a stout, casually dressed man ambled into his swim and began talking as if they had known each other for years.

"Hello! Good to see yer. Any of 'em boitin'?" came the strange greeting. Buzz fumbled for a reply before stuttering, "Er, yes. I mean, errm, no!"

This seemed to be quite acceptable to the visitor, and he carried on in similar vein, "So, 'ave yer sin 'em yet, young fella? Sin them girt big ol' boys. Hah!"

The last was almost coughed out and startled Buzz, who jumped back a little. This was a weird one!

"Well, last week I saw a good fish, probably low thirties, I would think."

This was a conservative estimate, but he didn't want to sound too foolish in front of this man, even though he seemed to have the monopoly on anything less than sane around here!

"Hah! No, young'un, them's the small'uns. I mean the girt'uns, big as a suckling sow, 'n' no mistake!"

'Oh, please take him away somebody. Please!' thought the trapped angler, but it seemed that his visitor had no inclination to leave in the foreseeable future, and continued his strange diatribe.

"Worms!" he growled. "That's what yer needs to catch 'em. Girt bigg'uns, loik snakes. Ol' Ted hooked 'un way back on a girt worm. Did for 'im, it did. Took all his loin, 'ook 'n' all. Busted 'im good 'n' proper. Big as a pig, 'e said, bloody girt pig!"

With that, he turned on his heel and exited the swim, as strangely as he had entered, and called over his shoulder, "More'n one, mind. Two girt'uns if I ain't mistaken, both as big as girt pigs. Put a saddle on 'em 'n' roid 'im, yer could. You be lucky, young'un," and with that he strode off into the woods behind the Reedy Bay.

Buzz stood there stunned, before barking out a laugh and shouting, "Worms!" The rest of the evening was spent mulling over the strange but possibly informative meeting until, as the sun disappeared to his left and turned the sky a rosy pink, he retired to bed to dream of girt carp as big as pigs!

A three-quarter full moon lit his rods and the surrounding ground with a milky light and Buzz sleepily pondered whether another nocturnal leaper had woken him. Looking out into the strange light he could see no ripples so assumed that he had just nodded awake when, from behind, he heard soft footsteps. He wondered if the weird fellow had returned with old Ted and the boys to re-enact that 'squeal like a pig' scene from the film Deliverance!

He was a very big, strong man but he wasn't stupid, so reached behind his bedchair and wrapped his fingers around a bankstick lying there. The noise came again, but sounded too soft for a footfall, then he sat stock still as a fox crept stealthily into the moonlight dappling the ground on the far side of the swim. Buzz held his breath and watched, motionless, as the animal sniffed the ground and moved slowly towards the recumbent angler. 'Camera! Camera!' thought Buzz, but knew that any movement would scare his wild visitor away, so gazed intently, hoping to burn the sight onto his retina. The fox moved slowly across the ground, edging ever closer to Buzz, until the mesmerised angler could have reached out and touched the beast. At that point, the fox seemed to realise Buzz's presence and, for the second time in as many weeks, the natural world stood still for the merest of moments. Then, completely at ease with the situation and showing no fear, the fox sniffed the air disdainfully before turning and ambling casually across the moonlit swim to disappear into the foliage opposite.

Buzz's heart was beating like a steam hammer, and he lay there for many minutes gazing at his rods in the eerie light, hoping that this visitor might return, but it was not to be and it was the golden light of the sun that he next gazed at, hours later.

"Got that kettle on, boy?" asked Chris, as he strode through the dew soaked grass.

Buzz had seen him arrive ten minutes earlier so did, indeed, have the kettle on.

The sun had been up less than an hour, as had Buzz, and as they sat gazing across the lake, he related his strange encounters of the previous day to Chris. After much chuckling and innuendo, Chris took a walk around the Reedy Bay and onto the far bank, where he thought he had seen some movement. Tench proved to be the culprits, so he continued his early morning stroll around the lake, arriving back with Buzz an hour later and demanding more tea. His search had been fruitless but, with so few carp in such an expanse of water, he wasn't about to guess their whereabouts and so, after downing another mug of the amber nectar, he began another circuit of the lake.

Fortunately, he had only travelled a few hundred yards, anti-clockwise this time, when he spotted some movement in the same reedbed where Buzz had spied the carp a week previously. Creeping further along to the first copse of trees that marked the start of the woods, he quickly scaled a convenient willow and was able to view the marginal shelf from above. As his eyes adjusted, he saw two fish cruising slowly along the margins, away from him, but he got a good enough view to be able to estimate their size.

"One was probably mid-twenties," he told Buzz whilst gulping in huge lungfuls of air. "The other was probably about three or four pounds bigger."

Once the fish had drifted from view, he had quickly descended and hightailed it round to The Point to inform Buzz.

"Where were they headed?" asked the char lady, whilst removing the teabags from another brew. Gaining his breath, Chris slowed down a little, and replied, "Out towards the pads, I suppose. But they seemed to have been interested by something in that margin. I'm gonna go and grab a rod and some corn and see what I can see."

With that, he drained the cup and hurried back to his car for the necessary items of tackle but, despite stealth and patience, by mid-afternoon he remained fishless and had seen no further sign of the early morning browsers. Sid and Stan would soon be arriving, so he had to decide on a swim for the night and he went through the usual mental evaluations. Buzz, although still on The Point, had moved around to the left and was fishing into the Reedy Bay, from where he had heard a large fish crash earlier in the day. That left, as the main possibilities, the swim he was in, The Pads and the right side of The Point - oh, decisions, decisions! He strolled onto the end of The Point and surveyed the area to the right, The Pads Bay, and as he stood there, a flash of sunlight on metal caught his eye. Peering down the length of the lake, he saw another flash of light as a closing car door once again caught the sunlight. It was either Sid or Stan and he knew he had about five minutes to make up his mind, which now resembled a spin dryer!

'Here or The Pads? Here or The Pads? Oh, shit, somebody help me!' His tortured mind screamed at him until, out of desperation, he shouted aloud.

Buzz ran around the trees and asked, bewildered, "What? What's up, have you seen one?"

"No, nothing as simple as that. I just don't know where to go. It's either here or The Pads. Help me! Please help me!"

His pleading made Buzz smile, so he bent down and picked up a stone, then put both of his hands behind his back, before bringing the two clenched fists in front of him and saying, "Choose. The stone means you fish here, no stone and you fish The Pads."

Chris looked intently at the huge paws, then at the smiling, bearded face before returning the grin and tapping one hand with his finger.

Buzz turned it upright to reveal the pebble and said, "Here it is, then. Better get the rest of your gear before you change your mind."

With that, Chris turned and made his way to the car, meeting Sid on the path through the woods and filling him in on the events of the day. With this knowledge, Sid decided to fish in The Pads swim, and Chris felt a cold finger run along his spine. Despite the friends that they all were, and the joy they felt for their mates if they caught a good carp, they all still preferred to be the object of that joy. Chris returned to his swim a little later still unsure as to whether he had made the right choice.

Stan arrived an hour or so later than Sid and, having moved back to Wimbledon to work, had a two hour journey to look forward to every Friday to reach the lake. At least there wouldn't be the rush for swims that there was on all the other lakes he had fished, but arriving fourth could pose its own problems. For the night, Stan set up on the end of The Point, fishing out into the main part of the lake as Buzz had done on the previous night and, with an hour of daylight remaining, they were all ready and had their traps set. Buzz regaled them with the events of the previous day, embellishing them sufficiently to bring gales of laughter from the others. Coupled with the story that Dean had told them, however, the tale of the 'girt pigs' interested as well as amused them, and they all went to bed to dream bizarre dreams.

The sun glinted off the mist-shrouded pads, and Stan and Chris drank there first cuppa of the day whilst peering at the green leaves through shaded lenses. For the previous ten minutes, they had watched ripples issuing from them, small patches of bubbles peppering the still surface, and waited expectantly for one of Chris's buzzers to burst into life. Then, as they gazed at the gap between the two sets of pads that Sid was fishing, forty yards away, a long, bronze body silently turned over and left them slack jawed, its passing marked by a froth of bubbles. They looked at each other without a word, then Stan turned to put the kettle onto the cooker once more.

A buzzer screamed and he turned back rapidly, expecting to see his friend leaping into action, but saw only Chris's rigid back as he craned his neck in order to see over the reeds to where Sid was creating chaos. As the pony-tailed sleeper was rudely awoken, another line of bubbles fizzed to the surface and indicated the path of something leaving the area in a hurry. Sid's strike did little to slow its departure, and the two watchers heard the clutch scream and saw the line cut though the surface film like a laser beam through glass. Buzz had also heard the take, and followed the rapidly disappearing backs of his friends into Sid's swim, where chaos had been replaced by controlled panic. The fish had stopped taking line, but the problem now was how to manoeuvre it back down the ten yard wide channel between the two sets of pads.

Buzz, as usual, was ready to go wading, but the lake bed was quite silty here and they doubted whether he would gain much ground. However, the merest foot might make all the difference so, whilst Sid did his best to let the fish tire itself out on a long line, Buzz slipped into the lake and squealed as the water passed the usual comfort zone! He managed to creep a couple of yards into the lake before the water reached his chest and the silt below threatened to suck him deeper.

"That's as far as I can go, Sid. You'll have to do the best you can to stop it from getting in the pads," he called.

The fish was now on the edge of the pads, fifteen yards from Buzz, and Sid was beginning to panic. They had yet to see it, but the vortices its tail was sending up indicated that it was not a small fish, and the stories from the previous night were still fresh in the combatant's mind.

"Try to confuse it, y'know, left hand side strain, right hand side strain," suggested Stan. "It can sometimes work."

"Have you tried it then, Quill?" asked Sid, running the idea over in his head.

"Well, err, no. But I read it in a book somewhere and apparently it does work!"

"Oh great. Bloke down the pub told you about it, did he!" groaned Sid, disheartened.

"What other idea have you got then!" returned Stan, a little disgruntled. Sid shrugged and, with the carp nearing the first of the pads, flicked his rod sharply to the left and employed its full test curve. As the fish moved with the strain, he repeated the manoeuvre to the right. Then to the left, and, amazingly, the carp just zig-zagged down the channel and into the waiting arms of the outstretched net, the whole procedure taking no more than thirty seconds. Stan smiled smugly as the others stared silently at the net, then they all went mad.

The rising sun lit the carp like a bar of gold and the four anglers gazed down reverently on Sid's capture. It was a long, torpedo-like mirror carp with two or three small scales on its left hand flank, the opposite flank being almost devoid of scales except beneath its dorsal. The chestnut brown colouration contrasted sharply with the green unhooking mat and surrounding grass, and they shook their heads in awe.

"I wonder if it's a Leney?" pondered Stan.

"Certainly looks like one. Bloody hell, Sid, that's not a bad way to open your account!" commented Buzz, and the captor just carried on smiling.

At twenty eight pounds, it was not the monster that they had anticipated, but size mattered little with a carp of that quality and they all stared enviously as Sid let it slip from his hands back into the lake.

They spent the rest of the session vigilantly scanning all parts of the lake for further signs of fish, their enthusiasm quadrupled by Sid's success but, by the end of the weekend they had seen no more carp, just a few margin feeding tench, one of which Chris caught on a float-fished worm on Sunday morning. At seven pounds, it was a worthy catch and they pondered the size of some of the other green demons they had seen.

The weather then changed dramatically and on their return, a week later, a strong southerly was coursing the length of the lake, the waves crashing into the North Bank like a North Atlantic swell. The chance of seeing any carp in the margins was slim, but Buzz and Chris braved the wind and squally rain showers to circumnavigate the lake a couple of times on Thursday before convincing themselves of the futility of that course of action.

"It's not exactly overfished, is it? I reckon we should go by the book and fish with the wind in our faces."

Buzz's suggestion was met with pensive silence from Chris and the constant drumming of rain on the roof of his van. They sat staring through the steadily misting window at the wind bent trees in front of them and mused over their next move. The North Bank would, indeed, be the best option but to set up in the horrendous conditions outside would be very trying so they sat for a while until the storm abated.

As is usual with summer storms, once the rain stopped and clouds galloped across the sky, the sun once again beamed down and, within an hour, they were both gazing at the waves crashing towards them. An area that offered some good possibilities, and also some shelter from the brunt of the wind, was the top of the West Bank looking out onto the Banana Island. The snags to the left were also very inviting so they decided to set up along there, Chris fishing a small gap close to the snags and Buzz a further fifty yards down the bank in a swim that faced the southern-most tip of the island.

By late afternoon, the wind had dropped considerably, but the sky still threatened rain, the sun intermittently appearing between huge, billowing clouds. Chris battled through the brambles to get to the edge of the snag, and there he found a small tree to climb which offered a better view of the lake bed. Five yards to the right of the prehistoric limbs of the dead oak he could just make out the glow of a small, clear area of lake bed. Possibly sand, possibly gravel, but definitely clean and well worth a bait for the night but, just as he was about to descend and retrieve some bait from his swim, out of the corner of his eye he saw the patch go dark.

Turning back, he peered carefully into the water and saw the shape of a large tail flick off the clear patch towards the snags. Descending quickly, he thrashed as quietly as possible through the undergrowth to the overhanging limb that he had climbed a few weeks earlier. Edging carefully along the still damp branch, he wrapped his arms around its girth and looked intently into the rippling water below. He thought he could discern movement, but it was too dark to be sure, and he then thought about how he was going to shin backwards along his precarious perch, when the sun appeared from behind a cloud and lit the scene below him. Beneath him were four carp; a common of about twenty pounds, a mirror that was considerably larger, probably by ten pounds, and two other carp that he could not quite make out, as they were a foot or so below the others. The common flicked its tail, moving away a little, and the sunbeam sought out the deeper pair of carp - and they weren't.

In the time that it took for him to realise what he was seeing, Chris replayed in his head the part of Chris Yates's 'Casting at the Sun' where he described seeing three fish at Redmire become one huge common carp. There, below him, was almost the identical thing, only this was two fish turning into one. 'Big as a girt pig'! Buzz's words came back to him, and below him was just that - a common carp as big as a pig, if not bigger! He clutched tightly to the branch, for fear that his thumping heart would shake him from his perch, and tried, as Buzz had done with the fox, to burn this sight into his mind forever. The carp hung motionless except for the occasional balancing flick of a pectoral, and the sunlight glinted off scales as big as saucers. The mirror slid slowly alongside the great fish, giving Chris a clear idea of how much larger the common was and he doubted that anyone would believe his conclusions.

He had to get Buzz. Somehow he found himself on dry land and scurried through the trees and brambles to Buzz's swim, breathless once again.

"Now! Come! Come now, quick!" was the extent of his vocabulary, but Buzz could tell from the look on Chris's face that he should follow immediately. Slowing as they neared the snag tree, Chris turned and held his finger to his lips before explaining, in a gasping whisper, what he had seen. He then ushered the big man through the last few brambles to the edge of the tree where he waved him onto the branch. The sun had, once again, disappeared from view so Buzz had to peer intently into the mirk below, more concerned that he might descend, fully clothed, into the lake unless he was careful.

"What can you see?" whispered Chris, as loudly as he dare. Buzz concentrated harder, then saw a small common drift into view from the left, followed closely by a larger mirror carp. Risking releasing his grip for a second, he raised his hand behind his back and held up two fingers.

"Oh, cheers!" said Chris, then realised what it meant. "Oh. Two. Right."

Buzz hung above the water for a few more minutes in the hope that either the sun or the monster that Chris had seen would return but eventually, convinced that neither would happen, he began to carefully inch himself backwards. He had moved no more than a foot when a movement to his right caught his eye and he halted his retreat. A dark fish slid slowly into view, obscuring the other two fish, and Buzz's heart beat stopped. The carp swam ever so slowly beneath the goggle-eyed angler and, just as it was about to disappear from view, flashed onto its side to reveal an enormous flank with one large scale in the middle of it - then it was gone. Buzz could barely breathe and, like Chris before him, clutched tightly to the branch. He stared down into the depths, willing the fish to return but, after a couple more minutes, realised that the light had worsened and that he could barely see the sub-surface branches.

His wild, staring eyes told Chris all he needed to know and they crept back through the tangle of thorns to Chris's swim where they just sat down and looked at each other in disbelief. Chris put the kettle on before asking, needlessly, "Did you see it?"

Buzz continued staring straight ahead, before replying, "Oh yeah, I saw it alright. But it's a mirror, not a common."

This baffled Chris completely and he looked quizzically at his friend.

"Mirror? No, it was definitely a common, boy. Definitely," he said, adamantly. "You sure you didn't see that small mirror under there?"

Buzz snorted derisively and shook his head.

"Oh no. This was no small mirror, Rhodie. This was mahoosive, boy! It flashed on its side before it disappeared, one big scale on its flank. Oh, no, that was definitely a mirror. You sure you saw a common?"

The interrogation continued for two cups of tea before it slowly dawned on them that they may well have seen two huge fish - the two that Dean had spoken of.

Then Buzz really put the cat amongst the pigeons when he said, "Neither of them was the fish I saw the other week!"

Chris took this news quietly, then said, "If that's the case, Buzz, I think we need a bigger boat!"

Buzz smiled and nodded his head before rising and returning to his swim to put on some stronger line!

Chris could barely sleep that night, almost scared that the fish that was emblazoned in his memory should visit during the night, and it was late when he blearily took in the grey light of a new day. Despite returning on numerous occasions to the snag tree, none of them saw the mythical monsters that Buzz and Chris had seen, and Stan and Sid began casting doubts on their friends' sanity! The small common returned on a couple of occasions, as did another larger mirror but, of the monsters, there was no sign and they left on Sunday with nothing to show from a wet and windy weekend's angling.

Chris phoned Stan three or four times a day during the following week, unable to stop thinking about the sight he had beheld beneath the snag tree, and Stan knew his friend well enough to realise that he was very serious about it.

Once again, they arrived to totally different conditions, and barely a ripple disturbed the lake's surface as Stan arrived to join his two friends. Sid was working, once again, and was unsure whether he would be able to get down at all so Stan was quite surprised to see three cars in the car park on his arrival. Having seen the conditions, he knew the others would be on or near The Point, so loaded up his gear and began the strenuous journey to the far end of the lake. Halfway through the woods he spied a brolly in a swim they called the Creaking Tree, for obvious reasons, so took the opportunity to drop his tackle and wandered along for a chat with the occupant.

The guy was about Stan's age and build, but about six inches taller, his grey hair poking out from beneath a beige beanie hat. Stan squatted down next to his chair and chatted for about ten minutes. It seemed that the guy, Clive, had fished the lake on and off for about five years, but was only interested in the bream and tench. He had taken, apparently, bream to fourteen pounds and tench to ten and was convinced there was much bigger of both species in the lake.

When the subject moved to carp, he said, "Oh, you'll be after the two biggies, then."

Stan nodded, and began probing gently.

"You seen 'em, then, mate?" he asked casually, whilst watching two damsel flies hovering above Clive's rods.

"I've seen one big fish, but I couldn't say how big," he began.

Stan nodded, and let the question remain hanging. The ploy worked.

"Yeah. It was last year. I was fishing this swim, as usual, and had just woken up. It was early in the season so it was quite light, probably about five, half five. I was looking at my spot out there, about fifty yards out on the edge of the stream bed, when this carp just launched itself out of the water. About twenty yards behind my baits it was, bloody great thing. Like I say, I couldn't put a weight on it but I've fished lakes with forties in so I know what a big carp looks like, and that was one. I was just praying I didn't get a take from it. I've only got six pound line on so I don't think I would have stood much of a chance."

Stan chatted a little longer before bidding him good luck and continuing his journey. Clive had said, in the last couple of minutes, that he knew of a couple of people who had carp fished the lake over the years, but they didn't seem to stay long. The general consensus being that there was no more than twelve to fifteen carp in the lake and that they were practically uncatchable - the largest he had heard of being a thirty one a couple of years ago.

On reaching The Point, where Buzz and Chris were fishing, Stan imparted this new information to them whilst settling down with a welcome beer.

They told him that they had seen three good fish jump that morning, all out in the middle of the lake at long distance, well over a hundred yards, and so both had a bait as far as they could cast. Stan pondered his options, as usual, before electing to fish round in the Reedy Bay. The reeds were dying back a little, now, and a swim had made itself fishable halfway back down the side of The Point.

The bay was relatively shallow, with average depths of three foot over most of its five or six acres, but Stan hoped that the fish would like the warmer water and would venture into the bay to sunbathe. He waded out as far as he could and flicked a lead along the front of the reeds to his left, feeling it sink into the silt, another six or seven casts producing the same result. Then, through frustration, he cast the lead thirty yards further back into the bay and was amazed as the lead thudded down, sending a shudder along the rod. Extracting his plumbing rod from the bag, he cast the float to the same area and felt it land with the same resonance, dragging it back a few yards before he felt it pull into some weed. That would do nicely. He cast a birdfood boilie just behind the marker, then scampered down the bank to throw hemp and boilies over the reeds to pepper the spot. Happy with that rod, he flicked around in front of him to see if he could find a similar spot in the mouth of the bay. This was not so easy and he eventually elected to put out a slow sinking boilie that would eventually settle on top of the silkweed. Once he was content that his baits were positioned as well as they could be, he strolled along to the end of The Point for some much needed sustenance. Chris had brought the ingredients for a huge stir fry, and they ate until they could eat no more, before eventually retiring as the owls began to call.

Stan had had to put his rod rests out into the lake as far as he could so that his line did not snag on the reeds and that was the reason that he found himself up to his knees in water and sleeping bag at three in the morning! His alarm had screamed and he had leapt, instinctively, into the lake to strike but had failed to relieve himself of the sleeping bag, which was gradually filling with water. Of more concern was the grating he could feel on the other end as something was making an escape bid. It felt as if whatever it was had gone through the reeds and Stan had no idea what to do. Unfortunately, the fish was giving him little time to think and the rod was bucking violently in his hands, the clutch whining as it grudgingly gave up line.

Stan unwrapped himself from his sopping bag and managed to throw it onto dry ground, before edging himself further out towards the edge of the reeds. By the time he reached that point, the water was up to his chest and he dared go no further, so began the slow process of line retrieval. A resounding splash echoed from the depths of the reeds, sixty yards away, and the rod tip pulled round alarmingly. With slow, steady pressure, Stan began gaining line and felt that the fish must have tired itself out with the initial exertions, but the grating sensation was still very evident and the fish was obviously still in the reeds. Unsure of what to do, he was just about to shout for some help when another great crash shattered the night's silence. Stan felt the rod pull back, then stop. There was no further sensation. Not of fish nor grating reeds, and he stood chest deep in the water with the rod held high, not entirely sure what was happening. The waves from the splashing fish lapped against his steadily chilling body and he knew that something had to happen soon so, winding down, he heaved as hard as he dared but gained nothing. This he repeated a couple of times when, suddenly, the rod sprang back and he thought that he had lost everything. As he wound in, dejectedly, he could feel something on the end and it felt like it was kiting back and forth.

'Surely not a bream,' he thought, 'not with all that splashing.' Then it all became clear as he wound the hooklink in and found the hook impaled in a six foot long reed stem. The fish had obviously thrown the hook with that last crash and it had pulled straight into a reed. Stan slumped to the ground in absolute devastation, soaking wet, freezing cold and having lost a carp of who knew what size?

He had no dry clothing with him, it being in his car a quarter of a mile away, and his sleeping bag was a sponge, so he walked, shivering, to The Point and woke Chris to tell him of his plight. Buzz woke as well and, between them, they managed to find Stan some dry clothes, Buzz giving the slowly warming angler the keys to his car where he could find a blanket to see him through the night. After a cup of tea, Stan made the slow trek through the dark to the car park, returning twenty minutes later and falling straight away into a deep sleep.

The day was still young when Buzz heard a buzzer, and he ran down to find Stan up to his knees in the lake whilst playing a fish on his right hand rod. This felt nothing like the fish of a few hours earlier and, when he saw the flash of dark green, he knew it was a tench and hauled it unceremoniously into the waiting net.

"Bloody hell, Quill, that's a bit of a whacker," commented Buzz.

"Yeah, whatever," came Stan's disconsolate reply as he searched, once more, for a towel.

"I'll weigh this for you, boy," continued Buzz; and before Stan could protest, the sling was being zeroed and the tench hoisted up on the scales.

"Bloody hell, that is a whacker, Quill. Ten pounds six ounces. boy!" exclaimed Buzz.

"What, a carp?" asked Chris on entering the swim.

"No, a bloody tench. Just stick it back, Buzz. I'm gonna have to go back to the car for some more clothes," and with that he slouched off through the bushes. Buzz did as he was told but, later that day, when he recovered his usual equilibrium, Stan wished he had taken a photograph of the fish. Maybe there would be another one.

There was no further action that weekend, and Stan spent many hours the following week daydreaming about what could have happened and what he could have landed. But the outcome was still the same, the fish was gone and he would never know.

With the weather remaining much the same for the foreseeable future, Stan fancied getting into the Reeds Swim again and made this well known to his mates on more than one occasion. Leaving work at four on Friday afternoon he looked forward to strolling down the bank in a couple of hours, trying his best to blank out the journey to the lake, but two hours later he was less than silently fuming in his stationary vehicle, just outside Basingstoke.

The cause of the miles of tailback became obvious an hour or so later when he crawled past three cars that were trying to occupy the same space in the fast lane! So it was that he drove down the dirt track to the lake with less than an hour's daylight left and, parking his car next to Chris's, angrily bundled out of it and dragged the minimum of tackle from the back. Loading himself up for the ball-breaking trek to the far end of the lake, he was just about to cross the stile when he heard another vehicle arriving. Looking round, he saw a tractor with some strange piece of farm machinery in tow heading slowly towards him, so decided to wait in order to utilise the open gate. On jumping from the cab, the young farm hand strolled to the gate and pulled it open, before turning to Stan, smiling, "A'roight, mate. Fishin' then?"

Although begging for a tongue full of sarcasm, Stan just nodded and forced a smile to his lips.

"You c'n droive roight roun', if yer want, ol' mate," the brawny lad said as he pulled himself up into the cab, "Jus' mek sure you closes the gate." With that, he touched his cap and trundled off in a cloud of dust.

Stan could do nothing but stare at the retreating dust cloud for a few seconds. Then, with a "Yes!" he slipped the rucksack from his shoulders and loaded it back into the car, before springing into the driver's seat and manoeuvring the vehicle through the gateway, leaping out to close the gate as requested. The track to the left initially went away from the lake but, then, curved back to the right and took him along the eastern edge of the woods, bringing him out just by the outlet stream a few minutes later. His black mood had, by now, completely disappeared and he smiled grandly as he strolled jauntily into the Pads Swim and was confronted by an openmouthed

Chris.

"Wha... ! I mean, how did you ... ? The car. How did, y'know, how ...?"

No more sense came from his friend's lips so Stan nonchalantly replied, "Oh, you mean that. I just had a word with the farmer and he said, 'Woi, you'm that there Stan Peacock, irin't yer? Course you kin use that ol' track, fella. Be moy guest!' so I just drove it round. Didn't you try that then?"

The glint in his eyes gave him away, and he could hide his smile no longer. "Nah, I just saw this geezer on a tractor going through the gate and he said we can use the track as long as we keep the gate closed after."

This news was very well received, as was the cold beer that Buzz gave him a few minutes later. He was fishing The Point, once more, having moved from the outlet swim that morning after seeing a fish jump at long distance again. Sid was on the far side of the Reedy Bay, in a swim they had dubbed the Dead Man Standing Swim, due to the skeletal appearance of a dead tree at its rear. This meant that Stan could move into the Reeds Swim he had fished the previous week and, having carefully plumbed it before leaving, had found a small, hard area ten yards closer than before. Donning the waders he had thought to bring, he reached the edge of the reeds and flicked the tiger nut bait twenty yards to his left, feeling the lead thud down satisfactorily. He repeated the same procedure with the other rod, but this was baited with a buoyant birdfood bait and was cast five yards to the right of the first bait. That done, he set his rods up as close to the bank as possible, pulling out the furthest reed stems in order for the line to enter the water close to the left hand edge of the reeds. He then laid out his bedchair near to the rods and slid his sleeping bag into the cover he had tied to the chair - he had prepared himself well and was praying for just one more chance. Thirty six hours later it came and, just as he was preparing to brew his last cup of tea of the session, his tiger nut rod burst into life and he was on it in a flash.

After the initial burst of power, the fish just stopped and Stan dragged it back to the waiting net. At first, on seeing the scales on its side, he thought it was a bream but when Chris took the net from him, he exclaimed, "It's a bloody carp, Quill!"

Buzz peered over his shoulder and chuckled in agreement and, once he had extricated himself from the cloying silt, Stan squelched over to confirm this news. It was very much a carp, but on a much smaller scale than Chris's monster common.

"Blimey, it's not even a double, is it?" asked Stan, before reaching into his rucksack and producing the sling and scales. His estimate was proved correct as the dial swung round between nine and ten pounds. It was a long, skinny wildie which he was about to return without a photo, but his friends' protests soon ensured that he was posing for the camera.

"Still a carp, Quill," commented Sid, "and better than those two have done," he added. With that, Stan smiled and Buzz re-named Sid, unflatteringly!

It was a carp, all the same, and although nowhere near the size he had regularly dreamed of, it was one of only a dozen or so in the lake, which was merit in itself. The week couldn't pass quickly enough for Stan, who was bursting with confidence. Two runs in two weeks meant that he was definitely doing something right and it would not be long, surely, before he contacted one of the mythical monsters of the lake. But he had much to learn about the lake and its carp and it was many weeks before he encountered his next action.

Not so the others, though, and the next fortnight saw their emotions peak, then plummet to the depths of despair.

Buzz and Chris did their usual circuit of the lake, starting and finishing in the snag tree. The days were shortening and the first leaves were beginning to change colour, so they reasoned that the carp could have moved into the slightly deeper water of the northern end of the lake. Although they had seen nothing amongst the tangle of branches, Chris still felt the urge to set up in the swim to the right of the snags and when the wind almost blew his brolly away in the night, he felt certain that he had made the right decision. Buzz was fishing along the North Bank, casting to the back of the Top Island, but the increase in wind strength had made that task much more difficult, and he was contemplating a move, when a leaping carp just to the right of the island convinced him to stay. By the time that Stan arrived, Sid had moved into the top of the Top Bay, a swim they called the South Westerly, as that wind blew straight into there, so Stan set up to Chris's right in the Top Banana swim. The evening was dry, but the light was quickly fading and he had little time to position his baits before nightfall, and was then joined by Chris for an hour of chat and a few beers. Sid and Buzz were loathe to wander too far from their rods, so spent the evening a few hundred yards away, their occasional laughter drifting across in the darkness.

An uneventful night gave way to a dull, grey dawn and Stan was, once again, joined by Chris who demanded tea. As they sat there, pondering the coming day, they heard a short burst from a buzzer which sounded like it had emanated from the far bank. The Banana Island obscured their view of Buzz's swim, so they picked up their cups and made their way carefully through the gradually dying undergrowth to Chris's swim, which would offer a better vantage point. As he entered his swim, Chris sensed something was not right, but could not put his finger on it.

Then Stan said, "Why's your rod on the ground, Rhodie?"

Chris looked at his left hand rod and realised, in a flash, what had happened. It was his buzzer they had heard, before the rod had been wrenched off the rest, and his stomach turned over as if he were on a roller coaster when the possibilities dawned on him. Picking up the rod, he gingerly pulled the tip round to the right until it reached its full test curve, the taut line beginning to sing. He looked at Stan, and his pained expression was like a blow to his friend.

"What's happened, boy?" he asked, needlessly. Chris tentatively eased the rod top back a little more, then it was pulled forward with a jolt and he realised that he was still in contact.

"I dunno, but whatever it is, it's still attached."

The rod tip pulled down once more and, just in time, Chris loosened the clutch, hearing it spin as the fish sought its freedom. The line was grating on one of the branches beneath the tree, which was acting as a fulcrum, as the fish moved off steadily away from the tree. After a few minutes, Chris managed to gain a little line but he could still feel the fish protesting strongly at the pressure and knew he would need a huge amount of luck if he was to land this one. Stan had crept into the branches of the snag and was peering intently into the mirky water below, hoping to catch a glimpse of the fish or the grasping branch, but the water was dark and he could discern very little. Then Chris gasped as the line went slack, fearing the worst, and was just about to scream in anguish when the rod tip pulled round to the right and the clutch screamed once more.

"The branch just broke!" exclaimed Stan as he bundled into the swim. "I saw it snap underwater. Just like that. You still in contact?"

"Oh, yes. Oh, I'm still in contact, Quill!" replied Chris as he desperately hung on to his tortured rod. The clutch was screaming and a mist of water droplets rose from the spinning spool.

"It's trying to get to the bloody island now," he grunted whilst tentatively tightening the clutch a notch or two. Then, as the fish slowed a little, he put his middle finger on the spool and lifted the rod high, reeling quickly as he smoothly lowered the rod tip and gained a few precious yards. This seemed to stop the carp's charge to the island and a wave of confidence suddenly washed over Chris. The carp was becoming very ponderous in its movements and, as Stan picked up the net for the first time, Chris could feel the fish rising in the water and prepared himself for the first sight of his foe.

"Jesus!" Stan breathed, scared to talk louder in case he broke the spell.

There, on the surface in front of them, a huge flank rolled over, revealing one large scale and, in a split second, Chris knew that Buzz had not lied. But there is more than one split second, and the next brought with it the wailing of a million tortured souls as the pair of anglers watched, in total disbelief, the lead float slowly through the air and into the bushes behind them. The great carp was merely a boil on the surface, then that too was gone, and they stared hopelessly into the deep, blue water.

"I don't believe it!" Chris said, quietly. Then he screamed it at the top of his voice, punctuated by many expletives.

Stan was at a total loss for words, not only because of his friend's loss, but also at the sight that was still very clear in his mind of the massive flank he had just seen. He stared into the water for a few more seconds before daring to look round at his friend, then turned away again as he saw the emotion welling up in Chris's eyes. A few minutes later, Buzz and Sid ran into the swim, before being ushered away by Stan, who then told them the whole, torrid tale.

Chris joined them twenty minutes later, slumping into a chair before accepting a cup of tea, but it was many days before he could accept the loss as readily. How do you explain the feeling to someone who has never felt the stomach-churning sensation of that sudden absence of weight on the end of the line? The same way that you could never explain the mind-bending elation of landing a fish as big as a sack of potatoes to the very same person.

But why bother? You know what it feels like, and that is all that matters.

The carp felt a sudden release of tension and, suddenly aware that it was free from its tether to the island on the far side, tore across the lake to the island on the far side, slowing to a halt as it reached a tangle of branches beneath a large willow. The irritation in its lip caused the carp to bury its face in the silt beneath its sanctuary. The dull ache faded after a few days, as did the memory of the trauma, and the fish was soon feeding confidently again with its large companions.

A few days later Buzz was driving down the track to their new car park, watching the rabbits scatter at the unaccustomed early morning intrusion. The days were steadily cooling as summer made preparations to leave for warmer climes, and a light mist covered the grass and crept from the woods to his right.

Parking the car, he got out and took in a great lungful of air. 'I love this time of day,' he thought, then coughed and wheezed like an old tramp as the cold air reached his lungs. A coot cackled at the sound and another rabbit skittered through the undergrowth and off into a nearby hedgerow. He slowly strolled past the gradually withering pads, keeping his eye on them for any telltale movements, then turned the corner and strode along to The Point.

The world was coming to life noisily about him, and he donned his shades to cut out the sun's reflected glare. Ripples expanded here and there to mark the waking of roach and perch, then an energetic tench splashed loudly in the left hand margins. This was the time to see carp, and he swung his head slowly back and forth like a bearded lighthouse beacon. After ten minutes, and his second cigarette, he was about to continue his early morning constitutional when a thunderous splash echoed across the lake. Turning quickly, he saw the aftermath of droplets and bubbles not twenty yards from his car, in front of the reeds where he and Chris had recently spied carp. He stared intently for a few seconds in the hope that the fish would repeat its own constitutional, but could wait no longer and hurried back to the car as fast as he could.

Minutes later, he was creeping slowly to the water's edge with two baited rods, each of which he lowered carefully on the far side of the reeds, before laying the rods down on the damp grass and loosening the bait-runners. Crouching on his haunches, he willed his heart to slow down, then carefully lit another cigarette to assist the process. Large bubbles marked the spot where the fish had leaped and Buzz concentrated on them in the hope that it might show itself again. Ten minutes passed, and he had to stand to rid himself of the cramp in his legs. A further ten minutes, and he realised that he was parched and was in dire need of a cup of tea, but he daren't leave the rods lest a fish should fall for his trap. A further five minutes passed before he eventually gave in to his thirst and returned to the car to grab the necessary tea making equipment, a couple of buzzers and a chair, then crept back to the rods in a half-crouch. Halfway back he thought he heard a faint buzzing sound, but put it down to the myriad of insects that inhabited the lake's margins. A few steps further, however, the noise was louder and very puzzling. The penny dropped in a graduated fashion. First he noticed the reeds bending over to the right, but there was no wind. Then he saw his rod butt, seemingly with a life of its own, gradually slide across the grass. And, finally but within a millisecond of the other two occurrences, he noticed small droplets of dew flying into the air above his rapidly spinning reel. The tea making paraphernalia clattered to the floor as the big man leapt the last few yards to his rod, picking it up gingerly and remarkably calmly applied pressure to the spool with his finger. The dew acted as a lubricant, but not for long, then as the spool dried its metal began to heat Buzz's finger.

This fish was not hanging around and it was almost a minute later before the dry mouthed angler was able to slow it in its headlong dash for the far bank. The next quarter of an hour was a blur to Buzz. He knew that this could very well be the fish of his dreams and he so wished that one of his mates could be there to help, but they were probably still asleep so he slipped the net into the water in preparation for the inevitable - he hoped. The carp rolled just below the surface, moving a vast amount of water in the process, and Buzz suddenly felt very small and very lonely. When it repeated the roll a few seconds later, Buzz was in the water with the net in front of him, his heart either having stopped or going so fast that there was no discernible gap between beats!

The third roll was the last, the net engulfing what was, undoubtedly, a truly mahoosive mirror carp, and Buzz screamed his elation with such force that farmers in a nearby field stopped their toils and stared in puzzlement at the skies. A colony of rooks in the nearby woods took to the air in fright, and coots, moorhens and mallards all complained heatedly about the noise! In case there was anyone unaware of the event in the surrounding countryside, Buzz repeated the cry seconds later before hauling himself and his prize out of the lake. Once on the bank, he bit the line and threw his rod into the reeds before laying the net carefully on the grass and parting the mesh. He could not believe his eyes.

The carp was indeed mahoosive and, for a moment, the totally opposite emotion to that which Chris had felt a few days earlier had a very similar affect on Buzz's eyes. Lowering the net into the margins, he quickly gathered mat, sling and scales and prepared himself for the truth.

The hook was firmly embedded in the lower lip but there was no other, hook nor hook mark, which indicated that this was not the fish that Chris had lost. Still disbelieving the carp's size, Buzz watched, mesmerised, as the needle swung slowly round - past forty, past forty five, forty seven, forty eight. There it hovered, tantalisingly, before remaining as steady as his muscular arms could hold it. Exactly forty eight pounds.

He lowered the fish carefully back onto the mat before throwing his head back and howling at the top of his voice, "Yes! You bloody beauty!"

('Bloody noisy neighbours, more like!' squawked an indignant mother coot).

He calmed himself sufficiently in order to sack the fish safely, before the next major problem presented itself. Who would take the photographs? It was seven thirty on a Wednesday morning and the nearest person that he knew was Sid, and he was thirty odd miles away. What to do?

He walked around in total confusion for a couple of minutes, then decided to drive to the nearby phone box. He needed to tell someone, that was for sure, and maybe he would bump into another angler on this or the smaller lake up the road. So, with a final check on the fish, he jumped into his car and drove back along the track a mite faster than he had a couple of hours earlier.

The phone box was a mile away and thankfully, unlike many of its kind in less rural areas, was in perfect working order and did not smell like a urinal! The first number he called was Sid's and he gave a relieved sigh when it was picked up on the third ring.

"Hello?" came a muffled female voice.

"Hi, is Sid there?" asked Buzz, almost bursting with the scream that was bubbling inside him.

"Sid? No, sorry, you must have the wrong number," and, with that, the phone went dead.

Buzz was sure he had dialled the right number but as he finished redialling, he realised his mistake.

"Hello?" came the slightly gruffer response. "Sorry, darling, I meant Rick. It's Buzz."

"Hold on," came the equally short reply, followed by a brief conversation and shuffling of the telephone.

"Buzz?" came Sid's querying tone.

"Yeahhh!" he screamed, and Sid nearly fell off the bed.

"Jesus, man! What's happened?" he managed.

"I've caught a bloody great mirror carp, boy. That's what's happened," came the reply. He then proceeded to tell the whole story before coming to the final part. "But I've got nobody to take the photographs."

There was barely a pause, then Sid said, "I'll be there in...forty minutes. Have the kettle on, boy."

"You are a god, Sid, even with that pony tail," and with that he hung up, before repeating the call twice more, to Stan and Chris, but leaving out the last bit.

Sid was good to his word, arriving in a cloud of dust three quarters of an hour later and shaking Buzz's hand vigorously, before demanding his cup of tea.

In the sunlight, the huge carp glowed and Buzz had trouble lifting it, needing a helping hand from the photographer on a couple of occasions, who was totally gob smacked by the size of the beast. Utilising two cameras, they swiftly took the photographs before Buzz slipped into the lake with the fish and gave it one final kiss, then watched it swim slowly away before raising his arms in triumph and howling at the moon, the sun and all the stars!

By the weekend the weather had changed and, far from the north, overcast ranks advanced. Chris had, once again, set up in the Snag Swim but, once again it proved to be a disastrous move as his hook was pulled from another carp's mouth in the early hours of Saturday morning. It had not been attached for more than a few minutes and he was unsure of its size, but the loss did little to cheer him after the previous week's events, despite the sight of Buzz's photos that Sid had brought with him.

Chris moved on Saturday morning, unwilling to risk another loss, and vowed never to fish the swim again. He moved into the South-Westerly in the Top Bay, just along from Stan who was fishing the first swim on the East Bank, and they both put a bait out to the island. It was Chris's that was picked up later on that windy Saturday afternoon but, within seconds of hooking the fish, he knew it would not compare to the two he had recently lost and rather dejectedly peered down on a nineteen pound common a few minutes later.

"Still a carp, Rhodie," said Stan, "and twice the size of mine. All you need to do now is catch one twice the size of Buzz's!"

Chris grunted, but his mood lightened a little and by the end of the session he was almost back to his normal, sarcastic self.

The sight of Buzz's carp had fired all of them, especially when they realised that there were still two other carp of that size swimming in the lake, but they elected not to send the shots to the papers for a while in case someone put two and two together. They had almost the whole of September in front of them. This was their favourite month, and they fancied their chances of a few more carp. The fickle finger of fate dictated otherwise.

A month later, with a carpet of green, gold, red and brown on the ground, all they had to show for their continued efforts was one night of bream madness for Sid.

He had fished Dead Man Standing, and had landed four massive double figure slabs, the largest tipping the scales at just under fourteen pounds, but the carp had, seemingly, done the off. The sun had been replaced by wind, rain and clouds and the carp moved from the margins to the vast open spaces in the middle of the lake and out of casting range of the anglers.

Not that they had a clue where their quarry were hiding due to the carp's reticence to show themselves and, by the time that the sun came out again in early October, its strength was considerably diminished, as were the hours between its rising and setting.

Stan sat in a swim that they had dubbed The Post Office, due to a strange slot that had been cut into one of the trees. 'Probably by a woodpecker with a set square' Sid had suggested, but whatever, it looked for all the world like a letter box, hence the name. To the left was the Top Island and Stan had managed to cast two baits under the multi-coloured boughs that drooped invitingly along its margins. The banks were awash with colour and Stan loved this time of year, desperately trying to capture Mother Nature's artistry on camera, but the lens never did her justice and he wished he had even a modicum of talent with a paintbrush. As the setting sun turned the island's trees into flaming balls of colour he heard a piping call and watched, enthralled, as the avian concord swept past in a flash of iridescent blue en route to the same island. To his right, twenty yards away, Buzz was admiring the Banana Island in a similar frame of mind, confident that his recently cast baits would entice an unsuspecting carp. For once, they were the only two on the lake, Chris taking a hastily arranged holiday to Turkey and Sid, once again, having to work. Buzz had decided to cut his sessions down as the winter approached and had arrived half a dozen hours before Stan. Over the previous few weeks the four of them had fished many different areas in a bid to track down the elusive dozen or so carp, and this area, covering both islands, seemed to offer a better chance than most.

The pair had just finished listening to the football on the radio, neither of them happy at the results of their respective teams, and had then set about preparing for the night. Stan's right hand bait had been cast one hundred and ten yards to the far end of the island, where they had discovered a small, gravel plateau a few weeks earlier. He was not about to reel it in and recast, as he had serious doubts as to whether he could repeat the feat! His left-hand bait was an easier recast, being just eighty five yards to a convenient bay between two overhanging trees so, happy with both, he began preparing the evening's meal for them.

Buzz had a tad further to cast his furthest rod, by ten yards or so, but a similar clean area made the effort worthwhile, and the memory of a carp leaping in that spot three weeks earlier was enough to convince him to put a bait there again. His other rod was flicked along the right hand margin towards the Snag Corner, but was at least fifty yards from that spot, Buzz not wishing to repeat Chris's mistakes.

They sat in Stan's swim as the final rays of the sun disappeared to their right and discussed their campaign so far.

"Seven fish we've hooked," said Stan around a mouthful of curried chicken, "and if there are as few fish in here as we think, they ain't bad statistics, boy."

Buzz nodded and washed his own mouthful down with a gulp of red wine.

"Also," continued Stan, "we've hooked at least two of the biggies, which means that they don't mind a bit of trough, so what's the chances of us hitting into the common?"

This was a regular topic of conversation, and the thought meandered for the next couple of hours, becoming more vociferous and brash as further wine was consumed.

Finally, Buzz hoisted himself unsteadily to his feet and declared, "Quill, my old mate, I will leave you with this thought. One of us, you and me, is gonna catch a carp of biblical proportions, of that there is no doubt. And, if it should be tonight, we will whoop and holler so loud, Rhodie will hear us in Turkey!" Stan rose and clanked his cup against Buzz's in salute to that, then slapped him on the shoulder and replied, "Amen to that, son, and boy will we get pissed!"

They both chortled heartily at that, then Buzz waved a hand in the air as he tottered off through the trees to his swim, leaving a grinning Stan to sit quietly for a few minutes before retiring to bed himself.

The sun tiptoed carefully across the eastern skyline, trying desperately not to wake the sleeping anglers, but in its haste it disturbed a colony of dozing rooks who exploded into the sky in a raucous symphony. Stan opened one baleful eye and groaned. He looked at his clock, it said eight twenty five and he thought, 'Oh God, I'm still alive!'

Slowly, he raised himself and sought out a carton of juice, which he gulped greedily. Then, massaging his temples, he looked around for the kettle and put it onto the stove. A few minutes later, the steam clouding his gaze indicated that the water was ready and he filled two cups, taking them along to Buzz. He was also semiconscious and almost cried at the sight of the cup of tea, the two of them sitting quietly whilst the hot liquid coursed through their bodies and stirred some semblance of life. A second cup, in Stan's swim ten minutes later, began slowly to bring them round and they muttered a few words here and there.

Stan's right-hand buzzer bleeped once and they both swung their gaze in that direction. A second bleep had Stan rising to his feet, his eyes fixed on the indicator. As it moved up a fraction, the buzzer sounded a third time and, checking to see that there was no bird life in the vicinity of his bait, he picked up the rod and struck fiercely. The rod bent over wickedly and, out by the island, a large tail thrashed the surface.

"Shit!" said Buzz, both at the strike and at the reaction it had caused.

Stan held the rod high and gave no line, trying to get the fish to kite away from the island, however the fish had other ideas and began moving to the left along the island's tree-lined margins. Winding furiously, the angler struggled to keep up, and he held the rod far out to his right, employing its full test curve in a bid to coax the fish away from the island. Steadily, the pressure began to tell and he began gaining line as the distance between them lessened. The battle was, effectively, over, Stan remaining as calm as he could as he cajoled the carp carefully towards the waiting net and, ten minutes after it began, the fight was finished and Buzz echoed Stan's shout as a long, bronze mirror carp slipped into the net. The perfect hangover cure!

They quickly set about weighing the stunning looking linear and Stan was elated at a weight of thirty one pounds. Against the autumnal backdrop, the picture was simply awesome and Buzz gasped as he snapped away, doing Stan proud with the resulting photographs.

The news fired Sid and, a few days later, Chris, and they hoped for one final feeding spell before winter set in but, once again, the lake proved to them that they still had a lot to learn. The first frosts, a month later, found them with only one solitary tench to show for their efforts.

A couple of pre-Christmas sessions did little to fire their enthusiasm for a concerted winter campaign so they said farewell to the lake and its monsters for that year, looking forward to returning a couple of months later with the onset of spring. The lake and its inhabitants licked their wounds and spent the next couple of months in recuperation and quiet reflection. There were still treasures to be given up. It was just a matter of whether there was an Indiana Jones to find them.

There had been more angling pressure on the water in the previous few months than there had been since the turn of the decade. Three of the group of four matriarchs had felt the sting of steel during the summer but, due to luck and mussel-encrusted branches, only one had succumbed fully, but the others had learnt a valuable lesson. The problem was that, as the months passed, the lesson was remembered less and less and the quantity of tasty new food items more and more readily available. The test would be whether the carp could avoid temptation in the future, or else need to rely on outside influences to avoid capture. The close season would make this more difficult.

Chapter Fifteen - A Bigger Boat

"Seen the Angling Times?" asked Stan as he strolled into the swim.

His three friends were sitting outside Buzz's bivvy, in the Post Office, drinking tea and they all turned as Stan entered the swim, waving the aforementioned paper.

Sid shook his head and asked, "What's in it, Quill?"

Stan opened the paper to the desired page and held it for all of them to see.

"Our old mate, Micky, with a bloody great mirror carp!" he declared, then handed the paper over for the others to peruse. Micky had caught the one fish that had eluded them at Kingfisher, the Big Linear, at a lake record forty five pounds, and they were all mightily pleased with the news. Even though they no longer fished there, they still tried to keep in touch with the news and one or another of them regularly phoned Dean to let him know of their results, or otherwise.

The winter had been cold and slow with barely any action to their rods on their 'easier' waters, and it had been with some relief that they all agreed to return to Felcham for the final four weeks of the season. The first week had produced nothing, and the cold north easterly wind had made the whole session very uncomfortable, but the slight change in wind direction from east to west had brought with it brighter weather and renewed enthusiasm. The next week saw the first hints of spring, with the lake's many waterfowl preening themselves for the coming mating Olympics, and busily preparing nests for the year's newcomers. Roach, tench and bream were also very active, as were the lake's small population of pike, for their mating rituals were soon to begin. But of the carp there was no sign, and the session proved fruitless in that respect. However, a few days prior to Stan's arrival as a newsboy, Sid had paid a visit to the lake after dropping a car off in Salisbury, and his stroll around the sun dappled banks proved very fortuitous.

Looking up the lake from The Point, Sid spotted someone in the Creaking Tree so carried on round in the hope of cadging a cup of tea. He strolled into the swim whistling, to announce himself to the angler, and recognised the battered hat of Clive, the bream angler.

"Hello mate. How's it going?" he asked as the angler turned round.

"Oh. Hello there. Didn't expect to see anyone today. You fishing?"

Glancing less than subtly at Clive's kettle, Sid coughed before answering. "No, just dropped a car off so I thought I'd come for a quick look. Had any luck, cough... cough?"

Clive looked thoughtful, then bent to fill the kettle before answering, "Well, no. But you might be interested in something I saw this morning."

Well pleased that the dry throat routine had worked, Sid relaxed and pondered Clive's statement before replying. "Really, and what might that be? Three naked women being hotly pursued by a panda car full of sheep!"

Clive looked totally perplexed by this line of questioning, so chose to ignore it completely, and carried on as if uninterrupted.

"Well, it was about half nine this morning. I'd seen a few bream and the odd tench showing off to my right, so I took a stroll along to The Lawn and, as I was standing there, looking out towards the island, a bloody great carp hurled itself out of the water."

Totally engrossed by now, Sid's next question was much less flippant, "Yeah? Where? Where did it jump?"

"Out by the corner of the island," came Clive's muffled reply, as he was bending to remove the steaming kettle from the cooker. "Probably five yards from it, I would think. Looked like a good fish, as well."

This information was logged, then Sid accepted the cup of tea and continued gently probing the angler, before handing him back the empty cup, thanking him, and turning to walk through the woods in the direction of The Lawn.

The Lawn was at the north end of the small woods and looked out on the same point of the Top Island as the Post Office did from the opposite bank. The westerly wind was blowing across the lake towards him, so Sid had to button his coat to keep out the chill whilst he looked out at the island, a hundred yards away, and contemplated the possibilities. They had fished this swim on a couple of occasions, so he knew a little about it. Though very inviting, the island margin on The Lawn side was quite steep and dropped to six feet quite sharply, unlike the other side which had the small gravel plateau that Stan had caught the thirty one from. Nonetheless, the wind told of low temperatures, and it might just be that the fish were sheltering behind the island in the deeper water there. Sid elected to keep his findings to himself for the moment - at least until he had the opportunity to set up in the swim on Friday. He had walked twenty yards, and his view of the lake was marred by the skeletal trees still in their winter garb, when he heard a splash. Running back quickly to The Lawn, he could just make out the flat spot where a fish had jumped, towards the middle of the island and no more than five yards from it. That made his mind up, the island it was! All he needed to do now was to convince his boss to let him leave a little earlier.

So it was that, when Stan arrived, Sid was in the swim they called Island Two, to the right of The Lawn and facing the middle of the island. Chris was to his right, in Island One and Buzz in the Post Office, so Stan had two logical choices - The Lawn or the South Westerly. After some chat and some tea, he took a quick walk round to look at the swims before night fell, he also having begged a few hours off work in order to get to the lake before nightfall. Of the two, the South Westerly looked the better bet and so, with the help of the others, he was firmly ensconced in there just before dark. The weather was warming considerably, and this seemed to spur all manner of fish into a frenzy of leaping and jumping, including three carp, which Buzz and Chris had seen earlier that day in front of their respective swims. Sid had relented a little and had told them over the phone of his sightings, but had warned them all that he wished to fish The Lawn or Island Two to which everybody was quite happy. Early the next morning, however, no one was happier than Buzz.

He had put one bait onto the '31' spot and it was that which was picked up an hour or so before dawn. The fish did very little, and at first he thought it was a tench but, as it slid into the net, he saw a large expanse of flesh and whooped with joy as he realised what had occurred. At twenty seven pounds twelve, the fish was a real bonus and they all thought that it must be Sid's '28', the scaling and colouration being very similar. It mattered not, of course, and Buzz's elation was infectious, his beaming smile bringing chuckles and grins from all of them during the day. The fish was, in fact, a different one and was their sixth from the lake, and their last for the season, the next and final weekend of the season bringing nothing but a small tench to Chris and a handful of perch in their end of season spinning match.

What a bizarre season it had been.

Banned from their first choice of lake. Dragging dead fifty pounders out of their second choice, then stumbling on a lake of unbelievable potential which produced a forty eight pound carp to one of them, and the loss of similar to another.

There was little doubt where they would be fishing the following season, or so they hoped, so they began making plans for what could be a momentous year.

Bait was their first consideration, and they considered whether it would play a large part in their planning. With only a dozen or so carp in the lake and so much natural food for them to gorge themselves on, the four of them could not introduce enough to make a difference to the food chain. However, with the tench and bream as well, a certain amount might not go amiss so the next question was 'What bait?'

They were all very happy with the bird food boilies as a food source, but not with the large size, so they decided to make a few enquiries of their supplier to see if the bait could be made much smaller. The other obvious choice was tiger nuts. The tench and bream, for the most part, seemed to leave them alone, as did the birds, but the carp still loved them and it was possible to leave them out for a whole session in the knowledge that they would be perfectly presented. Other stalking baits like corn, maggots, worms or bread, would be entirely up to the individual so, with that decision made it was left to Chris to find out about the mini boilies.

At first it seemed that their quest would be fruitless, then Chris waved a forty eight pound carp under the company's nose, and things suddenly took a turn for the better!

"Fifty kilos," said Chris, over the phone, "that's all we'll get for now, but if we only bait up with the bigger boilies in the close season, they should last us well into the season."

Stan agreed wholeheartedly, and the deal was struck, Chris taking delivery in the last month of the close season.

That last month was spent, as usual, walking the banks of their chosen water for many hours and the sights they saw left them gibbering and speechless. Two occasions stood out in their memories, and their telling would warm many a winter's night in the years to come.

The first was on a warm May afternoon, less than a month before the season began. The four had met a few hours earlier and had chosen to walk in pairs around the lake, meeting at the far end in The Point Swim. Stan and Chris had gone via Chris's favourite haunt, The Snags, and had spent twenty minutes in the branches there, watching three common carp of very different proportions. Stan's nine pounder and Chris's nineteen were regularly seen in the haven of underwater branches, but this time they were joined by a much larger fish. Although not the mythical beast that Chris had seen the previous year, it was still a substantial carp which they estimated at mid-thirties. They stayed in the tree in the hope that one or more of the larger carp would join the trio but it was not to be, so they slowly moved on and twenty minutes later they were creeping through the muddy margins at the bottom of the Reedy Bay, the reeds just beginning to poke through. They had seen Sid and Buzz in the Pad Bay a little earlier, so assumed that they would be sitting on The Point awaiting their arrival, however, a call from the far side of the Reedy Bay alerted Stan and Chris to Sid's presence in one of the trees lining the bank. As they extricated themselves from the mud, they were met by a highly excitable Buzz, his eyes almost bulging out of his head and his lips moving so fast that the words were tripping over themselves.

"Ssssh! Just down there, about twenty yards," he whispered dementedly. "Two of the biggest bleeding carp you have ever seen!" With that, he turned and motioned them to follow - as if they were going to do anything else! As they rounded a bush, Buzz motioned, with his hand behind his back, for them to stop. From above, they heard, "Psssst!" and, looking up, saw Sid perched fifteen feet above them, grinning like a fool.

He motioned for them to join him, so Stan followed Chris who was already halfway up the tree. As they found a suitable branch to cling to, Sid whispered, "Just down there, to the right. See that patch of weed," they followed the direction he was pointing, then nodded in unison. "Well just watch it for a few seconds," he suggested.

Stan squinted through his sunglasses and tried to make out what sort of weed it was, then it started moving slowly towards him. It was a carp, and a massive one at that! It slowly meandered across the silt, seemingly unaware of its audience, then casually flipped onto its side and threw up a small cloud of silt. They gasped at the sight of a huge scale on the flank, and Chris felt a sudden pang of anguish as his loss was brought forcefully back to him. Then from the left, a movement caught their eyes, and they turned to see another huge carp drifting into view. The two fish came together like a pair of ponderous oil tankers, brushing alongside each other as though the sensation was most pleasurable, and the contrast in size was clear, the second fish appearing a few pounds smaller than Big Scale.

"That's Buzz's fish," Sid pointed out, and the proportions became clearer. The other fish was obviously over fifty pounds, but what of Buzz's fish? If that was holding spawn...

They watched for a further few minutes before the fish, apparently bored with the adulation, flicked their great tails and drifted off across the bay, leaving the four anglers dumb-struck.

When they were eventually able to speak again, the incident fuelled their every conversation and they arrived at the lake on each subsequent occasion in the hope that the sight would be repeated. They did see a couple of fish over the next few visits, although nothing to compare with the two monsters in the Reedy Bay, but on their final trip before the start of the season they witnessed a sight that would stay with them for the rest of their lives.

Chris and Sid had been at the lake for most of the morning but, despite doing a couple of circuits, had seen nothing to excite them. The morning was dull and overcast, which did not lend itself to fish spotting but, as Buzz cruised into the car park just before midday, the first ray of sun broke through the clouds and sparkled on the rippling waters.

The trio sat in the Back Banana and gazed across the glistening waters of the lake, smoking a much needed cigarette and supping from a welcome can of lager that Buzz had dispensed. Stan had said he would be down just after twelve, and when Buzz had phoned him an hour earlier, his wife had said that he was well on his way. They sat with their backs against the trees and chatted about the start of the season, four days away. Where would they start, who would have the first fish, had they put enough bait in, would they catch one of the Myths, who did kill Kennedy? These and many other questions they pondered whilst awaiting the arrival of the fourth member of their happy band.

Just as their patience was being stretched, they heard the familiar chugging of Stan's diesel engine and slowly rose, stretched and made to walk through the woods to meet him.

Suddenly, Sid exclaimed, "Jesus! Did you see that?"

Buzz and Chris turned from their intended route and stared across the lake.

"Down there, in front of Dead Man Standing. A bloody great fish just left the water. Loik a girt pig, 'e were!"

Sid pointed in the direction, and the others watched to see if the act would be repeated but, by the time Stan joined them in the swim, they had seen no more.

"Wassup?" asked the newcomer, himself pulling the ring from a cold can of juice.

"Just seen a fish in front of Dead Man Standing," explained Sid, "best we go and investigate, me-thinks."

With that, they set off through the trees, past the snags and down towards the swim. They stood there for a few minutes, studying the water, then Chris wandered off in search of a suitable climbing tree. Twenty yards to the right of the swim, separated from it by a small stand of wispy birches, was a small patch of lily pads and it was above these that they found Chris, in the branches of a slightly sturdier oak tree. He was peering intently into the water below but had obviously seen nothing.

Then, with a single word, he had their attention, "Shit!" he exclaimed.

Three heads tipped back and looked up at the lofty angler, then back down and in the direction he was staring. From ground level they could see very little, then Stan thought he saw a glimpse of grey.

"There," said Sid, pointing to the spot that Stan was watching. "Two of 'em, I think. Bloody hell, the one at the front looks a good 'un."

"You wanna get your arses up here, boys. There are two very large carp down there," called Chris, and before he had a chance to repeat the offer, the others were scrabbling to be first on the ladder. Within minutes they each had their own limb and were gazing through the foliage and into the clear water below. The leaves made viewing difficult, but bobbing from side to side they all got the view they wanted. Two large carp, both mirrors, were lazily drifting through the upper layers towards the small lily bed and the watchers in the sky were becoming more and more astonished the nearer they drew.

"That's Buzz's fish at the back, innit?" whispered Stan.

Chris agreed, quietly, then they all tried to work out the identity of the other fish. The angle of the sun was not good so it was fairly difficult to make out any markings or scales, however it did not seem as though the fish was Big Scale. If that was the case, what on earth could it be? It was considerably larger than the other, identifiable fish. This would make it at least low fifties. It had to be Big Scale, surely?

Then Buzz said, "Look!" and pointed to their left, away from the pads.

Another grey shape was making its way along the margins towards the pads and the voyeurs all held their breath - it must surely be the common. As it disappeared from view, behind some marginal rushes, they all craned their necks in order to get a better view then, as one, gasped an expletive - it was Big Scale, as plain as day, the shadow of the trees aiding their vision and highlighting the huge scale. Totally mesmerised by now, all they could do was ogle at the sight below them as all three carp came together to the right of the tree and grubbed around near the lilies, sending up small puffs of silt. The watchers suddenly became aware that this was one of the spots they had been baiting regularly over the previous few weeks and, just a few hours earlier, Sid and Chris had deposited about half a kilo of tiger nuts and mini boilies in the area. They had no idea what was thrilling them more, the sight of three huge carp or the fact that they were feeding confidently on the anglers' choice of bait. The casual feast carried on for about ten minutes then, gradually, the fish moved away, back into the deeper water and, pretty soon, all that was left to look at was the slowly rocking pads and a small tench nosing around in the silt where once were monsters.

The next that happened was like the classic scene from Close Encounters of the Third Kind when all the scientists at the mountain congratulated each other after watching the parade of flying saucers - then the Mother ship emerges from behind the mountain and leaves them all slack-jawed and speechless.

"What a bloody sight!" cried Buzz, grinning from ear to ear and shaking his head in disbelief.

"Four of 'em. There must be four of 'em," muttered Sid. "Are you sure the one you saw was a common, Rhodie?"

A shadow of doubt had entered Chris's mind, the other fish down there had been almost a leather, and in the wrong light well, you could make mistakes.

"Yeah, I'm pretty sure. But, well, you know. Oh I'm really baffled now!" he snapped.

Stan had kept out of the discussion and was still gazing in wonderment at the small tench, overlaying the picture of three carp ten times its size in his mind's eye. Then he caught a movement to the right and squinted into the shining water,

"Sssh! There's another one. Just coming along the margins from the reeds," he advised.

The others fell quiet and waited for the carp to come out of the glare. Then they saw its head. Then its body. Then more of its body. Then more! Then its tail. Then, ever so slowly, it swam underneath the pads to join the tench on the other side, dwarfing it like a whale would a roach. It was The Common, and it was so large that there wasn't a word big enough to describe it!

Enunciating every word as if it were a sentence, Stan said "Oh My God!" and hoped beyond hope that it was not a dream.

The others felt exactly the same, but were incapable of coherent thought at the time, so merely dribbled from their open mouths.

The carp fed casually in the silt, next to the tench, for a couple of minutes that seemed to stretch on forever. Then, as a final gift to the watchers, it slowly rolled one flank along the bottom, stirring up a great cloud of silt, before erupting from the water like a whale. The sound, as it crashed back down, was like that of a thousand thunderclaps, and brought gasps and flinches from the four stunned anglers. Then, all that was left was the rocking water and the memory.

They sat in the tree quietly for a few more minutes before, in wordless agreement, descending and walking into the sunlight. Chris lit a cigarette and drew on it expansively, and Stan wished that, for once, he too smoked.

"How big was that?" Buzz asked quietly. They had sat silently for a few minutes, none of them daring to ask that question and, now, no one dared answer.

"It was, my old mate, truly mahoosive!" ventured Stan, eventually, and that brought grunts and nods of agreement.

After a while they continued their walk, but they saw nothing which could compare to that which they had just witnessed, so they made their way back to the cars and left for home, the journey passing in a dream and a flash of scales.

To say that they looked forward to the start of the season would have been the grossest understatement, and in the three days following their amazing sightings, British Telecom's share value must have doubled!

The main topic of conversation, apart from the obvious, was who was going to fish Dead Man Standing and they eventually agreed that there could only be one way to decide that - by spoofing for it. By begging, grovelling and the performance of acts so depraved it is impossible to talk about, they all managed to secure the necessary time off. With six hours of the close season remaining, they sat in the outlet corner next to the cars and prepared to spoof for the privilege of fishing for monsters. The ritual frowning, gasping and groaning preceded or followed every call but, after five minutes, it was left to Sid and Buzz to fight for the right.

Two null games heightened the suspense then, with a stunning call of 'Spoof', Sid was victorious and howled at the moon as if already having landed one of the Myths.

The next couple of hours was spent preparing for the off in their respective swims, the south end of the lake being the preferred area for all of them. Stan had chosen The Pads, Buzz The Reedy Point and Chris The 48 and once they were settled they gathered on The Point to toast the start of what they hoped would be a momentous season. As the witching hour loomed, the bravado increased and huge predictions were made.

"I'm telling you, boys. I, Sid Bladderwort Barrett, will be the first among us, not only to land a fifty pound carp, but a fifty pound common carp!"

"Ah, forgive my poor, deluded, pony-tailed friend, gentlemen," expounded an increasingly wobbly Buzz, "he is but a child and knows not what he says."

"Much the same as yourself, then, Chewwie," commented Chris, to which Buzz chortled and raised his can.

"Touche, my friend. I look forward to pulling your arm from its socket when next we wrestle!"

"Yeah, but as you well know, talk is, indeed, cheap!" retorted Chris.

"Half eleven, boys," broke in Stan, "way past your bedtimes. Let's get on and do the do, shall we?"

With that he rose and lifted his can at arm's length. "To carp of biblical proportions, for all of us," he declared.

This was answered with the clanking of cans and cries of, "Hear, hear!"

They made their way, slightly unsteadily, back to their chosen swims and, a few minutes before the allotted time, the plop of leads and the muffled bleeps of alarms intruded on the peace of the night.

"What was that?"

Sid rolled over and peered into the grey light of pre-dawn. Something large had crashed out in front of him and woken him from a fitful sleep. He watched, sleepily, whilst the pads to his right rocked in the waves from the fish's re-entry, then pulled the bag up over his head and willed himself back to sleep.

On The Point, Buzz sat up on the edge of his bedchair and rubbed his eyes. Was that a fish he had just heard? He peered into the gloom in an effort to pick out the ripples and, within a minute, watched them lap against the reeds to his left. Looking at his watch, he groaned before leaning over and firing up the Coleman for the first cuppa of the new season.

The sky behind him was gradually turning from gun-metal grey to burgundy and the first birds were clearing their throats for the day's beginning. By the time that the first brew was in his hand, he could just make out the far bank and Sid's brolly, nestled beneath the tree that they had so recently witnessed monsters from. There was no sign of life beneath the canvas, and he wondered who was the wiser at that moment.

The first rays of the new day reflected from the pads and straight into Stan's face, causing him to groan and turn over at the same time, not even daring to open his eyes. He would know soon enough if something out there wanted to come and play.

Undisturbed by jumping fish, errant sunbeams and squabbling birds, Chris slept on contentedly, oblivious to the goings on of the new day.

Buzz was staring into space, still only semi-conscious, when the shrill tone of a buzzer rocked him from his reverie, his tea spilling over his hand and waking him fully. Where from? He looked across at the pads and saw the now vertical Sid hanging onto his rod whilst something on the other end did its best to put many yards between itself and the angler. From a hundred yards away, Buzz could hear the whine of the clutch whilst watching the line cut through the water at speed so, quickly dropping his cup, he made off rapidly towards Sid's swim to see if he could assist.

"Was that a buzzer?' thought Stan, sleepily, and rolled over to look across at Chris. No movement there. Peering backwards towards The Point, he saw Buzz hurrying along in front of the reeds and slowly put the pieces together. Sid!

By the time that he reached the swim, Stan was also semi-conscious, but became more awake when he glimpsed the scene before him. Sid's rod was bent into its full test curve and the click of the clutch confirmed that this fight was far from over. Buzz stood by his side offering helpful advice but, as is usually the way with these things, Sid heard nothing except the voice in his head which was saying, 'Don't lose it! Don't lose it! Oh, please don't let me lose it!'

"How long's it been on?" asked Stan, whilst scanning the ground for a cooker and a kettle. Boy, did he need a cup of tea!

"Six or seven minutes, I would think," replied Buzz. "He hasn't been able to gain any line, yet." The clutch clicked another half dozen times in affirmation of that, and Sid began to feel a little scared. What on earth had he hooked? Surely not the... No, don't even think about that!

Stan found the necessary items and soon had the kettle on, searching now for cups and tea bags.

"Shit!" gasped Sid as the line 'pinged' off the fish's dorsal.

Then it was his turn to take line as, at last, the carp's run slowed and it began to kite slowly to the left. Over the next ten minutes or so, Sid managed to regain many yards of line, but the fish was kiting nearer and nearer to the left hand bank and its overhanging trees. For the second time in half an hour, Buzz gave up a warm cup of tea for an early morning jog, and made his way along the bank in an effort to spook the fish from the margins.

Passing the Dead Man Standing, he could see the line cutting through the water and knew that the fish must be very close to the outer branches, so hurried through the next copse of trees and up to the water's edge. The line was just off the edge of the trees and he peered into the water to see if he could glimpse the carp. A swirl five yards to his left gave away its position, so Buzz picked up a rotten branch and thrashed it against the surface of the water. The fish boiled again and Buzz thrashed once more, this time with better effect and he watched with satisfaction as the line began cutting away from the bank. He followed the carp's passage along the margins towards Sid, just in case it needed another thrashing, then stared, goggle-eyed, as it rolled in front of the Dead Man Standing, the rising sun picking out perfectly its one huge scale.

Stan looked round at him as he entered the swim and saw the big man mouth, silently, 'Big Scale!'

Stan's eyes went wide but he remained quiet, concentrating even more on the netting job in hand.

"There it is," said Buzz, needlessly, as the fish swirled just below the surface, ten yards to their left, and all the time Sid said nothing.

The next couple of minutes passed as if through treacle, then it rolled again and Stan stretched as far forward as he could and lifted the net cord upwards. For an eternity, the fish hovered halfway between net and lake then, with a final flick of the wrist, Stan coaxed it into the net. The morning was, suddenly, broken!

They had all seen the scale as the fish was balancing on the cord, so no identification was needed and Sid leapt five yards out into the lake, screaming all the while!

Chris woke with a start. What on earth was that bloody noise? His head hurt a lot and that confounded din coming from somewhere was not helping. Peeling back the sleeping bag, he opened one bleary eye and peeked out into the world. As he focused he thought that he could see a beach party going on across the lake, people leaping in and out of the water, screaming and hollering. Then his fuddled brain began putting the pieces together and the puzzle came out looking like a great big carp.

By the time Chris had got himself together enough to join his friends, the party was in full swing. The fish had been weighed and sacked in preparation for the photographs and the kettle was boiling for the third time. Sid's beaming smile greeted Chris, and he held his arms up, victoriously.

"Rhodie! I've caught a fifty pound carp!" he crowed, then accepted Chris's hand, which he shook vigorously.

"Bloody well done, boy. Which one? How big? Is one of those cups for me?" replied Chris, accepting the steaming mug of liquid lifesaver whilst listening to the full story of the fight, which culminated with, "... Big Scale. Fifty two twelve!"

"Bloody hell! Fifty two. So what does that make the others?"

This question had already been mooted, and the answers were a bit daunting. But, for the moment, they had the privilege of photographing one of the largest carp in England.

The fish was immense in every respect, from the two inch long barbules to the massive paddle of a tail. The scale by which it was named was like half a saucer, with a couple more nestling underneath it. The great, bronze flank faded to cream on the belly, which hung down between Sid's hands as he held the fish balanced on his knees. His muscles twitched under the strain and his shoulders ached but it was the most pleasurable pain he had ever felt and, as he let the carp slip from his grasp next to the pads, he slapped the water ecstatically and screamed his elation.

The day deteriorated swiftly after that and by early evening they had each taken a rod round to The Point whilst they continued to celebrate Sid's capture. Every now and then, between the laughs and the jokes, Sid would raise himself unsteadily and declare, "I hear that, correct me if I'm wrong, somebody around these here parts has caught a carp in excess of fifty pounds! In excess of fifty, I say! Now, whoever he is, he must be one hell of an angler, that's all I can say!"

This was met with derision and flying lager cans, which all just added to the width of Sid's smile.

The lake, like the anglers, seemed to take the next few days to recover and nothing, not even a tench, came out to play, and they left tired but very happy on Sunday morning.

They vowed that the next weekend would be taken much more seriously and indeed it was. Buzz and Chris arrived on Thursday and spent nearly all day patrolling the margins in search of the carp but, by the time that Sid and Stan arrived, a day later, their search had been fruitless. Buzz was fishing the Dead Man Standing, in the hope that the fish might still patrol the margins there, and Chris was in the swim he had vowed never to fish again, to the right of the snags. Stan arrived not long after Sid and they spent an hour walking and talking and ogling at the prints of the massive carp. Eventually, Stan decided to fish The Pads, again, feeling certain that he had missed out on a chance the previous week, and Sid set up in The 48 to Stan's right.

The night was uneventful but, as they were scattered so far apart, also very sober and they were all up early the next morning in the hope of seeing some carp moving. By seven in the morning, Stan had become restless, having seen nothing but a few tench in the pads to his right, so reeled in his baits and took a slow stroll in the direction of the Reedy Bay. His eventual destination was Buzz's swim where he knew the kettle would be full, but as he strolled slowly behind the wall of reeds that surrounded the bay, he saw a number of stems twitch as something moved through them and out into the lake. Treading ever so carefully, he crept to the tree that they had watched the two huge carp from earlier in the year and climbed towards its canopy. The sun had not penetrated the branches, here, so all was still in shadow and it took a couple of minutes before his eyes could adjust to the light, then he saw a small movement to his right, just in front of the reeds that he had seen moving. Staring intently, he willed a huge mirror carp to appear, and nearly fell from his perch when it did!

Moving very slowly along the edge of the reeds was a large carp, but what it was he could not say, only that it was very obviously feeding. It was stopping every couple of feet and grubbing in the silt, small clouds of the stuff puffing up around its head. Stan did not know whether to stay or go. The sight before him was magical but the thought of hooking the fish even more exhilarating. What was he thinking? 'Get your bloody rod, Peacock!' he thought, so descended the tree as quietly as he could and legged it back to his rods.

'Float rod! Float rod!' he kept telling himself, as he neared his swim.

He kept a float rod made up at all times for just this occasion but had never found the opportunity to use it, until now. It was a nine foot, 2lb test curve stalking rod with a small baitrunner loaded with ten pound line. A peacock quill was held in place by float rubbers and two swan shot were pinched on the line, six inches from the size 8 hook. His hands were like a bunch of bananas as he clumsily put together a small selection of tackle and bait, before running off to do battle. Halfway to the reeds he realised that he had forgotten his net so had to spin round and return for it. His mind was a blur. 'It'll be gone by now. I should have had my rod with me first time, bloody idiot! What bait? Tigers? Corn? Boilie? What about worms, ol' Ted lost one on worms.'

That last made him smile and brought a tad of sanity to the situation.

As he reached the reeds he slowed to a tiptoe and crept up to the tree, laying his tackle quietly next to it before carefully ascending. From his perch he could see that which he had feared the most - the fish was gone. He stared intently, once more, but could see no movement in the cloudy water below. A silt cloud to the left seemed to indicate the path that the fish had taken so Stan scoured that possible route but, after a couple of tense minutes, admitted defeat and began to slowly descend. He stopped at the branch below to see if he could get a better angle, and was greeted with the sight of a tail lobe waving lazily above a huge cloud of silt, ten yards to his right. The fish was obviously patrolling the whole length of the reed bed for whatever tasty morsels the silt held.

This was his chance. Whilst the carp was preoccupied he could drop his float fished bait into its path and await the outcome. But what bait? His mind wouldn't sit still long enough for him to catch a coherent thought, so he dove into the bag and grabbed the first thing that came to hand - it was a Tupperware container full of sweetcorn. That would do nicely. He wasted a dozen grains before he could actually get two to stay on the hook, then lost both of them when his first cast ended up around a reed stem. This was going to be a disaster, why didn't he just pack up now and go round to Buzz for a cup of tea? Thirty seconds later another two yellow grains were nestling onto the silt, two feet below the quill.

Laying his rod on the ground, he adjusted the clutch then sat next to the rod. Then got up and peered through the reeds.

Then sat down again.

This was repeated a couple of times before he could take no more and quickly climbed the tree. The red tip of the float seemed much further out than he had thought and he wondered if the carp had passed between it and the reeds. Then, a yard to the right of the float, he saw a small puff of silt billow towards the surface and knew that his bait was in the middle of route one!

His descent of the tree was almost fatal, his foot slipping and threatening to dump him on the floor, which would have definitely put an end to the whole affair. A quick grab with his hand, however, left him dangling a foot above the grass and he carefully lowered himself from there, turning quickly to search out his float.

He saw it through the reeds - then he didn't!

'A float is pleasing in appearance and disappearance' a strangely calm voice in his head quoted, but a nano-second later that voice was replaced by one that was screaming, 'Bloody hell, it's taken it!'

As his hand reached for the rod he heard the bait-runner begin its scream and looked up to see a huge bow wave move steadily across the bay, away from him. What now? He hadn't thought as far ahead as to what he would do if he actually hooked a carp, now every second would count.

Picking up the rod, he waded straight into the lake and out to the edge of the reeds where the water reached his waist. The silt, however, sucked at his feet and he felt himself slowly sinking, whilst all the time the hiss of the line through the rings was reminding him of the more pressing problem. The bow wave was now some fifty yards away and receding, the time for action was now! Putting a finger on the spool, he steadily applied pressure, whilst tightening his clutch with the other hand and the bow wave began to slow. The water was, by now, up to his chest but he had stopped sinking, the only problem was how he was going to extract himself from the lake to net the fish, his landing net lying conveniently up against the tree ten yards away. That problem would have to wait, first he had to get some control of the carp. Hooking carp in shallow water, ain't it just dandy?

Slowly and ponderously, Stan began gaining line, the fish kiting slowly right and left but for no more than five yards in either direction and, soon, it was no more than fifteen yards away. Now came the netting problem. Stan had tentatively tried to extricate one or other of his feet from the cloying silt, but they seemed firmly wedged for the moment and there seemed little option now, other than to yell at the top of his voice.

After three loud shouts, he had heard no reply and began to think that he might have to wrestle the beast into submission!

"'s that you, Quill?" Sid's voice came from behind him and he called again.

"Sid! Sid, over here. By the Climbing Tree."

Seconds later, Sid's voice came from right behind him,

"What you doing out there, boy?" he asked, incredulously.

"Well, I heard that the silt was good for athlete's foot, so I thought I'd give it a try! What d'you think I'm doing out here, Einstein, I'm playing a bloody carp!"

Sid laughed aloud, then picked up the net, "So I s'pose you'll be wanting this then, Einstein!"

Stan grimaced, but daren't turn to see his friend's grinning face as the carp was doing a very good impression of a carp that wanted to get into some reeds. He pulled the rod way over to the left, but the test curve was not enough to stop the fish from reaching its destination and Stan swore aloud as he felt the line grating along a reed stem. He slackened off the clutch a little in the hope that the carp might swim out, then heard a great splashing and, looking farther to his right, saw Sid wading into the reed bed with net held high. Stan didn't know what to do next, he just hoped that his friend did, so held the rod out as far as he could and waited for some sensation to come back down the line. There was suddenly a lot of splashing and muttered curses before Sid's voice cried out,

"Yesss! Big fat mirror, Quill!"

Stan was still unsure as to what had happened so called to his friend, "What? Have you got it, or what?"

"Oh, we've got it Quill! We certainly have got it and it's a bloody whacker!"

Stan stood, glued to the spot, and howled like a mad dog! On the far side of the bay he could see Buzz's head bobbing up and down behind the reeds as he made his way quickly around the margins to the soaking but happy anglers. With his help, they managed to drag Stan from the clinging silt, one of his trainers becoming a permanent feature of the lake bed there.

Chris arrived in time for the weighing this time, and the identification. The carp was the same that Buzz had caught nine months earlier, but weighed just eight ounces short of fifty pounds, this time.

Happiness was, once again, unconfined and Stan smiled royally for the camera. What a lake this was, but what was amazing was that there were three carp larger than this one swimming in it!

All agreed that the celebrations should be postponed until later that evening, the feeling being that there may be a chance of another margin browsing carp, so they all went off in search of stalking rods and feeding carp, leaving Stan to grin inanely. There was one thing left to do, though, and he jumped into the car and drove to the phone box to tell Jean the news. She had come to enjoy fishing - 'If you can't beat 'em, join 'em' she would say in answer to her friends' baffled stares - but she had little time to get out, normally. But Stan knew she would understand how he felt, and also that she would be a bit aggrieved if he didn't phone her with the news.

She was, as anticipated, ecstatic and her joy made him realise that it was very much the right thing to do. She left him with, 'go and catch another' ringing in his ears, but his thirst was quenched for the day and he returned to relax and run the whole battle over in his mind again and again.

The other three, however, were much more determined and spent the rest of the day in search of carp and, in the early evening, Chris's determination was rewarded.

From a tree behind the Post Office, he had spied two or three fish cruising just below the surface at the far end of the Top Island. They were too far for him to cast to and also looked as though they would treat a bottom bait with some disdain but, as he watched intently for the next hour, he saw them mouthing a few floating items beneath the branches of the island's trees. Very slowly, they made their way along the margins of the island towards the nearest tip, eighty yards from the bank. Plans were formed and then dismissed in Chris's head, but when he saw another two fish join them from his right, he knew this was a chance not to be missed.

He ran to his car and extracted a piece of equipment he thought he would never need on here, a spod rod, and returned armed with that and a box of Chum Mixer. A steady southerly breeze was blowing down the lake and he thought that if he could get a stream of bait moving past the carp it might entice them to feed and also follow it into the margins of the bay. Putting a stone in the bottom of the spod, he aimed at the middle of the island and watched with satisfaction as the white plastic tip bobbed to the surface ten yards from the island. He repeated this a dozen times, then rescaled the tree to watch events unfold through his binoculars.

The carp were still present, seemingly unperturbed by the disturbance, and he watched carefully as the first of the mixers drifted over their heads, unmolested. After five minutes he thought that his plan had failed, then a fish swirled on the surface. Then another. It was working.

In the time it took him to descend from the tree he had seen another four mixers disappear into a small whirlpool and, by the time he had crept round to the South Westerly, the first drift of mixers were bobbing in the margins. Scooping them up, he fired the sodden biscuits back out into the lake and saw them land thirty yards distant, a few yards short of another small vortex on the surface. He had had the foresight to thread a couple of mixers onto his rig, knowing full well that if the situation should arise, he would also be guilty of gorilla fingers! Dunking the hook into the water, he waited for a few more signs of feeding fish and when he saw two mixers disappear at the same time, yards apart, he knew that the time was right. Unlike Stan's disasters a few hours earlier, Chris's plan came together perfectly.

The weighted controller sailed out perfectly, the hook avoiding the grasping branches above. It landed with a plop, forty yards distant and amongst a large patch of drifting mixers. The hooklink was not coiled up, but extending to almost all of its four feet, and Chris watched breathlessly as first one then another of the patch of mixers disappeared.

Then his.

There was no abortive take and swirl away.

There was no nose-balancing like a performing seal.

There was just no hookbait, and as the line snaked across the surface he struck firmly and watched the water erupt in front of him. The battle was frantic but, fortunately, took place mainly on the surface and the only problem came when he saw the flash of a large flank covered in scales - a common, and a big one at that!

Within ten minutes, the battle was over and he roared as loudly as his friends had done recently.

It was a common, and a big one. A personal best by some way, but it was not the Myth and for that he felt strangely relieved. When that was caught it would surely be the ultimate battle, all four of them present on a misty dawn as angler and carp gave their all.

That was for some other time, though. Now was the time for much celebration, and the others soon gathered, alerted by his victory cries. At thirty six pounds it was the largest common any of them had seen on the bank and was a stunning example of that strain.

Its mouth was perfect, the recent hookhold showing as a small red dot. It was long, so long and each scale looked as though it had been hand crafted and placed precisely by an ancient Japanese craftsman. The evening sun glinted off its flank and reflected a golden hue on the surroundings. What a day! What a day!

The celebrations were long and joyful and they left the next day with sore heads but very happy hearts.

Over the next few weeks the fish became conspicuous by their absence, the only evidence of their existence being the occasional thunderous splash in the middle of the night but, by mid-July, no further carp had fallen to their baits and they were becoming a little frustrated. A procession of suicidal tench did little to enthuse them and it was becoming very clear that the mini boilies were proving more of a hindrance than a help. So it was that Buzz arrived on a Wednesday in the middle of the month armed with the recently purchased twenty two millimetre sized baits. The weather was cool and the south westerly breeze eventually pushed Buzz into the swim of that name. The baits went out well, so he put fifty or sixty in the margins of the island, his hookbait dropping perfectly at the same distance. His other rod was dropped into the right hand margin where he had found a shallow shelf and that was baited with tiger nuts.

As the evening turned to night, he thought he saw a carp roll just to the right of his island bait and so, when a screaming buzzer woke him at the other end of the night, he automatically struck the island rod. His sleep befuddled brain took a few seconds to realize that the buzzer was still screaming and that the rod he had picked up felt lifeless. Suddenly becoming aware of his folly, he dropped the rod and snatched the other from the rests, the tip pulling round alarmingly as the fish continued on its path, unimpressed by the new pressure. The reel handle clattered against his knuckles as he tried desperately to slow the carp's charge along the margins, and eventually he managed to grab the foolish thing and bring a slowing to the carp's retreat. With the rod tip beneath the water, he could feel the grating of the line on an unseen snag and used the test curve of the rod to ease the carp back to the snag. Minutes later he had succeeded in returning it to the point of contact, but there was a definite grating of line against something and, with the plethora of shelled food in the lake, he was loathe to abuse the line any more than he had to.

For the next five minutes he tried all that he could think of. Slack lining. Pinging the taut line and then letting it fall slack in a bid to spook the carp out from the margins. Hurling rocks into the lake in a bid to affect the same, but each time the fish moved off he inevitably brought it back to the snag. There was only one thing for it - he had to go in.

The sun was a little higher in the sky, but the east woods hid its light from view, so Buzz would have to rely on touch, something he was very adept at beneath mirky North Atlantic seas. Slipping into the water he was suddenly awake, gasping at the feel of the water on his semi naked body. He had set the clutch loosely and was following the line along to where he thought the snag might be then, filling his huge lungs with as much air as possible, he dived below the surface. Following the line for a few yards brought him, shortly, to the offending branch and he carefully tested its strength before returning to the surface to refill his lungs. He trod water for a few seconds pondering his next move, then felt the line pull through his fingers as the carp moved away once more, the clutch on his reel clicking to his left. No time to think so, with a huge breath, he disappeared once more. The line was still pulling through his fingers so he lowered himself to the branch, which felt about as thick as a banana, and, letting go of the line, put both hands around it and pulled. It gave so easily he nearly gasped in a lungful of water, then kicked himself to the surface and back towards his steadily spinning reel. Clambering out like the Neptune that his friends had described him as, he quickly picked up the rod and was relieved to see the line pull round at right angles and away from the bank.

It had worked! The only worry now was how much damage had been done to the line, so he played the un-tethered carp very gingerly for the next couple of minutes. He had glimpsed a dark figure below the surface that had given him the impression of size, so he didn't want to lose it after all of his hard work, then something hit the surface ten yards out and he could see that it was the branch. The line must have wrapped around it, so how far behind it was the fish?

This fight was a long way from over, that was for sure and as the branch came closer, Buzz saw another swirl five yards behind it and knew that the fish was not far away. To land the fish he would have to remove the branch, but he had no idea what state the line was in, nor the extent of the tangle. Then, all of a sudden, the problem was solved for him.

The fish rolled on the surface and he saw a large, brown flank turn over - a mirror, and a large one at that. As it rolled over it flicked its huge tail for one final time and caught Buzz unawares, the line tightening too rapidly. There was a deafening 'crack' and the branch splashed onto the surface, in two pieces. Just as this was registering in the big man's head, another softer noise registered the final extent of punishment for his line and he looked in astonishment as one end of it flapped uselessly from his rod tip. His howl of anguish was almost palpable and, like Chris and Stan before him, it took many weeks for him to recover from the pain of such a loss.

One final flick of the tail was all the strength that was left in the big mirror, then it was sliding back beneath the waves, the stinging sensation still remaining, but the pressure gone. Slowly it gained its equilibrium and moved away from the bank, a thin thread trailing from its aching mouth. Bemused for a while, it cruised into deeper water before eventually regaining its bearings and moving slightly more purposefully towards the sanctuary of the snag tree, where it would rest uneasily for a few days until the sensation in its mouth was gone.

The food was nutritious and tasty, but once in a while strange things happened. Unfortunately for the carp, it took little time for them to forget the strange happenings and it was not long before the temptation was too great once more.

The news of Buzz's loss put a bit of a dampener on the following weekend's fishing and even Sid's capture of a twenty six pound mirror could not put the smile back on the big man's face for long. Sid had caught it from Dead Man Standing, having seen a fish roll in front of there on the previous morning, and it proved to be the same fish that Buzz had caught at the end of the previous season. The sense of loss became even greater when, first Stan, then Chris also lost fish over the next couple of weekends.

Stan's was in the Reedy Bay and was lost from the spot that he had landed the 49 from. Once again he was float fishing, having seen three fish patrolling the edge of the reeds and, although none of them were the real biggies, he saw one fish that he estimated at about mid-thirties. The float had slid under as before but, before he had a chance to repeat his leap into the water, the rod sprang back and he watched forlornly as the spooked carp bow waved across the bay to freedom. On retrieving his float he saw that the hook was missing, the line cut clean through above the split shot. He had no idea which fish he had lost but any fish was a worthy prize from Felcham and he felt depressed all the same.

Although elated with his common, Chris felt a little left out as all of his peers seemed to be getting in on the whacker act. So, when he saw two large carp leap from the water in front of the Creaking Tree, he set up confidently on the Saturday morning following Stan's loss, and fired out a dozen or so of the large baits around his hookbait, fifty yards distant.

The take came later that afternoon and was a real belter, the fish taking thirty yards of line in its first run before leaping like a dolphin in the middle of the lake. Chris stood transfixed at the sight, as did Buzz and Stan who had both heard the take, then he could only gawp incredulously as the fish crashed back down and tore off to the left. The rod was wrenched round, then sprang back lifeless as the acrobatics succeeded in ridding the carp of the hook. Chris sat very quietly for the next few hours, spurning any company, and trying to work out what he had done to so annoy the Carp Gods.

Mistake! Once again the bountiful supply of food had produced a most unwelcome sensation of pain and pressure. The carp's initial reaction was to hurl itself from the lake, as it would to rid itself of the many tics and bugs that caused it irritation at certain times of the year. The tactic worked successfully, and the momentary irritation was soon forgotten, although the desire to feed was not as great for a day or two.

The run of bad luck came to an end in the middle of a very warm August, when Buzz finally made sure that the hook stayed in not one but two carp.

His first came from frustration, his second inspiration, but both were warmly received.

"Another hot day in paradise, Quill," sighed Buzz, as the pair of them sat in the shade of a large oak tree.

The temperatures were in the mid-eighties once more, and the carp did not want to come out to play. Sid and Chris were at the far end of the lake, in The Pads and The Reedy Bay respectively, but there was little shade there, so Buzz and Stan had elected to fish the north end. They sat in Buzz's swim, The Back Banana, and gazed lazily across the glass calm lake. Nothing seemed to stir, barring the odd acrobatic rudd, and the two anglers had long since run out of things to say. Then Stan squinted and looked carefully towards the end of the Banana Island.

"Is that a dorsal?" he asked, whilst pointing to a small, moving dot on the surface.

"Nah, just another water boatman, boy." With that, Buzz pulled his cap over his eyes and laid down on his bedchair, trying to ignore the stifling heat.

"Wake me when I've bagged one, will you?" he requested, and closed his eyes. Stan peered more intently at the dot, then saw it flick up and become a small sail.

"It is a bloody dorsal, look!" he exclaimed, whilst shaking the recumbent giant. Buzz lifted his cap up with one finger and squinted one eye in the direction of the island, ready to scoff at his pal, but saw the totally unexpected - a carp roll on the surface.

"Bloody hell, Quill, you're right. It's a bloody carp!"

He jumped up and hit his head on one of the brolly spokes, cursing as he did so, then stood erect and grabbed for his binoculars. Concentrating hard, he could make out two shapes just below the surface moving very lethargically, but they were a long way out. The tip of the island was a hundred and forty yards away and the fish were slightly beyond it.

He thought about moving round to the Top Banana swim on the right hand bank, but just the idea of all that moving made him break out in a sweat so he opted for the next best thing - the big chuck! Breaking out the spool with eight-pound line and a twenty five pound leader, he slipped on a four and a half ounce lead, a short six inch nylon hooklink, and a small pop up and eyed up the target.

His plan was to drop the bait onto the shallow gravel plateau at the far tip of the island. With the creaking of carbon, straining of sinews and wincing of his companion, he hurled the lead with all his might and watched it fly through the midsummer air, willing it a yard or two further. It landed with an audible splash, five yards to the left of the island, and the same short of the far end. An admirable cast, but was it good enough?

Stan thought not and, when Buzz turned to him with a questioning glance, he shrugged his shoulders in reply. "Yep, you're right. Need another couple of yards," and with that he reeled the lead back in.

The next cast went the same distance but was much closer to the island and Stan watched the rod tip shudder as the lead touched down. 'That's the one,' he thought, and nodded his approval as Buzz turned again. They watched through the binoculars for the next ten minutes, but the carp stayed frustratingly ten yards further than the tip of the island and Buzz began to wonder whether he should have moved.

"What's that?" asked Stan, and Buzz raised the glasses to his eyes, focusing on the disturbance near his hookbait. It looked like a tail pattern, but the angle of the sun had changed so he could see nothing below the surface.

Then the water seemed to boil and erupt and, at the same instant, his buzzer coughed into life. Buzz dropped the binoculars and picked up the rod, striking with all his might, and once more Stan winced. The water above the plateau exploded as a carp's tail thrashed the surface.

The fight was uneventful and it was obvious to both of them that this was no monster, but when it went into the net, Buzz roared just the same, this being his first of the season. The carp was the nineteen pound common that Chris had caught the previous year and was mightily welcome and royally toasted later that evening. Thirsty work, summer carp fishing!

The following week's capture was as different as two could be.

Buzz was fishing the Reedy Point and had woken early on Friday morning. Chris had arrived the previous evening and had elected to fish opposite, in Sid's Pads (as Sid had dubbed them!) but, at that time of the morning, was nowhere to be seen. Buzz had his usual early morning cup of tea before doing anything else, then took a slow stroll along the back of the reeds to Quill's Tree (as Stan had dubbed it!). There seemed little activity there and Buzz thought that it might be a little early for the carp to move down there, the sun having barely breached the far horizon. As he strode back to his swim he heard a splash and the complaint of an angry coot in the reeds ahead, so crept closer to see what was happening. Through the stems he could discern some movement, but put it down to the tench which they regularly saw in there.

Then a tail the size of a hand waved at him and he nearly wet himself! If that was a tench it was a bloody record, and he turned rapidly on his heel and headed swiftly back to his rods. There was no time for the fancy float fishing stuff, the fish was so close he could lower his lead from the rod tip without a sound, so quickly wound in one of his baits. There was no time to replace it, it was perfectly sound and may even benefit from a lack of smell so, grabbing his net, he crouched down and returned to the scene of the crime. The reeds were still moving and he could just discern a small vortex where the tail was moving, just below the surface. If that was the tail then the head must be... there. With that, he inched the rod tip carefully through the reed stems, the lead wound right up to the tip, and once over the desired spot oh so carefully lowered it down, a yard in front of where he thought the fish was.

The next few minutes passed like days and he wondered if his heart could take the strain. The reeds to the left of his bait, inches away, moved to one side as something substantial pushed past them. The line hung limply from the rod tip, Buzz concentrating feverishly on it lest it should twitch. Twitch? Oh it twitched, alright! It twitched like a runaway train on a downhill slope, hissing through the rings as the startled carp smashed through the reeds and made off across the lake. Buzz stared open mouthed as the bow wave grew, afraid to even pick the rod up, but soon panic took over and he hoisted the rod up, flicking the bale arm over and waiting for the 'snap'. It didn't come, however, and after a few minutes of thrashing and complaining, the carp slid slowly into the waiting net, the captor up to his knees in water and screaming like a banshee.

The fish weighed thirty three pounds and was the same as Stan's '31', and in its bottom lip was embedded another hook with a short piece of line attached. It later proved to be the fish that Stan had lost in the reeds a month earlier, which made Stan feel a little better, but none of that mattered to Buzz. He was elated and, like his friends before him, thought that he was at last getting something right.

Ah, carp fishing, don't you just love it!

The steady introduction of boilies, not only by the carp anglers, but also the occasional tench and bream anglers, was a welcome supplement to the carp's diet and they began to show the benefits of this extra nutrition as the year progressed. The downside was that, once in a while, their guard would drop and they would fall for the anglers' traps, as three of them had done on more than one occasion in the past year. The Common, however, had avoided any confrontation, its greedier cohorts normally beating it to the bait and therefore the hook. But it was surely only a matter of time before it made its perennial mistake, and only a matter of luck whether it was landed or not.

Chapter Sixteen - the Myth

Thunder rolled ominously in the distance and the wind suddenly increased in strength, hissing through the gradually dying leaves. This was the first noticeable change in the weather for a couple of weeks and, after steady high pressure and consistent calm and sunny days, the promise of wind, rain and low pressure was music to the ears of a small minority of the population.

It was the middle of September, their favourite month, and almost a month since Buzz's success. A month that had seen them search endlessly for the ever more elusive carp in the mere, but with little success. Sid had spied a couple of fish in The Snags, but they were not feeding and remained there for a day, totally oblivious to their audience. That had been at the turn of the month. A fortnight later, the promise of a change of conditions renewed the anglers' confidence. So much so that both Sid and Stan had taken a couple of day's holiday in order to be at the lake, just in case the fish turned on.

The forecast was for thundery rain and strong southerly winds and all four of them knew where they wanted to be - in the Top Bay. Stan and Sid arrived after work on Wednesday evening, and found the other pair sitting in Buzz's swim, the Post Office, sheltering from the wind in Buzz's bivvy.

"Alright boys," called Sid, "got that kettle on?"

Stan ducked past a wind-beaten bush and into the shelter of the bivvy before Sid could take another step, seating himself on the floor and. taking a quick slurp from Chris's still warm mug of tea.

"Bloody hell, Quill. You're a bit sprightly for an old 'un, boy!" came Sid's whining cry. "Save us a bit of that tea."

Stan turned the cup upside down and smiled, "No chance of that, young 'un. You'll have to ask your Uncle Buzz to make you a fresh one, won't you?"

"More like Uncle Buck," muttered Chris, and received a thump on his shoulder for the remark.

"I heard that," said Buzz, needlessly, then flicked his lighter to ignite the flame.

"So, where is it, then?" asked Sid. The remark needed no explanation, the charade having been carried out for many years.

"Oh, we slipped 'em back, boy. Took a couple of quick snaps on the mat then -whoosh!"

Chris flung his arms to one side like somebody passing a rugby ball, indicating the fate of the fantasy carp. Stan smiled, leaning forward with his elbows on his knees and peering out at the wind tossed lake.

"Where you fishing then, Rhodie?" he asked, knowing full well the answer, but then taken by surprise when it came.

"Island One."

"Yeah? Why not the South Westerly, it must look prime in these conditions," came Stan's puzzled response.

Chris just winked at him, bending to pick up his empty cup and passing it to Buzz to refill. Stan frowned at him before picking up the bait. "What you seen then, boy. Come on. Tell, tell!"

With that he turned and jabbed his hand into Chris's armpit making him squeal and squirm like an infant.

"Okay! Okay!" he begged, huddling against the big man to his right for assistance, but all he got was a gruff, "Mind out! The bloody tea!"

Stan and Sid laughed, Stan feigning another dig to Chris's ribs.

"D'you wanna drink this tea or wear it!" Buzz growled, but the seriousness was lost on the others.

"Sorry Dad," tittered Stan, then accepted a fresh brew from the scowling man. "So, Mr. Rhodes, what enticed you to venture into the aforementioned swim?" he continued.

Chris smiled once more, but was not about to go through the tickling torture again, so answered swiftly.

"Well, I might have seen a carp, I suppose!"

Stan nodded at him, appreciatively, then looked to Buzz as he said, "And I suppose I might have seen one as well!"

The newcomers listened intently, whilst sipping the welcome brew, as Chris and Buzz told of at least three sightings of carp over the previous few hours. Buzz had seen two fish, both near the far tip of the island, and had managed to get a bait to the plateau before the wind made it impossible.

"That's staying there until we go home or until a mahoosive carp runs off with it," he stated, firmly.

Chris had, in fact, been set up in the South Westerly until a few hours earlier, but then he had seen a good fish leap clear of the water halfway up the left hand side of the island, so had quickly packed away and moved into his present swim. The fish had showed ten yards from the island so he had put one bait at that distance and the other beneath an inviting overhanging tree on the right hand side of the island.

With this knowledge, Stan and Sid pondered their next moves.

Island Two and the South Westerly seemed the obvious choices but, just as

Stan was about to call for a spoof Sid said, "I fancy Island Two, what about you?"

"South Westerly. Job done then, boy," replied Stan, and with that they drained their cups and returned to their cars.

The wind was building towards gale force, the rumbling thunder advancing towards them, so the four of them lent a hand to erect the two remaining bivvies, the wind whipping the material from their hands on numerous occasions before both were safely pegged down.

'Drop 'em in the edge,' thought Stan, and did just that, one to the right, one to the left and both landing on firm bottom five yards out. Sid attempted to reach the island, but the vicious side wind was causing him grief and, eventually, he adopted the same ploy as Stan, just for the night. That was advancing rapidly, also, and it was in the last vestiges of evening that they all gathered in Buzz's bivvy for a huge curry and a few ales. The wild night was temporarily forgotten, and they listened intently to another of Buzz's stories.

"One of the most amazing sights I ever saw was when we were in Belize a few years back," he began.

"We were due to do an early morning dive over this wreck that was supposed to have some bullion on it, or some such bollocks! Anyway, we were staying in these little grass hut things near to the beach, bloody paradise it was, and on this particular morning I was up just before dawn."

"She's such a lazy cow, ain't she!" chipped in Sid, as usual, and got the usual derisive response.

"Yeah, well anyway. I got up just before the sun had appeared over the horizon," continued Buzz whilst eyeing Sid carefully. "We had an hour or so before embarking, so I took a stroll along the beach to watch the sunrise. As I stood there, having a quick fag, I saw this thing slide up out of the water and I thought 'that's a bleeding blanket!' Then I saw another, and another, and I realised that they were Manta rays. Now I've seen Manta's when I've been diving and they are tremendous creatures. So graceful. But I had never witnessed anything like this, and as the sun came up it turned them all gold. It was the most unbelievable sight I have ever seen in my life. It continued for about twenty minutes then, as the sun got higher, they just stopped. I must have seen nearly a hundred, just sliding silently in and out of the water. I went back the next day, and the next, but I never saw it again and I've only ever spoken to one other person that has seen it. I'll never forget that."

The story left them with a warm glow, although that could have been the wine, and they spent the rest of the windswept evening relating similar tales, before Buzz advised them, like Zebidee, that it was time for bed.

The night was not wild anymore, it was bloody furious! Stan checked all of his bivvy pegs, stamping two or three back down where they had been worked loose, before snuggling down into the warmth of the sleeping bag. He took some time to drift off to sleep, but was soon dreaming of flying golden blankets called Dawn!

She arrived soon enough, but instead of flying blankets she brought with her carp a-leaping, and large ones at that. Stan peered out across the lake and watched another huge, golden body crash back into the waves, sending up a plume of spray to be whipped away by the wind, and wished that he had cast a little further the previous evening. The fish were showing to the left of the island, about ninety yards distant, but the wind would make a cast to there very difficult and, besides, Chris was fishing not very far from there and was probably feeling just a little confident.

Chris sat on the edge of his bed drinking a hot cup of tea and could not help feeling just a little confident as he watched yet another golden body leap from the waves. The fish were a few yards to the right of his right hand bait, although also a few yards out from the island, and he wondered if one would venture beneath the trees for an early morning muffin. He had managed to get a few baits out on the previous evening, but a lot of them had fallen in the vicinity of the leaping carp and he considered the risk of a recast.

His right hand buzzer bleeped, once again, as some more weed collected on the line, and he vowed to remove it in a second after he had finished his tea. As he peered at the conglomeration of weed on the line, he gradually realised that it was moving, of its own volition, against the flow of the wind and, when another bleep emitted from the buzzer, it dawned on him that something else might be to blame. Picking up his rod, he flicked the weed from the line before winding in the bow in the line and striking forcefully, feeling a satisfying thump on the other end as the hook found purchase. The fish continued to kite slowly to the left and Chris carefully applied pressure to it, coaxing it away from the island and into the open water in front of him. The tree to his left would pose a problem, but that was yet to come. For the moment he could concentrate on keeping a firm pressure on the fish and guiding it ever closer to the net. The pressure began to tell and the fish turned back the way it had come, but twenty yards closer, and by the time it had passed in front of him again, it was thirty yards out. The vision of a huge common carp would not leave him, and he began to shake, then the vision of a huge common carp leaping out of the water fifty yards behind the hooked carp caused him to shake for a different reason. Was it one of the big mirrors, then? The question was moot, first he had to get it into the net, then he could get picky!

The fish rolled in the waves, but it was difficult to discern size or shape in the huge swell and Chris just concentrated on netting the fish first time. A minute later he failed at that and the carp, a mirror of some stature, rolled backwards and flicked its tail. Chris groaned and let the reel backwind a little, composing himself for another go. The carp rolled slowly in front of him once again, and this time he did not miss, feeling the satisfying kick as the carp fought against the mesh. Dropping the rod he screamed his delight, pulling the net towards him so as to have a better look inside. He knew that his friends would soon arrive to lend a hand.

Stan propped himself on one elbow, the better to look through the bivvy door, then stared wordlessly as a huge common carp slid gracefully out of the deeps. 'Just like a manta ray,' he thought, 'wonder if Rhodie saw it?'

He stared at the spot hopefully for a few more minutes, but nothing further showed itself, so he inched himself out of bed and stood to relieve his distended bladder when, from his left, he heard a triumphant scream.

'Rhodie,' he thought, and visions of monster commons flashed before his eyes. "What you had, boy?" screamed Sid as he bundled into the swim, seeing Chris holding the net in the margins.

"A bloody great mirror carp, Sid, my old mate," came the beaming reply." Give us a hand, will you?"

Sid grabbed the folded net and helped Chris heave it from the lake and onto the mat. Stan arrived as the mesh was peeled back to reveal the stunning frame of a long, muscular, almost linear mirror. "Bloody hell, which one is that?" he gasped.

Chris shook his head, smiling, and replied, "Who bloody cares, boy? Look at it, it's fantastic! Look at the length of it, it must be three feet long!"

It proved to be one inch short of that, but was one of the most beautiful carp any of them had ever seen. The weight of forty two pounds seemed immaterial and the subsequent photographs could easily have been of a carp five pounds heavier. Chris was elated beyond belief. Oh, sure, it wasn't one of the Myths but it was a totally unknown carp that had probably never been caught before and the quality of it meant more than pounds and ounces ever could.

"Best we get a few beers in, boys," said Chris, whilst watching the fish disappear into the depths, "I think there's gonna be a party!"

With that, he hoorahed at the skies, the others chorusing that, then bursting out laughing.

The Common leapt from the lake, landing with a satisfying splash before diving back down to its larder. The water was greatly disturbed around the island and many food items were suspended in mid water, an easy mouthful for the group of cruising carp. As well as these smaller items, the lake bed was littered with many larger items of food which were much appreciated, and the carp began to feed with abandon, the change in pressure bringing with it a need to replenish valuable energy. The Common cruised further into the bay, in search of more sustenance, its hunger once again lowering its defences.

By early evening the wind had abated somewhat, but was still pushing into the bay, which was fortunate because none of the anglers felt any desire to move. They had spent the morning toasting Chris's capture with mugs of tea but, by early afternoon, the need for a more serious celebration was called for and the first beers had been quaffed. Still, they had taken it easy, especially as the weakening wind meant that they could get their baits exactly where they wanted them.

Sid's cast to the island margin was perfect and his subsequent addition of sixty or so baits likewise.

Chris was happy with the position of his baits, naturally, just adding a scattering of freebies to the area for good measure.

Stan took the opportunity to put a bait on the tip of the island, happy with the solid thump of the lead as it landed a yard from the island margins. The larger baits made it easier to be accurate when catapulting and he watched with pleasure as the boilies plopped, one after another, within yards of his baited hook.

Buzz felt no need to recast, his baits were untouched and were both in the island margins so could be recast no better. As for freebies, he would not be able to reach the far bait but had already pulted out a hundred baits, a day previously, to his left hand rod which he was very happy with.

The evening was a good one, everybody on top form, and Chris's capture was saluted again and again. Buzz regaled them with more stories, but with verbal abuse raining down on him constantly, eventually gave up, content to sit back and get slowly drunk. The night was middle aged when they finally left Stan's bivvy and returned unsteadily to their own, wishing each other the very best of luck before settling in to a sound sleep.

As the sunlight gradually filtered through the leaves, the carp began cruising slowly along the island margins, picking up baits that were scattered hither and yon. Of the six fish, three were huge and intent on getting even bigger, so relished the small patches of food they found at regular intervals on their travels. Greed began to take over as the food steadily diminished and one of Nature's primal laws took over. Only the strong survive.

Bleep!

The noise registered at a subconscious level but the angler barely stirred.

Bleep!

This brought a ruffling of bedclothes and the gradual opening of one, red rimmed eye. He peered out into the morning light and tried to work out what had woken him.

Bleep! Bleep!

The red light shone once more and it registered on him that it was the island rod. Raising himself carefully onto one elbow, he searched beneath his bedchair for the carton of juice, gulping down half of its contents before lowering it back down. Better. He swung his legs round and sat on the edge of the bedchair, frowning at the rod. Was the tip pulling round or was it his imagination?

Bleep! Bleep!

Onto his feet.

Bleep!

Two steps towards the rods.

Bleeeeeeeeep!

The tip pulled round to the right. The clutch screamed before he could bend to grab the rod, the buzzer continuing its wail long after battle was joined. It acted as a clarion call to the other three who soon joined him in the swim, in different stages of wakefulness and well-being.

The line hissed through the rings and he felt trepidation at the thought of trying to stop the carp's charge. They all watched as the line cut through the water, like a cheese wire, and then looked at the ashen angler before one of them said,

"Don't you think you should try to slow that down a bit, boy?"

"Thanks for the advice, I never thought of that! Now, stick the kettle on, there's a good chap!"

Shrugging, he did as he was bade and the others licked their lips in anticipation. The rod still bent alarmingly, he applied gradual pressure to the spool, but succeeded only in severely singeing that digit! Trying again, this time with a spit dampened finger, he achieved a little respite and watched as the line cut more to the right. There was at least a hundred yards between him and the carp and the thought of that made him shudder. This was a powerful fish. Very powerful. He wondered if it was one of the Myths, then dismissed that thought immediately and replaced it with one of a steaming cup of tea.

"Jeez, has that kettle boiled yet? I'm gagging here," he demanded, and was rewarded with a cup of steaming liquid thrust in front of his face.

"Want me to blow it for you, sir!"

"Urr, yeah, I s'pose you'd better," he replied, seriously.

"Yeah, kiss my ass, bucko!" came the less than impressive reply. The carp had slowed somewhat, allowing him to gain a few valuable yards, and he reeled vigourously for as long as he could before the fish took umbrage and kited back out to the left.

"Shit, this is a good fish, boys," he muttered, and behind him the others did a silent war dance and held their heads theatrically in anticipation of the celebration that would follow.

The tea was tepid when next he had a chance to sample it, but that was all the better and allowed him to gulp it down and turn the desert that was his mouth back into an oasis. The carp was now about forty yards out and merely holding station whilst recuperating. He bent the rod a little more and felt it creak under the weight, then the pressure began to tell and he sensed the carp gradually moving towards him. They all watched, transfixed, as the line cut upwards through the water as if it was attached to a whale that was about to sound. Then their mouths gaped as the sun lit upon a huge flank covered in golden sovereigns- it was a huge common carp, and the smell of adrenaline filled the air!

Ten more minutes passed with the knowledge that, at any minute, the hook could pull from one of the largest carp in England, and that required more than tea to moisten the desert! Nobody had spoken a word since they had seen that flank, but they now moved with purpose as the end of the battle drew nigh. The net was dipped into the water, the netsman crouching low and extending the pole into the lake. An overhanging branch was pulled back lest the rod should foul against it and a gentle mantra was spoken, almost inaudible.

"Nice and easy, son. Nice and easy. We're nearly there now, just take your time. This is in the bag, just take your time."

The words meant little, just the fact that they were being spoken was enough, and he used them to blank out the voice in his head that was stammering, 'Please don't fall off. Please don't fall off!'

Three yards out it rolled again and they wondered if it would fit in the net.

'I think we need a bigger net!' thought one of them, absently, then continued the mantra.

Everything slowed to a quarter speed and the huge fish seemed to be a still frame from a silent movie. The next frame showed it bent almost in half as it hung on the net cord. And the next frame? That showed it engulfed in a black mesh and a solid wall of water.

Then full speed was resumed and utter mayhem ensued.

When Gary Lineker equalised against West Germany in the 1990 semi-final, eighteen million people were sent into ecstasy and the combined noise must have been massive. It would not have matched the ecstasy and volume of the next twenty seconds on that lake in September.

They had done it. They had landed the Myth and none of them dare look into the net just in case they were wrong. But they weren't wrong. There it was, filling the landing net with a million sovereigns and it took all four of them to lift it from the lake and onto the suddenly insignificant mat. A sleeping bag was grabbed and thrust beneath it as extra protection, then they watched, like small boys seeing a stocking removed for the first time, as the mesh revealed their prize.

They were speechless. It was huge.

A huge, pristine, mythical common carp, the sun glinting off every scale. There were tears in their eyes, maybe from the sun, maybe not, and they just looked at each other and shook their heads in disbelief.

Unsurprisingly, the sixty pound scales proved insufficient and they beamed at each other proudly. The fish was sacked up very carefully whilst they worked out what to do. There was a tackle shop a few miles away that would have larger scales, match fishing scales with a tripod, so one of them would go to get them.

But first, a cup of tea.

They were still shell-shocked, then Sid said, "You know what this means?"

They stared at him quizzically, unsure of what it did mean.

"The monster commons in all those lakes; they're catchable!"

This brought smiles and nods of agreement before Stan, looking at the sack cord disappearing into the margins, replied, "Best we go and catch them, then."

*****

THE END?

*****

About the Author

Keith has been writing in fishing magazines for over two decades, and his 'Made in England' column has achieved quite a following.

Originally from South London, Keith has lived in Crawley, with his wife Linda, and children, Vincent and Christine for almost thirty years, and the recent additions to his family of granddaughters Ayla, Willow and Ebony has made his life complete.

Now, his weekends are split between going fishing, being a granddad or cruising around on his beloved trike. What with all that, music, reading, and writing it's a wonder he had time to write a book at all!

Oh well, as Ian Anderson once said, 'You're never too old to rock'n'roll.'

*****

*****

Also Available
The Keeper - By Keith Jenkins

Almost a decade after the much acclaimed 'Myth', comes the sequel that many people have been awaiting. Beginning as the last book ends; 'The Keeper' takes us on a decade-spanning journey with faces old and new, and encounters of more than just the fishing kind.

Once again, Keith has drawn from real life, so the main characters are a melange of personalities that we have all met, either on the bankside, or elsewhere, and as usual, fact is always more colourful than fiction.

This isn't just a book about fishing, although that has always been the thread that stitches everything together. The span has broadened here, and once again reflects what we see but sometimes fail to recognize. The changing of the seasons; the constant battle for survival – both animal and human survival; the many and varied characters and personalities we encounter in our lives, and who inevitably mould us into who we eventually become. But there are always the fish –

Small fish; to enchant a young boy with his first encounter.

Big fish; that bring smiles and adulation to the most seasoned of anglers.

And the fish of dreams – those mythical creatures that exist on the periphery of vision, and hope; legends that are tantalisingly out of reach, but if you could just stretch that little bit further…

All the characters, above and below the water line, face major changes and, as Old Ted is all too well aware, only the strong will survive.

Young Smiffy has to learn to adjust to life in the country, after having spent his first dozen years in the confines of boarding schools or his parents' Chelsea home. But maybe an equally young Neil (Posh) Becks can help with that adjustment, and show Smiffy the wonders that Mother Nature has laid before them.

Stan strides from The Myth into The Keeper full of confidence, but his world is soon tipped upside down and he, also, has to readjust and re-learn if he is to move forward. Fortunately, his old buddies, Rhodie, Sid and Buzz are on hand to assist, if only to ensure that their future is secured as well.

Then there's Old Ted. His is the wisdom of the trees, the knowledge of a true countryman. His history is mysterious, and its memory both grieves and soothes him, but his goal is simple – to ensure that everyone survives. But, as he knows too well, that outcome is never quite certain.

This isn't 'Son of Myth', this is the Myth's big brother, and he's got an attitude. In short, this is life, pretty much as we all know it – and then some.

... Welcome to the world of Old Ted – The Keeper.

*****

'This book picks up from where the Myth left off, However things are seen through the eyes of a different group of people...some nice and some just downright nasty but all with one aim. to catch a monster carp. Trials and tribulations along the way by everyone involved are woven into a charming and delightful tale. Again we have the story told from the carp's point of view. A guardian angel in the form of an 'enigmatic' man gives his name to this tale. He almost thinks carp, knowing where and when they will be certain places when anglers around thrash the water to a foam. I really enjoyed this story..more so than the original. Its definitely worth reading.' - Andy Garner

'A truly fantastic, exhilarating read. Every time I picked it up it excited me and touched a place in my own adventurous heart. I could relate to it on just about every level, if only the world we lived in were more like that, it's there, but most don't see it. Of course, I'm a ruffy tuffy soldier, not of Ted's ilk mind, but still, there was no evidence of any lump in my throat!' - Carl Bullock

'After reading The Myth the expectation of getting into The Keeper was high. I had heard the content was strikingly similar to a water I was once a member of and I wasn't disappointed. The maturing of the two young lads and their progress through life and their fishing was a joy and having started at an early age myself brought back many pleasant memories. This is a wonderful book which quite rightly highlights the beauty of the countryside, which passes so many unfortunates by. But it's so much more than that. It's about respect, right and wrong, and just a little bit of luck. I can't recommend this highly enough and I will be looking to purchase the hardback as soon as is possible.' - A. Nash

'The Keeper by Keith Jenkins has been the first fictional fishing book I've read and I can honestly say I enjoyed it from start to finish. I found the writing style very descriptive and easy to read, which helps transport the reader into the magical world of the mere. Throughout the book it reminds you that fishing is not all about catching fish and is often more about just being outside enjoying nature in all its beauty. Full of likeable characters, each with a different piece of the story to play out, which means you never get bored reading about one character and instead are left wanting more, whilst wondering what's going to happen to each of the characters next. Overall a great book that begs not to be put down, highly recommended. Whether you're an angler or not you'll love this book.' - Kev Mitchell

*****

*****

Also Available

The Keeper - By Keith Jenkins

Available online:
Amazon Kindle, iBookstore,
and Limited Edition Hardback

*****

Printed in Great Britain
by Amazon.co.uk, Ltd.,
Marston Gate.